PRAISE FOR CHRISTI CALDWELL

"Christi Caldwell's *The Vixen* shows readers a darker, grittier version of Regency London than most romance novels . . . Caldwell's more realistic version of London is a particularly gripping backdrop for this enemies-to-lovers romance, and it's heartening to read a story where love triumphs even in the darkest places."

—NPR on *The Vixen*

"In addition to a strong plot, this story boasts actualized characters whose personal demons are clear and credible. The chemistry between the protagonists is seductive and palpable, with their family history of hatred played against their personal similarities and growing attraction to create an atmospheric and captivating romance."

—*Publishers Weekly* on *The Hellion*

"Christi Caldwell is a master of words and *The Hellion* is so descriptive and vibrant that she redefines high definition. Readers will be left panting, craving, and rooting for their favorite characters as unexpected lovers find their happy ending."

—*RT Book Reviews* on *The Hellion*

"Christi Caldwell is a Must Read."

—*New York Times* bestselling author Mary Balogh

"A Christi Caldwell book never fails to touch the heart!"

—*New York Times* bestselling author Tessa Dare

"Two people so very broken in different ways, and their journey to becoming whole again. This is Christi Caldwell at her absolute best!"

—Kathryn Bullivant

"One of [Christi] Caldwell's strengths is creating deep, sympathetic characters, and this book is no exception . . ."

—Courtney Tonokawa

The SPITFIRE

OTHER TITLES BY CHRISTI CALDWELL

To Tempt a Scoundrel

The
SPITFIRE

CHRISTI CALDWELL

Montlake
Romance

Published by Montlake Romance, Seattle

www.apub.com

Amazon, the Amazon logo, and Montlake Romance are trademarks of Amazon.com, Inc., or its affiliates.

ISBN-13: 9781503905313
ISBN-10: 1503905314

Cover design by Erin Dameron-Hill

Cover illustration by Chris Cocozza

Printed in the United States of America

My Wicked Wallflowers series was set to be complete at four books. That is, until one morning—more specifically, in the dead of night, which is the time when all great ideas come to me—a character slipped forward. She stole my sleep that night and in the nights to come, demanding that I tell her story. That character was Clara Winters. Clara is a secondary character in my book The Scoundrel's Honor. *From the moment I met her, I was intrigued by her. She was strong, direct, and honorable. There was, however, a vulnerability to her as well. She was a woman with a past. Her past does not make her any less worthy of a happily-ever-after.*

Fortunately, my editor agreed.
Alison, when I came to you needing to tell Clara's story, you were as supportive as you've always been. Thank you for believing in her as a heroine and in me as an author. Clara's story is for you.

PART I

The Storm

Chapter 1

East London
England
1826

Henry March, the Earl of Waterson, lived a well-ordered existence. Every minute of his every day was carefully laid out, organized in a neat schedule that he devoutly followed.

Even with the meticulous planning he'd put into every part of his existence, there was one area he'd never given much thought to: how he'd die.

If he *had* thought of it, given the life he'd led as a staid, proper, ever-vigilant lord, dutiful son, and devoted brother, he'd have expected to be one of those doddering lords who lived long after eyesight and hearing failed.

Mayhap there would be a wife and a pair of sons—the whole requisite "heir and the spare" to preserve the title—at his side. Of course, a nobleman would have to be married in order to leave behind either a loving widow or children.

In the end, in *his* end, it would turn out that Henry would meet his maker with no one at his side, and dying not in the comfort of his four-poster bed but in the unlikeliest of places—on the dank, grimy cobblestones of St. Giles, facedown, and with his cheek submerged in a puddle.

Henry lay there, on the hard, unforgiving London street, with his eyes closed.

I'm dead.

It had come so fast, so unexpectedly. From behind in the form of two masked brutes—a blade slicing through his flesh and then blackness.

And all because he'd been bent on good. Even in death, the irony of his demise was not lost on him. That he, leading MP, determined to see a universal constable force throughout the whole of England, should be cut down in his research of London's most dangerous parts.

Except . . .

Henry forced his left eye—the one not submerged in water—open.

Surely in death one wouldn't feel pain. Unless one found oneself cast out of heaven and into hell. Which, given the mistakes he'd made in life, mayhap made hell his final resting place. And there could be no doubting his left side burnt with a searing viciousness that sent vomit climbing up his throat. The agony pulsing at his side caused his whole body to radiate pain.

From the attack. His flight. And then his collapse, here.

Now, the icy chill that came from lying wet upon the unforgiving streets of East London.

But in death one was released from feeling . . . anything.

So Henry wasn't dead. He was dying.

The frantic beat of footfalls came from around the corner.

Closing his eye, Henry said a prayer to a God he'd been woefully neglectful of attending in his life that it was a constable.

But the steps were too unsteady. They bore down on him, crashing through puddles.

"Jaysus. There 'e is."

And it appeared there'd be no intervention from the Lord this night.

"Oi told ya 'e couldn't have gone far," the other man said, his voice rasping and breathless. "I nicked him good."

Henry's two assailants staggered to a stop over his prone form.

"Is 'e dead?" That coarse Cockney slashed across the otherwise quiet London air.

That appeared to be the question of Henry's night.

"Oi don't know." The admission, gravelly and rough, emerged almost hesitantly.

The pair of masked brutes who'd taken him down leaned over him. He felt them rather than saw them, blotting out the faint slash of moonlight that periodically peeked out from behind the thick clouds that rolled past.

"Oi stuck 'im in 'is ribs. Ya stick 'im if ya wanna be sure."

"Ya do it."

"Oi already did. It's yar turn."

They were going to shove another blade into him. That realization came with the usual matter-of-factness that had been part of Henry. Only this time, there was a blessed numbness to that realization.

One of his attackers grunted as his partner in crime pushed him. "Ya just want me to be the one to 'ave killed a nob. Only fair that ya stab 'im, too."

"'e's dead anyway," the other man groused. "Ain't no need for me to do it, too."

As the pair fought, darkness plucked at Henry's consciousness, muting the argument unfolding between the pair so that their words rolled together into an incoherent jumble that ultimately faded completely.

And still, he fought that pull of unconsciousness. Knowing with an innate sense that if he gave himself over to the inky blackness, he'd never open his eyes again. Knowing that he didn't want to die like this. Not here. Not now.

And then . . . it was too much. The world went dark.

When Henry came to, a thick haze of confusion clouded his head and his eyes felt as if they were weighted shut. He struggled to open them.

Where in blazes was he? And why did his side hurt like the Devil had touched a pitchfork to it?

"Didn't say that we 'ad . . ."

And with the guttural Cockney penetrating the confusion, it trickled in: his meeting with several MPs who were at odds with him on cleaning up the streets of East London, surveying those same streets, and then parting ways.

The first thing Henry registered . . . was a voice. An unfamiliar one. Except . . . it wasn't completely unfamiliar. Why did he know it? Why should he know a coarse East London Cockney? And then it came rushing back.

The attack. The assault he'd suffered on the streets.

He must have gone black for just a moment. And then a groan escaped him, piteous and—worse than that—damning.

His assailants went silent.

"Wot was that?"

There was a grunt, followed by a curse. "Wot in 'ell do ya think it was? It was 'im."

And through the agony lancing at the wound he'd sustained, there was something more—terror, and a hungering to escape.

I cannot die here . . .

Digging deep for one last grasp at a fight to survive, Henry pressed his gloved palms against the cobbles and struggled to push himself to a stand. Only one thought compelled him: *flee.*

Alas, Fate or God or, mayhap, the Devil had other plans for him this night.

His body collapsed, weak from his earlier attack. Struggling to lift a hand but knowing his very life, or what remained of it, depended on the movement, Henry grabbed the purse from inside his jacket. "Money," he rasped. "I have money." He tossed the bag weakly at the pair, and it landed with a jingle that sent greed dancing in his assailants' eyes.

The pair exchanged a look, and then as one, they made a grab for it.

The bulkier of the two beat his partner to it and then cuffed the other man about the ears for attempting to best him.

When he spoke, his reedy voice contained a whine to it. "Oi told ya 'e wasn't dead," he complained, stuffing Henry's purse inside his tattered and patched wool jacket.

"Ya didn't. Ya asked, and Oi said if ya wanted to kill 'im that ya should see to it."

"You don't have to do this," Henry said, his voice thin, weak, barely audible to his own ears. *Please don't do this.* It was an entreaty that, because of a lifetime of honor ground into him as a peer of the realm, he couldn't bring himself to utter. Not even with death facing him.

"Ya don't tell us what we 'ave to do or not." With a growl, the burlier of his attackers buried his foot in Henry's bleeding side.

Henry cried out, the sound weak and threadbare, but the other assailant kicked him in the face. "Shut yar damned mouth," he warned Henry, skittering his gaze about.

The metallic bite of blood tinged Henry's mouth and ran down his throat. He choked and spit into the muddy puddle already aswirl with crimson.

"Oh, foine. Oi'll do it," one of the brutes muttered. There was a sharp hiss, the whine of a blade being unsheathed.

Henry closed his eyes. This was it. They intended to finish him off, after all. Now. In this instance, with another blade to his body. "Don't," he whispered, determined that his last word come forward as a command and not as a plea.

Then in the distance, the echo of a horse's hooves sounded, and he was spared.

At least, temporarily.

"Bloody 'ell. We can't do this 'ere," the scrawnier of the pair muttered. "Get 'is legs."

"Ya take 'is legs. Oi'll get 'is arms."

"Stop foighting about everything. Do ya want to be seen?"

And as one of them grabbed Henry roughly under the arms, the darkness inched back over his eyes, pulling it across his vision like a curtain descending.

"Bloody 'ell. 'e's 'eavier than 'e looks."

"I can pay you more," he whispered weakly as they struggled to lift him. Henry would likely end up with another knife wound before this night was through and felt desperation clutching at him through the pain, but he'd be damned if he humbled himself in his final moments by begging.

"Pay us more?" One of the men snorted. "Wot do ya intend? To 'ave us join ya at yar townhouse, where ya'll give us a fortune?" The thug grunted, panting from his exertions. "We'll settle for yar purse." He paused, bringing Henry's dragging body to a brief stop. "Ya got a timepiece?"

A gold timepiece. A signet ring. A silver carrier with his cards in it. They'd take it all and end him anyway.

"Will ya 'urry up?" the other man whined. "Oi 'eard someone, and yar blabbering 'ere with this nob?" As if to punish Henry for that annoyance, he punched him.

This time there was a sickening crack, followed by the spray of blood.

His assailant chortled. "Ain't such a foine-looking nob now with a crooked nose."

Digging deep for a last bit of strength, Henry struggled, kicking. That unexpected showing startled the attacker carrying his legs into dropping him. The added weight sent the one at his shoulder stumbling, and he lost his hold on Henry.

With a Herculean strength that could come only from a primitive place that lived within all to survive at all costs, Henry found his feet. Clutching at his side, he took off running once more. Blood soaked through his fingers, coating his gloves, the sticky warmth penetrating the thin leather. His breath rasping loudly, Henry staggered, and his legs weakened.

All his life's energy drained from him.

He stumbled, and too weak to even hold the agonizing wound seeping blood from his side, he collapsed to his knees.

And sensed the blow before it even landed.

One of his attackers clubbed him hard at the back of his head.

Light danced behind Henry's eyes, flickering, vivid, bright specks that twinkled like false stars in the miserable St. Giles night sky. He fell forward, his cheek slamming hard into a broken cobblestone. Its jagged edge shredded the flesh.

This time, as the pair of thugs grabbed him and began dragging him off, he surrendered the fight and turned himself over to the inevitable fate that awaited him.

And he remembered nothing more.

Chapter 2

A person who'd lived and survived in the streets of East London knew one truth to be certain: never involve oneself in another person's affairs.

No matter how perilous a person's situation might be, nothing good could come from interfering. Martyrdom only saw a person dead, and not much more.

As such, Clara Winters, former whore, madam, and now, at last, a woman with a future, knew above all else that she should leave. That she should turn and walk away from the trouble unfolding twenty paces ahead, where two brutish thugs dragged a limp figure by his arms and legs.

And she planned to leave. She planned to turn on her heel and take an alternate path to the modest apartments she rented and avoid whatever evil was unfolding.

In the end, she was unable to for the unlikeliest of reasons—boots.

A pair that, but for the mud splattering them, fairly gleamed, with a lone gold tassel still dangling from the top of one of them.

And the realization hit her. It wasn't just another London street drunk knocked down in a brawl, but rather a nob—some fancy dandy playing in streets that devoured men of all stations and sizes.

He isn't your problem.

In fact, Clara had problems enough where she didn't need to add any—and certainly not anyone else's.

The pair reached an alley intersecting two dilapidated buildings and proceeded to drag their prize down the row.

And when they disappeared from sight, Clara knew precisely the fate that awaited the unconscious stranger. Because regardless of whatever rules drove Polite Society, all of them ceased to mean anything the moment those peers entered these streets.

Bloody hell on Sunday.

Tugging her skirts up, Clara removed the pistol tucked in her boot, and breaking into a run, she started after the trio.

Nothing good could come of this. Nothing good.

Even as that litany pounded in her ears, she pressed forward, not stopping until she reached the building at the corner of Earl Street Great & Little.

"We're far enough. No one will . . . get it done quick . . ." The remainder of the hulking brute's words were lost.

Her chest heaving, Clara took care to slow her breaths, keeping them still and silent. There was a way out of this.

If one of the well-known rules of St. Giles was to never interfere in another person's affairs, it was just as well known that if one was caught in the middle of a crime, it was best to flee and save one's hide. Squinting, Clara did a quick survey of the ground. The pervasive London fog blanketed the uneven cobblestones. Bending down, she fished through the muck and wrested loose a piece of makeshift stone.

Clara tossed the improvised projectile down the alley. It bounced and clattered, echoing between the dilapidated buildings.

A terror-laden whisper went up. "Wot was that?"

"It was nuffin'. Get on with it."

"Someone's 'ere."

"No one's 'ere," the other man barked. "Forget it, ya damned coward. If ya won't stab 'im this toime, Oi'll do it again."

Do it again.

As the blighters, both posturing as only men could, launched into a quarrel about which one of them would deliver the next blow, Clara waged a battle with herself.

The thugs had already stabbed the stranger, then. Limp as he'd been since she'd first caught sight of him being dragged through the streets, it was likely he was already dead. Which made her intervention here all the more foolhardy. Little good could come from sticking her nose into business that wasn't hers . . . and nothing good could come from aiding a dead man.

"Well, get on with it, if ya're gonna off 'im."

She briefly closed her eyes. *Damnation.*

She'd always been weak. That weakness had been her failing too many times.

Clara opened her eyes. "He is right," she called out, remaining cloaked in the shadows. "Someone is here."

Silence met her echoed warning, followed a moment later by frantic whispers. "Told ya. Oh, Christ. We're gonna 'ang."

"We ain't goin' to 'ang, ya blathering idiot. It ain't a constable. It's a damned woman," he said, stuffing his mask into the front of his jacket.

"Back away from the gentleman," she demanded over their back-and-forth. "Continue on your way." So she could continue on hers.

Her command was met by a chortling laugh. "Get out of 'ere, ya daft slut, or ya'll be next."

"Slut" was what she'd been for seven miserable years, but even when a woman ceased collecting coin for trading sexual favors, she remained a whore because of what she'd done. Even so, Clara would walk through hell barefoot before allowing a London street thug to shred her. Raising her pistol, Clara stepped into the entrance of the alleyway. She immediately found the pair in dark, tattered garments—hulking, bearish men who would make Satan think twice before tangling with them.

Clara, however, had engaged in far too many dealings with equally black souls. A hated face flitted before her eyes. A man who'd enslaved countless souls to make his family fortune . . . and then he'd sought to strip Clara of both choice and freedom.

One of the men whistled slowly. "Ya *are* daft."

She shifted the muzzle of her pistol in his direction. "I may be," she conceded and, drifting closer, sized them up. Their bald heads dripping sweat onto heavily bearded cheeks, they would have appeared to be identical twins in everything down to the patches in their wool trousers if it weren't for the size disparity between them. She stopped close enough to guarantee her shot. "But if I'm mad, what does that make you two, refusing to move even with a gun trained on you?" she asked coolly.

"She ain't going to shoot us, Judge." Except a thread of uncertainty crept into the brute's tone, turning a statement into a question.

Judge. Thug One was Judge, then.

It also spoke to either their arrogance or stupidity that they'd use their names before her.

Or then, mayhap it was just unneeded evidence of all the ways in which women were underestimated by men—of all stations.

"An' she only 'as one bullet."

"I'm a quick shot and an even faster reloader," she drawled in icy tones that sent the color leaching from Judge's cheeks.

"Did ya 'ear w-wot she said?" the more cowardly—or mayhap the more clever—of the two stammered.

His partner punched him in the shoulder. "Ya damned fool. Of course she ain't gonna shoot and reload. Handle him, and Oi'll deal with her."

Deal with her.

A steely calm went through her when any other sane person would have turned on their heel and fled. Instead of remaining here, taking a stand for a man whose body hadn't moved once since she'd come upon him. "Stop," she warned as the hulking brute began his approach.

"Or what?" he jeered. "Or ya'll shoot me?"

Clara drew the hammer back, the click echoing her warning for the pair, bringing the assailant to a stop. "Precisely."

Judge smiled, flashing yellow teeth and an empty space where his top two front ones had been. And then he started forward.

Steadying her hand, Clara fired the flintlock pistol. She braced her feet against the powerful recoil. The loud report of that shot blended with the ungodly screech emitted by the man set to deal with her. He crumpled to the ground, his fingers clutching at his shoulder. "Ya bitch," he croaked, his eyes oozing fear and pain.

And with rapid movements as familiar as brushing her hair, Clara had her powder out, loaded, and another ball on top before the nameless one could even speak. "Now, I'll not say it again. Leave the man alone." She curled her lips up in a taunting smile. "Or continue as you were, and I'll deal with—"

The bastard was already charging for his partner. Collecting him under the shoulders, he kept them close to the opposite wall and made a path around Clara.

She kept her weapon trained on their retreating backs until the pair of them had disappeared, the tread of their footsteps echoing, then fading altogether.

Dropping the weapon inside the pocket sewn along the front of her cloak, she raced over to the prone figure. And then stopped.

Her initial assumptions had been wrong; the man sprawled face down on the ground was no dandy. Dandies wore garish satins and brightly colored trousers. With his face buried in the pavement and his hair caked with blood and mud, she couldn't get a gauge of his age. But by the sheer size of him, she was certain of one thing: this wasn't one of the bewhiskered boys from university, carousing about town and reveling in the dangers that saner, more desperate men knew to run from.

"But apparently, stupidity runs in all ages of the nobility," she muttered, sinking to a knee beside him.

Clara searched his back for a hint of movement and, when she saw none, slipped her hands under the stranger. With a grunt, she rolled him over. Blood and mud had caked his face in a dark grime; there was a crooked bend to his nose with blood spilling from the surely once noble appendage.

At some point in his struggles, the buttons had come loose from his jacket. Pushing the garment aside, she rested a palm against his chest.

And then she saw it: faint, so faint she had to squint in the dark to see it . . .

But the slightest up-and-down movement.

He was alive.

But barely.

Bloody hell.

Several strands of her hair had slipped free of her combs, and she gave them an impatient shove, tucking them back behind her ears.

Straightening, Clara surveyed the victim at her feet and did a sweep.

What in blazes was she to do *now*?

She couldn't very well leave him here. His fate would be sealed if she were to do so. But to summon a constable would only end badly for her, a former courtesan and madam discovered in an alley with a near-dead gentleman.

Clara peered at him and came to the grim acceptance that she had just one option available that wouldn't result in her landing in Newgate: get him from this place, care for his wounds, and then send him on his way.

And what happens in the meantime if he dies on your watch? He was barely breathing, bruised, and bloodied, and yet, he could not die.

"You were always a damned fool," she muttered into the quiet. "But you can do this." After all, there'd been any number of unconscious persons she'd helped through the streets of London. And there was nothing she could not do—except avoid landing herself in trouble, that was.

Of course, those persons she'd helped had been women, and none had possessed the solid weight of muscle that this stranger did. She had, however, too much experience in displacing drunken men whose weight had felt dead after they'd collapsed from drink. Resolved, Clara pulled her serviceable leather gloves on, came 'round the top of the stranger, and sank to her haunches.

Sliding her hands gently under his head, Clara tipped it forward until his chin was pressed against his chest. Then, sliding her knee under his left shoulder, she rolled the man onto his side.

Bloody, bloody hell.

Noblemen weren't supposed to be broad, heavily muscled figures.

Nay, they weren't broad and heavily muscled. Not in the experience Clara had with them. And her experience had been unfortunately vast. Most padded their garments, and the others? The others were either portly from their taste for drinks and sweets or painfully slender.

Clara made to move both knees under the prone figure.

Except—

Pausing, she stopped to dust the back of her arm over her perspiring brow. Mayhap she'd been altogether incorrect in her supposition. Oh, by the quality of his garments, the unfortunate, bloodied figure was certainly one in possession of wealth. But perhaps he was one of those self-made men. It would explain why he might be in the East End of London. It would also explain his physique.

And for the first time since she'd shoved her nose into circumstances that belonged to another, she felt a giddy wave of relief. It filled her with a burst of strength and a renewed determination to get him out of this place.

Self-made men and women Clara could relate to, and she feared them a great deal less than the ever-undependable peerage.

Scooting both knees under the stranger, she braced herself. Even knowing his strength, having wrestled it for the past several minutes, she was still unprepared for that added weight. Her knees sagged, and she braced her booted feet, stabilizing them.

The back of her right heel snagged on her cloak. She choked and struggled to right herself.

Who was the person who'd decreed that skirts of any sort were the garments a woman must wear? Impractical, cumbersome, they were solely designed to look pretty while putting a woman's figure on display.

"A man," she mumbled. Only a man could be responsible for such obtuseness. Fetching her pistol and case from inside the pocket, she returned them to her boot, and unfastening the clasp at her throat, she released the wool garment. The heavy, velvet-lined cloak fluttered to the ground in a whispery heap.

She cast it a brief, regretful look. Mayhap it would still be here when she returned for it. Except, given the men, women, and children who crept along every crevice and corner of East London in search of shelter, security, or another crime to commit, she had little hope for recovering the article. And having lost five years' savings to a bastard who'd swindled her, and having since invested the remaining ones she did have in an establishment of her own, there were hardly coins to go about for luxuries such as replacing one of her just two cloaks.

With a sigh, Clara redirected her attentions back to the silent figure, literally at her feet. She reached for the underside of his arms and again stopped.

Was he even breathing still?

And perhaps it was exhaustion from another endless day of working and the late-night hour combined, but her heart knocked against her rib cage, a foreign response that she'd ceased to have. That she'd believed herself incapable of feeling: pity . . . and sadness for a man.

She quickly pressed her fingertips against his neck. The faintest pulse throbbed beneath them. "All right, you are alive," she said quietly, talking herself through the impossible task before her more than addressing the man who was knocked out cold. "I need to get you to your feet," she explained.

And then what? Drag him the remaining way to her residence?

No. Even if she got him up, she couldn't single-handedly carry him home.

"Sir." She tapped her palm lightly against his cheek; his nose, which had stopped bleeding, reopened its wound. Blood ran in slow crimson rivulets over her fingers, turning her purple gloves black. "Sir," she repeated, giving him another, this time stronger, tap.

Men didn't help a woman when standing on their own two legs. Why should they prove any more obliging unconscious?

Determined to get the gentleman onto his feet and from this alley, with her knees directly under his shoulder blades, she used her legs as leverage and propelled him forward so that he was seated upright.

"You are deuced heavy, you know?" she panted, briefly pausing.

And then the faintest groan filtered from his lips.

Her heart hammered. *Thank God.*

Clara shook his arm in a bid to further rouse him. "Sir?" she asked again. "Can you hear me? I need your help."

Thick, dark lashes trembled slightly as if he struggled to open his swollen eyes, eyes that had already begun to turn black from the blows dealt to his face. And then, they opened. The faintest, slightest crack, but it was enough to indicate he was conscious, at least for now.

"Help," he whispered. His voice, hoarse and ragged, did nothing to disguise the cultured tones conveyed in that single syllable.

"Precisely. I'm trying to help you," she said in the calm tones she adopted with the whores who had also been bloodied beyond recognition and were too terrified to let Clara near. "But I need you to help me. I'm going to get you to your feet, and when I do, I'll need you to wrap your arm about my shoulders. Can you do that?"

Because if he couldn't, she was lost as to how to get him from this place.

His cracked and bloodied lips tried to move, but no words came out. Taking that as his agreement, Clara used all her strength to push herself to standing and, with her weight, propelled the gentleman forward and up.

He staggered, and his entire body pitched.

Clara caught him around the waist and, gasping from the effort it took to keep the man upright, braced her legs on the pavement to steady the both of them. And when neither of them tumbled facedown, a sense of accomplishment filled her. "You are standing," she said, reassuring the both of them.

His head lolled sideways and rolled forward like the rag doll she'd never been without as a child. "Sir?" she demanded, lightly nudging her elbow into his side.

An agonized moan pealed from his lips. He'd been beaten there, too. And another wave of sympathy washed over her. She might be hardened by all she'd done, witnessed, and suffered through, but she was not so heartless that she didn't know what it was like to hurt precisely as this man was hurting: a bloodied nose, a broken rib, swollen eyes and cheeks. She'd endured all. Granted, never at the same time, as was the nameless man against her now.

"I need you to move with me," she said more loudly. "We'll go slowly. One foot in front of the other. You do not even have to lift them. Drag them as I bear your weight." His weight, which was already sagging her shoulders. Couldn't he have been one of the slender dandies? "Can you do that?" She searched his face for any indication that he had heard her.

His lashes, caked in blood, lifted again. "I . . . can . . ."

By the threadbare quality to that assurance, Clara wasn't altogether sure he'd committed in the affirmative, and yet, neither did she have a choice.

And so, inch by agonizing inch, she, with the gentleman's limp frame borrowing support from her own, made her way down the remainder of the alley and out through the streets of St. Giles.

Periodically, she'd stop and allow them both a break. Breathing. Focusing. And then walking once more. It was a steady pattern that kept her moving. That, despite the strain of every muscle in her body, kept her on her feet and walking forward. Past pickpockets and whores plying their trade, and drunken men and women stumbling by to find their corner to sleep in for the remainder of the night. None would dare look twice at a man and woman stumbling through St. Giles arm in arm. Even beaten as he was, the stranger and Clara blended so much with the landscape of these godforsaken streets as to not even attract any notice.

At last, she and the badly wounded stranger reached her apartments.

"We're here," she panted, her breath coming hard and fast. Keeping her right arm around his middle, she reached into the bodice of her gown and found the chain hanging there. She fished out the attached key and unlocked the door, letting herself and the gentleman inside.

Fighting for one last wave of strength, she straightened and shoved the door closed with the heel of her boot, then led her unwanted visitor to the one bedroom in her apartments. The moment they reached the bed, all the energy she'd managed faded. She collapsed and managed to shift the stranger sideways so when he fell, he landed in her lumpy-but-tidy bed.

Groaning, Clara rolled onto her back and stretched her arms out in a futile bid to ease the ache in her muscles.

Well, none of this evening had gone according to plan.

After overseeing the builders at her recently purchased music hall, she was to have returned to her apartments, sought out her bed, and claimed some desperately needed rest.

She was not to have rescued and then recovered a damned stranger in fancy garments, one ragged breath away from death.

Angling her head toward her now-occupied bed, Clara stared at her burden, sprawled and still unmoving, facedown.

Now what?

Chapter 3

Death was a peculiar thing.

Despite being freed of all control of one's body, one was still capable of pain.

And for Henry, every corner of his being throbbed and ached. It was a vicious, numbing agony so intense he floated between awareness and unawareness, reduced to only the pinpricks of pain that radiated throughout his body. For surely it wasn't consciousness. Consciousness would indicate Henry was still alive.

In his death, however, he'd learned there was a transitional process. One where a person lingered in the moment when they'd last drawn breath, and hovered there. A place where one neither dwelled in the fiery bowels of hell nor attained that eternal peace in heaven . . . but rather an in-between purgatory.

And in it there was, in place of clear thought, only pain.

Nay, not only pain.

"It will get better, I promise . . ."

Through the agony, there was also something else—something more—something that only served as a confirmation of his death. A voice.

Silvery and sultry, it lilted as she spoke, rising in a musical intonation that, when he heard it, kept him from the misery of his suffering and fixed on her voice. Her words. They called him.

And Henry ached to open his eyes. Even as he knew when he did, it would signal the absolute end of his existence and mark his full immersion into heaven or hell, or whatever came after death.

"You cannot keep your eyes closed forever . . . ," that voice murmured, and contained within was an impatience at odds with her dulcet tones. "The longer you do, the . . ."

Whatever insight she imparted was lost to another crippling wave of misery.

Something cold touched his face, wet and unforgiving as it poured over him, a hellish baptism into eternal suffering. He twisted and turned in a bid to escape it. But there was no escaping; there was only more torture.

Stop. Please.

Henry tried to force words out. To plead for an end.

Except words were impossible.

He whimpered.

"*Shh,*" that angel—or devil?—cajoled, and regardless of whether the Lord or Lucifer had sent her, she had her magical, calming effect still.

Henry quieted, and something soft but lumpy met his back.

And while that angel or devil continued to alternately work between soothing and torturing, Henry let the inky blackness suck him under once more. Until mercifully, there was nothing.

Everything hurt.

Every inch of his being. Even parts of Henry that he'd believed incapable of feeling—from the roots of his hair to the soles of his feet—throbbed.

Not unlike the time he'd been a boy at university and gone out with a crowd of fellows whom he'd made a habit of avoiding until he'd joined them at a seedy hell, drunk too much, and realized just why he'd avoided such company.

And such vices. Aside from the occasional brandy he'd partaken with respectable gentlemen through the years, Henry made it a point to avoid all such indulgences.

Which made the fact that he was so damned foxed bloody peculiar.

Except . . . there was no recollection of overindulging . . . ?

And then it all came back to him.

His visit to St. Giles. Taking leave of his MP counterparts. The attack.

Henry's eyes flew open. Or one of them did. A flash of bright light blinded his one eye, and his stomach pitched. He closed his eye once more. Vomit climbed his throat, and he gagged. Even that movement sent another wave of pain shooting through him. His side throbbed. He concentrated on breathing through the torture that came from the simple task of drawing air into his lungs, all the while forcing himself to remain motionless.

When his nausea abated, Henry tried again and slowly opened the eye capable of sight.

Cracked plaster, in desperate need of paint and appearing dangerously close to tumbling down, met his gaze.

Except he was not a man with cracked plaster. In full command of a sizable fortune that he himself had meticulously overseen through the years, there was not so much as a Chippendale piece of furniture out of place in any of his seven residences.

The smell—a blend of moisture and old leather books that had paid the price of too many years of exposure to that dampness—filled his nostrils. Those dank scents belonging to a place he'd never been, and certainly none that he owned.

Where in blazes was he?

On the heel of that came a swift rush of panic. Where had his assailants taken him?

Fighting through the pain, he squinted his one good eye and did a furtive search for his captors. However, the cramped quarters he'd been carried to at some point were conspicuously empty. . . and more ominously. . . silent. It rang in his ears, an incessant whine that wreaked havoc on his already throbbing head.

Alone.

They'd left him alone.

Slowly closing his eye, Henry focused on drawing even breaths through the pain. He had to leave, now.

Henry forced himself up by his elbows.

Creeeak.

His stomach pitched, and he stilled—that absolute cessation of movement a product of both the damning announcement that he'd awakened and the aching toll exacted with even the most infinitesimal movements.

He waited with a sick, heightened anticipation of the men who'd rush the room.

And yet . . . only more silence accompanied that previous groan of the mattress. Nonetheless, Henry continued waiting, refusing to fall into any additional traps this night. Time ceased to mean anything in this instance.

When still no one came, Henry slid the surprisingly soft sheet down his person and brought one leg over the side of the bed.

Oh, God.

That movement nearly cost him whatever contents remained in his stomach.

Sweating, Henry clenched his eyes shut, and promptly winced, but then forced himself to push through that nauseating pain. As he set his feet down on the floor, the coolness of the room was like a balm upon his hot skin.

His mind, dulled from confusion, pain, and terror, sought to make sense of his missing garments.

He was naked, and yet, something had been wrapped around his middle.

Henry touched a palm against his waist, and his fingers brushed the tight bandage that had been wrapped around him.

That was right. He'd been stabbed. And at some point, his assailants had not only moved him from the streets but also bandaged him up.

Only—that didn't make sense.

None of this did.

Why should the pair of miscreants who'd fought over the dubious assignment of issuing the final death blow have done . . . either of those? Regardless of who was responsible for his current naked state and bringing him to this place, Henry had no intention of remaining to find out.

He came to his feet.

And the floor promptly rushed up to meet him.

Henry put his palms out to keep from smashing face-first into the floor, but his reflexes were still dulled. His cheek smashed into the threadbare rug, and his nose began bleeding. He groaned as that hated darkness threatened. It wavered behind his eyes, and Henry struggled against its pull. Terrified of what would happen if he surrendered to it. But coward that he was in this moment, he craved a surcease from all pain and feeling.

Blood continued to stream from his nose and coated his lips with that same vile metallic tinge that had assaulted his senses on the streets. With the last sliver of strength, he rolled onto his back, stared at that foreign-to-him plaster overhead, and slept.

Or he attempted to.

"Hello? Hullo?" someone was saying. Nay, not someone. This had become a familiar voice. "You really shouldn't have tried to . . . You aren't doing yourself . . ."

And there it was. That soft singsong voice; it beckoned.

He fought to open his eyes and gaze upon the owner of those dulcet tones but could not manage that now Herculean feat. As she spoke, he found himself lulled deeper and deeper to a place of peace.

"I'm here to help you," she murmured, and here, for the first time since he'd been felled in the streets, Henry believed that promise. Believed *her*.

And it was that inherent trust that gave him the strength to again force his eye open.

With her hair a tangle of pale-blonde curls, her lips a perfect cherub's bow, and her skin a pale cream white, he at last had confirmation to the question that had whispered through his mind during points of consciousness and unconsciousness.

"You are . . ." Saucer-size eyes, great big crystalline pools that beckoned, darkened with a question. "An angel," he managed to whisper, his voice coming as if from down a long hall.

That full mouth quivered up in a slow smile that dimpled one cheek.

And even as the efforts of that caused his lips to crack open and bleed, Henry grinned before resting his head on the floor and surrendering to sleep once more.

❧

Given that Clara had interrupted an almost-murder and spent the better part of the night and now morning tending the stranger, there'd been little to laugh about.

But being mistaken for an angel was enough to stir amusement from even the deepest place of exhaustion.

Yes, "angel" was the last thing anyone would confuse her for. And those opinions were all well deserved. She was no angel. She wasn't even remotely good.

And if her lifetime of sins wasn't proof enough, her impatience with the unconscious stranger was.

"Blasted lummox," she muttered. After her struggle to get him from the streets to her residence, and after the time she'd spent bandaging his middle and cleaning his bruises, he'd gone and undone all those efforts. His nose had resumed bleeding; the gash in his side now soaked through the bandages at his waist.

Dropping to a knee, she rolled the gentleman over and used her body to bring him upright. "I shouldn't have to do this again," she panted, blowing a curl back that had fallen across her eyes. "You've one job: stay in your bed and continue breathing. That is—*iiiiit.*" With that grunt, she heaved him up and rolled him onto her mattress.

Clara fell back on her buttocks and drew in several breaths, studying the burden she'd brought home.

The gentleman lay there, his arm hung over the side, his fingers grazing the floor and his face buried in her pillow, soaking the floral pillowcase with blood.

Lest her intention was to smother him to death, she could hardly leave him that way. Clara gently angled his head, so he faced the doorway. "There." She picked up his arm and rested it alongside him. And then, as an afterthought, drew her floral coverlet over his naked frame.

Another woman might have averted her gaze and blushed at the naked display of the male form before her. Over the years, however, Clara had developed a pragmatic understanding of nudity and sexual congress that didn't elevate either state. A body was just a body.

Though . . . that wasn't altogether true.

Her gaze, of its own volition, crept back to the slumbering form in her bed.

In her quest to care for the man, she also had failed to properly appreciate his masculine physique: narrow hips, a flat, muscular stomach. Equally muscular buttocks and tree-trunk-thick thighs confirming once again she'd not, despite her earliest fears, brought home a fancy lord to convalesce.

A small, piteous groan spilled from his lips, snapping her to the moment.

Her cheeks smarting at having been ogling him like a pathetic girl who was still impressed by men, Clara jumped up and diverted her focus to caring for the stranger. Hurrying from the room, she fetched the bowls of water she'd been readying when she'd heard his collapse. She set the chipped porcelain washbasin onto the lone nightstand and then rushed off to retrieve the bag she kept of medical supplies.

Gathering up a wet cloth, Clara rang out the excess water, and shaking it out, she held the damp cloth to his nose until the steady flow of blood had abated. Exchanging the rag for another, she washed his face so she could better assess the extent of his injuries.

Head wounds, she'd learned from too-rough clientele, were often the most perilous of all the injuries.

Clara continued cleaning him, switching bloodstained rags for cleaner ones. She dragged another through his close-cropped hair. With the blood and mud previously caking it now gone, she revealed dark strands with the faintest trace of silver at his temples.

He wasn't a young man, but neither was he old. The chiseled planes of his face, now riddled with blacks and blues, didn't bear a hint of a wrinkle. He was nothing short of masculine beauty; the recent bend to his broken nose, however, didn't detract from his handsomeness but rather added a ruggedness to him. Clara squeezed water from another rag and shook it out.

In her lifetime, she'd learned to look at beauty as a thing removed from a person's character. Some of the most breathtaking men had displayed a streak of cruelty that had left her and too many other young women with scars as reminders. And then the physically ugliest had proven the kindest and gentlest.

As she laid the damp cloth over his face, he moaned.

Blood continued to seep through the bandage around his waist.

She loosened the fabric enough to get another look at the gash left by one of his assailants' knives.

The wound, a deep, vertical line that ran three inches down his side, needed to be stitched up, and soon. "I trust someone will be looking for you," she noted, tucking the bandages back into place. "A wife, perhaps?" Only silence met her announcement and question. "A business partner?" And if Clara could locate said individual, then she could pass on the remaining responsibilities of his care. She'd done more than enough. Certainly more than anyone else in St. Giles would have.

Quitting her place at his bedside, she went to the pile of garments she'd cut from him before she'd tended his injuries. She fell to a knee and began searching through the exquisitely tailored articles. Her fingers collided with cool metal, and she drew the timepiece from the gentleman's trousers. The watch heavy in her hand, Clara studied it. The diamond, enamel, and gold cover of the hunter-case watch bore two initials: *HM*. She carefully set it down on the floor beside her and resumed her search.

All gentlemen, regardless of whether they'd been born into the peerage or outside those vaunted ranks, carried calling cards. Switching her efforts to the sapphire tailcoat, she searched through the inner pockets—and found a small case. "You have a name," she murmured gratefully as she drew the silver-and-gold-inlaid tortoiseshell piece out. She unhooked the tiny latch and removed a card. "Let us see who you are, Mr. . . . *Oh, hell.*"

Her stomach flipped over.

With horror sweeping through her, she forced her gaze from the damning card over to the unconscious man who occupied her bed. The unconscious man on the cusp of death.

And who now wasn't just a man, but a man with a name . . . and a title.

The Earl of Waterson.

A bloody *earl.*

"Damn it." Clara dropped the scraps in her hand, and they fell into the pile of Lord Waterson's garments with a muted thump. This was bad. Very bad. No good could ever come from a former whore being found with a nearly dead nobleman. What she saw or rescued him from would be irrelevant in the eyes of Polite Society. Society trusted not at all people of the streets. They trusted women even less.

Clara swiped her palms over her face. "All right," she said aloud in a bid to ward off the panic buffeting her. "So you found an earl." Coming to her feet, she proceeded to pace a distracting path across her small chambers. "After all, you well knew when you came upon him that he was likely a nobleman."

You just convinced yourself by his appearance and lack of servants about that he'd been born outside those powerful ranks.

Summoning the constables and regaling them with the story of what had happened last night was simply not an option to even consider. Nor could she reach out to the Countess of Waterson, of which there was certainly one. A gentleman whose hair was peppered with grey, with the rank of earl, would have not only a wife but also the requisite heir and a spare by this point.

"Think," she muttered and then came to a stop. Clara stared squarely at the bounder responsible for all her woes this morn. She had to care for him. Despite wanting to turn him over to another, the reality was . . . she simply couldn't do so without risking her very neck.

She'd stitch his side, clean his wounds, and tend his bruises. And when he was awake and able to walk on his own two legs without need of her assistance, Clara would send him on his way.

With a resolute determination, Clara shoved the sleeves of her violet muslin dress up to her elbows.

And rejoining her unwanted patient, she set to work.

Chapter 4

He was alive.

Henry had come to that conclusion not only by the agonizing pain that had gripped him and continued to hold him under its spell . . . but also because of her.

The angel, who, between Henry's moments of hallucination and clarity, proved herself very much of this world.

And even as words failed and he found himself incapable of anything but an animalistic groan that reverberated in his temples, there was also a calm that came from the woman's realness.

In any day of any year, Henry, one of society's most refined and proper lords, would have been horrified by that string of thoughts.

Real in this instance, however, meant alive. And as long as she was cursing him and his title, Henry was very much . . . breathing.

And for the first time since the nightmare had begun, he managed to open his eyes—both of them.

Henry winced as the rush of bright morning light sent a vicious stabbing behind his eyes, and he briefly closed them. He tried again, this time more slowly, more measured. And when keeping his lids open no longer sent nausea roiling in his gut, Henry allowed himself to take in his surroundings. The cracked plaster overhead and dank scent of moisture were not familiar.

With a bed, nightstand, chair, dressing mirror, and armoire, the small room was made all the more cramped for space. For the starkness of the whitewashed walls, there were also unexpected touches to the space that added a level of cheer and brightness.

On the nightstand, a small porcelain vase painted with yellow, blue, pink, and green blooms rested alongside the washbasin. Within the vase a lone rose, now wilting, hung over the edge. That floral theme continued onto the chintz quilt, each square displaying an arrangement of some flower or another.

Everything within the room bespoke the feminine touch of a woman and not the crass type of place that would be occupied by men like his assailants.

From somewhere outside the small quarters where he'd been—at some point—deposited, came the tread of heavy, determined footfalls . . . and then she entered. He closed his eyes and feigned sleep as he sought to place her: this woman, a stranger to him, whose voice and—amorphous in slumber—form had worked her way into his dreams. With a tangle of pale-blonde curls artfully arranged and held in place by a pair of enamel-and-gold hair combs, the woman was Spartan in her height. And yet Henry's mysterious caregiver also possessed a lush frame, rounded in all the places he, a proper gentleman, shouldn't notice but as a still living, breathing man could not help but appreciate, even in his misery.

She stopped beside the nightstand, hovering over his bed. Even with his eyes closed, he felt her stare as she moved it over his person. His . . . unclad person. "You are awake," she said with a blunt matter-of-factness. "Anytime you are ready to finish feigning sleep, please let me know," she drawled, moving the vase at his bedside to the floor. With that, she left the room. She returned a moment later with a pitcher.

Henry forced his eyes open, and the air lodged somewhere between his chest and his throat at the sight of her. And it was a testament to the depth of her exquisiteness that pain could be forgotten—he flinched as she pressed a hand to his forehead. He'd been wrong. Pain could not be forgotten.

"Friend or foe?" he asked, his voice coming out strangulated by a parched throat.

"If you were foe, I'd have left you for dead in the streets," she said flatly. "But you are awake, which, given your head wound, is promising," she announced, probing at a knot at his temple.

Everything—time, how he'd come to be here, what exactly had happened—was murky in his mind, blurred moments he struggled, and failed, to piece together. "How long have I been here?" he croaked.

The woman collected a pitcher and proceeded to pour water into a glass. "Twelve hours."

He pushed himself up onto his elbows. "Twelve hours?" Henry collapsed into the lumpy mattress under him.

"Here." Sitting at the edge of the bed, she helped him lift his head and then brought the glass to his lips. Too weak and thirsty to protest, Henry gulped the cool liquid, welcoming the balm as it slid down his sore throat. How had he failed to properly appreciate that sustaining drink until now? "Slower, my lord," she urged, a thread of impatience to that directive. Henry forced himself to swallow in moderation.

The exertion of keeping his head up proved too much a chore. He again laid his head down. "What happened?" he asked as she set aside the glass.

"I don't know your business, my lord," she said crisply.

His chest rose and fell rapidly from the toll this simplest of tasks—speaking—was taking on him. And yet . . . he needed to know . . . who she was and how he'd come to be here. "But you know I'm a lord." When he was uninjured and not weak as a babe, he'd have managed a coolness to his tones. He'd been stripped of all strength in the attack upon him.

The Spartan beauty lifted her shoulders in a shrug. "It didn't take much to read your calling card."

He frowned, the muscles of his mouth protesting even that slightest strain. So she'd gathered his identity . . . and kept him here anyway. With his gaze, Henry did another sweep of the room. Wherever "here" happened to be.

"I came upon you as you were being dragged off by two men, one named Judge?" *Judge?* He searched his clouded mind and came up empty. "They had beaten you badly. Stabbed you." She pointed to his waist. "And based on what I overheard, they intended to kill you." Otherwise, why not just make off with his purse and valuables?

"I don't know anyone by that name," he squeezed out past dry lips.

She shrugged. "You've got enemies. Who'd hate you enough to hire thugs to kill you?"

In his years as MP, he'd drafted legislation that had been controversial—laws and acts that had earned the fury of the masses, and unpopular ones that men and women of all stations had chafed at. "It's a long list," he whispered. "You helped me, though."

"Because I'm a fool," she mumbled, and that self-annoyance coating her tone erased all possibility that she'd been involved in his attack. Or it should. His doubts persisted.

"You know my identity . . ." And yet . . .

"You are wondering why I didn't summon your wife or family."

There was no wife. There should have been. Long ago. This attack and his near death on the streets only served as a reminder of all the years he'd neglected his responsibilities to the Waterson title. Except when he'd been lying there dying, choking on his own blood . . . it hadn't been a title he'd thought of. Rather, it had been all the things he'd not done in his life.

The woman claimed a spot beside him; the mattress dipped slightly under her weight. "Nothing good could have come from notifying anyone that I'd discovered you."

No. Had she sent word for his mother, Countess of Waterson and leading hostess of the *ton*, she would have reacted only to his circumstances and asked questions . . . not at all.

"I have to inspect your wound," the woman stated, taking charge, already reaching for his bandages, not seeking permission. "Are you able to turn slightly onto your side?"

He wasn't sure. Henry, however, was too proud to admit a hint of weakness. "I am." Strength had been ingrained into him by his late father, his tutors, and the university professors to come after. "I can sit up." It was another lie, as he wasn't wholly confident he could manage that feat. He attempted it anyway.

The air hissed between his teeth, as he swung one leg over the side of the bed. He promptly collapsed back, sweating.

"You've lost a lot of blood," she said, matter-of-fact when every woman of his acquaintance would have dissolved into a fit of tears at the mere mention of it. "You've suffered a head injury. Standing, sitting, or walking is hardly wise at this point." She unwrapped his makeshift bandages, damp with blood, with a methodical precision. Falling into perfect time to her movements, he shifted as she needed to unwind the cloth around his waist.

And it was a testament to his weakness that he found himself nearly naked, now being stripped to the waist by a stranger—and a woman, at that. "Do you have a name?" he asked, panting.

His mysterious caregiver paused, allowing him a brief break. "Clara."

Clara.

Just that. Her Christian name—a further scandal he'd not have tolerated . . . ever.

"Clara . . . ?"

"You don't need my last name," she said crisply. "Here, turn," she urged. In a bid to deflect from his question?

He obliged. "I can hardly call you by your given name."

"Says who? I'm not one of your fancy ladies." And yet her tones were as polished and cultured as any woman of the peerage.

"It isn't . . . proper." He grimaced, and this time it wasn't pain but rather . . . embarrassment. As soon as the odd sentiment slipped in, he quashed it. There was no shame to be had from being . . . proper.

The woman—Clara—snorted as if she'd heard that silent assurance he sought to make himself. "You want a title, call me Nurse Clara," she drawled. "There." Clara tossed aside the bloodstained bandages. The debate over how they might address one another was promptly ended.

Their brief conversation and his back-and-forth shifting had depleted him of the small surge of energy he'd found upon waking that morn. Henry closed his eyes and lay there, concentrating on breathing to keep from focusing on the pain. "How bad is it?" he whispered.

There was a slight pause, and then . . . "Bad."

Despite the fire burning at his side, Henry found his lips twitching in the faintest trace of a smile. "You are nothing if not honest, Clara."

"I have no reason to lie. Just like I don't have any reason to be 'Madam' or 'Miss' or 'Mrs.' to you."

He wanted to point out that she also didn't recognize sarcasm but could not muster the energy to debate her on that point.

The mattress squeaked, and he forced his eyes open to find her striding across the room. "I thought I might not have to stitch it."

His stomach roiled. "Stitch it?"

Clara glanced back over her shoulder. "Your side," she elucidated, mistaking the reason for his unease.

When other boys at Eton and then Oxford had taken a perverse thrill Henry himself had never understood in beating one another to the point that they'd required stitches, Henry had been calculated in that regard, too. His physical activities had all been as measured as his life: riding, fencing, and when he'd been younger, boxing with Gentleman Jackson himself. Never had he been risky in those pursuits.

"You've never had stitches," his caregiver remarked with a dawning understanding in her sultry tones.

Henry gave his head a slight shake.

"They're not pleasant," she went on with that blunt directness he was fast learning to be a part of this peculiar woman. "But in your case, they are necessary. Your wound is still bleeding." She stopped beside an oddly shaped bag that rested in the corner of the room.

Carrying the black leather article over, she set it down on the now-empty nightstand.

She quit the rooms and returned a moment later with a bowl, sloshing water back and forth as she walked, before setting it down with a *thunk*.

Dipping her hands inside the bowl, she proceeded to wash them.

He followed those movements. "I have a family doctor," he said, his voice threadbare to his own ears.

She snorted. "One of those fine doctors who'll do what?" Clara winged a perfectly arched brow up. "Bleed you and the infection?"

Yes, that was precisely what Dr. Quimbley would do. "And you know so much of medicine, Clara?" he asked without any malice.

Dusting her hands on a clean linen towel, she returned the cloth to the corner of her makeshift workspace. "And do you?" she began, turning his question on him. "That there is a result of your injuries."

He struggled to turn his head and follow her gesture . . . over to the opposite corner of his—her—rooms. A pile of discarded cloths, all stained with dried blood, rested there.

"All that blood of yours . . . lost. Now tell me, do you truly feel better for losing all that blood?" she murmured.

No. He felt weak as a damned babe, wholly incapable of forming proper words or managing the slightest movements.

"As you were," he said weakly, his chest rising and falling fast.

Clara went back to withdrawing her medical equipment. Next, she pulled from her bag a sewing kit and needle. She lined them all up in a neat row, pausing to straighten the ball of thread.

He should be fixing on the fact that this woman, whom he knew not at all: one, had managed to convince him not to summon his family doctor, and two, intended to thread that needle and slide it through his skin.

And yet . . . there was a greater . . . fascination with her. And her experience and strength and confidence. "How did you come by your experience?" he asked, briefly closing his eyes once more.

"Would you care to see my letters of reference?" she offered with an increasingly familiar drollness.

"Call it curiosity about the woman who is going to sew my skin up . . . ," he returned, his voice trailing off from the taxation of speaking too much.

A little laugh escaped her, as unexpected as everything proved with this woman. Husky and warm and inviting. A siren's laugh. When Henry had never been so weak as to be captivated by anyone. He managed his desire with as tight a control as he did his finances and dealings in Parliament. Something about this woman, however, said she wasn't one to be managed . . . in any way.

Despite his requests, she ignored his question. She turned her attention to tending his injury. Collecting a cloth, she began cleaning the remnants of blood from his side.

He winced and then made himself go still.

"Men and your refusal to show emotion," she chided as she went about that task.

Henry wanted to respond with a clever, snappy retort, but he'd been reduced to the burning at his side. His breath came hard and fast, and he clutched the damp sheets in his frail grip.

Wipe, rinse, wring out—repeat. Each drag of the cloth over the knife wound, the water seeping in and then the injury being cleaned, sent nausea climbing up his throat.

Clara tossed aside another rag and then reached for her needle and thread.

He focused on breathing. In and out.

"You are going to make yourself faint," she said gently.

"I don't faint," he said with as much indignation as he could muster on his back, incapable of lifting his head for any real duration of time.

"You also haven't had stitches, Lord Waterson."

Lord Waterson.

It was the proper form of address and one he'd have insisted upon with any woman, regardless of station, out of propriety's sake.

And yet . . .

"My name is Henry. Considering my current state and the unexpected intimacy of our situation, I trust it is safe to dispense with formalities." It must be the pain. There was no other accounting for his dispensing with proper decorum.

A smile formed on her full lips; it was not the more jaded expression of mirth she'd worn earlier, but rather real and sincere and lit her eyes, only elevating her beauty. And mayhap it was the loss of blood, but that smile had a dizzying effect on him. "You are certain my referring to you by your given name is . . . proper."

"Hmm?" It took a moment for her words to register. *She is making light of me.*

"You are teasing."

She leaned close, and the whisper of lavender filled his senses as she placed her lips close to his ear. "I trust you're not altogether familiar with being teased."

"Or . . . or . . ."

"Teasing," she supplied for him. "It's hardly blasphemy to say the word."

"Teasing," he finished, his neck going hot, not with embarrassment but rather with her assumptions about him and his existence. He was nearly forty-two years of age, and his days were alternately spent overseeing the March estates and finances and drafting legislation from his offices at Parliament. "There simply isn't a place for it in my world."

"How very . . . sad." The slight pause there conveyed more pity than the word itself.

His head pounded like the devil from a conversation that had gone on entirely too long. *Go to sleep. Close your eyes, and let her start and finish sewing you up.* And yet . . . "It is not sad." When he'd been a younger man, fresh out of university, his father had passed, and along with his death, all responsibilities had shifted to Henry—including the care of his mother and siblings. There was no shame to be had in taking on that role for his family. And his pride proved as great as his threshold for pain. "I assure you, my existence is . . . quite purposeful." Never dangerous before now. Even as that pathetic-to-his-own-ears defense left him, he grimaced.

"I'm sure it is."

Another time, Henry might have been piqued at finding himself the source of any person's judgment. In this instance, as he struggled to remain alert while maintaining his pride, and suffered through the injuries he'd sustained in his attack, her response proved the perfect distraction. "Carry on, Clara," he said as coolly as he could manage.

"I'm going slow deliberately." Of course the spitfire would challenge him at every turn. "You've never before had stitches, Henry. The first time, many faint."

He opened his mouth to disabuse her of the notion that he'd do something as weak as faint . . . and yet, since his attack, he'd been largely without control of his faculties. "And have you?" he asked gruffly.

"Fainted or had stitches?" she asked without hesitation.

"Both."

"I've sewn up enough people to know the two often go hand in hand."

As she reclaimed a spot at his bedside, it did not escape his notice that she'd failed to answer his question. No doubt deliberately. The woman clung tight to her secrets.

He stiffened.

Clara pierced his skin with the needle, and he winced. Bile churned in his belly and climbed his throat. "Easy, Henry," she murmured, as if testing those two syllables. Nay, as if tasting the feel of them on her tongue, wrapped in sultry tones more potent than the drag of her needle. "It will go easier if you're relaxed. I won't rush," she vowed in those same gentling tones. "I'll go slowly."

In the end, it was the soothing quality of her voice that released some of the tension from his frame.

She worked in silence for a long moment. "I trust your illustrious name comes from one of England's great King Henrys?" she asked, directing that question to his injured side.

She was trying to distract him. And he appreciated those efforts. He concentrated on breathing. "There are only nine previous monarchs named Henry. First through second, and then Henry, the young king, who was a"—he flinched as Clara inserted the needle into his skin once more—"junior king to Henry the Second, and from there, we resume the proper count of three up through the last monarch named Henry— Henry the Eighth."

"Yes, well. I trust the legacy of nobility is much diminished when one goes about killing one's wives," she said dryly.

"There is that," he muttered. "My namesake, however, is the first Earl of Waterson."

"Who was undoubtedly named after one of those nine great monarchs."

Undoubtedly?

He frowned. It was surely the height of folly to challenge the very person responsible for one's care, who even now had a needle in one hand and his flesh in the other. Nonetheless, that thinly veiled disapproval rankled. "By your tones, you take umbrage with my respecting a distinguished lineage."

Clara paused and brushed the back of her spare hand over her brow. "I take greater umbrage with men and women who don't place proper respect where it is due."

What in blazes is that supposed to mean?

"It means, Henry, that my respect is reserved for those who make their own fortunes and build their own empires." And not ones who were passed those privileges.

The words rang as clear as if she'd spoken them aloud. Her charges and scandalous opinions proved distracting. "Your respect is reserved, then, for self-made men." Those rabble-rousers who'd rioted at Manchester and sent guns firing into a crowd, without caring about the welfare of the passersby. Tension snapped through him, and the suddenness of that movement sent a hiss slipping through his teeth.

"Try not to move," Clara urged, and he made himself go still once more. "Nor is my respect reserved for self-made men," she went on, continuing to stitch his wound.

"That is reassuring."

"I also have great—mayhap greater—respect for self-made women."

Self-made . . . ? He laughed, and that expression of mirth cut off on a gasp as his whole body screamed in protest to those exertions. He glanced up to find Clara's eyes narrowed on him, and the truth slammed into him.

"You were *not* jesting."

"I was *not*."

Henry creased his brow. If she'd sought to distract him, she was succeeding beyond her greatest expectations. He studied her face, her high brow, devoid of any wrinkles of amusement, killing all possibility that she was teasing.

"I trust you've little experience with self-made women." More of her pitying tones.

He pounced. "Is that what you are?"

There was the slightest of pauses. "You know my rules, Henry."

Yes, that was right. She clung to her secrets and her life like most noble families protected familial heirlooms. Mayhap that was the reason for the intrigue swirling through him, intensifying with every question she evaded or detail she inadvertently revealed.

"I'm going to continue," she said in gentle warning, but before she touched the needle to his side, she stared down at him. Waiting. Allowing him some control.

Henry nodded.

Only this time, the original horror of being stuck with a needle now realized, he focused on the surprising lack of sensation.

"The edge of the wound becomes numb," she explained, inserting the needle downward. "The idea is to start with the closest edge of the wound to you. Face and sew away from yourself." She shifted slightly. "Now I'm going to level off the needle and venture through the wound and to the adjacent wall of the injury."

He breathed through clenched lips. "You're certain you aren't a nurse?" he whispered, directing that question up at the ceiling. More than half hoping she was.

"I am quite certain." She spoke with a finality that indicated she neither expected nor wanted further questions about her past. "Relax," she murmured, not lifting her gaze from her task. "It is worse if you tense up."

While she saw to his wound, Henry remained with his eyes closed, dozing between sleep and being pulled awake by the occasional tug as Clara brought the needle through his skin.

"There," she murmured, tying off the knot. "You were lucky last night."

"This is lucky?" he asked, his voice beginning to fade.

"You aren't dead, Henry. As such, I'd suggest you count your blessings. In the meantime, perhaps you'd care to send word to your family?"

His family. Yes, of course. His mother would even now be frantic. His sisters would be intrigued that he'd gone missing. His fellow MPs would be scandalized that Henry had failed to appear in his offices at Parliament.

Later. He would see to it later.

"Please," he whispered, his eyes heavy.

"My lord?" Clara asked, her voice growing distant.

"Do not leave."

And then he slept.

Chapter 5

Do not leave.

Those words, stated as a plea from the now silently slumbering gentleman. Just as he'd been slumbering since she'd brought him back.

"Nay, Henry," Clara said into the quiet as she hung the last previously bloodstained, now clean, rag along the drying rack in her kitchen.

She glanced back toward the rooms where Henry still slept.

Bloody, bloody hell.

She'd bathed, changed her garments, arranged her hair, tidied her apartments, including his—her—rooms, and he'd not roused through any of it.

He'd remained absolutely motionless. So still, in fact, that there had been four times where she'd had to force herself to search for his pulse, fearing what she'd find. Or rather, fearing what she would *not* find.

And then where would she be?

Clara grimaced. Though in actuality, it was not solely self-preservation responsible for that reaction. Death, dying, and murder were moments the people of East London viewed with the same casualness they did breathing and eating.

She, however, despite all the time she'd lived amongst them, had never been accustomed to or so comfortable with the idea of a person—man or woman—drawing their last breath. There was a finality to it. An end that represented no hope for anything better.

Quitting the kitchen, Clara returned to her doorway and checked on the gentleman once more. The previous coverlet—her favorite article of chintz flowers—now dirtied, had been replaced with a simple white linen sheet. Ever so faintly, it rose and fell in cadence with his shallow breaths.

Clara worried her lower lip, wishing she were more jaded. After all, she had every reason to hate mankind and the world they ruled so ruthlessly as much as any other whore. But this hadn't always been her world. Which no doubt accounted for her weakness.

That weakness was why she remained here, making sure he continued to breathe, even as there was work to be done at her music hall, set to open in two months' time.

A frustrated sigh escaped her.

"I'll have you know this is not ideal timing for me," she called quietly over to the earl. "I have my own affairs to see to."

Only silence met her chastisement. The longer she kept a nobleman here, the more perilous it was for her. Now that he had awakened and was able to report for himself on what had befallen him on the streets she was safe.

And if he dies still? How will you explain having the battered body of a nobleman in your apartments?

A chill scraped along her spine, and she forced aside the silent voice needling at her.

Heading to the Adam-style writing desk in the living area of her apartments, Clara opened the center drawer and removed her notes and folio there. She slammed them down with a hard thwack. Then, gripping both sides of the desk, she proceeded to drag it around until she had a view of her bedroom and her patient.

Through the noise of the wood legs scraping the floor, Henry remained still.

And as he slept, Clara focused her energies on something that was within her control: her music hall. Neither a saloon nor a theatre, what she and her only real friend in the world, Regina Killoran, intended to provide was a venue unlike any other. But also, it represented something more: a business of her own. Run with the help of another woman. Meant to employ women so they needn't sell their bodies as Clara had been forced to do. *Just as the women who worked under you were forced to do.*

Remorse burnt her throat, a raw, all-too-familiar emotion. Clara stared blankly ahead, over the top of the sleeping earl. Through the years she'd sought to erase the guilt that came with being responsible for young women selling their bodies to survive.

Survival was what it had been. And a job was also what it had been. She'd told herself that enough over the years that she'd even allowed herself to believe it—for a while. One could only lie to oneself so long before the lie caught up with them.

From her earliest days as the daughter of London's most famed actress, Clara had made so many mistakes. She'd angered the wrong man for the right reasons. She'd taken a moral stand against one who'd stood for evil. That right decision had been met with disastrous results, caused by the man who had ruined any hope Clara had for an honorable future.

"Enough," she whispered, forcing her fingers to pick up her pencil. She'd not allow her past to occupy any more of her life.

The past couldn't be changed. Only one's future could.

She stared at the names of the performers whom she had managed to commit to a contract: five women.

That was all.

Two ballerinas. Two singers at Drury Lane. And one actress.

Former performers, who, like Clara, had become whores and now wanted a new life . . . a new way.

That number represented the only women who'd been willing to walk away from the security of their posts to take a chance on a new establishment . . . run by two women.

Clara's gaze went to the note from her builder.

And until they opened, the women would continue to be without pay. *All the while, you're off playing nursemaid to a nobleman.*

A pit formed low in her belly as the enormity of that obligation and responsibility weighted her shoulders.

Focus on what you can control . . .

Those words, her mother's, who'd always been in such control and masterful with everything, echoed in her mind. Providing strength.

Clara set to work constructing the performance schedule and routines for the music hall's opening. The struggle remained in striking a balance: gentlemen largely came to the theatre to find their next mistress. Ladies attended for the gossip. Therefore, to be successful, one must create an experience so grandiose, so magnificent, that the latter focuses became secondary and forgotten.

Clara's pencil flew over the page, and she paused periodically to strike a line through an idea. She worked until her muscles ached, and then she continued working.

Sometime later, Clara took a break. She was arching her neck, first left and then right, stretching the muscles there . . . when she registered the touch of a stare upon her.

Her gaze went to the sleeping earl.

And she gasped at finding his hooded eyes on her. "Hullo."

The pencil fell from her fingers, and she hurried to her feet. Oh, thank the God in heaven who proved Himself real, after all. "You are awake." She was already stalking over to her unlikely patient.

Using his elbows, Henry struggled to push himself upright, and she increased her pace.

"You should take care to avoid hasty movements. You'll open your stitches."

"How long was I sleeping?" he asked. Even with his voice ragged and weak, there was a husky timbre to it. Melodic tones spoken in his crisp King's English. It was an unnecessary reminder of his station and the dangerous game she'd unwittingly made herself a player in during a moment of weakness.

She consulted the timepiece at her breast. "A long time."

He closed his eyes, and she thought he'd sleep once more, but then he again spoke. "What time is it?"

"It is late," she murmured as she reached for his sheet.

He caught her wrist in a surprisingly strong and yet somehow still-tender grip that sent tiny shivers, delicious ones that held her frozen, radiating up her arm.

In the years in which Clara had turned herself into a gentleman's plaything, she'd come to learn all manner of the human touch: The commanding one. The violent one. One that was purposeful, devoid of warmth, and sought just one thing from her.

Only to find here, with Henry's fingers twined about her wrist, that she'd been . . . wrong. There was another touch.

Unnerved by that awareness when she'd long ago ceased being aware of any man, she drew her hand back. And surprisingly, when another man might have fought for control, this earl released her. "I am checking your injury," she said softly.

He eyed her with a proper degree of wariness but then gave a small nod.

Clara gathered the edges of the sheet once more and folded the linen down. Trying not to notice the contoured planes of his chest and hard muscles of his flat stomach.

Because she didn't want to notice that her body was responding to his masculine perfection. She preferred when she was simply the jaded courtesan who long ago had ceased to be affected by any man.

Focusing on her task, she inspected her stitchwork and the area around his wound.

"You're quite skilled with a needle," he said, his voice so hushed she barely caught his words.

"I told you. I've had extensive work with one," she murmured without thinking. Before realizing she'd said too much. This time, unlike the prior one when he'd awakened, he did not press her for information. She finished checking the other injuries he'd sustained: around his head, his broken nose—pausing at that slightly crooked appendage.

Her heart tugged. There could be no disputing the once sharp and perfect lines of that noble nose.

"It is broken?"

"Your nose? Yes," she said softly and drew the sheet back over him. "But it adds character." Of course, he hadn't needed character. At least not physically. Hers, however, was a rote response she'd given to young women who'd been left with scars by too-rough patrons, who'd sobbed at the damage done to their beauty.

Where noblemen were concerned, it wouldn't matter whether one had two heads or none, as long as one had a title.

That was the unfairness of the world.

"Do you have a mirror?" he asked.

She hesitated. With each passing hour his bruises had set, the color changing and deepening so that his cheeks were a canvas of purple, green, black, and blue. "Across the room," she finally relented.

He followed her stare over to the floor-length piece in question. "Will you help me stand?"

Clara dug her heels in. Men of the streets were accustomed to sporting all number of breaks and bruises. Every last gentleman she'd had dealings with who'd suffered the slightest injury had dissolved into blubbering panic. "I don't think that is a wise idea, Henry." Given the state of his head injuries and stitches, he couldn't afford the upset.

"Because of my injuries or because of how I look?"

"Both," she said with a reflexive honesty that brought another faint grin to his swollen lips. They parted enough to reveal two flawless rows of even white teeth. And she found an odd relief that that perfection remained unmarred.

The earl pushed himself upright; a sheen glistened on his body from that exertion.

"Oh, you stubborn man," she gritted out. "You are going to undo all the progress you've made." He answered by setting his bare feet on the floor. "Stay as you are." Rushing over to the French cheval, gold-trimmed mirror, Clara dragged the piece over. She took care to keep the glass reversed, facing the door until she could be beside the obstinate lout. She made one more appeal. "You have nothing to gain in looking at yourself in this condition."

"You'd expect me to hide the truth from myself, then?"

"Actually, yes. Yes, I would." Gentlemen didn't squarely face anything unpleasant. At the first hint of discomfort, they turned on their fancy, fine heels and took off running for the comforts they took as their due.

"I'm not one who hides from anything." With his swollen lips, those words emerged slightly garbled.

She sighed and reluctantly brought the mirror around.

He stared at his visage. The clock at her breast loudly ticked the passing seconds. No words were said. Through that study, Henry's expression remained impassive. And then he gave a slight nod. "Thank you."

Clara rushed to move the mirror back into place in its usual position beside her armoire.

"I cannot return home like this."

It took a moment for that statement to register.

She blinked slowly. "Beg pardon?"

"My family"—his wife and children—"cannot see me in this state."

"You cannot stay here," she blurted. "That is . . . I cannot stay on here as your caregiver. Your wounds, those bruises? They'll take weeks to heal. If you become infected, you can die. Anything might happen." And she'd be held responsible for his death.

"I thought you didn't trust my . . . fancy doctor."

"I don't. Just tell him not to bleed you, to keep the wounds clean, and to wash his hands, and you'll be fine." She shook her head. "But I cannot be your nurse." The care he would require was constant, and time was not a luxury Clara had. Not with the work still to be done with her music hall . . . not when so many women were reliant upon the money they'd earn once it opened.

"A week."

"No."

"Three days," he persisted.

Good God, he is tenacious. "What will that do?" she implored. "You'll still have the look of one who was dragged facedown through London, which is what, in fact, happened to you." She swiped her palms down her face and then let her arms fall to her sides. Once more, Clara tried to reason with him. "You have a family who is worried about you." How long had it been since she herself had family who loved her and cared for her? The closest she'd come since her mother's passing had been Regina, whom she'd known just three years. Clara sat on the edge of the mattress, close to the earl's broad shoulder. "They will care less about what you look like than that you are home safe, my lord."

"They'll worry about me."

He sought to protect his family, then. "You do them no favors by shielding them from the darkness. Inevitably, night always falls."

"That isn't a code by which a gentleman lives his life."

"Neither, I trust, is wandering the streets of the Dials at night, and that is what you were doing," she pointed out.

"My family cannot see me in this state," he repeated with an impressive cool for one incapable of sitting up or lifting his head for any duration.

Clara contemplated the earl and his insistence. All the gentlemen she had known had been unfaithful to their wives and eventually returned to those respectable spouses after taking their pleasures with Clara or the girls she'd overseen. And yet, here was apparently the one man in the whole of the realm who cared more about protecting his family. It was . . . wholly foreign. She felt herself wavering and fought that lapse in judgment.

"I'll not ask or expect you to care for me," he pressed. "Just allow me to remain."

No good can come from his being here. Send him away.

She made one more attempt. "You're so very worried about alarming your family. How will they be when you do not return home?"

His hesitation was palpable, not a product of his flagging energy but of the point she'd raised. "I can pen a note and have you see that it is sent to my residence."

"You do the women in your life a disservice, my lord," she said crisply. "Women do not need to be coddled. They need to be armed with the truth and allowed the ability to act without interference."

"Perhaps." By the incredulity brimming in his pain-filled gaze, he was of a different opinion and wouldn't ever see reason. "Not, however, these women."

Clara felt herself weakening and resisted.

Mad. This was utter madness. For the truth remained, despite his insistence, that as long as he *was* here, he was her responsibility. His care. His living. His dying. Any infection to his injuries. All of it . . . fell to her. He was a complication she couldn't afford. Not when she'd already had too many to count where her new business was concerned. And how very typical it was for a nobleman to ask her to make those sacrifices. That truth alone should break through her weakening resolve.

"Two days." The offer slipped forward before she could call it back. "You are free to remain two days, and then you leave." She braced for a continued fight . . . that surprisingly did not come.

Clara had started for the door when he called out, his voice weak, "Thank you."

She nodded once, and as she left, she closed the door behind her.

She'd risked much by rescuing him from the streets and bringing him to her apartments. One could never trust a man. She knew that well enough, having learned in the most difficult way to never allow an earl who'd been dragged through the streets of the Dials to make her home a place to hide. So why did she allow him to remain despite all that?

As she returned to her work for the Muses, she could not stave off the sliver of dread that she'd made yet another unpardonable mistake.

Chapter 6

After a restless night's sleep, Henry felt a healthy modicum of shame as he admitted that he'd never properly appreciated the simplest luxuries for the gifts they were.

A fire—he missed his hearth. The blazing, always well-stoked ones that warmed every room his staff correctly anticipated he'd enter in the course of a day.

A raise. The whole lot of them deserved and would receive a damned raise.

Teeth chattering, Henry shifted under the thin blankets. His side twinged in protest, wringing a gasp from him. Fire burnt from his wound. So hot, and yet, damned if he wasn't bloody freezing. "A-and c-coverlets," he stammered into the quiet, hating the distorted quality to his words, that product of his swollen lips. He missed the heavy, lined, high-quality coverlets that he'd also never given due thought to. Never again. He'd recall this instance every time henceforth when he climbed into his four-poster bed with warmed sheets.

The need for heat greater than the need to avoid further pain, Henry burrowed deeper into the mattress, taking whatever warmth he could from Clara's bed.

When this was done . . . he was sending the woman a mattress. A fine one.

And imagine how that should appear to Polite Society if . . . when . . . the ton *learned of that morsel of gossip?*

Henry, the stodgy, always proper Earl of Waterson, ordering a bed for a woman in the Dials. He chuckled, the sound emerging strained and hoarse to his own ears.

There was the soft tread of footfalls outside his temporary rooms, and then without so much as a knock, the door handle turned and the panel opened. Clara ducked into the room with a tray in her hand. "I am leaving for the—" She stopped abruptly, and even in the darkened space, he caught the frown on her lips. "Are you all right?" There was a faint thread of impatience underlying that question.

And once again he found that honesty . . . refreshing. She wasn't one who took to serving him and hadn't backed down in her determination to send him on his way. It was hard not to admire someone who had convictions. Nor had she sought money in exchange for her premises.

"It is deuced c-cold," he managed between his chattering teeth.

"Cold?" He may as well have asked her to set her own residence on fire for the shock in that question. Clara came over and set the tray down on the nightstand next to him. "It is summer."

"A cold summer night."

"No. No, not at all. It's warm. Quite warm, really. And furthermore," she went on, pouring him a glass of water, the steady stream of liquid oddly calming, "it's hardly night."

Hardly night? Ignoring the glass she held out, Henry reached around it, making a slow grab for his timepiece. Struggling to see through swollen eyes, he sought to bring the numbers into focus.

"Just after four o'clock," she supplied for him.

"This is hardly morning," he managed, collapsing back onto the mattress. It was an ungodly hour.

His reluctant caregiver snorted. "For the working class it is, my lord."

For the working class. Nor did it escape his notice that she'd wrapped that form of address as a thinly veiled insult. "Yours is not an unfamiliar response."

"And what is that?"

"Disdainful. The work I do as MP is not always appreciated." Especially by those he sought to help most.

"You expect pretty thank-yous for the laws you draft?"

"I'm quite content without any expressions of gratitude." He managed a wry grin. "I'd settle for simply not having an occasional brick thrown through my window at Parliament."

Her head whipped up. "Someone threw a . . . brick through your window?"

There was a shockingly breathless quality to her voice. One that was totally at odds with the bold directness he'd come to expect from the one who'd stitched his side and tended his wounds.

"No," he corrected. "Someone threw *five* bricks through my window while I was in the stages of negotiating legislation some took exception to." An act he'd put forward to abolish slavery had been met with fierce resistance from men who'd ultimately proven their greed was greater than their sense of moral right.

"And so now you look with distrust upon all the working class because of the treatment of some." Hers was both a statement and a fair point.

As Clara set down the pitcher, he followed those work-roughened hands; her nails short, her fingers callused, they were not the hands of a lady.

Odd, he'd spent all his adult years drafting legislation and debating on some of the most essential laws that would govern the kingdom. And after his sister's near death during the Peterloo Massacre, Henry had spent the past seven of them attempting to bring order to that working class. To prevent struggle. Never, however, had he considered their lot.

"Here, Henry."

Unnerved, he struggled up onto his elbows as she brought the glass toward his lips. She laid her hand gently along the back of his sweat-dampened head and braced him so he had support to keep himself upright while he drank.

"Slower," she murmured as his throat worked. She'd indicated she had no intention of being a caregiver, and yet that was precisely what she'd either unknowingly or knowingly made herself. After he'd finished swallowing, she made to remove her hand.

A frown puckered the place between her brows. She hurriedly pressed the back of her spare palm against his brow. She blanched. "Bloody hell," she whispered.

"Wh-what?"

"You've a fever." There was an accusatory thread there.

Damn it. "I cannot help it that I h-have a fever." But he could have helped it by leaving as she'd wished so she needn't care for him any further. And it spoke volumes of the woman that she didn't throw that very fact back in his face.

With another inventive curse, Clara unfastened her fine silk cloak and returned it to her armoire. Henry took in the pink satin piping along the trim of her silk dress, the iridescent shine of that high-quality fabric.

That dress was so wholly at odds with this place and these streets. As were her tones. And for not the first time since he'd come to and found her hovering over him, he wondered about the woman who had found him. Nay, who'd saved him.

"What are you doing?" he asked faintly, struggling to draw the coverlet close to his chin.

"I am playing nursemaid, after all," she muttered. "I can't very well have you go and die on me."

He managed a weak chuckle. "I promise I shan't die."

Another inelegant snort escaped her as she pushed the sleeves of her gown up. "How very typical of you noblemen to believe you can command even death."

"You've a low opinion of the n-nobility." His voice came out raspy, and he burrowed deeper under the blankets.

"I have a low opinion of all men. Those sentiments are not reserved for the peerage." Clara fetched another blanket and covered him with the floral article.

"Wh-what of your respect for the self-made man?"

"And self-made woman," she reminded. "I respect what they manage to do. That is altogether different from respecting a person for who they are."

As she continued caring for him, Henry tried to make sense of her pronouncement. Who a man was, was intrinsically connected to what he accomplished. Or, at least, that was the way he saw the world. As such, Clara and her peculiar views were a confounding contradiction.

Throughout the remainder of the day, Clara proceeded to apply cool compresses to his head and under his arms. The chill of those damp cloths stung as much as the scrapes he'd earned from his attack. And as she cared for him, Henry lay there and came to an unexpected reckoning: how very inadequate he was in so many ways. On the streets, he'd been helpless to defend himself. Neither his rank nor wealth nor his work in Parliament had been his salvation that day, but instead, this tall, spirited woman. A woman who was also as skilled at stitching skin as she was at bringing down a fever. And all he knew was that whenever she was near, he wasn't focusing on the pain ravaging his body, but rather . . . her.

She was the angel who kept him from the precipice of darkness. Or mayhap she was a siren. Either way, her pull was magnetic and called to him. His teeth chattered. "Who are y-you?"

She stiffened. "I don't know—"

"Y-you've the speech of a lady and the gowns, as well." But for the streets she lived in, and the interior of her residence, she may as well have been any lady in Mayfair's fine parlors or rooms.

"You asked to stay," she said bluntly. "I didn't, however, allow you questions." Her eyes flashed.

She was a woman who cloaked herself in secrets, and it added a layer of intrigue to her. It filled him with a desire to know who she was.

"You should leave," she said quietly. "You should return to your wife and children."

Once again, those responsibilities he'd put off for too long. "Th-there is no wife or children." And given his current circumstances, there might never be. Desolation swept through him.

Clara picked her head up quickly. Suspicion and confusion both rolled together in her clear gaze. "But . . . you indicated your family."

"I was speaking of my two sisters and my m-mother," he explained, rubbing his arms in a bid to bring warmth into the trembling limbs. Honoring that end of his responsibilities was something which had, after Lila's near death and then descent into reclusiveness, been secondary to his other goals. "M-my mother was scheduled to leave for the country with one of my sisters, who is expecting. I simply sought to remain here until they left."

"And your other sister?"

His stomach muscles clenched. Clara with her million-and-one secrets had given him every reason and permission to answer not a single question she had about him. "She doesn't leave"—*the townhouse*—"London." Despite the fact this woman had witnessed him at his most vulnerable, he still could not bring himself to confide the state of his sister's well-being with her. As she removed the cool compresses from his person and returned them to the now tepid bowl of water, he followed her movements. Searching her face. "N-no further qu-questions?"

She lifted one shoulder in a shrug. "Every person has their secrets. The nobility is no different in that regard." She spoke as one who had a familiarity with the *ton*, only stirring intrigue all the more in Clara With-No-Surname-She-Cared-To-Give. "You didn't wish to say anything further on your sister, and as such, I'd not press you. That is your information. Not mine."

Here, when the ladies of Polite Society had found almost a vicious glee in spreading ideas and questions through London's parlors and ballrooms about Henry's sister. And mayhap it was the fever. Or mayhap it was the fact that she was a stranger who belonged to an entirely different world and when he left, their paths would never again cross, but he found himself wanting to share that tragic secret not even discussed between Henry and his family. "She was at the Peterloo Massacre."

Clara briefly paused with another wet cloth midway between Henry and the washbasin. The rag hung there in her fingers, dripping water onto the hardwood floor.

He rolled onto his back and angled his face, eyes closed, toward the ceiling overhead. "Y-you're wondering what a lady was doing in Manchester." Henry's breath came ragged; his chest moved up and down at a frantic pace while sweat, mingled with the remnants of cool water at his brow, dripped down his cheek. "She'd gone to visit her friend. There had been talk of impending insurrection . . . in Parliament." The talks and tales of the peril unfolding in that bustling corner of England had filled every chamber. There had been a false sense of control over a situation that had been a powder keg of doom, with an explosion by the masses imminent. "I summoned her." *But I didn't go to gather her myself.*

And that was the greatest mistake and the gravest sin he'd take with him to his grave.

In Clara's thirty-three years on this earth, she'd sat with or beside four people as they'd prepared to meet their makers. One had been her mother, London's greatest stage actress since Sarah Siddons. Two had been young whores who'd perished in childbirth. The other had been a child pickpocket from the first club she'd worked at, who'd suffered a knife wound to his belly.

She recalled each moment with each person. There was a vivid clarity to those exchanges still, where a person—even the most jaded—could not ever forget what it was like when a person prepared to draw their last breath.

It was why she knew with every bit of information Henry, the Earl of Waterson, shared about his family, that his words came forward as a confession; he was a man seeking a benediction.

Her heart thudded with a sick, dull beat—the same dread that had kept her company while she'd sat beside the four before him.

He could not die.

A beaten and battered earl dead in her rooms was the last thing she could afford.

And yet, peculiarly, that was not the sole reason for her worry.

She didn't want to have his death added to the vast number of sins she carried.

Clara sighed and grabbed a chair, sliding it closer to the side of his bed. "What happened to your sister wasn't your fault," she said, giving him the words he needed to hear.

His lips twisted into a pained smile. "She is my responsibility."

She frowned. That is certainly what he . . . and all men believed. Women were their responsibilities; in the case of the nobility, their women were prized possessions to be watched over and guarded like fine silver. "Did you introduce her to her friend?"

His feverish eyes registered confusion.

"Whomever it was she was visiting? I trust that friendship was one you carefully coordinated. Mayhap your families are friends?"

"I . . ." Shame flashed in his gaze, replacing that earlier perplexity. "I was not familiar with the young woman. She attended finishing school with my sister."

"Ah, so it is your fault, then, because your sister knew this woman from finishing school. Had you not sent her on, they would have never met, and she would have never been traveling that road of the massacre."

Closing his eyes, he drew in a ragged breath. "I'm usually sharper than this. My wit's been dulled from the attack. Say whatever it is you're saying that I'm missing."

Clara rested her palms on her knees and leaned forward, the chair groaning under her shifted weight. "I'm saying that you, like every other man, takes ownership of women . . . including their decisions and fates and futures. Sometimes accidents happen, and they aren't things you could prevent or alter." She grinned wryly. "Unless you are Father Time with your fingertips on the handle of a clock." She stared at his bruised face. "No streets are safe, Henry," she murmured, schooling him on a lesson he still hadn't gleaned, even with his beating. "Just because she was a woman . . . a lady . . . doesn't mean she's any more immune to the darkness that any other man or woman faces."

He shivered. "Th-thank y-you." Another shudder racked his frame, and she damned the state of helplessness that came with a fever. Henry's thick lashes drifted open. They were magnificent lashes. Which was, of course, a preposterous detail to note at this precise moment in time, and yet . . . she was riveted by those thick, dark strands. "Am I going t-to die?" he whispered, and through her pathetic musings, Clara blinked slowly. Was he . . . ?

And if she'd still been an innocent, admiring a nearly unconscious man as she was would certainly have been grounds for a blush. "No," she said dryly. "You aren't going to die."

He stretched his hand out and caught her fingers in his, clinging to her palm as if it were a lifeline to the living. His touch burnt hot, sending warmth spiraling through her. It was the fever. His fever. That was the only way one could account for that heat. "How confident you a-are, Clara."

"You're too stubborn to die, Henry." The smallest of smiles ghosted his lips, and then he closed his eyes.

Panic brought her shooting to her feet. "Henry?" she asked, her voice pitched as she moved over him.

His eyes opened, and this time there was a flash of something unexpected in their feverish depths—amusement. "Not as confident as you let on, Clara With-No-Surname," he murmured.

She didn't blink for several moments. "Why . . . why . . . You were teasing me."

He lay there, silent, for a long while, not replying. "I am fearful of d-dying," he finally said through teeth that still chattered. "I've too m-much business to set in order to go about dying."

Ah, to be as arrogant as the nobility. "When I'm confronting my own mortality, I'll not be thinking about business or finances." As such, it was an indication that either the man before her was a good deal away from that dark fate, or his life was as empty as those of so many of the noblemen who'd entered every club she'd ever worked in.

"And what will you be thinking of?" he asked, his voice weak.

Clara started, both at the unexpectedness of that question and also at the truth . . . She'd never given much thought to when she'd die. She'd been so focused on simply surviving that she'd barely been living. What would she be thinking? Would there be family? As soon as the thought slid in, she pushed it aside. For there to be children, there would have to be a man. And she'd resolved long, long ago to never let any man into her life. Not again.

The earl kept an unwavering stare on her; for one so weak, his gaze was so focused. What would the Earl of Waterson be like fully lucid, not racked with pain and ravaged by fever? A little chill scraped along her spine, an unnecessary but still welcome reminder of the perils posed by all men.

"I don't—"

"Reveal personal parts of your life," he finished for her, his chest rising and falling. "Y-yes. I am quite familiar w-with your opinions on saying too much."

Nay, on saying anything.

"Indulge me?" There was a thread of desperation to that query, and the realization slammed into her—he was afraid to stop talking. He feared if he did that he'd never again awaken.

Biting the inside of her lower lip, Clara warred with herself before settling into her previously abandoned chair. "I've not given much thought to how I would die," she grudgingly conceded.

"N-neither have I. U-until last night. Until I was confronted with it."

Clara drew her legs up and rested her chin atop her knees, contemplating the earl. What would she be thinking of when the time of her death came? There'd be no family. It was unlikely that there would even really be friends. Her only friend, Reggie, would have her own family, a husband and children, so even as she'd likely mourn Clara's passing, she also would have her own life.

"I shall hope that my life was a happy one," she said quietly. She would hope that at some point, the struggles would end and she'd have stability and security provided because of what she had done and managed and not because of anything she'd relied upon from any male. "But I'll certainly not be thinking about title, rank, or business ventures."

Henry rested his bruised hands on his chest, as if every breath he drew caused him agony and he sought to lessen the struggle. "Fair enough, b-but those ventures a-also see my family cared for, and so they matter."

"No, they don't, Henry," she murmured, rubbing her chin back and forth along the smooth fabric of her silk skirts. "How you live your life will have mattered, and not what you left behind."

"Then we shall agree to d-disagree on some of that."

"Fair enough."

They shared a small smile, and his mouth immediately twisted in a grimace, shattering that fleeting connection.

Clara immediately came out of her seat. Except . . . She wrung her hands together.

There was nothing left for her to do. She'd changed his dressings, applied cool compresses. The fever had to run its course. *And you sitting here, chatting amiably with a nobleman, can only lead to problems.* "You should rest, my lord," she said quietly, resurrecting that barrier on the class divide between them. Clara started for the door.

"Will you stay with me?"

That request came so softly, so quietly, she could continue on and very well maintain the illusion that she'd not heard him.

Bloody hell. She'd been a fool too many times where men were concerned.

And you've not learned your damned lesson yet.

Cursing herself ten times to Sunday, she returned to the chair and, sitting beside him, waited.

Chapter 7

When Henry awakened the following morning, the first thing he registered was heat.

So much heat.

Nor was it the agonizing blaze of the fever that had racked his body in the early-morn hours.

This was a different kind of heat. A pleasant one. Soft. Soothing. Much like lying under the Leeds summer sky and basking in the sun's rays.

Henry didn't want to open his eyes. He wanted to remain in this cocoon of unawareness, devoid of the hurt that came with his injuries.

He forced one eye open, and promptly winced. Streams of sunlight filtered through the leaded-glass windowpanes and bathed his rooms in a blindingly bright glow. *Bloody hell.* He closed his eye once more.

His side throbbed like the devil, and yet even that pain was secondary to that delicious warmth blanketing him; it was like a soft weight that kept him anchored while a curtain of silk lay draped over his skin.

Henry lay there and welcomed the soothing calm . . . until a faint snore split the quiet. He stiffened and noted the details that had previously escaped him: the slender, toned leg draped across his thighs. The arm flung across his middle.

He swallowed and, this time ignoring the sting of sunlight, opened his eyes.

All the air lodged in his chest, making it impossible to draw a proper breath.

At some point Clara had joined him in bed. She lay curled against his side, twined around him with one of her legs slipped through his like clinging ivy.

You are a gentleman . . . You are a gentleman . . .

"By God, you are a gentleman," he mouthed into the quiet, praying for strength. Drawing forth every moral scruple and devotion to propriety.

And failing miserably.

Swallowing hard, Henry peeked . . . lower . . . lower . . . lower.

Clara's gown had become tangled about her hips, leaving her long limbs exposed. Her legs, a pale cream white, went on forever.

His pulse thudded hard and fast in his ears.

Hell. I am going to hell.

And he deserved that fiery fate. For he stared on, unable to look away. He'd prided himself on being a gentleman. On conducting himself honorably and respectably . . . with everyone and in every endeavor . . . and yet here he lay, the woman who'd cared for him pressed against his side, ogling her like some damned lech.

Disgusted with himself, Henry struggled to free his arm from under her trim waist.

With a little sigh, Clara burrowed deeper into his side—his injured side. And damned if he didn't feel anything . . . except her.

"Clara," he whispered, tapping her lightly on the shoulder.

"Mmm," she murmured, her lips moving against his shoulder in an unwitting kiss. She rolled onto her side and then flung a toned calf across his lower limbs.

His shaft jumped in response, and he closed his eyes once more, fighting his basest urges, fighting a hungering for the temptress asleep beside him.

Think of something. Think of anything.

Whereas divers Acts of Parliament have been passed and Provisions have been made in Acts of Parliament from Time to Time, for the Reduction of the National Debt, he silently spoke the first provision of the National Debt Act of 1823. He glanced down at the slumbering woman in his arms. Her generous breasts teased the edge of her deep neckline, testing his self-control and his strength. His mouth went dry, and he jerked his focus up toward her plaster ceiling. *And be it further enacted,* Henry whispered, *that all Capital Stock, save and except the Capital Stock hereinafter directed to, be carried to a new and separate account and all annuities for terms of years, which on the fifth day* . . . Of its own volition, his gaze slid downward once more.

Think of Parliament. Think of the legislation you are drafting.

He tried again. "Miss . . ." Henry grimaced. "Clara," he urged again, in firmer tones.

With a delicate shuddery snore, Clara rolled onto her back.

Cursing, he tossed an arm over her waist to keep her from tumbling off the bed, that effort stretching the neat row of stitches sewn by the temptress in his arms.

A little frown marred Clara's lips, drawing his attentions thankfully away from one temptation . . . and promptly over to another.

In his previous state of first unconsciousness and then fever, he'd failed to pay proper due to the fullness of her mouth, the crimson flesh slightly pouty in sleep.

"How is it possible for a person to sleep so deeply?" he muttered through still badly swollen lips.

Thick, golden lashes fluttered and then swept up, revealing heavy, sleep-filled eyes. Clara blinked slowly, and then horror lit up riveting, greenish-blue eyes. She scrambled to put distance between them, and before he could reach for her, she landed with a hard thud on the floor, and he winced.

It hardly did anything to a man's pride to have a woman willing to throw herself at the damned floor to escape his company.

"How long did I nap?" Her contralto, husked by sleep, conjured all manner of wicked thoughts, testing every last vestige of strength.

"I am not certain," he croaked, following her frantic movements out of the corner of his eye.

"What time is it?"

"I'm uncertain on that score as well," he managed, and then she hopped up in one fluid motion.

Her rumpled silk skirts slid down her legs, stealing the sinfully delectable view of her long limbs but leaving her ankles on display.

They were just ankles. Trim, naked ankles that just moments ago had been draped over him.

Henry squeezed his eyes shut and proceeded to run through the remainder of the National Debt Act.

Or he attempted to.

Only to find for the first time in all the years that he'd served in Parliament . . . he couldn't think of a damned word. He, who had endless passages of countless acts committed to memory, couldn't dredge up a single—

"This is bad," she was muttering.

Yes, it was.

Clara rushed across the room, the floorboards creaking and groaning as she found her way to the armoire situated directly opposite him. She tossed the doors open and grabbed a dark-emerald gown with black overlay. Silver undergarments followed.

By virtue of any Act or Acts now in force, shall, on and from the said 5th day of April, one thousand eight hundred—.

And then she proceeded to disrobe.

"What are you doing?" he croaked.

"I trust it should be obvious," she muttered.

Actually, it was. Beyond obvious.

Clara shimmied out of her gown, and the elegant garment fell to the floor in a puddle of purple silk.

Henry hastily averted his gaze, training it on the opposite wall. Only to find a mirror positioned there and putting her nearly naked form directly before him just as she reached for the edges of her chemise and began to pull the garment overhead. He quickly angled his head, allowing Clara her privacy.

"I want to assure you," he called over in surprisingly steady tones, "last evening and this morn, at no time did I behave in any way that was untoward." *Even as I wanted to. Even as it challenged every shred of self-control I possess.*

"That is . . . reassuring," she said dryly.

Henry scowled. What in blazes was the meaning behind her tone?

"You needn't worry," she whispered, holding her garments against her chest. "I've no intention of trapping you into marriage."

"I assure you," he said, studiously avoiding the minx, "I was not worried—"

"I was teasing, Lord Proper," she drawled.

Teasing him . . . yet again. She was making light of him, their situation—perhaps, a healthy bit of both—when no one ever teased him. He looked over to the entrancing spitfire.

And froze.

Bare naked, her body on full display in the bevel mirror, Clara With-No-Last-Name was a study in female beauty. Curved in every place a woman should be curved, she was a lush fertility goddess. Sprinting over to the nightstand, she grabbed for the porcelain-and-gold timepiece there. She consulted the broach and launched into a stream of curses. "Nine o'clock," she groaned. And as she hurriedly set down the exquisite piece and resumed dressing, it hit him square in the chest: she hadn't been horrified at awakening in his arms but rather the time in which she'd been sleeping. "Are you able to move your fingers?"

He angled his head. "Move my . . . ?"

"Fingers?" she repeated, impatience threading that word. Clara waggled her right hand. "Your knuckles. Are they too bruised to—"

"My knuckles are just fine," he assured her. Most of his body was bruised and swollen, and his hands revealed scrapes from when he'd been dragged, but he still had use of his fingers.

"Well?" She stretched that single syllable into three long beats of annoyance.

Alas, his mind was still dulled from his ordeal these past three days. "Well?" he echoed, knowing he sounded like a damned lackwit.

"If you would get on with it, then?" Spinning around, Clara presented her back to Henry.

The satin day dress lay agape, exposing the expanse of her narrow back; she was cream white all over. Every inch of exposed skin. And Henry ached with the need to stroke his fingers over her, to the dip at the base of her—

Angling her head, Clara scowled. "I know you've never done this, but surely you might manage buttons and laces."

And where laws and thought of Parliament had failed, that condescending opinion and tone penetrated the haze of lust that had held him ensnared since he'd awakened. He bristled. "I assure you," he began, swinging his legs over the side of the bed, "I know how to"—manage? handle?—"*do* buttons and laces."

Clara muttered something that sounded a good deal like, "That remains to be seen."

Henry brought his hands up and caught the exquisite French lace in fingers that trembled, their quake having nothing to do with his bruised knuckles and everything to do with the tempting beauty before him. "An actress?" he put forward hoarsely in a bid to distract himself from . . . her.

"Hmm?"

"Are you an actress?"

It would explain the quality of her garments and the condition of her furnishings.

"I . . . I . . ." She glanced back with stricken eyes. But then as quick as that weakening had come it was gone, so that he was left to wonder if he'd merely imagined it. "I am no actress."

Which likely meant . . . she was either: one, the widow of a wealthy merchant, or two . . . his mind shied away from the remainder of that. Not wanting to think of how a woman who resided in this end of London with extravagant garments and furnishings came to be in possession of them. Henry didn't press her further. He finished buttoning the long row of tiny buttons.

"There," he murmured.

"Henry."

And without a word of thanks or backward glance, his entrancing nursemaid dashed from the room.

A moment later, he heard the jingle of locks being turned. The slam of the door. And then she was gone.

Henry sat there long after she'd gone.

Well . . . that certainly had been a first.

All of it.

All of this.

From his attack on the streets to the company he'd kept with a woman in her apartments.

With yet another first in his life—he'd been ordered about by a woman.

I know you've never done this, but surely you might manage buttons and laces . . .

He grinned.

And insulted—he'd been insulted by her, too. Insults which not a single man or woman had ever dared hurl at him. And oddly, there was something invigoratingly real in being treated like any other person. Of course, he would vastly have preferred that it hadn't taken being beaten within an inch of his life to know that realness, but that was something that had come from this.

On the heel of that ridiculous romanticism of his circumstances, reality came traipsing in.

Here with Clara at his side, and under her care, he'd not thought of the men who'd attacked him. *Nay, you didn't let yourself think of them.*

When he hadn't alternated between sleeping or being unconscious, he'd lost himself in the blessed distraction Clara had posed.

Now, with her gone and him alone, with the loud hum of silence, he confronted all the ugliness that had befallen him.

Ruthless attacks carried out by violent thugs in deliberate acts.

And in that, he was not unlike his sister Lila, who'd survived her own hell at the hands of the masses. He stared at the note that had been started, written in Clara's hand, but never completed or sent to his family. He'd sought to stay here until he was fully recovered to spare his family from worrying.

But a new purpose beckoned and took precedence over his family's sensibilities—bringing some order to these streets that were so lacking in it. Gathering the charcoal pencil from Clara's nightstand, Henry turned the unfinished letter over and, using the other side of it, proceeded to write a note.

He forced himself up, slowly, onto still-unsteady legs. And unlike his attempts yesterday and two days before, he did not come crashing down. Every step and every movement taxed his muscles, but he hurriedly shoved one leg into his trousers.

Henry winced.

You should take care to avoid hasty movements. You'll open your stitches . . .

He forced himself to move through his ablutions with his usual measured calm. Even so, his injuries screamed in protest, but he persisted through it. Gathering up his clothes, still bloodied but now neatly sewn and folded, Henry sat in the same chair Clara had occupied and proceeded to dress.

His breathing came in quick, sporadic spurts.

Henry reached for his boots and swallowed a cry.

Sweat rolled down his cheeks as he collapsed in his chair.

Bloody hell, he hurt everywhere.

I know you've never done this, but surely you might manage buttons and laces . . .

And even through the pain and struggle of beginning his trek home to Mayfair, he found himself smiling.

Chapter 8

As Clara entered the Muses a short while later, she was greeted with a series of frowns.

From her business partner, Reggie, to the builder and men who worked for him, to the performers on the stage as Clara rushed through the entrance of the Muses.

And why shouldn't they be upset?

You've been negligent. Derelict in your duties.

And all because you were playing at nursemaid for a blasted nobleman. "I know," she said by way of greeting as she shrugged out of her last remaining cloak. Sidestepping the worktables littering the cluttered theatre, Clara hurried to meet her partner. "I am late," she called over the noise of banging hammers and—she winced—the slightly out-of-tune pianoforte that the singers still practiced at.

Just another issue to be corrected.

Reggie said something quietly to the builder. He lifted a heavily muscled arm.

In unison, his crew immediately stopped their various jobs throughout the theatre.

Splendid.

They'd put Clara on display, then.

"You are never late," Reggie said as Clara met her and Martin Phippen at the center of the Muses.

Shame sat low in her belly, an unwanted, uncomfortable niggling. Nay, she never was late. She was first and foremost a businesswoman. Be it when she'd served in the role of actress, and then courtesan, then madam, before ultimately finding a place as head of the female staff at the Devil's Den, business guided her decisions. And she was always and only ever punctual.

Reggie's frown deepened, the downturn of her lips highlighting the strain in Clara's friend's pale cheeks. "Where have you been?"

"I . . ." *Saved an earl and brought him to recover at my apartments. Instead of attending the music hall, I was tending him.* And as close a friend as she considered this woman, Clara was not so very close that she could bring herself to make any of those admissions. Nay, not when they'd bring more questions and concerns than she wished to take. "Had business to see to," she settled for, giving a pointed look at a still-silent Phippen.

Reggie peered at her. "Related to the Muses?"

"Different business," she assured her. Which wasn't an untruth. Henry, the prim Earl of Waterson, had become an issue Clara had to deal with. Henry, the prim earl with his now deliciously crooked, aquiline nose and flat belly and tapered hips and—

Phippen, their architect and builder, held up his leather folio, interrupting those wicked musings about her current patient. "And you missed our meeting yesterday." The sharp planes of his face were a study in annoyance. "With the additions you both requested, we are already three weeks behind. And when I'm delayed with your project, I'm delayed with the projects following yours." He jabbed his folder toward the other workers silently watching the exchange.

"Mr. Phippen," Reggie began in her typical no-nonsense speech, "I am certain—"

"I know that, Mr. Phippen," Clara said in those sultry temptress tones that had never failed to sway a man. She ran a gloved fingertip along the jewel-encrusted bodice of her gown. "I won't allow it to happen again," she murmured.

From the corner of her eye, she caught Reggie's scowl.

Crimson color splotched Phippen's cheeks as his gaze drifted lower, following her deliberately distracting movements, each back-and-forth glide of her fingertip.

"You have my word." It was a shamefully wicked technique . . . if one were capable of shame. Clara leaned close and placed her lips near the tall worker's ear. "It will not happen again," she vowed.

Reggie shoved an elbow into her side, pulling a grunt from her and knocking her arm loose.

And shattering the trance she'd sought to cast.

The builder's leather book fell to the floor with a loud thwack, and as he hurried to retrieve it, Reggie cast her a warning, side-eyed look. "Enough," she mouthed.

Clara touched a palm to her breast in false affront. "I didn't do anything," she returned silently.

Her friend lifted a brow in a perfect display of jaded skepticism. "Really?"

Well, mayhap she had. Using her wiles to sway an annoyed employee. Regardless, Clara wouldn't make apologies. Everything in the world came down to survival, and where women were given little power and even less influence, she'd employ whatever tactics she could to survive.

As Phippen straightened, he made a show of opening his folio. "Er, yes, as I was saying." He spoke in gravelly tones that contained traces of Cockney buried underneath. "Given the unexpected . . . situations that have arisen with the project, we've already been significantly delayed."

The builder focused all his attentions on the book in his hand like it contained the answer to life.

Clara's lips twitched with amusement, and she fought the need to point out that his work was, in fact, upside down.

Reggie gave her another nudge.

"What?" Clara mouthed.

"Stop it."

"As I was saying," Phippen went on, hurriedly righting his records. "We've faced unexpected setbacks."

Setbacks. Yes, they had. Truly, from the start, even before the renowned builder had agreed to take on the assignment of two women with limited funds. Back to when she'd been swindled out of her life savings by a damned man playing at proprietor. Hatred brought her hands into tight, painful fists at her side.

"Expanding the stage, as you know, resulted in the front flooring caving in. I'm still awaiting the lumber to arrive." With his spare hand, he doffed his hat and swiped it across his slightly perspiring brow. "There's also the problem with the chandeliers."

As one, they glanced up to the sizable hole in the ceiling. Covered with a specialized drapery to prevent the elements from raining in, the clear fabric still allowed the sunlight to stream through the two-foot gap.

Clara's stomach sank. "What happened there?"

"Haunted is what it is," old Maeve O'Beirne, the once great actress long past her prime, called from her position at the center of the stage.

"Oh, hush, Maeve. There's no such thing as hauntings," Clara replied loudly for the benefit of the younger girls cowering alongside the dowager of their group. "Furthermore, mind your affairs. You should be practicing."

"Can't practice in a haunted club."

When she'd played second to Clara's mother on the stage, Maeve had been superstitious. With the passage of time, she'd only become increasingly eccentric. "Do not make me send you back to Drury Lane," Clara warned without inflection.

Maeve snorted. "You won't send me off."

Nay, she wouldn't. One, because they were short of performers. And two . . . weakness or not, the older woman had once been like a second mother to her. The moment she'd shown up at the Muses, Clara had known she couldn't turn the old woman out. "Go back to your performance," she called out again.

With a beleaguered sigh that rolled around the quiet, Maeve clapped her hands once, and all the performers gathered close.

Waiting several moments until the five were fully engrossed in their practice, Clara spoke to her partner and builder. "What happened?" she repeated, this time in hushed tones. The last thing she could afford was nonsensical talk about haunted theatres and bad luck.

"Bad luck is what it was," Phippen explained, pointing his notebook up at the ceiling. "Do you see there?"

Clara and Reggie tilted their heads back.

"The load-bearing beam that we affixed the lighting to proved not so very load bearing. There was a small hole in the roof that allowed water in. Over time that portion of the ceiling was weakened by age and rot."

"And it ripped open a hole in the ceiling," Reggie finished.

"Precisely." Phippen nodded, returning his cap to his head. "There is, of course, the matter of the beam that will also need to be replaced, along with the lighting."

Clara's gut clenched as she mentally tabulated the previous expense for the chandelier and work . . . and on top there was the additional timing. "How long?"

The stocky builder ran his palm along a cheek thick with stubble and in desperate need of a razor. "A fortnight."

"A fortnight?" Clara exclaimed, too loud, earning another bevy of stares from the performers.

Reggie offered a smile and a wave and waited once more until the group's attention was on whichever number they currently rehearsed.

"It could be sooner," Phippen was explaining. "A fortnight, I hope, is the absolute latest. In that time, I've allowed for the possibility of weather delays. Rain," he added, as if the matter of England's island weather required any further clarification. "As it is, given the structural break occurred two days ago and I've not had an opportunity to make a decision as to how to proceed, it is—"

"Fourteen days," Reggie murmured. Her friend sighed.

A sigh that sent waves of guilt pummeling at Clara. Reggie had recently announced she was expecting, constantly nauseous, and always exhausted. As such, Clara had assured her friend that she would take on overseeing their project for that week.

And now Phippen had summoned Reggie.

And Clara had failed her.

Because of a gentleman whom was nothing more than Henry, a stranger she'd found in the streets.

"It will be fine, Clara," Reggie said, catching her hand and lightly squeezing. Offering comfort and forgiveness that Clara didn't deserve. "So it is just another two weeks, then. There's nothing else to be done."

As Phippen opened his folio and proceeded to go over the new plans for the lighting, Clara's attention wandered off. Her eyes, still tired from two nearly sleepless nights, went to the women on the stage.

Two more weeks.

Yes, it was just fourteen more days. That on top of the time they'd already lost for the construction problems with the stage and flooring. Each day they delayed the opening was another day that moved them further and further from independence. Reggie, married to one of the most successful gaming hell owners in England, had personal security, but that was different from establishing and maintaining a business of one's own. This venture represented a salvation for so many. Until it opened, their performers were having to work doubly between other clubs and theatres, then come to the Muses to put their time in here. And that was those who still had employment.

Not just Clara but also the women at the front of the theatre.

"No."

Phippen stopped speaking midsentence.

Clara faced her partner and builder. "We've already lost enough time." And money. There was that, too.

"Clara," her friend began.

Not allowing Reggie to defend the adjusted construction schedule, Clara walked toward that gaping hole in the ceiling. "All right. I give you that cannot remain, but closing up the ceiling and adding a beam are surely not the only options."

Another builder, and any other man, would have likely taken exception at having his craft challenged by a female. After all, how many others had turned down working with Clara and Reggie? Or overpriced their bids.

"What are you thinking?" Phippen asked.

She tilted her head back and measured the space with her hands. "I've"—lived in—"been inside an establishment that had a portion of the ceiling removed and a window put in its place."

Phippen caught his chin in his hand. "A skylight," he said slowly in contemplative tones. "It could work."

A thrill of relief and triumph shot through her but was quelled a moment later.

"And if we are to hold performances in the day as we'd originally spoken of?" Reggie reminded her. The unheard-of afternoon performances represented an opportunity to increase their income and open the hall to people who might not otherwise afford entrance to the evening shows. "If there are skylights, then we cannot control the lighting."

Clara chewed at her fingernail. No. That wouldn't do.

"I can develop a pulley system with a curtain that can be drawn over it."

They looked over at the builder.

Phippen already had his sketchpad open. Pulling out the piece of charcoal tucked behind his ear, he proceeded to create a rough drawing. His fingers flew over the page as he mocked up a model of the proposed ceiling revision. A moment later, he turned the quick but impressively detailed rendering around for their inspection.

Clara accepted the notebook, and after studying the drawing, she passed it over to Reggie.

The other woman glanced between the sketch and the ceiling overhead.

"There will, of course, need to be more than the one," Phippen added, tapping the page. "Balance is important." He flashed a crooked grin. "Otherwise, it will look like the mistake we tried to conceal, as opposed to a deliberate aesthetic design."

"This will work," Reggie murmured, handing the folio back to Phippen. "And are there any other concerns?"

"The oak floors. The lumber has come in above cost. And the diamond-and-herringbone pattern you wanted in parquet finish"—it did not escape her notice that he spoke in past tense—"will put you over budget."

"Bloody hell. Can *nothing* go right?" Clara muttered. Tension radiated at the base of her neck, a product of a cramped sleep alongside a surprisingly broadly built lord and the stress of an increasingly complicated business venture. She let her arms fall to her side. "How much over?" she asked tightly.

Phippen turned his folio out once more.

Clara cursed roundly, drowning out Reggie's more demure sigh.

And it was likely a testament to the manner of people the builder dealt with that he didn't so much as flinch at the crude language spilling from Clara's lips.

Unlike Henry. Wholly proper and committed to responsibility and decorum, the Earl of Waterson would only have ever been scandalized by such utterances. *But said proper gentleman also was stealing glances at you in the mirror. Stop thinking of him . . . You've problems to focus on.* Pushing aside thoughts of the gentleman convalescing in her apartments, she focused all her attentions on this latest setback. "What can be done?"

"Carpets remain your most affordable option."

"I meant to preserve the parquet flooring," she snapped.

"You might still consider the Axminster carpet."

Given Mr. Phippen was not obtuse and had proven only too willing to work with their vision, his deliberate evasion could only mean there was no alternative to preserve the flooring she'd sought.

Reggie rested a hand on her shoulder. "Carpets will be fine."

Frustration thrumming through her, Clara shrugged off her friend's touch. "And what happens when boots are muddied?" Not allowing her to answer, she turned to Phippen. "Or wet slippers mark the carpets?" All inevitable certainties, based on London's wet weather. "It is a cost savings now. But in time the fabric would show its wear and age and require replacement."

"By that point, we will be profitable and able to reinvest," Reggie murmured, the regret in her tone meeting her eyes and indicating the matter was settled. "Is there anything else, Mr. Phippen?"

He hesitated.

Warning bells went off, a product of too many years of being wholly attuned to a person's every response. "What is it?"

"Someone broke a window." *Again.*

Her stomach clenched. "Which window?" she asked, already knowing before he confirmed it.

He hesitated. "Yours, ma'am. Likely just a coincidence," he assured, tucking the pencil back behind his ear.

She and the Earl of Waterson made grand company. Between the two of them, they'd live in a windowless world. "It is not," Clara said tightly. Whoever had thrown that second brick had done so with great specificity.

Reggie held her gaze. "Why do you say that?"

"Because I do not believe in coincidences. Because there are any number of establishments in the Dials that remain free of vandalism. Because it is . . ." *My window . . . What if it is him, again?* What if he'd returned? She curled her hands tight. *Nay.* It couldn't be him. Years had passed. He'd moved on.

Hadn't he?

"Clara?" her friend asked, resting a hand on her shoulder, and she jumped. "What is it?"

"It is just that there are men and women in and out of this building every day, and yet someone is willingly risking discovery."

"Perhaps it is the previous owner?" Reggie put forward tentatively. "He expressed concerns that he'd been swindled out of his property."

Swindled out of his property. A sound of annoyance escaped Clara. Blaming a woman for his own decisions would be a typically male response. "*He* chose to sell it." Except . . . her friend's rationale still didn't make sense. "Furthermore, the sale went to Broderick. As such, his anger would be reserved for your husband."

"He might see me as an extension of my husband?"

Because such was *also* the way of the world. But neither was it Reggie's office window that had been broken for a second time.

"Regardless, at this point, we can only speculate. I'd suggest you hire someone to be stationed outside. At least, during the early-morn hours when the building is vacant," Phippen suggested.

Clara's stomach plummeted. Yet another expense.

"Broderick can spare a guard each night."

A protest sprang to her lips, but her friend cut off any response on Clara's part. "Would you rather continue fixing and then refixing the front of the hall?" she shot back.

No, she wouldn't. But neither did she want to take charity from . . . anyone. This venture represented the one thing she'd done without the interference or involvement of a man. And the moment she . . . and Reggie . . . took assistance, Clara became what she'd always been—a woman whose existence and survival came at the hands of a man. "Very well," she grudgingly conceded. "A guard. But not more than that."

"Fine," Reggie quickly said, as if she feared Clara might change her mind.

"Is there anything else, Mr. Phippen?" Clara put to their builder.

He shook his head. "That is all."

For now.

It hung there as clear as if he'd spoken it aloud. Because in any building project, problems continually cropped up, and costs rose. As soon as the burly builder had gone and the activity resumed in the theatre, Reggie looked to her. "Clara, I know you are determined—"

"No," Clara said tightly.

Her friend's brow scrunched up. "I didn't even finish my thought."

"You didn't have to. You were going to suggest we borrow funds from your husband." A guilty blush splotched her friend's cheeks. So Clara had been correct. "I do not want your husband's money, Reggie." Drifting closer, so she needn't shout amidst the renewed noise, she spoke into her friend's ear. "We agreed we would do this on our own."

"It can be a loan," the other woman persisted. "I have already—" Reggie promptly closed her mouth.

She'd already spoken to her husband. Tugging off her gloves, Clara beat them together. "Tell me, Reggie, would Broderick Killoran have given you the funds had you not been married?"

There was a heartbeat's worth of hesitation, but it was enough.

"No. I'll answer for you. He wouldn't. We know he wouldn't because before we could even purchase this hall, he bought it out from under us and sought to charge us a higher purchase price."

"That was different," her friend muttered.

"I agreed to taking on a guard from the Devil's Den. Taking anything more?" She shook her head. "I'll not do it, Reggie."

"You are more stubborn than God himself," Reggie muttered, borrowing one of Clara's favorite phrases.

"We will make this work." Clara gave her a long look. "We will." Jamming her gloves into the front of her pocket, Clara started through the theatre, bypassing the actresses going through an agonizingly over-dramatic rendition of *Love in a Village*. Clara brought them round to the next problem they faced, unrelated to the construction of the hall. "We need actors."

Reggie hurried to catch up and adjusted her stride to meet Clara's. "We have—"

"We have actresses. We need the male counterparts. Otherwise, none of this makes sense. A performance about a woman and her betrothed"— she slashed her hand through the air—"without *the betrothed*."

"If we take a loan from Broderick . . ."

Clara should have known better than to trust Reggie's easy capitulation on the matter. "I already said no, Reggie," she said tightly as she walked into her office behind the stage.

"Unless you set your pride aside and accept help, then we'll continue to struggle along." Had there been a sting of recrimination there, it would have been easier than her friend's quiet acceptance. "Regardless, I—" The remainder of whatever Reggie intended to say ended on a sharp gasp. "Clara, your hand."

Blankly, she followed her friend's horrified gaze and swallowed a curse. "It is nothing," she said, clasping her hands behind her back.

Undeterred, Reggie reached behind her.

Clara danced out of her reach. "I said it is nothing."

"If it were nothing, you wouldn't be hiding your hands from me." Her friend slipped behind her and caught her wrist.

Together, they stared at the dried blood on the tops of her hands. At some point that morn, between awakening in Henry's arms and hastily changing her garments and rushing off, she'd gotten his blood on her fingers.

"What happened?" Reggie asked quietly.

"I don't know."

"Clara," her friend implored, searching for the source of that injury . . . which she'd never find, because the wounds belonged to another. "Is this the reason you've been . . . missing these past three days?"

"Two days and just late today," she mumbled. "And it is fine," she promised, and tried to tug her hands back. "I am unhurt."

Reggie tightened her hold. "I am not only your business partner, Clara, I am your friend," she implored. "Tell me what is happening to you. I can help. That is what friends do. You were the one who told me that."

Yes, she had. Back when Reggie had been helplessly in love with the gaming hell owner, Broderick Killoran, who'd been too thick to see her. Clara had invited her to leave and start anew somewhere else.

"Please, Clara."

This time, Clara managed to disentangle her fingers. "*Nothing* is happening to me, and nothing happened to me." *Liar. Henry stumbling into your life was not "nothing."* Both unable to lie to Reggie and not wanting to, she offered Reggie something. "I came upon a man in the streets in the midst of being attacked."

"What?" Reggie gasped, stifling that exclamation behind her fingertips. It was a reminder that Reggie had come from a gentler, more refined existence that hadn't been erased by all her time in St. Giles.

"Two and a half days ago." Clara proceeded to give an accounting of what she'd witnessed, her subsequent rescue, and her more recent care for the man. All the while, through her telling, she sidestepped the truth about the gentleman's birthright.

Reggie rocked back on her heels. "You were caring for him."

Shame filled her. "I was." *I still am.* What did it say about her as a person and a friend that she'd not given thought to those dependent upon her when she'd been off caring for Henry? And more . . . what did it say about him as a man that despite the beating he'd taken, he'd thought only of his kin?

"Why didn't you tell me that?" her friend persisted. "I would have helped you."

Which was precisely why she hadn't told her.

Reggie narrowed her eyes. "Why *didn't* you tell me?" she asked, suspicion brimming in her blue eyes. "And why do I believe you're keeping something from me?"

Because as it was, Clara had already worried her friend enough. She'd not further add to that with mention of the earl she still harbored in her apartments. "It was nothing, Reggie. I've cared for countless men and women. You need to take care of you and your babe first."

Reggie pressed a palm against her slightly rounding belly in an almost reflexive touch. "It is possible for a woman to be both: a mother and a friend. You needn't do everything alone, Clara. Not with our music hall. Not with the stranger you found."

"I know." Her answer came more reflexively than anything. A bid to halt the flow of any more probing on Reggie's part. Alone was all she'd ever known. It was all she'd ever be.

"Miss Winters?"

She and Reggie glanced over.

Belle, the prettiest and most talented of their performers, stared back.

"What is it, Belle?" Clara asked the youngest of the other women. Not even two inches beyond five feet and in possession of the palest blonde hair, there was a fey quality to the young woman that lent her an otherworldly quality. She would have been plucked from the theatres of Drury Lane in no time and swiftly converted into some lord's plaything.

"We are wondering if we could go through each performance in order. There is some . . . concern that . . . ," she murmured in a lilting, singsong voice. A pretty blush pinkened the singer's cheeks.

"What are the concerns?" Clara gently urged.

"There are concerns that the order of performers should be changed."

She sighed. In short, no one wished to fall in the middle. The coveted opening and closing numbers. "I'll be along shortly."

The other woman nodded and rushed off, leaving Clara and Reggie alone once more.

"Is he going to be all right, then?" the other woman pressed.

And the worry that had dogged her since she'd helped him from the streets of St. Giles to her apartments gnawed at her gut. Would Henry be all right? Only this . . . fear . . . didn't come from the possibility of what would happen to her should he die. But rather, an aching sadness at the loss of him. A man who'd rather recover in Clara's cramped, modest apartments instead of his own likely lavish residence, all to spare his family from worry.

I cannot die . . .

Arrogant in his supposition that he was more powerful than death, there had also been something . . . comforting, reassuring in that confidence. The men she'd generally found herself playing mistress to had been weak, men who'd sought to be propped up with words of their greatness and strength.

"Clara?" Reggie prodded.

"He will be fine."

"Very well. But you must promise me that should you require any assistance, any at all . . . that you'll tell me."

"You have my word," Clara vowed.

"Go." Reggie gave her shoulder a light shove. "See to him. I have this."

Nonetheless, Clara still hesitated. "You're certain?"

"Gooo," Reggie repeated, softening that stern echo with a smile.

As Clara donned her gloves and took her leave of the Muses, she walked with measured steps. The moment she was free of her friend's unswerving focus, Clara took off running through the streets until she reached her apartments.

Winded from her efforts, she staggered inside to an empty silence.

Her heart thumping hard against her rib cage, Clara pushed the door shut behind her. "Henry?" she called out.

Only an answering quiet, underlined by the passing carriages and errant shouts outside, met her question. Unease sent her heart into a triple beat. She ran to her chambers and then skidded to a stop in the doorway.

Clara did a sweep of the rooms, but knew immediately . . .

Gone.

He'd . . . left?

It was, of course, what she'd wanted him to do since he'd become her burden. And yet, neither had she expected he'd leave early. Not when he'd pressed her to stay.

"This is . . . ideal," she said aloud, drifting over to the bed, rumpled from where he'd slept these past days. "Now you can go about your own business, and you needn't worry about an earl dying on your watch."

So what accounted for . . . this . . . odd regret?

"Don't be silly," she muttered, sinking onto the edge of her mattress. "Of course you don't want . . ." Her gaze snagged on the note resting against an empty glass.

Clara grabbed for the page, written in an elegant scrawl, and read through the handful of lines, signed by . . .

Clara,

I am deeply appreciative of your generous care these past days. My sincerest apologies for inconveniencing you. Please accept this as a token of my gratitude.

Henry.

She turned the page over in her hands, set it down, and froze.

The sun's rays slashing through the windowpane glinted off the timepiece he'd left behind.

He was gone.

Clara set to work tidying her rooms and then, afterward, bathed. All the while, she acknowledged the truth at last to herself: all company she'd kept with men prior to Henry had ultimately been sexual in nature, and she'd not appreciated until he was gone how splendid it had been, matching wits with someone who wasn't expecting to use her body as repayment.

Chapter 9

"Oh, my God, you are . . . you are . . . d-dying."

Henry winced.

It was a thought he himself had had numerous times since the attack upon him on the streets of St. Giles. With the throbbing in his temples, exacerbated by his overdramatic mother, he almost wished he were, however.

Almost.

"I assure you, I am not dying." That swift assurance—the same one he'd made to his mother, the Countess of Waterson, eight times prior to this one—was met with another round of blubbering tears and cries. How very different this woman was from another. And prior to meeting Clara With-No-Surname, Henry had believed all women would react . . . well, as his mother had. It was why he'd delayed coming home. Now, he rethought the wisdom of his change of heart.

"I have no intention of dying, Mother," he said in placating tones as the family doctor, Quimbley, fluttered around Henry's bed, trying to find a spot beside him but prevented from doing so by the Countess of Waterson, who blocked the older man's path.

"You look like d-death," she whispered, catching another sob in her fingers.

You do the women in your life a disservice, my lord... Women do not need to be coddled. They need to be armed with the truth and allowed the ability to act without interference...

For Clara's confidence in his family's response, she'd proven woefully off the mark. When he'd entered, he'd been greeted by tears from his younger sisters and incoherent sobbing from his mother.

"I will not die," he repeated.

How very typical of you noblemen to believe you can command even death...

"How can you smile about this, Henry Winston James March the Fifth?"

I trust your illustrious name comes from one of England's great King Henrys...

"Why are you smiling?" she cried, before swiftly turning to the loyal March family doctor. "Why is he smiling, Quimbley?"

"I am afraid I am unable to say, my lady." The ancient doctor's voice shook with age as he spoke before he sidestepped the countess yet again. Henry continued to ignore her, thinking about the previous person responsible for looking after him.

Clara would have ordered his mother gone, slammed the door in her wake, then locked it for good measure. She certainly wouldn't have ceded the place at his side, putting his care second to propriety.

And despite the strain placed on his mouth with every upward tilt of his lips, Henry found his grin deepening.

"Please tell me you've not been . . . a . . . a . . . *ahhhhhhhdled.*" The Countess of Waterson buried her face in her hands. "H-He is *ad-adddled,* isn't he, Quimbley?"

"He is not," the doctor vowed in his nasal tones. Wise enough to know just how to answer the countess.

"Though, in fairness, you cannot truly be certain," Henry drawled, his split, swollen lip beginning to bleed. "You've not even evaluated me, Quimbley."

Countess and doctor stared at him as if he'd sprouted a second and third head for good measure.

"Are you . . . you . . . are you"—his mother dropped her voice to a still ridiculously loud whisper—"*teasing*, Henry?" By the horror filling her eyes, she may as well have called him out for treason.

He sat back in his bed. "Do you know? I believe I am."

His mother promptly burst into tears. "He is a-a—"

"I believe the word you are looking for"—again—"is *addled*?"

"Addled," she wailed, her voice echoing around his chambers. "He suffered damage to his head."

No one had ever spoken about him as though he weren't there. And . . . it grated. Furthermore . . .

A frown pulled at his lips, splitting the wounded flesh once more, and he pressed his kerchief against the bleeding skin. Is that . . . truly what the world thought of him? Nay, worse . . . his own mother? That he was so stodgy that any hint of mirth on his part must be a mark of madness?

"May I suggest, Your Ladyship, that you step outside a moment so I might inspect Lord Waterson's injuries?"

His mother was immediately in full control. "You already are inspecting them, Quimbley."

The small, rotund doctor blinked slowly.

"Actually, Mother, Quimbley hasn't been able to step near the bed," Henry delighted in pointing out. How had he failed to appreciate just how much fun it was . . . baiting the stuffy woman?

She folded her arms at her chest and looked between her son and the doctor. "I am not leaving."

"Then we are at an impasse," Henry said drolly around the fabric of his kerchief. "Because I've no intention of disrobing in front of my mother."

His mother turned ten shades of red. And then with her eyebrows shooting to her forehead, she spun on her heel and bolted.

As soon as she'd closed the door hard behind her, Henry closed his eyes.

"Thank you, my lord," Quimbley whispered.

"I'm hardly a saint, Quimbley," he returned in measured tones and forced his eyes open once more. "I did it for the both of us."

And unexpected of all the unexpecteds, the stuffy, serious-eyed family doctor's gaze twinkled with amusement. "If I may, my lord?" Immediately all business, Quimbley was already reaching for the sides of Henry's stained and ripped lawn shirt.

I know you've never done this, but surely you might manage buttons and laces . . .

"I have it."

Quimbley's fingers hovered in the air, lingering there. *"What?"*

"I'm capable of removing my own shirt." He dropped his voice to another whisper. "I even dressed myself this morning."

"My . . . lord."

And Henry couldn't sort out whether it was a form of address or prayer that fell from the other man's lips. Shifting himself to an upright position, Henry caught the edges of his tattered shirt and drew it overhead. The doctor unwound the bandages Clara had wrapped around his middle.

Quimbley went silent for a long while. "Oh . . . my."

"It is hardly reassuring when one's own doctor is horrified," Henry said dryly.

Pushing his spectacles farther back on the bridge of his bulbous nose, Quimbley made to touch the neat row of stitches Clara had sewn into his skin.

Just tell him not to bleed you, to keep the wounds clean, and to wash his hands, and you'll be fine . . .

Henry held a staying hand up. "I'd ask that you wash your hands first."

Quimbley opened and closed his mouth several times. And then . . . "Yes. Yes. Of course, my lord." Pushing his sleeves up, the old doctor approached the washstand that had been immediately filled by dutiful servants the moment Henry had staggered through the front door, nearly an hour earlier. Quimbley rinsed, and then, drying his hands on a neatly folded linen cloth, he returned. Wordlessly, with his high brow wrinkled from his level of concentration, Quimbley prodded the edges of the injury. "There is some redness here," the man murmured, directing that observation to the wound. "But whoever tended you did an impressive job with his stitchwork."

His.

I trust you've little experience with self-made women . . .

It was on the tip of Henry's tongue to give credit where credit was due. A woman had been the one who'd not only saved him from his assailants but also saved him from certain death from the injuries they'd inflicted.

Nor was it his wounded male pride that kept Henry silent, but rather the certainty that such a revelation would inevitably find its way to his mother. And he was not so much a glutton for torture that he'd willingly subject himself to *that.*

Finishing his inspection of Henry's side, Dr. Quimbley straightened and then turned his focus to Henry's mangled face. *"Tsk. Tsk."* The loyal family physician periodically clucked, and Henry forced himself to remain motionless through the additional poking and prodding. "Your nose, my lord. I am afraid"—Quimbley's voice cracked—"it is . . ."

"Broken?" he drolly supplied, arching an eyebrow and then promptly wincing as pain throbbed at his forehead.

"Yes, broken. And you've quite the knot at the back of your head."

"So my mother was correct in her fears, and I *am* addled?"

"Oh, I would not say that, Lord Waterson," the doctor continued on a rush. "It's hardly a mark of madness or severe deficits to your faculties."

"I was jesting, Quimbley."

"Oh, uh . . . er . . . right, my lord. Of course."

This is surely how Clara had felt whenever she'd teased him and he'd met her with a confounding somberness. How had Henry failed to appreciate just how very . . . tiring that solemnity, in fact, was?

Turning to the leather bag resting on the table at Henry's bedside, the doctor proceeded to take out a small kidney-shaped bowl and a gleaming razorlike instrument. "What is that?" Henry asked, pushing himself up all the more.

"I have to bleed you, my lord."

"You have to bleed me?"

"There is the swelling." Quimbley gestured to the lump at the back of Henry's head.

Just tell him not to bleed you, to keep the wounds clean, and to wash his hands, and you'll be fine . . .

"There'll be no bleeding," he said quickly as the physician came at him again with his damned knife.

"But . . . my lord—"

"No bleeding."

Affronted by that challenge, Quimbley's bushy white brows came together. "Very well, my lord," he said stiffly. "If you'll not allow me to see to the treatment I see best, at this time, there is nothing more I can do to help you. I will return later this evening to see if you've changed your mind."

I will not. "Thank you."

As soon as the physician had taken his leave and closed the carved oak panel behind him, Henry lay down once more. The exertions of the past days . . . his struggle from Clara's to Mayfair, took their toll, and he closed his eyes—

Rap-Rap-Rap-Rap.

That frantic knocking brought his eyes open, killing all hope of rest. "I assure you, Mother," he said as the door opened. "I am not allowing Quimbley to . . . oh—Sylvia."

The elder of his sisters lingered behind the door, clinging to the handle, the oak panel partially obscuring her belly, slightly rounded with child. "Henry. May I come in?"

"Of course." He was already reaching for his shirt and drawing it on when she faced him.

"You . . . look terrible."

"I'm sorry."

A sad little smile played on her lips. All her smiles since her husband's passing had been the sad sort. "You would apologize to me? Who do you take me for? Mother?"

"Hardly," he said automatically. Sylvia had only ever put others' comfort and happiness before her own. And she'd done so this time . . . for him.

"You should have gone," he said gruffly as she carried a chair over and sat beside him. Since her husband's death, she'd wanted no part of London.

Sylvia scoffed. "With you missing? You expected me to simply leave?" Settling herself into the chair, she rested her hands on her distended belly. "Then you really don't know me, Henry."

He did know her, though. It was why he'd wanted to write the note and remain in hiding at Clara's. If he'd done both, his widowed-too-young sister would be in Leeds until her babe was eventually born, just as she'd wanted since her husband's death.

"Furthermore, I've time before the babe arrives. Certainly enough to see my brother is well cared for and make the journey to Leeds."

"I should come with you."

"You know you cannot do that. Lila needs you here."

His throat constricted as the weight of his own uselessness and failings came rushing up. He couldn't be everything both of his sisters needed him to be at the same time. Reclusive Lila, who refused to leave the townhouse, and who, following Peterloo, had become a silent figure who preferred being invisible to joining the company of others. Only these past two years had she begun to say . . . *any* words.

"Furthermore, I'm quite capable of caring for myself."

Women do not need to be coddled. They need to be armed with the truth and allowed the ability to act without interference . . .

Sylvia pulled her chair closer to the bed, and the scrape of the legs on the hardwood floor slashed across those remembrances of Clara's words. Sylvia stopped so that her knees brushed the side of the coverlet. "Does it . . ." Her lower lip quivered, and she caught that flesh between her teeth.

Henry stilled, allowing her the time.

His sister closed her eyes and, when she opened them, drew a deep breath. "Hurt much?" she finished. "Did it hurt badly?" Her slightly swollen fingers trembling, Sylvia motioned to Henry's bruised face.

Like the Devil. Agonizing enough that he'd thought himself on the edge of death and, in his weakest moment, prayed for it.

Henry knew his sister loved him and did not doubt her worry for him these past days, or even in this instance. Nor did Henry, however, presume to believe that Sylvia's response—her worrying—came solely out of concern for him. It didn't. It went to the tragic fate of her husband, who'd suffered one errant blow at Gentleman Jackson's that had seen him dead. "It—"

Sylvia turned her right palm out forcefully. "I don't want your lies for protection, Henry. I want to know if it hurt y-you." Her voice cracked. *"Please."*

You do them no favors by shielding them from the darkness. Inevitably, night always falls . . .

"I was beaten, Sylvia," he finally said—quietly, lest there was anyone passing in the hall. "Badly. I was stabbed." Tears filled her eyes and then rolled in crystalline trails down her cheeks.

She swiped at them, almost angrily.

"I was dragged throughout St. Giles. And it hurt. Badly." He reached for her hand, and his sister slowly placed her palm in his scraped one. "But your husband"—a man whom she'd loved beyond reason—"he suffered a single blow, Sylvia. It was rotted luck. And from what I understand, from those who were with him? Instantaneous."

Sylvia sucked in a shuddery sob. And then exhaled slowly through her lips. "Thank you." Giving her head a slight shake, his sister drew her hand back and patted at her cheeks. "I'll have you know," she said with a decisive shift in discourse, "that my visiting now is because I was most concerned with you and not for any information I sought."

"I know that, Sylvia," he said quietly.

"I should also allow you to rest," she said, sweeping to her feet. "I trust it will not be long before Mother returns and Quimbley attempts to bleed you."

He winced. So she'd been listening at the door. She was now a grown woman, but the deviltry that had been such a part of her as a girl hadn't faded with time. "You heard all of that."

"Indeed." And for the first time since the unexpected death of her husband, a playful glimmer sparkled in her eyes. "And I heard your teasing, too. I will say that it was . . . unlike you." Leaning down, his sister kissed his cheek. "And I quite prefer that side of you. It leaves me to wonder if you weren't taken away and cared for by Iaso herself and healed in every way."

He chuckled, the sound of that mirth hoarse with emotion. Since her husband's death, Sylvia had been a shell of her usual self, losing her ability to tease and laugh.

Until now.

Then the meaning of what she suggested belatedly registered. He bristled. "Are you suggesting I'm not right in the head?"

"That you *weren't*." She winked. "It's altogether different. You are quite fine now, thanks to your Iaso."

Iaso, the Greek goddess of healing and recuperation.

It was an unwittingly apt homage to the woman who'd cared for him.

"Henry?"

He glanced up.

"I am so happy you are home."

When she'd taken her leave, Henry lay down once more. And where sleep had beckoned before, now it eluded him. He stared at the seat his sister had occupied moments ago, her presence having reminded him of his responsibilities.

Except . . . that is how he'd couched every aspect of his life, including his sisters and mother.

They were, of course, responsibilities, women he had an obligation to . . . but they were more. They were also family. And in one sudden attack, he'd nearly been killed, only to be left with the valuable reminder of everything he still had to do: for his family, for himself . . . and for the world as a whole.

As ideas began taking shape in his mind, Henry at last surrendered himself to sleep.

PART II

After the Storm

Chapter 10

Two months later
London, England

For Henry, there were few joys in life greater than drinking his morning coffee alone, except for the footmen in the breakfast room, while he read through the day's news.

Which is what made the determined pair of footfalls echoing outside the breakfast room at that very moment so painful.

Blocking out the din of activity, Henry scanned an article in the *Times*, underlining the names mentioned in the respective piece, and then he went back to his reading.

Today marked the day his mother and sister would finally depart for the country. Mayhap the servants rushing about, packing the final trunks, and loading the carriages were—

"Henry," the countess said by way of greeting, dashing any such hope.

Lowering his paper, he came to his feet and greeted his mother and Sylvia. "Good morning." They waved him back down. "I trust you both have much to see to this"—as one, his mother and Sylvia took up a place on either side of him—"this day," he finished after the pair of liveried footmen returned to their respective posts alongside the wall.

Sylvia dragged her Louis XIV dining chair closer to the table. "Do not try to be rid of us. We're leaving soon enough," she drawled.

"I'm not trying to be rid of you." Sylvia, he was comfortable enough having around. His mother? Now, the Countess of Waterson was an entirely different animal.

"We do have much to do," his mother said, lifting a gloved palm with a flare of her usual impatience.

Another servant immediately scrambled to make the countess's customary plate of three rashers of back bacon, two slices of fried and toasted bread, and a small porcelain bowl of black pudding.

The countess settled a linen napkin on her lap and picked up her silver spoon. "That will be all," she announced.

With an ease of the King's Army, the servants promptly fell into a neat line and filed from the room.

Oh, bloody hell. Sending away the servants? This was never good.

Henry himself, however, ever the dutiful, most reliable of her three children, had never been on the receiving end of the "dismissed servants." "I have a meeting short—"

"With that street-born investigator fellow," his mother muttered.

"Mr. Steele," Sylvia supplied. After his attack, Henry had hired the services of Connor Steele to locate and question the men responsible for his assault. The men had been found—both dead, which had stalled Steele's search.

"Yes, *him*." The countess wrinkled her nose in distaste. "Could you not even go about hiring a *proper* constable to investigate *L'incident*."

L'incident. Only his mother would seek to elevate the beating he'd taken. "Yes, how uncouth of me to choose the most *skilled* individual to investigate the matter over a proper English constable."

"Bah, those fiends are . . . are . . ."

"Dead?" Henry and Sylvia offered in unison.

Their mother waved a hand in front of her face and her eyes rolled back. "My salts. My—"

A dutiful maid was already across the room, having instantly appeared from the hall with smelling salts that she passed under the countess's nose. Sniffling, the countess sat upright once more. "I've not come to speak about *L'incident*. Those responsible were discovered, and you've come to no harm since. As such, I'd have you move on to matters of more import."

"More important than my life?" he asked in droll tones.

"Do not be theatrical, Henry," his mother snapped. "No further harm has befallen you."

And yet . . . it had. In the form of a broken axle on his carriage just a fortnight ago. In his work it could be any number of angry people. He'd received nasty letters at Parliament about his police-force legislation and his antislavery bills.

For the Countess of Waterson, however, only one matter superseded every other concern. *Bloody hell.* Henry pushed his chair back. "If you'll excuse me—"

"Sit, Henry," their mother commanded.

Reluctantly reclaiming his seat, Henry dragged it closer to the table.

His sister's eyes danced with far too much amusement.

"I'm so happy you're enjoying this," he said from the side of his mouth as their mother focused on smearing butter over first one piece of toast, then the other.

"You wound me," his sister said, touching a hand to her chest. "Furthermore, you should thank me. I am here to help you."

Seeking fortitude from the remainder of his cup of bitter black coffee, Henry took a long sip. "What is it? Have out with it already."

His mother pursed her lips, that little moue of displeasure highlighting the wrinkles in her cheeks, reminding Henry that she was no longer a young woman. "This is precisely what I've come to speak with you on. This . . ." She waved her silver knife in his direction, and he angled away from that intentional . . . or unintentional threat? Given he still hadn't a clue as to the purpose of her meeting, it was too soon to tell. "Meeting with investigators," she whispered. "You . . . rushing a person to speak. Me, of all people." She lowered her voice to an angry whisper. *"Teasing."*

"Have I been teasing?"

"Since the attack?" Sylvia gave an enthusiastic nod. "Quite often. I rather appreciate it."

He inclined his head. "Why, thank you."

Their mother tapped her knife against the side of her teacup. "That will be enough." She scowled at Sylvia. "From the both of you."

Brother and sister fell silent.

Folding her hands primly on her lap, Sylvia trained all her energies on those locked digits, avoiding his gaze, when she'd only ever confronted . . . anyone and anything head-on.

"I have been . . . patient with you, Henry."

"Thank you."

She continued over that droll response. "I have appreciated your devotion to the March finances and estates, and your work in Parliament."

"Why does this not sound as though it is a compliment, then?"

Sylvia leaned in. "Because it is not," she whispered.

At last, his mother ceased buttering a thoroughly smeared slice of toast and set her knife down on the side of her plate. "You have become consumed in your *work*." Her mouth twisted in a grimace, as if she'd scorched her tongue just uttering that word. "And it concerns me, Henry, because you might be angering the masses again, and that isn't healthy for anyone."

Not "might be."

He was.

People failed to see the need. Especially if it gained them enemies. Henry, however, collected enemies the way an old gentleman collected snuffboxes.

"That is not all that concerns me. So much of your life has become work, and it is uncouth. Unnatural."

While she went on cataloguing the reasons for her worrying, his mind drifted.

It means, Henry, that my respect is reserved for those who make their own fortunes and build their own empires . . .

At the oddest times, she would slip in—her. *Clara.*

In the days following his recovery, when he was able to walk and breathe without needing a nap like a babe, he'd sought her out, returning to the streets of his attack. Wanting to bring her some payment greater than the timepiece he'd left for her, even though she'd never asked for either. Needing to express his gratitude to the woman who'd saved him. Only to find those apartments . . . empty. So that he'd been left to wonder if he'd merely imagined her, the angel who'd tended his injuries.

"Are you listening to me?" His mother looked to Sylvia. "Is he listening to me?"

"I do not believe so," his sister said unhelpfully.

"Traitor," he mouthed.

She winked.

"That is another thing, Henry. Since *L'incident*, you have not been yourself."

How could he be? "No, I have not," he acknowledged gravely, his gaze going to a point beyond his mother's head. Following his attack— for that was ultimately what it was and what could never be glossed over with prettier words as his mother and the papers sought—Henry had been changed . . . irrevocably. Just as he'd been impacted by Lila's near-death incident at Peterloo, so, too, had his assault left an indelible mark upon his life.

"You are a man driven, Henry. So, so focused on your legislation."

Since his return to Parliament, Henry's previous commitment to establishing legislation that would allow for an English police force had taken on an even greater meaning. Every moment of every day was spent writing laws and attempting to earn votes, a process which had proven painstakingly slow. After all, people failed to see the value of drafting new laws—until it was an issue that impacted them personally. Then everyone put forward their energies. He was as guilty as the rest of society. "And do you see there being something wrong with that focus, Mother?" he asked coolly, picking up his coffee and taking a sip. Forcing a casualness he did not feel.

"I do when it prevents you from properly seeing to your responsibilities as earl."

A charged energy hummed around the room.

Sylvia directed her gaze to her lap.

And at last, it made sense. Henry sat back in his chair. "So this is the reason for your meeting this morning? The Earl of Waterson line." He should have known. In fact, this talk was nearly ten years overdue, and given what had unfolded a few months ago, he would have expected it to come sooner.

"You could have died, Henry."

"But he did not, Mother," Sylvia murmured.

In a remarkable break from her usual control, the countess snapped. "And if he had?" she pressed her eldest daughter. "What would have happened to you? Or me?" His mother leveled her gaze on him. "Or Lila."

A muscle pulsed in his jaw. "Don't you trust that I've seen you properly settled"—he glanced out the corner of his eye at his widowed sister—"if anything should happen to me?" he asked, deliberately exchanging his word choice.

"Three women, Henry? On our own. And now, Sylvia's babe? While the title, the entailed properties, and most of the wealth passes to some distant cousin?"

"My husband has left me a comfortable enough settlement that I would not have Henry make any sacrifices for me," Sylvia said, giving him a small, encouraging smile. His sister, entirely more loyal than he deserved.

"So my marriage, then? That is what you are seeking?" Because she certainly was not asking.

"I'm not so heartless that I would have you set aside your greater purposes."

He stilled, fully attending her now. "Go on?"

Reaching for a small folded page that he'd failed to note resting beside her plate, she slid it over to him. "I can help you."

"What is this?" he asked, already unfolding the scrap, revealing two names: Lord Peerson and Miss Newton.

His mother beamed. "Or rather I should say, I *did* help you."

His sister avoided his gaze.

The countess leaned over and tapped the page. "Though there are two ways in which I'm helping you there. Lord Peerson is attempting to push through legislation that will update laws pertaining to virtue and—"

"I'm aware of his latest legislative efforts," he said curtly. "Since when did you become interested in politics?"

"Since I wanted my son married."

He leaned close. "Come again?" It had sounded as though his mother had said . . .

With a groan, Sylvia pressed a palm against her forehead.

"You are making no headway with your police-force business."

Nay, still in the draft stages of a bill, he'd not made much progress in three years now. "It is not *my* business," he said tightly, refolding the page along its neat, decisive crease. Is that what his mother . . . the world . . . thought about him and his endeavors? That all his efforts were because of his own interests? "Furthermore, the change is long overdue.

The Statute of Winchester was drafted in 1285, nearly six hundred years ago, and as such—"

"I ceased paying attention at 'the Statute of Winchester,'" the countess cut in.

"An organized police force would be for the good—"

"Of all England," she slipped in the line that had become his when speaking to peers in Parliament whose votes he sought in both the House of Commons and the House of Lords. Back and forth both houses had gone, making change after change. And still no closer to the formation of a police force. "You needn't convince me, Henry. Why, you need to convince your peers." She gestured to the notes he'd been taking that morn. "Lord Peerson, as you know, has not been a friend of yours in the process."

His jaw tightened. No, the viscount hadn't. Henry drummed his fingertips on the table. Perhaps he'd approached this the wrong way. Mayhap he should consider an act of taxation that would provide for a professional police force. It would be a roundabout way of avoiding having to secure permission from both houses.

"Do pay attention," Sylvia whispered. "She's going to become upset. And neither of us want that."

"Peerson is a pompous ass who believes he knows what is best for all," Henry muttered.

"He's not unlike his wife. They'll always do something that might advance their goals."

Henry narrowed his eyes. "Go on."

Shielding her mouth with her napkin, Sylvia spoke from around the fabric. "I cannot believe you are indulging her."

Ignoring that sisterly disapproval, he trained his attention on his mother. For the first time in his life, he found himself wholly vested and interested in what his mother had to say. In fairness, this time, she wasn't prattling on about gowns, her allowance, or some social gathering or another. Acts and bills in Parliament and those lords drafting them, however, always commanded his full focus.

"Lord Peerson is closer than you in securing the votes for his act, but he is not quite there. And he may be willing to consider a partnership."

His jaw fell open, and he tried to form words.

The countess positively beamed. "Go on," she urged, patting the back of her immaculate coiffure. "You may say it."

"You managed that?"

Her smile deepened, dimpling her cheek and giving a hint of the younger woman she'd once been. "Dear boy, do you still not realize your mother can manage anything?"

"When it serves you," Sylvia muttered, wandering over to the sideboard to make herself a plate.

"Oh, pooh. I'll not allow you to rain on my flowers, Sylvia."

"Rain on flowers is desired, Mother," his sister called as she heaped a healthy portion of fried whiting and stewed figs onto her plate. "It helps them to grow."

"Not in excess. Have you seen my prized rosebushes? The rain quite drowned them, it has."

While his mother and sister carried on bickering over the right amount of water for a healthy garden, Henry picked up the page written in his mother's elegant scrawl. Who would have imagined the Countess of Waterson should have so neatly coordinated a potential political alliance between Henry . . . and anyone?

And yet . . .

"Miss Newton?" he asked abruptly, and both women turned back. Henry lifted the small scrap of paper. "Why is Lord Peerson's daughter here?"

His mother rolled her eyes skyward. "La, Henry. You disappoint me. I've never taken you for thick. Alas, you've been a bachelor so long you only think like a bachelor now. Granted, a respectful, honorable bachelor, but a bachelor nonetheless."

"Mother," he warned impatiently.

"You're only just now wondering why our mother has waded into your politics, Henry?"

"They are all our politics," Henry said, nearly mechanical in that familiar phrase. And actually, he was.

His mother set aside her napkin and pressed her palms together, a study in piety. "Why, your sister is correct."

The uneasy feeling reared its head once more. This time stronger. The countess had never conceded that either of her daughters had been correct in any regard.

"Surely you don't believe, after your near-death incident, that I'll simply depart for the country without ensuring your future is secure?"

"My future?" he echoed dumbly, giving his suddenly tightening cravat a tug. Alas, the feeling he was choking persisted. And he eyed the doorway.

"You're concerned with your police force, dear boy."

"A police force. Ours." He gave his head a clearing shake. That was all irrelevant now.

"The only way to ensure a political dynasty is through not your legislation but"—Oh, God. *Marriage*. His mother was talking—"marriage," she concluded with an entirely-too-pleased-with-herself grin.

"I told you," Sylvia muttered, setting her plate down hard, and the porcelain dish clattered back and forth before settling into place.

Henry fell back into his seat.

"Oh, come, Henry," his mother chided, adding another smear of butter to her already drenched toast. "You're forty-two."

"Forty-one." *Almost* forty-two. "I'm hardly a doddering fellow," he grumbled, giving his cravat another pull.

"You've done irreparable harm to the knot," Sylvia murmured. "I tried to warn you."

"Thank you," he said from the side of his mouth.

"You have grey hair."

Henry blinked several times. Was his mother continuing to make her case for all his deficits?

"Why, even your only friend has five babes now. Five. An heir, two spares, and two girls." As if he needed some elucidation, the countess lifted her right hand and wiggled those five fingers back and forth.

Chafed at the continued insults, he shifted in his seat. "Waverly isn't my only friend."

The March women both gave him a pointed look.

"Is it truly a sin to be discriminating with one's friends?"

His mother pounced. "No, it *is* a sin to be a forty-two-year-old—"

"Forty-one," Henry and Sylvia said together.

"—bachelor without a wife."

"I'd be remiss if I failed to point out the redundancy there," his sister intoned. "By its very nature, the word 'bachelor' denotes the absence of a wife."

"Do hush. This isn't something to jest about, Sylvia. We're speaking of your brother's wedded state."

"Of course," Sylvia said with mock solemnity that was belied by the amusement brimming in her eyes. "How could I forget the seriousness of such a topic?"

"Now, where was I?"

Henry cleared his throat. "I believe you were debating the merits of watering flowers?" he ventured hopefully.

"No, that was quite settled. We were speaking of you and a potential dynastic alliance with Lord Peerson."

"Mother," he began.

"Lord Peerson will be awaiting a meeting with you at White's"— the countess consulted the longcase clock at the opposite wall—"at ten o'clock. I expect you'll be there. It is settled, Henry. It is time you marry. If it is not Miss Newton, find another." She hardened her mouth.

"*Soon.*" His mother shoved back her chair and stood. "Now, if you'll excuse me. I need to oversee the remainder of our travel arrangements. Come along, Sylvia."

Sylvia hesitated a moment and then, with a silently mouthed apology, came to her feet. His sister followed after the countess, but when their mother had taken her leave, Sylvia lingered.

"What is it?" he asked, remembering to stand.

His sister fiddled with her widow's weeds. "It is just . . . marriage is not all bad, you know. Quite the opposite." Her gaze grew distant. "In fact, it was oftentimes . . . splendid," she said with a wistful, faraway quality that cleaved at his heart for all she'd lost. "Marriage should also be to a person one deeply loves."

Marriage to a person one deeply loves.

It was . . . a foreign concept to the peerage. Matches weren't made for love. They were made for the very reasons his mother had mentioned: connections, influence. Securing family lines and fortunes.

Henry had been committed to all those principles, and yet . . . marriage had been the last responsibility he'd undertaken.

"Henry?" his sister called out.

"Yes?"

"There is no saying Miss Newton might not make you a perfectly splendid match." She paused. "But neither is it a certainty, either. And I'd ask you to not put your political aspirations or Mother's expectations for you over your own happiness."

"Thank you, Sylvia," he murmured.

She narrowed her eyes. "You are going to go forward with it anyway."

Henry rested his elbow along the back of his chair. "I didn't say as much."

"You didn't have to," she muttered. "I know you. Your sense of duty is nauseatingly predictable and as much a part of you as your blood."

"Despite that ill opinion," he called as she turned to go, "I still love you."

Sylvia snorted. "Goodbye, Henry."

The moment she'd gone, Henry grabbed for the notes he'd taken that morning, along with those from his mother, and prepared for his meeting with Lord Peerson.

Chapter 11

One week later

"Mayhap it isn't . . . haunted, after all," Old Maeve of the Muses breathed into the absolute stillness of the at-last-completed music hall.

And Clara, sitting on the velvet-upholstered seating at the front row of the theatre, rather found herself agreeing with Old Maeve, who walked in a slow circle around the center of the stage.

The other performers, all wearing like expressions of awe on their painted features, took in the Muses. Even the cynical, occasionally drunk actors they'd managed to lure away from Covent Garden appeared suitably impressed. Tremaine Anderson and Ferguson Graham stared on in wide-eyed wonderment at the recently affixed crystal chandeliers that hung overhead.

The burly Scot whistled. "Dinna think ye crazy birds were gonna finish," he murmured in his thick brogue.

And in the same gruff manner she'd treated the young stage-hands at London Theatre, Old Maeve slapped the back of his head.

Ferguson grunted. "'Course we were going to finish, you surly Scot," she snapped.

"*Ye* dinna finish anything. Mrs. Killoran and Miss Winters are responsible."

"A theatre belongs as much to the performers as the owners." Maeve punctuated that long-known truth in the acting world with the bottom of her cane. "Now, let us begin practicing for our first performances."

Birdie, one of the two theatre leads, took up her place at the center of the stage and signaled the recently hired pianist to begin playing.

As the singer's deep contralto soared to the rafters, Clara briefly closed her eyes and allowed the music . . . this moment . . . all of it, to wash over her. How very long it had been since she'd set foot inside a theatre. After she'd found herself trading her work as a singer for the work of a mistress, she'd vowed to never set foot inside a theatre again. Not when doing so forced her to remember how she'd never been good like her mother had been. Not when the theatre, which she'd loved, had come to represent her greatest mistake, one moment of weakness that had seen her life forever changed.

Mistakes she'd made because she was naive and believed she could have scruples. But of course a man who made his livelihood in the sale of human flesh would have pursued her with a like ruthlessness. And with that naivete she'd underestimated him. He'd pursued her. Stalked her. And ruined her hopes for an honest future.

Until now.

Now, her life had changed once more. For the good. Nay, *the best*.

"The Muses," Clara breathed.

"The Muses," her partner, Reggie, echoed with equal reverence and wonderment.

Breathing deeply, filling her lungs with the crisp, clean scent of freshly carved wood, Clara sat back in her chair and stretched her arms out, resting them along the backs of the seating.

It was done.

After months of toil and delay and vandals wreaking havoc at the front of the establishment, the culmination of her greatest dreams, dreams which had seemed so very impossible, had come . . . true.

An arm came to wrap about her shoulders, and Clara glanced over at her partner.

Reggie smiled back. "We did it."

Clara's lips curved up in a slow, wide grin that she felt all the way inside her chest. "We did."

They, two women, on their own, had purchased, built, and created something of their own—a *business* of their own. Everything that had come before this: her past. The ten thousand pounds that she'd been swindled out of. Broderick Killoran buying this place out from under them. Clara having to swallow her pride and give up her own apartments and return to living at the Devil's Den to preserve funds. *All of it* had brought them to this moment, and the triumph of it all, after all the struggles, brought an unutterable joy. A feeling that was intangible and yet so very potent in its power. There'd been those determined to see her fail in life. Men who'd sought to possess her at all costs. And in the end, Clara had won.

"She is splendid," Reggie murmured, bringing Clara back to Birdie's moving performance.

> "When shawes beene sheene, and
> shradds full fayre,
> And leeves both large and longe,
> It is merry, walking in the fayre fforrest,
> To heare the small birds songe.
>
> The woodweele sang, and wold not cease,
> Amongst the leaves a lyne:
> And it is by two wight yeomen,
> By deare God, that I meane.

Me thought they did mee beate and binde,
And tooke my bow mee froe;
If I bee Robin a-live in this lande,
I'le be wrocken on both them towe."

"We are going to do well," Reggie said softly. "Without women having to sell themselves or gaming tables or spirits, we have made something so very special."

"Buske yee, bowne yee, my merry men all,
For John shall goe with mee;
For I'le goe seeke yond wight yeomen
In greenwood where they bee."

"We are going to do better than even that. We are going to thrive," Clara whispered.

"There were they ware of a wight yeoman,
His body leaned to a tree."

She would at last leave her mark on the world as something more than a whore. She would be the self-made woman she'd spoken of not so very long ago with a man who'd been a stranger. A man who'd listened with incredulity but who'd not disputed her claims.

Henry.

A wistful smile hovered on her lips. Sometimes, when she least expected it, her patient-for-a-brief-time, the Earl of Waterson, would slip into her thoughts, those fleeting days they'd spent together an increasingly distant memory.

He'd been injured and hurt, but even if he weren't, something told her the gentleman so very concerned with protecting those women dependent upon him would have never thought their relationship to move into that expected trope all men had for women.

Even if you would greatly like to know what it was to lie with Henry. Muscled in all the places gentlemen were not normally muscled, he possessed a masculine perfection that she would have ached to know.

"What has you smiling?" Reggie murmured.

And be damned if Clara didn't feel herself . . . blushing. *Blushing?* "I am just . . . happy."

Which was true. For the first time in the whole of her life, Clara was truly happy.

> "'Stand you still, master,' quoth Litle John,
>   'Under this trusty tree,
> And I will goe to yond wight yeomen,
>   To know his meaning trulye.'"

"Is there anything we need do for the remainder of the day?" Reggie rested her hands on her gently rounding belly.

And catching that maternal touch, softly caressing the place where her babe rested, Clara found an unexpected wave of regret . . . for what she would not have. What she would never know. There would be no loving husband or babes. "I'm going to have the crew move through the entire performance one more time," she said, feeling like the worst of friends for the envy that tugged at her breast.

> "It is noe cunning a knave to ken,
>   And a man but heare him speake;
> And itt were not for bursting of my bowe,
>   John, I wold thy head breake."

"We still have a week before opening. We've worked hard. It is late. We should return home. Tomorrow arrives quickly."

"You go along without me. I'll return after one more rehearsal. Go on," she urged at Reggie's hesitation. "I'll be fine."

"MacLeod will accompany you back," Reggie said, climbing to her feet. "I'll see you home soon."

Home.

After her friend had gone, Clara tested that word in her mind. *Home.* The Devil's Den, the club owned by Broderick Killoran, was now a home to Reggie. But it wasn't one to Clara. *Home* suggested family, a residence that would always be there and wasn't a transient property that a person would move into and then out of.

Which is precisely what the Devil's Den was for Clara. It was a temporary place in which she'd live. In fact, she'd never had a home—not truly. Not even when her mother had been alive, the then-revered actress of her time. They had moved about from apartment to apartment, depending on which theatre her mother had found herself performing at.

This . . . the Muses . . . was, however, the closest she'd ever have to a home. A place that belonged, and would always belong, to her. Drawing her knees to her chest, she looped her arms around them and followed Birdie's achingly poignant performance.

> "'Woe worth thee, wicked wood,' sayd Litle John,
> 'That ere thou grew on a tree!
> For this day thou art my bale,
> My boote when thou shold bee!'"

Clara stared on, riveted, allowing herself to become lost in the music.

When at the back of her mind, she registered the echo of the hall doors opening.

> "This shoote it was but looselye shott,
> The arrowe flew in vaine,

And it mett one of the sheriffes men;
Good William a Trent was slaine."

A little shiver worked along her spine at the dark turn of the song. "Did you forget something?" she asked upon Reggie's approach . . .

And stiffened.

The approaching footfalls, coming closer, were not the soft, delicate tread of Reggie's but rather heavier, more pronounced ones belonging to one unfamiliar with stealth in the Dials.

Unnerved, she came to her feet as a well-attired gentleman in a midnight-wool cloak approached. "Mrs. Killoran? Or Miss Winters?" he asked by way of greeting.

"Who are you?"

He peered down the length of his long, hawkish nose. "Are you or are you not one of the owners?"

"I am," she said crisply.

The stranger held out a small packet, sealed with a crimson wax mark.

She made herself take that official-looking item. "I fear you have me at a disadvantage. Who are you?" she demanded as fear, that most primitive of emotions she'd become so well acquainted with over the years, wound through her, a serpent spreading its venom.

"Sir Emory Stuart, madam. I am a solicitor."

Pinpricks of unease stabbed at her belly as she examined the official-looking packet in her hand. With fingers that shook, she slid a finger under the seal, breaking the wax legs of the lion affixed there.

"And it is sayd when men be mett,
Six can doe more than three:
And they have tane Litle John,
And bound him ffast to a tree."

Clara hastily scanned the page.

Her heart stopped. And then picked up a sick, panicky rhythm. *It is happening again* . . . She was going to lose everything because of some ruthless man. No! She couldn't. "What is this?" she whispered, the dull buzzing in her ears muting her own question and the sound of the solicitor's retreating footsteps.

> "'I seeke an outlaw,' quoth Sir Guye,
>   'Men call him Robin Hood;
> I had rather meet with him upon a day
>   Than forty pound of golde.'"

The solicitor reached the back of the auditorium, and just like that, the world came whizzing back in a rush of noise. "Halt!" Clara cried after him.

The piano struck a discordant strand and then fell silent, along with Birdie. "Do not stop singing," she shouted to her employees, her voice pitched with a sick dread. "Did I give you permission to stop?" she rasped, already sprinting off to meet the man who'd delivered a death knell to her hopes and dreams.

The pianist's fingers brought the mournful ballad to life once more, and Birdie continued singing.

Clara's long-legged strides easily ate away the distance placed by the solicitor—the damn coward. When she reached his side, she'd managed to regain control of her emotions—on the outside. Inside, her heart was thudding sickly against her rib cage. "I'll not ask you again, Sir Stuart. What. Is. This?" she demanded, shaking the page under his nose.

He gave her another one of those long looks—this one so patronizing and impatient she wanted to bloody his nose. "It is an order to cease and desist, which means—"

"I know what it means," she hissed. "I am asking *why* you are bringing me this."

"Because with your purchase of said establishment"—he jabbed a finger at the page as if there could be another establishment in question—"you are in direct violation of the Proclamation of Encouragement of Piety and Virtue, and for the Preventing and Punishing of Vice, Profaneness, and Immorality Act."

"The *what?*"

"The Proclamation of Encouragement of Piety and Virtue, and for the Preventing and Punishing of Vice, Profaneness, and Immorality."

The . . . ? Numbly, Clara glanced at the top page and then flipped through sheet after sheet . . . and realized Sir Emory was once more starting for the doors.

She rushed over and, placing herself in front of him, blocked his escape. "This is horse shite," she thundered, again shaking the pages at his face.

"It is the law." He stepped left.

She matched his movement. "It is horse shite. There is no immorality. There are no vices."

He cast a long, pointed glance at the front of the stage just as Collette stepped out as Maid Marian in full ballet regalia. The young woman proceeded to dance in time to Birdie's entrancing song.

"She is a ballet dancer," Clara clipped out through clenched teeth.

"She is indecent. Barely clad. Now if you would?" He was striding for the exit once more.

"And what of the gaming hells and clubs and bordellos?"

"Good night, Miss Winters," he called out in bored tones, not even bothering to spare a glance back in her direction.

Clara seethed. Oh, how very typical. That those places of real vice, run by men, preferred by men, should remain unscathed . . . while her venture they sought to dismantle because of the gender of the proprietors. *Over my lifeless body.* Clara took off flying and reached the double doors before he did. She tossed her arms back, pressing her palms against the heavy turquoise panels. "You do not simply get to leave, Sir Emory."

"There is nothing more for me to say. The person who sold you this property did so under fraudulent activities, and therefore all ownership you have of it, you must immediately cede back to the respective owner so he might . . . remove the immorality of your"—he pulled his lip back in a sneer—"business."

Cede it all back to the respective owner. Her arms fell limp at her sides. "That is it?" she croaked. "It is not possible." After all the monies and energy and efforts she and Reggie had put into making this once ramshackle hall a palace, some powerful strangers would simply yank it out from under them. She refused to believe it. Or accept it.

"It is quite possible."

"Who?" she breathed, rushing into the solicitor's path when he made to leave.

"Who?" he asked impatiently.

"Who is responsible for this . . . this . . . this . . . notice?" *Terrence Lowery.* It had to be him, again. The bastard who'd gone to any length to have her. Every time she believed she was free of him, he crept back. "Names, I want their names."

Sir Emory pursed his mouth, and for a long moment she thought he'd damn her and her request. But then—

"The issuance was set into motion by His Lordship, the Earl of Waterson."

"The Earl of . . ." All the air, life, and energy left her. Clara's entire body jolted forward and then fell back. Not . . . Lowery. *What?* *Impossible.* She'd heard this surly stranger wrong. It wasn't possible. It was . . .

"I assure you, quite possible," he said, and she stared at him with dazed eyes, not realizing she'd spoken aloud.

And this time, when he reached for the door handle, she let him walk out. The moment he'd gone, her gaze went back to the hated pages in her hands. She flipped through them. Her eyes tripped over the vile words reflected back in a kaleidoscope of black ink.

> "Check the spread of open vice and immorality, and more especially . . . to preserve the minds of the young from contamination by exposure to the corrupting influence of impure and licentious books, prints, and other publications . . ."

Her stomach churned.

I am going to be ill . . .

Clara focused on taking slow, steady breaths, swallowing back the bile creeping up her throat.

Henry had done this? How . . . ?

What did you really know about him? That voice jeered at the back of her mind. *No different from every other gentleman you've known—nay, any man—who took what he needed, saw to his own self-interests . . . and then discarded you for more important business.*

"Fool, fool, fool," she whispered to herself. There had to be a way out of this. Filled with a restlessness, Clara began to pace a frantic path over her just-completed parquet floors. The floors she'd fought so valiantly for, the elegant, meticulously nailed-together floorboards she had swallowed her pride and given up her own personal apartments for, moving into a gaming hell once again . . . had been for naught?

All because Lord Prim and Proper, with his blasted pathetic view of women and their capabilities, had wrought this upon her?

"'God's blessing on thy heart!' sayes Guye,
'Goode ffellow, thy shooting is goode;
For an thy hart be as good as thy hands,
Thou were better than Robin Hood."

Clara came to a jerky stop that sent her silk skirts snapping about her ankles. "Over my dead body," she breathed.

And grabbing her cloak, she set off to find the damned blighter who'd destroyed her only happiness.

Chapter 12

Since the Peterloo Massacre, Henry had set clear, specific priority for himself and his work in Parliament. His goal had been singular: enact legislation to prevent the dangerous activities of the masses. And in that, spare other men, women, and children the hell his own sister had survived through.

His establishment of a police force had represented the goal of achieving a greater security and peace—for all.

Seated at his desk, his fingers steepled under his chin, Henry studied his at-last-completed draft for the London Police Force Act; still shy of the necessary votes, he'd found himself close, with Lord Peerson having secured ones from the House of Commons that would have otherwise proven elusive.

He grinned wryly. And irony of ironies, such success was a product of the one he'd have least suspected—his mother.

But then, when an aging mother was determined to see her nearly forty-two-year-old bachelor son married, she was capable of anything.

Everything was going swimmingly.

Coming to his feet, he strolled to the sideboard, and under his breath sang a jaunty tune.

> "Let rogues and cheats prognosticate
> Concerning king's or kingdom's fate
> I think myself to be as wise
> As he that gazeth on the skies."

Humming the remainder of the tune under his breath, Henry passed his hand over the crystal decanters before settling on his oldest French brandy. He wasn't one to drink, but these circumstances necessitated a celebration. Plucking a glass from the neat row of bottles, he carried it and his decanter over to his desk to celebrate his triumphs.

Once more comfortably seated, he wiggled free the stopper and set it down parallel to his crystal inkwell. He proceeded to pour himself a glass. "To a police force," he murmured into the quiet. Henry lifted his glass in a lonely salute to all his life's efforts.

Footsteps sounded in the hall, and he lowered his glass just as Wright, his loyal butler, entered.

And momentary triumph forgotten, Henry sat up. "Wright?"

The young man came forward and, as he always did, stopped three paces from Henry's desk, clicked his heels together, and kept his gaze forward. "I have come with your nightly report on Lady Lila."

Lila, who moved throughout the household like a specter, taking care to avoid the world, her family . . . *me. She is avoiding me just as she has been since she returned from Manchester seven years ago.* She hadn't been able to meet his eyes that long-ago night, and she'd spoken but a handful of words to him in passing since. Agony lanced his soul. He'd been reduced to obtaining nightly reports from a handful of loyal servants. Their reports came at all different hours of the day, depending on when Lila left her rooms. *What does it say about you that your own sister cannot stand the sight of you and that you are unable to help her?*

"Shall I begin, my lord?" Wright ventured in his always tentative tones.

His earlier sense of victory deflated under the weight of his . . . of Lila's . . . reality, Henry set down his drink. "Please."

Withdrawing a folded scroll from inside his gold liveried jacket, Wright went on to give his accounting. "Lady Lila awakened before her maid, twenty minutes after four."

An ungodly hour for any person to be up.

"Twenty minutes after four, you say?" Henry murmured.

"Yes, my lord."

A memory traipsed in. Nay, *she* traipsed in, as she still sometimes did.

"Just after four o'clock."

"This is hardly morning," Henry said to his reluctant caregiver.

Clara snorted. "For the working class it is, my lord."

Those who awoke at ungodly hours were those whose lives were not without strife.

Not unlike Clara. And not unlike . . . Lila.

Over the years, with the passage of time, his sister's rest, her life, had become not easier but rather more tormented. Which meant her memories, the nightmares, were never fading. "What else, Wright?" he asked edgily, feeling a wave of guilt when the young man's cheeks went red.

"Y-yes, right, my lord." The butler snapped his heels together a second time. "Per her usual, Lady Lila spent the morning in the music room." That room from which haunting melodies were no longer played. She went to that place and sat in silence. "Following sunrise, she visited the gardens and remained there . . . until she retired to her rooms to take her meal." Wright folded the page. "And Lady Lila remained there ever since."

As she always did.

"Is there anything else you require, my lord?"

A family that was no longer broken. Sisters who were able to again smile. "No, that is all, Wright," he said. Henry glanced to the bracket clock atop his mantel. "You are dismissed for the evening."

"Thank you, my lord." With a sweeping bow, Wright backed out of the room with his usual flourish and drew the doors closed behind him.

The servant forgotten as well as his earlier celebration, Henry stared into the untouched contents of his drink. Occasionally, with the victories and accomplishments he found in Parliament, he managed to forget how very fractured the Marches had become.

Nay, he never truly forgot. Rather, he allowed himself to focus on those matters that were within his control. Areas in which he wasn't a failure and where he was able to help others.

With a long sigh, Henry picked up his glass once more, and this time lifted it in a mock salute.

"To—"

That toast was cut short yet again, but this time by the hard slam of a door. *What in blazes?*

"You cannot . . ." Wright's frantic cries went up, followed by the echoing shouts of several footmen. "Do you hear me? . . . You are not . . ." The remainder of the butler's reedy command was drowned out by the resounding boom of another door striking a wall.

Henry set his glass down hard; the liquid sloshed over the sides, soaking his papers. *What in hell . . . ?* Stalking over to the door, Henry drew it open and rushed into the hall as the cacophony of an approaching herd grew increasingly closer.

"What in hell is going on, Wri—" Henry thundered, just as a virago shouted to bring down the damned household and brought him up short.

"Where are you, Waterson?"

That voice, the husky contralto that commanded so many of his waking moments and still nearly every one of his sleeping ones since he'd seen her.

Clara.

And this was surely a dream. She was *here*? Now? The woman who'd saved him, whom he'd sought out without success, was before him now. A million questions all swirled with only one taking any crystalline clarity: *What* was she doing here?

His heart thumped.

Everything played out with both an infinite slowness and dizzying rapidity as time ceased to mean anything.

"Waterson?" she bellowed again, and his name, spoken on her lips, sprang him into movement. He made it five feet—before she turned the corner.

Then she stopped at the opposite end of the hall, her magnificent chest heaving—from emotion? From racing his servants? The quartet, trailing behind, from whom she'd put a small distance, caught up. Each servant collided into the back of the next man to keep from toppling over the Spartan beauty not even fifty paces from Henry.

Her enormous wide eyes, lined with charcoal, flashed.

Her usual cream-white cheeks were entrancingly flushed.

"Clara," he whispered, and she came sprinting forward.

He rushed to meet her.

She brought her arm back.

Henry grunted as her fist collided with his cheek in an impressive right jab that sent him flying, landing on his arse. Pain shot from his arse up to his damned ringing ears.

He opened and closed his mouth several times, testing the movement of his jaw.

Sure she'd broken it.

Bloody Gentleman Jackson himself couldn't have landed a finer blow.

Clara towered over him. "You bastard," she hissed, spitting in his face.

A heavy, thick tension descended upon the hall, filling it with a thrumming energy.

Spittle dripped down his cheek.

Wright was the first to act. "Summon the constable," he ordered, and as one of the footmen took off running in the opposite direction, Henry's butler grabbed Clara by the arm and wrenched the long limb sharply behind her back.

And even with her attack on him in his own home, a red haze of fury briefly blinded Henry that anyone would dare touch her. "Release her," he commanded over her sharp cry as he struggled to his feet.

But he should have known this woman, of all women, wouldn't require saving from him. Or from any man.

Jamming her heel back into his kneecap, Clara crumpled Wright's left leg.

The butler gasped, but she only turned and brought her knee up, catching the servant between the legs. With a shriek, Wright collapsed at her feet.

Henry, along with the two footmen—the two footmen slowly backing away from the impressive warrioress—all winced with commiserative misery for the poor fellow writhing on the floor.

Reaching inside his jacket, Henry slowly withdrew a neatly folded kerchief and wiped the remnants of her spit from his cheek. "You are dismissed."

Her eyes radiated a searing hatred that landed sharper than her previous physical blow. "If you think I am going anywhere—"

"Not you." Glancing pointedly at the trio of servants, he gave a slight nod.

"But—but . . . my lord," Wright whispered, stumbling awkwardly to his feet.

"I said, you are dismissed."

The ever-obedient butler bowed and then, with the two footmen flanking him, left.

As soon as they'd gone, Henry redirected all his attention to the woman before him. She said nothing. Instead, she continued to stare at him through eyes that burnt. Her shoulders rose and fell fast, from her emotion? From her exertions?

"Clara," he greeted, beginning again. "May I suggest we adjourn to my off—"

She charged at him, but this time he anticipated the attack and caught her wrist before she landed another blow.

"Release me, bastard," she hissed, bringing a knee up.

With his spare hand, Henry intercepted that affront, his fingers curving around her soft thigh. And his neck went hot under the evidence of his own depravity that he should notice her in this moment when the only thing she sought from him . . . was his blood.

"I trust there is another purpose for your visit than attempting to beat me senseless?" he whispered against her ear.

Lavender.

That floral scent of his dreams clung to her skin and filled his senses.

"Can I release you? That is, and have your word that we can talk?"

She hesitated and then gave a tight nod.

Henry released her. "Now, if you'll follow . . ." His former nurse was already marching into his office, head high, shoulders back, spine erect, like she was the owner of the household. ". . . me," he finished dryly.

After she'd disappeared through the doors, he lingered in the corridor a moment, attempting to get his tumultuous thoughts ordered. And failing.

Henry entered and found her positioned at the center of his room, in the middle of the diamond designed upon the parquetry flooring. As he carefully closed the door behind him, he didn't take his eyes from her; with her hands planted on her shapely hips, she looked one wrong word on his part away from flying across the room and planting him another facer.

He knew better than to speak. Instead, he allowed her control of the moment.

"Well?" she demanded, her breasts still heaving. "What do you have to say?"

"I don't . . . I'm sorry, I do not know what this is about."

"Don't know what this is about," she spat, reaching inside her cloak and drawing out a thick packet. Cursing his ancestry in impressively colorful language, she hurled the stack of notes across the room.

They landed atop his boots with a thump.

Keeping her in his sights, he bent down to retrieve the reason for her discontent, and with her breaths coming in fast, noisy spurts, Henry opened the packet . . . and recognized it on sight.

He frowned. "How did you come by this?" he demanded.

"How did I come by it?" she echoed, her voice shrill. Clara stalked over until only a pace separated them. *How did I come by it?*

The cease-and-desist letter he'd seen arranged and dispensed as part of his agreement with Lord Peerson. Something told him whatever answer he gave to that repeated question best be the right one, or she'd drop him again flat. A kernel of an unwanted idea took root at the back of his mind, and he fought it back. "These are legal papers."

"Yes, I *knowwww* what they are," she cried. "They are archaic, rubbish pieces of shite drafted by you pompous, priggish lords who fuck your whores by night and draft legislation on morality in the morning."

Heat splotched his cheeks. "Well, that is quite colorful."

Clara cracked her open palm across his cheek; the force of her slap sent his head ricocheting back. "Do n-not . . ." Her voice trembled with the strength of her emotion. "Do *not* play games with me, Henry March."

Cradling his wounded cheek in his palm, he waited several moments until the ringing in his ears dissipated. She had him at a disadvantage. It was an odd detail to note and lament over, given that, if she had a knife in hand, he didn't doubt she'd use it on him. And yet . . . there it was. Clara, his savior with no surname that he was aware of, knew far more about him than he knew about her.

"I don't know what this is about," he said quietly, and of anything he'd said or done since her arrival, that managed to bring her up short.

Clara opened and closed her mouth several times, those full crimson lips parting, but no words coming forth. And then: "So you are not the one who sent 'round a cease-and-desist letter to shut down my business."

Oh, bloody, bloody hell.

"Henry?" she prodded.

Ignoring her question, packet in hand, Henry wandered back toward his desk. All the while, every last discussion he'd had with this woman, every word exchanged, rolled through his mixed-up mind.

I also have great—mayhap greater respect—for self-made women . . . I trust you've little experience with self-made women . . .

He stopped with his back to her as it all at last made sense.

She was the self-made businesswoman . . . of—he skimmed through the packet—*the Muses.*

Owned and operated by Regina Broderick and . . .

Henry briefly closed his eyes. *Clara Winters.*

She, his savior, his angel of salvation, at last had a surname.

When he opened them, he picked up his drink and took a long, slow swallow, welcoming the fiery burn the brandy left in its wake. Setting it back down, he made himself face Clara.

"It would seem I was the one who shut down your business, after all, Miss Winters."

Chapter 13

It would seem I was the one who shut down your business, after all.

That is what he would say?

Those were the words he'd finally speak.

After everything she'd done for him, to save him, he would say *that*?

What was so very much worse was that he delivered that hated utterance in emotionless, measured tones.

And why, of all she'd survived, struggled through, and faced in her life, all the betrayals she'd known at the hands of a man, should this one hurt worse?

Because he was the one man you had any personal dealings with whom you never traded sexual favors for. For their short time together, he'd simply been a man.

Only for her to be presented with the ugly reminder that he was a man like all the rest. It was a reminder she hadn't needed. She'd had plenty reminders enough in the whole of her thirty-three years. Shaking from the inside out, Clara strode over to Henry's well-stocked sideboard and grabbed the first bottle her fingers touched.

Whiskey.

Clara stared blankly down at the brown liquid, and a half-mad giggle worked its way up her throat. How absolutely fitting. Of all the drinks she could have grabbed, it should be the one she despised most.

Whiskey . . .

"I cannot do this, Marley. I've changed my mind. I'm not looking to be any man's mis—"

"Some women are performers and some . . . are not. You aren't a singer, Clara," the owner of the theatre said with a brutal honesty. "You're the other reason gentlemen come to this theatre. Now drink up. The whiskey will help. Whiskey helps everything."

She gave her head a shake, dislodging the memory. How very fitting the drink was, too.

Whiskey was strong.

Whiskey was a reminder of what she'd lost long ago. Nay—her fingers closed tight around the bottle, clenching hard, draining the blood from her knuckles—then, that night when she'd made herself mistress for a nobleman, she'd made the choice.

This? What Henry had done? This was something that had been taken from her. And it made it all the worse.

"Clara," he murmured, that modulated baritone deep and smooth like the brandy in his glass, and damningly calm. He rested a hand on her shoulder, and she shrugged it off.

If he could be measured, so could she. "Do not touch me, my lord." And then, removing the stopper, poured herself a tall glass of whiskey. Clara tossed back a long swallow and grimaced at the dryness it left in her mouth. "Of course even your whiskey would be astringent and not sweet," she muttered, slamming the glass down. Needing some space between them, she moved away, restless . . . when she felt his stare on her. With a sneer, she made herself face him. "Have I horrified you, Lord Proper? I trust it is not every day a woman storms your office, knocks you on your arse, and downs your whiskey."

Henry laid his palms against his lapels. "Yes, well, you are at the very least the first."

"Are you . . . jesting?"

"Trying to, at the least," he put forward.

"Failing. You are failing."

"No one ever accused me of being amusing."

"And no one ever will." She whisked over and stood so close the tips of their shoes brushed. "They will, however, say you are a pompous—"

"Stodgy?"

"*Priggish* bastard."

"Yes, I'm certain there are those who say that, just not to my face."

She didn't know whether to laugh or cry at his total inability to: one, properly read a person's emotions, and two, form a suitable response based on those emotions.

"Will you sit, Clara?" There was a slight pause. "Please."

They stood there a long while, the fire hissing and crackling in the hearth, before Clara relented.

Wanting to unsettle the endlessly proper nobleman, Clara poured herself another whiskey and carried it over to one of the winged chairs before his desk.

And ever a gentleman, even to a woman responsible for his bruised cheek, Henry waited until she'd been seated before claiming that king-like red-upholstered mahogany chair.

Cradling her glass between her fingers, Clara stared across the top of her drink, studying the man she'd saved months ago. She didn't want to notice or appreciate how darkly magnificent he was. It had been pathetic before when she'd lusted for the battered man in her apartments. It was an altogether deeper level of pitifulness to appreciate the man who sought to ruin her. Even knowing that, even recognizing it, she could not stop herself from noting the difference in this version of Henry March, the Earl of Waterson, from the one she'd previously known.

Before, when he'd been beaten and unable to so much as sit up without struggling, he'd been splendid in his beauty. But this? Tall, broadly powerful with the corded muscles of his biceps straining the elegant fabric of his wool evening coat, he was a study in masculine elegance, a display of noble strength, but brimming with a raw vitality that she doubted he saw in himself.

"How have you been, Clara?" he asked, placing that hated packet at the center of whatever leather folio he'd been working from when she'd interrupted his nighttime pleasures.

"This isn't a social visit, Henry."

"No," he said gravely. "It isn't. But neither does it mean I can't ask how you've been these past months."

"You can ask, but it doesn't mean I have to answer."

"I came back for you."

Of anything he could have said . . . that had been the last she'd suspect. "What?" she whispered. He'd come back for her. What did that even mean? To what end? Why? The questions continued to come, but there wasn't a single answer she could land on in her mind.

Henry loosened his cravat, that slightest of hints that he was not in the control he wanted to be. "Rather, I went to see you." What accounted for the odd deflation at that clarification? "You were not there."

Bitterness swelled anew, rancid and biting. "No, I was not." And just like that, that weakening over his pronouncement was stamped out by the reminder of just why she'd had to move into the Devil's Den. "Do you know where I was?" she asked coolly, placing her drink on the mahogany arm of her chair.

"If I'd known, I would have found you before."

A laugh tore from her lips, shaking her frame, shocking her with the unexpectedness of it. "Are you daft?"

"That is *not* one of the deficits I've been accused of."

She groaned and shook her head. "Literal, Henry. You are literal in everything. Sometimes people speak figuratively."

His noble brow went up. "Figurative speech is a waste of speech. There is nothing direct in it, and it only serves as a source of confusion. For example, even now we should be speaking about the reason for your visit, but instead we're debating a rhetorical question you didn't ever really want an answer to."

Clara stared at the man opposite her, feeling like he'd spun her around in dizzying circles. "Maybe you are daft, after all," she breathed. Needing a drink more than ever, she took a sip of her whiskey. Thought better of it, and took a second swallow. And some of the tension dissolved, replacing it with a welcome warmth that soothed.

"Now, the matter of—" A frown played at the corners of his hard lips.

She followed his stare, searching for the source of that displeasure . . . to her knuckles.

"You were injured."

"What . . . ?"

And with something akin to disbelief, she stared on as he leapt out of his chair, crossed the room, and gave the bellpull there a tug.

An instant later the door opened.

"The constables are on their way, my lord," the young butler whispered, glancing over his employer's shoulder to where Clara sat turned around . . . taking in the latest bizarre tableau.

Borrowing one of the Killorans' favorite threats, Clara made a slashing motion at her throat.

The servant promptly collapsed into a choking spasm.

Whatever Henry's reply was, however, was lost, and a moment later his servant was gone.

"Now, where were we?"

"You destroying my future," she said as he slid back into the folds of his seat. "We were discussing how you destroyed my future. Unless"—hope kindled in her breast—"there was a mistake?"

Sighing, Henry opened up the packet and scanned through the pages one by one before pushing them away and picking up his brandy.

Liquid fortitude, he sought.

It was how she knew his response before he even answered.

"It was not a mistake. I intended to have the cease and desist drafted, Clara."

She nodded, waiting for him to finish the remainder of that thought.

And waited.

And continued waiting before she realized . . . "That is it?"

His face pulled in a grimace. "Your business—"

Surging to her feet, she slammed her palms down on his desk. "Is not indecent. It is not immoral. There are no vices." She knew; she'd been guilty of those very sins enough in her life.

"I know nothing about your business," he said calmly.

"And yet you ordered the closure of the Muses." She sought to make sense of the implications of that. "How can you shut down something you know nothing of?"

Henry passed his drink back and forth between his palms. Good, he was unnerved. He should be, the miserable blighter. "I draft bills and acts for the House of Lords," he finally said.

Straightening, Clara crossed her arms at her chest but made no attempt to reclaim her chair. "Go on."

"In Parliament, what an MP is able to pass is all dependent upon the support it receives."

"I do not require a civics lesson. A bill can start in the Commons or the Lords and must be approved in the same form by both houses before becoming an act. I quite know how Parliament works," she said irascibly.

Henry's powerful jaw dropped, even as his eyes radiated heat. And she fought off another round of laughter. Of all the men she'd charmed, they'd gazed upon her with that very look of desire because of the plunging trim of her neckline, because of the sway of her hips as she'd walked. Not a single man, however, had ever looked at her as Henry did now because of her grasp on British politics.

"Uh . . . yes . . . well, as I was saying." Henry downed his brandy in one fluid swallow, his throat working, that Adam's apple she'd failed to note before in their time together bobbing. "Everything is about securing votes for the passage of bills or acts."

Clara closed her eyes and counted to five. When she opened them, she spoke in measured tones. "What does that have to do with me and my music hall?"

"There are enough members of Parliament concerned with making revisions to the morality act. Passed in 1787, there are many who believe it did not go far enough."

"Far enough in doing what? Curtailing people's freedoms?" she snapped.

"In promoting an uncorrupted society," he put in smoothly.

"Are you one of them, Henry?" *Of course he would be.*

"That is not my focus, no," he said, and she struggled to mask her surprise. Not wanting him to upend her any more than she already was. "In order to secure votes for the bill I'm presenting, I pledged my support and my vote."

It did not escape her notice that he'd sidestepped his focus. Why in blazes should she care? *You don't care. It doesn't matter what his damned interests and efforts were.* What mattered is that he'd thwarted her dreams. Except . . . "What was your bill?" she asked with a grudging reluctance.

"My bill is . . ." Henry fiddled with that now-rumpled cravat until he caught her stare on that movement, and he abruptly stopped. "A universal police force for the whole of England."

"A—"

"Police force. The bill or act would appoint a police force to be under two commissioners, who will be justices of the peace. The constables would have power not only within London but also throughout

Middlesex, Surrey, Hertfordshire, Essex, and Kent." He sat forward in his chair, gesticulating as he spoke, and if she didn't want to slap him in his head again, she would have found that boyish enthusiasm for his damned politics endearing. "It is all about improving the presence of officers of the law who'll preserve order and—"

She'd heard enough. "You . . . traded votes, then." It was a statement, not a question.

"Beg pardon?" His dark brows stitched together in a line of confusion. Or was it disappointment that she cared not at all for his aspirations and everything about her own future and those who were dependent upon her.

"Traded. Votes. If you don't give a fig about the morality act— which my music hall does not violate—"

"I never said I did not care." He bristled.

"Then you traded votes to get something you wanted."

Henry scowled. "You make what I've done and my role as an MP . . . somehow dishonorable."

"No," she said with a calm she didn't feel. "Not what you do, but rather how you go about achieving your *goals* is dishonorable."

He thumped a hand on the desk. "It is the way things are done. The way bills and acts are made law."

Oh, the bloody nobility. Nay, it was men. Such black-and-white thinking was the way of men. They would never see eye to eye on this, and she didn't care to waste any time trying to make him see. Her purpose, her goal, was singular.

"What do you want, Clara?" he asked quietly, as if he'd followed the precise path of her thoughts.

She opened her mouth to launch her demands when she was interrupted by footfalls outside and a firm knock. She braced, prepared for the constable the servants had summoned. Only to find the tall, wiry butler she'd leveled earlier at the other side of the door.

A pair of maids, their arms laden with bowls of water and white linen cloths, scurried in.

"Please set it over by the hearth," Henry called over.

After they deposited their burdens and left, he came to his feet. "You were saying?" Henry asked, shrugging out of his jacket. He draped the immaculately cut black evening coat along the back of his chair and started across the room.

Her mouth went dry. "I . . ." Why had he removed his jacket? And what was more . . . why was his chest so broad, the width of his shoulders so . . . ? All the pompous gentlemen she'd known had never had physiques that belonged to working-class men.

Focus. You're not one to go weak-kneed over any man. What in blazes was wrong with her? Her earlier resolve and rightful outrage restored, she stormed over to where he'd positioned himself at the hearth. "You cannot simply just . . ." Henry captured her left wrist in a tender grip. Puzzling her brow, she stared at the top of his bent head. "What are you doing?"

"You were injured."

"I was . . ." Clara followed his attentions to her swollen knuckles, the product of knocking him on his arse.

"Here, sit."

And because he'd knocked her completely off-kilter that night, she sank onto the edge of the leather button sofa.

Wringing out a cloth, Henry then came and knelt beside her. Briefly shocked out of words, she stared on as he applied the cool compress to her throbbing knuckles. Knuckles which, in her outrage and fury, she hadn't realized even hurt. Knuckles that hurt because she'd planted him a facer.

And despite that, he took care of her anyway.

"I don't need you playing nursemaid for me, Henry," she said tiredly.

"I'm not playing nursemaid." He paused in his ministrations and, lifting his head, flashed a crooked grin. "That was your role."

She lowered her brows.

"Another poor attempt at a jest?"

"Undoubtedly," she said under her breath.

Henry returned the cloth to the bowl and dunked another scrap of linen. This time, when he returned, he claimed the spot beside her on the sofa. So close their knees brushed. And as he wrapped the cool cloth around her hand, she studied him.

Why was she allowing him to disarm her? She didn't want him to be concerned for her bruised knuckles or for him to care for her. It was a contradiction to what he'd done in shutting down her business.

My business. The reason why I am here . . .

She'd swayed countless men before him. Surely she could make this gentleman—one whom she'd rescued on the streets, no less—see reason. "I wanted to provide women without any options in life a new beginning," she said softly, and he froze, his hand upon hers. "I wanted there to be a place where women weren't required to use their bodies or feminine wiles, but rather their talents. The Muses?" Clara lifted her spare palm up. "That is what my establishment represents, Henry. Hope."

Emotion traversed the planes of his harshly beautiful face, and yet . . . she could not make sense of what he was thinking. Or feeling. Drawing in an uneven breath, Clara sought to explain all the ways in which her music hall was special. "Only, this, Henry, my music hall," she murmured, fiddling with the corners of her makeshift bandage. "It is about so much more. It is about the thrum of the orchestra's strains going through you."

Of their own volition, her eyes slid closed, and for the first time since she'd traded the theatre for whoring, her love of the theatre all came rushing back. "It is about how the music resonates from a place deep inside. Where it melts away anything but the feel of that song." Somewhere along the way, the intent of her words for him had shifted as her long-buried love of the theatre breathed to life once more. Still alive. Still there. Clara forced her eyes open and found Henry's hooded gaze trained on her. "Have you ever felt something like that, Henry?" she asked quietly without inflection. "Have you ever been so moved, so captivated by anything?"

His eyes darkened, the deep blue turning a shade darker, to sapphire. Then he looked down at her hand. "No, I've not." Henry refolded the damp cloth over her knuckles. "My life has been more"—*emotionless, calculated*—"focused, Clara."

"Focused?" she gently prodded.

"On my obligations as earl. Caring for my sisters and mother. Our landholdings. My responsibilities in Parliament."

And despite the rage that had sent her here, there was a stirring of pity for the cold, untouched life he'd lived. Henry went to remove the cloth, and Clara laid her palm over his, stopping him. "Have you been to the theatre?"

"Many times," he replied automatically.

"Many times, you say?" she murmured in echo. A wistful smile played at her lips. "No doubt you've a family box at every distinguished theatre. You're undoubtedly fashionably late but arrive early enough to take part in the social experience." An endearing splotch of color filled his cheeks. Ah, so she was right. "A box of your family's own." Even as most patrons couldn't afford that luxury, and many combined resources to have that pleasure. "Just off the center of the theatre."

"How do you—" He immediately closed his mouth in a firm line.

How did she know? She knew because all the peerage was the same. Clara angled herself so she could better face him. "A family of import such as yours would only ever have a box that signified that station, and yet, to be center would be too obvious, but to be too in the wings would deny you a view: of the stage, of the other patrons." His color deepened. Clara placed her mouth close to Henry's. So close their breath tangled. So close, their lips nearly touched. "But you don't really know, Henry," she whispered.

"Know?" he asked hoarsely, his voice entranced.

"You don't know what it is to feel passion, Henry." Their eyes locked, and she drew one of his hands close to her chest. "You've never had music move you, its strings taking you on a journey where you are someone else. *Somewhere* else. And who you are, along with the whole world you've been born to, just melts away so that, for a brief time, all you know is the glorious hum going through you that comes from being alive."

Henry angled his head, and for a moment, she believed he was going to kiss her. She felt his desire. It poured from him and seeped from the narrow slits of his passion-heavy eyes.

And yet—

Henry froze. Ever a master of self-control.

"It has to be about more than emotion, Clara," he whispered. "If there is no order, there is nothing."

If there is no order, there is nothing . . .

There is nothing.

That last two-syllable word reverberated in her mind.

Nothing.

Nothing.

It spoke to the great divide between her and this man who would never be swayed by impassioned words that had come from deep inside her. "You speak of nothing, Henry. You don't know the meaning of 'nothing,'" she spat. And the rage that had brought her racing here had her on her feet. "Nothing is whoring yourself in exchange for a roof over your head or food in your belly."

All the color leached from his cheeks, turning him a sickly, ashen shade of grey. "I didn't—"

"You didn't what?" she taunted. "Know that you'd been rescued by a former whore and one of London's most notorious madams?"

For a moment, it was hard to say who was more stunned by her admission. Clara's heart thumped an erratic pace. It was an admission of fact, one which she'd long ago come to terms with and accepted as what she'd done unashamedly in her quest to not only survive but also thrive.

Hadn't she? Why then, as Henry sank back, did her chest tighten so painfully?

She braced for the ever-proper Earl of Waterson to look away . . . in self-righteous disgust.

"No," he finally said, quietly. "I did not know anything about you, Clara. Because you were so very determined to keep your secrets."

Then she spied it. It was a deep glimmer in his eyes, faint but so sharp it burnt—pity. "I don't want your pity, Waterson." She hissed that title for the curse it was. *By God, he can take that sentiment and choke on it.*

With a frown, Henry straightened. "I didn't say anything about pitying you, Clara."

"You didn't need to, Henry," she said, her voice flat to her own ears. And God, she didn't know who she hated more in this moment: this man who'd somehow made her feel the long-remembered regret for how her life had turned out, or herself for trading her virtue and her soul for something *more*. "You didn't need to," she repeated. "Because everything you're thinking is there in your eyes." Regardless, how he felt about her or her past was irrelevant. "You had my business shut down." Before it had even opened. "Make it right, Henry." Clara tossed the makeshift bandage at him. The damp cloth landed with a thump on the crisp leather, soaking the side of his trousers.

Sighing, Henry scooped up the cloth and returned it to the bowl. "It isn't that . . . easy, Clara."

"But it was easy shutting down my music hall?" she demanded.

He scraped a hand through his hair, shoving back those slightly tousled brown locks. The light curl to those strands at odds with a man who coveted control. Then he let his arm fall back to his side. "Let me explain." Henry stalked over to his desk, and opening the center middle drawer, he pulled out . . .

"A deck of cards, Henry?" she asked, incredulity creeping in. Mad. He was mad. She'd surely addled him when she'd hit him. Or mayhap his madness went back to the assault he'd sustained in St. Giles months earlier. "This isn't the time for whist or hazard."

"I'm not a whist or hazard man. Bear with me," he murmured more to himself. "Drafting bills and acts requires reliance upon others. One can push nothing through by oneself. There are discussions." A card went up at the base. "This would be me." A king of hearts went into place at the bottom center of that geometric design, and Henry stabilized the foundation with his long fingers.

Unbidden, her legs were moving, carrying her back to his side. "That would be you and your . . . police force."

"Precisely." He briefly lifted his attention from the precariously balanced cards. "This represents Lord X's desire for banking reform." Yet another card found a place upon that growing pyramid. "Lord Y wishes for changes to the Enclosure Acts. And of course, Lord Z with a factory act that would address the shifting industry across England."

His hands flew rapidly at his task. "And so on and so on and so on until at last you have it." Keeping his fingers steady, barely touching and lightly steadying the card masterpiece he'd created.

"It?"

Henry stepped back. "A house of cards." As he spoke, his voice growing animated, Henry walked about his desk, motioning to the pyramid. "Every bill or act drafted requires support. Each MP needs the support of others, who require support for their ventures, and so on and so on." At last, he came to a stop directly across from her, with only the desk dividing them.

She shook her head slowly. "*That* is what you'd say?" He'd equate what he'd done and her now-uncertain future to a damned deck of cards?

"Surely you see that to undo one action"—he slashed a hand up and down at his pyramid of cards—"would bring it all falling down."

"The only thing I see, my lord, is that you've used the wrong card." Clara moved quickly and plucked the king of hearts from the bottom, and the whole deck came toppling down. "You have no heart." She flicked the card at him. It hit his chest before falling atop the rest of the cluttered mess of cards.

Henry stared at it a moment before retrieving that scrap she'd hurled. "The thing is, Clara," he murmured, staring at the card as he rotated it back and forth. Back and forth. The picture card to blank white. Over and over. "You proved my very point. When removing me from the pyramid, it all came crashing down."

Clara fought to breathe through the panic and desperation. She wandered away, giving her back to him. Not wanting him to see, not wanting to cede any more power, as she'd already had so much of her strength stripped away by this man. He was too logical to be compelled by a woman he knew not at all. Nay, that wasn't true. Making one more desperate attempt, she spun back. "I cared for you, Henry. I saved you in the streets and nursed you." She searched every angular plane of his face for some indication that her words meant anything.

"I looked for you in the days after," he said, repeating that first confession he'd made. Opening his drawer once more, Henry pulled out a small sheet and, coming around the desk, handed the official-looking page over to her.

"What is this?" she asked, already scanning the document. Already knowing before he spoke.

"One thousand pounds."

Her fingers curled around the edges of the page, noisily wrinkling it. "I see that. What. Is. It?"

"It was a token of my appreciation. Take that."

For your troubles.

Clara had been angry countless times in her life; usually a man was the reason for that ire. But this, the red-hot, acidic burn that seared through her veins had a tangible life force which she'd never before known.

"It is quite a generous offer . . ." Henry's words trailed off as Clara spun on her heel and stalked across the room. "What are you . . . ?"

Clara was already touching the corner of the payment he'd make to the fire. The moment the edges went black and curled up, a little flame fast crumpling the funds, she spun and faced him. "Is this what you'd offer me?" she cried. "Money for my *troubles*? Troubles which *you* are responsible for? You can take your generous offer and eat shite." She tossed the burning scrap down, and it immediately licked at the gold fringes of his Aubusson carpet.

Cursing, Henry rushed across the room and stomped out the small fire she'd set.

Clara surged forward, and he stiffened.

She caught him by the front of his shirt, and pulling him close, Clara pressed her mouth to Henry's. An explosion of heat greater than the flame that had nearly scorched her fingers blazed to life. Hotter than anything she'd known, and in that moment death by fire seemed quite the way to go.

Henry's entire body went motionless against her own suddenly still frame, and then he was kissing her back.

Moaning, Clara parted her lips, allowing him entry, and when he slid his tongue inside, stroking hers, she lashed the pink tip of flesh against his in a seductive move. She angled her head to better receive his kiss, and to kiss him in return. Then his hands were at her waist, his fingertips sinking into her hips as he drew her closer. Pressing her against the enormous hard ridge of his length. An ache settled between her legs as she, the seducer, became the seduced. And she fought the spell he wove, because by damn, she wasn't one who had spells woven over her. For everything she'd never been in command of, this was something she always—

Henry moved his lips lower, worshipping the trail of skin in his wake, settling his mouth against the place in her neck where her pulse erratically beat—for him.

A wanton moan filtered from her lips as she let her head fall back, and she opened herself to him. Tangling her fingers in his dark curls, still damp from when he'd run his wet fingers through them, she held him close. Allowing him his search and taking the pleasure he provided as her due.

She shifted, reclaiming his mouth in a savage kiss that pulled a guttural groan from him; it reverberated against her chest and filled her with a hedonist's triumph. He angled his head, deepening their kiss. Their embrace. And then, fighting the too-potent hold this man had held over her since she'd met him on the streets, Clara reached between them. Drawing back, she denied herself any more of his kiss, delighting in the heaviness of his thick, black lashes that did little to disguise the lust raging in his eyes.

She curled her lips up into a cool smile. "I'm going to destroy you, Henry March." And with that warning, she stormed from the room, leaving in her wake the man whose kiss still tingled on her lips.

Chapter 14

"You look like hell."

What was more, Henry felt like hell.

"Stuff it," Henry muttered as he joined his—as his mother had so unflatteringly pointed out—only friend in the world at his private table at White's.

"I trust you also feel like hell," the Marquess of Waverly put in with his usual pragmatism.

"Indeed," Henry mumbled. Nor did that feeling have anything to do with the impressive right hook Clara had landed last evening. It was everything she'd at last revealed about her past . . . and everything that had come thereafter. *That kept you awake last evening. You're thinking of the feel of her in your arms, her mouth against yours, her breasts pressed against your chest—*

Waverly sat forward, concern in his eyes. "They still haven't found your assailants."

"Steele did. Both men were dead." Henry didn't want to talk about the attack on him anymore. He didn't want to relive that horror and the terror of facing death, alone in the streets.

His friend, however, proved tenacious. "And the ones responsible for your latest attack?"

Henry puzzled his brow. His . . . ? And then his friend's words registered.

"I wasn't . . . attacked." Not in the way his friend was thinking. "That is . . . not by street toughs or thieves or . . ." *Bloody hell. Shut your mouth.*

His friend lounged in his seat. "Well, now, this is fascinating. Bruised, but not at the hands of some unknown assailants."

A woman. He'd been bruised by a woman. Granted, Clara wasn't like any other woman he'd known or would ever again know.

"Is that flush on your cheeks guilt or embarrassment?" Gabriel, the Marquess of Waverly, grinned. "Or mayhap both?"

His friend was only right on the former score. Henry was spared any more ribbing when the marquess motioned over a liveried servant. "A glass, please, and a bottle of something strong," he said to the young man. "Stronger than brandy," he called after the servant, who'd already rushed off. When the young man had gone, Waverly spoke in hushed, entirely too-amused tones. "Something tells me, given the state of your face, you require something stronger this day."

So he wasn't to be spared from Waverly's probing, after all. "Stuff it," he said for a second time, earning a boisterous laugh from his traitorous friend, along with glances from all the other gentlemen at White's.

"What happened to you?" Waverly paused. "Again."

Again. Yes, because this was not the first time his friend had seen him in a battered state. "I . . ." Henry felt his neck burning. After all, how in blazes was a gent to admit to even his best friend that he'd been knocked on his arse by a woman? Granted, a stunningly powerful Spartan warrioress whose kiss had robbed him of sleep and haunted his waking thoughts still. But a woman nonetheless. "Who's to say anything happened to me?" he hedged.

Waverly kicked back his chair so that he balanced precariously on the rear legs. "Oh, your bruised cheek. Your black eye. Your pathetic attempts at evading my questions. All pointed me toward that conclusion."

The waiter arrived with glass and bottle in hand, giving Henry another brief reprieve and chance to formulate an immediate reply. *Did you truly think Waverly of all people wouldn't have questions for you?*

Beginning to regret the hasty acceptance he'd sent to a meeting at White's, Henry devoted all his attention to making himself a drink.

His skin prickled with the stare Waverly trained on him. Of course, friends since Eton and closer than brothers, they'd known one another for decades. As such, Waverly wouldn't be content with a nonanswer, and Henry should be wholly comfortable in revealing . . . all . . . and yet . . . he could not.

Determined to put Clara from his mind, he raised the glass to his lips—and froze.

An image of Clara as she'd been last night, commandeering his sideboard and pouring herself a drink. Then she'd downed that whiskey with an impressive ease not a single gent of his acquaintance had. Given he was the stodgy lord she took such delight in reminding Henry he was, there should have been . . . disapproval. Disgust. Distaste. Any number of words with "dis" attached to them. Instead, even a day later, he was filled with a potent hungering.

He didn't know any woman—any person—could be so in command of oneself.

And yet, there had also been . . . a vulnerability to her when she'd revealed her past.

A past that had included men providing her security, for the gift of her body. Henry was suddenly besieged with a vitriolic hatred for those unknown bastards who'd known her in any way. In ways Henry ached to but without any payment involved which would reduce their relationship to a business transaction.

Growling, Henry tossed his drink back.

Of course even your whiskey would be astringent and not sweet . . .

"Whiskey," Henry groused. "It would be whiskey."

From behind the rim of his glass, he caught Waverly's grin. "I trust by that response whatever or whomever is responsible for that bruised cheek and black-and-blue eye is also responsible for your newfound hatred of whiskey."

Oh, hell. His experience with Parliament had taught him long ago, directness went a good deal further than sidestepping issues. "It was a woman."

Gabriel promptly choked; dissolving into a fit, his friend tried to get words out. "A . . . w . . ." The remainder was strangled off by that paroxysm of coughing.

Henry casually sipped at his whiskey. Yes, there was something to be said for always staying a step ahead of . . . everyone.

I'm going to destroy you, Henry March . . .

Remembering that huskily whispered threat Clara had breathed against his lips, he'd be wise to heed his own thoughts.

When he was able to at last breathe without strangling on his words, Waverly dragged his chair closer. "What woman would want to hit you?" Not *would* want to. Did. Altogether different.

Furthermore . . . "What is that supposed to mean?"

Waverly eyed him like he'd gone mad. "It means you do not offend women. Everyone knows that. Well, other than your mother, who wants to see you properly married—"

"Waverly," he warned.

"I digress. But you couldn't be improper if you tried."

His fingers curled around his glass, twitching with the wicked remembrance of Clara's hips, the generous curve of her buttocks. "Yes, well . . ." He cleared his throat. "This woman, I have offended." Henry went on to provide the details of his meeting with Clara, going back to their first.

When he'd finished, Waverly didn't say anything for a long while. Rather, he sat there with his high brow furrowed in displeasure, that response generally reserved for others and never Henry. "What?" Henry snapped.

"You were rescued by a woman."

Henry braced for the laughter that would follow. The marquess, however, continued on with an accounting of the key details Henry had just laid out the same way he presented arguments before Parliament. "She stitched your side. Nursed you back to health. Allowed you to remain with her . . . and this is only the first you're mentioning it?"

"Of all that I've told you regarding . . . Miss Winters, this is what you'd fix on?"

"Yes," Waverly said flatly. "Because it's the omission of Miss Winters before this point that tells me the most."

"T-tell . . ." Henry sputtered. "It doesn't *tell* anything. It was just . . . a detail I omitted."

Waverly snorted. "Indeed. Very well, I'll allow you your mere 'omitted detail.' Let us instead focus on the latter part of your telling: you betrayed the young woman."

"I've not betrayed anyone," he exclaimed . . . too loudly.

The marquess gave him a long look. "Haven't you, though?"

His friend's hushed retort may as well have been an echo of Henry's own guilty thoughts.

Whispers went up around the club, while the other patrons strained in their seats to catch a glimpse of Henry and Waverly. Miserable gossips.

His neck heating, Henry straightened his already immaculate cravat. Only, it wasn't the gossips. It was Henry's own discovered-too-late conscience.

Waverly eyed him a long moment before at last speaking. "You might not believe you've betrayed her, Waterson . . . but that is certainly how the young woman sees it."

Dragging his chair closer, Henry propped his elbows on the table, framing his face and blocking out the busybodies. "I do not need to lecture you of all people on the workings of Parliament."

"This isn't about Parliament." Waverly waved him off. "And I'm hardly lecturing you. Rather this is about understanding how a woman might feel about it." His friend dropped his voice and spoke in hushed tones. "I am simply pointing out that you can certainly see how the woman who, by your own words, saved you should take exception with your being the one to orchestrate the closure of her business."

And bloody hell, damned if his friend wasn't correct. Henry did see why Clara was upset. The rub of it was, he couldn't do anything about her or her situation.

And what would become of her when her music hall was shuttered? His stomach churned.

"I'll have you know, I offered her payment," Henry said defensively.

Waverly dissolved into another fit, bringing another bevy of stares their way, and while the marquess strangled on his own amusement, Henry scowled at him.

"What? It was a generous offer."

The other man dusted tears from his eyes. "Oh, indeed. Very generous. Given your directness over the years, I trust you even told her as much."

Henry shifted in his seat. "There is nothing *wrong* with being direct."

Waverly roared with hilarity.

"Oh, go to hell," Henry muttered, no longer giving a single damn about the riveted crowd around them. Of all the people he'd expect would defend a woman who owned and operated a music hall, Waverly would have been the last one. But then, this married version of Waverly was vastly different from the person he'd long known. Waverly, whose wife was bastard born and herself an owner of a finishing school for other bastard-born children.

To give his fingers something to do, Henry picked up his drink once more and stared into the dark contents of his glass.

"Well?"

At that question, Henry glanced over at Waverly quizzically.

"That is," the marquess clarified. "What do you intend to do?"

Mayhap it was a largely sleepless night, or the effects of the whiskey he'd consumed thus far, but Henry couldn't sort out what in blazes his friend was talking about. "What do I intend to do about what?"

"Not 'about what,' 'for *whommm*,'" Waverly clarified. "Your savior on the streets may have very well addled your brain, after all. Surely you intend to make some repayment." Henry opened his mouth to remind Waverly of the funds he'd offered. "Other than your first offer, that is."

"You don't even know her, and yet you're speaking of recompense for—"

"Saving your life and you shutting down her business," Waverly finished in somber tones. "That is precisely what I am recommending."

That quiet pronouncement was a mark of all the ways his lifetime friend had been changed by his marriage, and all the ways in which Henry and the marquess were now different. And yet, damned if he didn't find himself . . . agreeing with the other man. Hating it because of the complications it posed. Henry let out a sound of frustration.

"There is nothing that can be done. With the deals you've struck in the House of Lords, you know that better than anyone. Not without undoing everything I've done thus far to secure my votes. Removing my pledge of support for Peerson's morality bill would instantly result in him yanking his support of my legislation."

Waverly stared at him for a long moment and gave a slight shake of his head, barely noticeable, and yet, enough, and it conveyed such an abject disappointment in Henry that his disapproval couldn't have struck more had he put it into biting words.

Coward that he was, Henry opted to move them over to safer discourse. "You asked me to meet you?"

"Jane is expecting," his friend said without preamble.

"Again?" he blurted.

Waverly's cheeks grew flushed. "Nothing wrong with a large family."

"You've five children." And now a sixth on the way. It was a nonsensical statement to make, given the other man's announcement.

The right corner of his friend's mouth lifted in an amused half grin. "Yes, well, if you're advising me to give the sixth away, I've quite decided already on keeping her . . . or him."

"Forgive me," he said quickly. God, what a bloody horrid friend he was. "Congratulations. My sincerest congratulations to you and Lady Waverly." He lifted his glass and toasted his friend, taking a sip while his friend, who'd never bothered with spirits, sat there grinning with a besotted smile on his face. "I am very happy for the both of you."

And here you sit . . . without even one child. Without so much as a wife with whom to build a family. It was a detail that had been secondary for so long—behind Henry's greater goals for Parliament and his sisters' well-being—that he'd not allowed himself to think of all he'd not accomplished. *Or missed.* Miss Newton represented the clearest, easiest path to those goals. And yet, even with that, he'd not brought himself 'round to honoring that unspoken end of his agreement with Lord Peerson. There'd been an understanding they'd not discussed which would resolve that end of Henry's future and secure both his and Peerson's legislative wishes. *Because I want more. I want what Waverly has with his wife.*

Yes, it was official: sitting here envious of his friend and his news marked Henry the worst of friends.

"I asked you here to inquire if you'd be willing to serve in the role of godfather," his friend said, bringing him back from those pathetic musings.

"Godfather?" he repeated dumbly.

Waverly coughed into one of his fists. "If you'd rather not . . ."

"No, I . . ." *Godfather.* Henry responsible in some way for that child—granted, a child not yet born—but that responsibility now passed to him. And yet . . . also wanting more—for himself. "I am honored," he said quietly, meaning it. "I would be . . . will be . . . *am* honored."

Waverly's grin widened. "Thank you. And given the gossip I've heard, I trust such an announcement might not be so very far from you."

Henry's mind traveled down an unexpected path, imagining a tall, fearless woman with a solid right hook. What would it be like with such a woman in one's life? Certainly never dull. Always adventurous. Both truths that would have had him shudder—before Clara had saved him.

"Woolgathering about the lady is certainly the first telltale indication that you're close to the parson's mousetrap. Lord Peerson must be thoroughly elated at the prospect of a match."

The lady? Lord Peerson.

Then it slammed into him: the dynastic union his mother had spoken of and had helped broker the initial discussions between.

Miss Newton.

And while they moved thankfully on to safer, less volatile subjects of discussion, Henry couldn't rid his thoughts of Clara Winters . . . or their embrace in his office the previous night.

Chapter 15

It had been two minutes and thirty seconds since anyone had spoken.

And Clara knew only because ever since she'd revealed what had happened, her gaze had been fixed on the round clock at the back center of the Muses theatre for each passing moment.

Seated at the edge of the stage with her legs dangling down, she stared forward . . . unable to look at her friend on her left or the man who'd served as Clara's former employer to Reggie's other side.

Their silence was deafening and ominous.

Oh, in the immediacy of what she'd learned, and the vow she'd made to see Henry destroyed, the reality was, in the light of a new day . . . she saw no way out of this.

Connections trumped all.

Nobility trumped even more.

And despite what the Killorans had, and all Clara did not, they were no match for the peerage.

"I might have him killed," Broderick Killoran at last suggested, with forced brevity in his tones.

Reggie gasped. "Quiet," she ordered, jamming her elbow into his side. "You're not one to go about murdering people." Clara rather suspected at one point he had been, however. It was a detail his wife likely did not or could not want to see about the man who'd been so transformed.

Broderick grunted. "I was trying to ease some of the tension."

"You failed."

Actually . . . he hadn't. Not entirely. If she wasn't close to crying, and if she'd been capable of it, Clara would have managed a laugh at Broderick Killoran, ruthless gaming hell owner, jesting over offing a lord.

If that lord weren't Henry.

If she hadn't already witnessed the gentleman near death.

If he weren't a lord who genuinely cared about his sisters and mother—an all-too-rare sentiment amongst members of the peerage.

And also if you hadn't kissed Henry last night with a burning intensity you've never known from any other kiss.

Clara had not taken a lover in four years. And the last man she'd taken to her bed had been a business partner of another gaming hell. Not once in all the times he'd bedded her had that man kissed her mouth. And his denying that intimacy had been an indication that he'd believed her inferior. Undeserving of his kiss. Somehow less in his eyes, while he saved that special part of himself for someone he'd deemed deserving.

But Henry . . . he had devoured her with his mouth, kissed her like she was the only woman in the world and—

Stop, you pathetic fool. Here she sat, waxing silently on about the bastard's embrace while he sought to ruin her.

Nay, when he already had ruined her . . . and Reggie.

Reggie, however, would be fine. Able to begin again, and secure with the wealth and power marriage to Broderick Killoran afforded her.

"This cannot be it," Reggie said quietly, in an echo of what had reverberated in Clara's mind throughout a long, sleepless night.

"A nobleman talks, and the world listens. Do you truly believe they . . . he . . . any of them will alter their opinions out of a sense of honor?" Restless, Clara jumped up and proceeded to pace. "No. They've laid down the law, both literally and figuratively."

Figurative speech is a waste of speech. There is nothing direct in it, and it only serves as a source of confusion. For example, even now we should be speaking about the reason for your visit, but instead we're debating a rhetorical question you didn't ever really want an answer to . . .

She groaned. Damn him for intruding in her thoughts yet again.

"We'll speak to my solicitor," Broderick said quietly. "We'll develop a case against their case."

It was a generous offer from a man she'd clashed with many times over the years, first because they'd been employed by rival gaming hells. And then because she'd come to see him as a commanding, pompous man like all the others.

Reggie sighed. "And how long will that take? To fight them legally on a case—"

"We'll no doubt lose," Clara finished for her. And just like that, the life and energy drained from Clara, and she sank to the stage, her skirts spread around her. "Even if we somehow triumph, how long would the matter drag on? There are the women, men, and children now reliant upon work here." Employees who even now had no idea that their existence was about to be upended.

Because of me . . .

Reggie abandoned her husband's side and joined Clara. "We're not ones who are simply defeated, Clara," she said softly, sitting beside Clara. "When I believed all hope was lost, you were the one who would not let me simply accept defeat."

"Our opponent was Broderick," Clara muttered, dropping her chin atop her knees. "This is altogether different."

"I beg your pardon," the proprietor of the Devil's Den called over in affronted tones.

Reggie gave Clara a sly wink and then looped an arm around her. "Regardless, we did not accept the previous threat to our hall, and we should not accept it now."

Clara furrowed her brow. Her friend was correct. Surely there was some way out of this. Something they could do. Connections they could appeal to? After all, Reggie's sisters-in-law were all linked to the nobility in some way. Why, the eldest Killoran sister had recently married a marquess. Granted, the marquess had been—and still was—considered mad by Polite Society after the death of his first wife, but once a noble, always a noble.

"You are right," Clara breathed. "Why should we simply accept defeat?"

"That is the Clara Winters I'm accustomed to." Her friend beamed. "And you are correct: we shouldn't."

"There has to be someone who can intervene—"

Someone opened one of the front doors a fraction, sending light slashing through the slight gap and cutting across the remainder of Clara's sentence. She sprang to her feet while Broderick hurried over to help his wife stand.

"Can we help you?" Clara called when the figure on the other side still didn't enter.

There was a long pause, and then a small, hooded figure stepped inside and closed the door behind her.

Clara briefly took in the shine of the elegant satin cloak; the quality and cut all bespoke the wealth of its wearer. Silent as the grave, and motionless, the person made no attempt to move from her spot at the doorway.

Broderick started forward, but Clara held a hand up, staying him.

Hopping off the edge of the stage, Clara wandered toward the stranger in the shadows. "May I help you?" she repeated, this time in quieter, more calming tones.

Her repeated question was met with more silence and then—

All but hugging the entranceway with the left side of her body, the figure pushed the deep hood of her cloak back, revealing herself to be a young woman with dark curls and a slight dimple in her chin. There was something . . . familiar about her, and yet Clara searched her mind for any hint of remembrance. She was entirely too young to have been a woman who'd served under her when she'd been a madam. Furthermore, Clara had never before forgotten a person who'd worked with her. Who *was* she?

"You are Mrs. Winters," the girl murmured in dulcet tones. Only there was also a roughness to the tonality of her speech, as if she used her words sparingly, and in this instant was reluctant to do so.

It didn't escape Clara's notice that the young woman's words hadn't been a question. "I am," she answered anyway.

The mysterious stranger crept a gaze past Clara to the stage, where Reggie and Broderick silently watched on.

"I was wondering if I might speak with you," the girl whispered, when she moved her attention back to Clara. This time, she met Clara's gaze squarely.

And Clara paused.

The young woman bore a deep scar at the center of her forehead. The mark, jagged like lightning, had faded to a pale white, indicating she'd been injured long ago. It was also an unfamiliar mark, but one that should have—would have—placed her in Clara's mind. The stranger tipped her chin up in a silent challenge, one that indicated she'd noticed Clara's stare.

An appreciation for the peculiar stranger stirred in Clara's chest, and she offered the other woman a regretful smile. Wishing she could offer the girl what she likely sought. "I am afraid we are no longer hiring." And lest the young performer take that rejection as an indictment of her physical display, Clara quickly went on to explain. "Our venture has been temporarily suspended, and no new staff is being added to our employ." And all previous staff members were likely going to be sent on their way to find work until Clara's situation got sorted out. If it did. Clara reached past the young woman and collected the brass floral door handle, that added expense she'd insisted upon that now represented nothing more than lost funds and deadened dreams. "But I do wish you all the best in your endeavors," Clara said, her words wholly suitable for the both of them.

The dark-haired girl glanced from Clara's fingers to her face. "I am not looking for work, Mrs. Winters," she whispered.

Clara stiffened. *"Miss Winters,"* she corrected. "And I confess that you have me at a disadvantage. I do not recall us meeting."

"We haven't met. I . . . saw you . . ." Saw her? Clara hadn't performed upon a London stage in more than a decade, back when she'd been a girl of twenty. "Visiting with my brother."

Clara's cheeks flamed hot. So the young woman was a sister to one of Clara's past lovers? Impossible. She'd always been set up in townhouses away from respectable society. "I'm afraid I don't—"

"My brother, the Earl of Waterson."

Clara lost her grip on the door handle. "Beg pardon."

"Henry March, the Earl of Waterson," the girl repeated, in more halting tones.

The woman before her was . . . Henry's sister? Her mind raced. He'd revealed that he had two sisters; the only one he'd spoken of at some length, however, had been the woman trapped at the Peterloo Massacre. A woman he'd acknowledged had become a recluse. Therefore, this could not be that particular sister.

"May we speak?" the girl whispered. The girl—nay, not girl—woman, rather. For standing close as she did now, Clara noted that despite her initial assumption, she'd been wrong. With the previous distance she'd failed to notice the dark circles under world-wary eyes.

Or the sad frown lines etched in the corner of the woman's mouth. Nay, Henry's sister was no young girl, but rather a woman who carried her own struggles.

"I'm not certain that is wise, my lady." There was nothing Clara and the nameless young lady should have to discuss. They knew each other not at all. The lady's brother was her enemy.

"Please—Lila. Just Lila. And I promise, I'll not take too much of your time."

Clara went to war with logic and reason and her own strength before losing the battle. "Very well."

Lady Lila glanced over to where Broderick and Reggie still stood across the hall, observers in their exchange. "Alone."

Clara hesitated. There was a faint entreating there. And as she looked at the young lady . . . truly looked at her—the terror in Lady Lila's brown eyes, her grey complexion—it hit her.

She is Henry's reclusive sister.

The one he'd spoken of who'd rarely ventured out since Peterloo.

Clara turned to her friend and former employer. "Reggie, Mr. Killoran, will you excuse me a moment? I've . . . business to attend to." Holding her arm out, Clara urged the young woman to follow her.

Lady Lila stared at her extended elbow and gave a tiny shake of her head. There was more of that pleading in her eyes.

She doesn't wish to be touched . . .

Slowly, Clara lowered the rejected limb to her side. She donned the gentle smile she had always affixed for the most wounded, fearful prostitutes who'd come to her in desperate need of employment. Those women she'd insisted retire and instead found other work for—away from all people. Henry's sister trailed alongside, her slippered feet nearly silent upon the immaculate hardwood floors.

Unbidden, Clara's gaze went to the geometric diamond at the center of that parquetry. That flooring she'd been so determined to have that she'd swallowed her pride and set aside her valuable independence to live inside the Devil's Den once more.

Because of Henry . . . and his like-minded friends.

"Your floors are magnificent," Lady Lila whispered faintly.

"Yes, they are." Clara was unable to keep the sadness from creeping into that proud acknowledgment.

They didn't exchange any further words until they reached Clara's offices. Or what would soon become the previous owner's newly renovated offices. Clara quietly pushed the door closed behind them. "Won't you sit?" she encouraged, gesturing to the walnut chair, upholstered in deep orange pineapples that stood out vibrant and cheerful amidst the sandy background.

Not immediately accepting that offer, Lady Lila tentatively stroked the pineapple carved into the top of the chair. "Pineapples," she murmured.

"Yes. They are a symbol of generosity, hospitality, and wealth." All of which she'd intended the Muses to represent. "The—"

"Europeans tried to grow them outside their native tropical climate," Lady Lila put forward in a murmur. "But their propagation could only be achieved through greenhouse methods." She spoke as one who recited a familiar passage in a book. "The absence of a local supply and an increasing demand made them even more popular. I am . . . familiar with them," Henry's sister said absently, pulling off first one sturdy leather glove trimmed in wool, followed by another. The young woman stared at those articles in complete silence.

Clara had always believed one could tell much about a person by their hands. But more specifically . . . by their gloves.

Cotton ones were the cheapest of the gloves. Their advantage being that they were warm, they were therefore often worn by commoners.

The most preferred of the gloves amongst the nobility were the French white silk gloves: well made and elegant, they were a mark of wealth and prestige. The dandies preferred them cut in garish purple and fuchsias.

And then there were the respectable ladies married to those unfaithful lords. Those women, whom she passed at Bond Street and observed in theatres, donned the most luxurious fabric gloves: satin embroidered with silk. Seamless fingers. Ornate lace.

And yet Lady Lila's durable ones better suited a member of the working class than a woman of her station.

"I overheard you with my brother last evening."

The silence had gone on so long that it took a moment for that pronouncement to register. And when it did . . . Clara's mind ran through her entire discourse with Henry, everything from her inventive curses about his parentage to their embrace. Her mind shied away from that particular detail. "I . . . see," she finally said. Even as she didn't see anything.

"You were . . . quite direct with him in your speech. *No one* speaks to Henry like that."

Had her life depended upon it, even with the slight emphasis on those two words, Clara couldn't make a hint out of what the other woman was thinking. "I take it you took exception with my . . . words for your brother," she ventured. Is that what had brought her here? Sisterly loyalty for the devoted brother?

"Oh, no." The answer sprang automatically to Lady Lila's lips, refreshingly honest and sincere. "I quite enjoyed it, really. I thoroughly appreciated it. I . . ." The younger woman slid into the pineapple chair. "That is why I'm here. One of the reasons, that is."

Clara felt much the way she had during too many rehearsals calling out for a line because the ones in the script had escaped her. "You are here because I yelled at your brother and you *approved* of it?"

"I've never heard any woman speak like that to my brother . . . or any man. I once went toe to toe with him, but th-then"—her voice broke—"everything changed. I've forgotten how to be around people. The world."

Clara pulled the matching pineapple seat over and sat facing Henry's sister. "I am sorry, Lady Lila. I'm struggling to . . . follow."

"Until you came . . . I forgot what it was to be passionate about life and music and . . . anything. Last night, listening outside my brother's office . . ." She spoke without compunction at having listened in on a private conversation. "My mother, my sister, me, we've all gone meek with life. I don't want to be the person who hides anymore."

"And you think I can help you?" she asked slowly.

"I don't know," Lady Lila said with a raw honesty. "I don't know if anyone can. But I know that you reminded me that life has continued."

"And you want me to teach you how to stand up to your brother?"

"No." The first real sincere smile Clara had seen from the other woman turned Lady Lila's lips in the corner. "But that is a lovely thought. I want you to teach me how to sing."

Had Henry's sister asked her to school her on the lessons for being a courtesan, she couldn't have shocked her more.

"I heard everything you said to Henry," Lady Lila whispered. "About music. How the strings take one on a journey, where one is able to be someone else. *Somewhere* else. And who you are, along with the whole world you've been born to, just melts away so that, for a brief time, all you know is the glorious hum going through you that comes from being alive . . . you said that."

Clara remained stunned speechless. What else had the young woman heard? Either way . . .

"I don't . . . I wish I could help you. But I'm not . . ." Talented. Her lack of talent had been the reason Clara had found herself on her back and mistress to various noblemen. "I'm not the person who can help you."

The young woman frowned. "Surely you can. You spoke passionately about what music and dance, in fact, are. Defended the institutions that my brother and his stodgy friends see as licentious."

Clara shook her head. "I'm afraid you are incorrect." Even if she could help Henry's sister and provide her lessons in music and theatre that Clara had once so enjoyed, her life no longer allowed for it. Not when she was fighting for her survival and professional existence. "I'm no vocal teacher. I'm not even a performer."

Lady Lila's brow puckered, drawing that lightning-shaped scar at the center of her head into a jagged line. "You must have been a performer."

Clara stared back dumbly.

"Acted? Sang? Danced?" the young woman pressed. "For someone to speak as passionately as you did, and who now invested in and runs a theatre, you must have been involved somehow with the theatre."

"I did—"

"I knew it!" Lady Lila's whole face lit up, and for a moment Clara had a glimpse of who the young woman must have been before the bottom had fallen out from under her life. "As I said, only one who knows music and loves it so could speak so eloquently from the heart."

Henry had been incorrect about another matter: his sister was stronger, more capable, and more knowing than he credited. "I . . . it was a long time ago, my lady," she conceded gruffly, and as soon as that admission left her, Clara's toes curled into the soles of her boots. No one knew of her past. She spoke of it not at all.

"I would ask that you give me lessons." Henry's sister went on over Clara's immediate protestations. "And if you do, I am prepared to help you reclaim ownership of your theatre."

That avowal broke through Clara's gentle rejection.

Inhaling through her compressed lips, Lady Lila explained, "My brother would deny me nothing." No, he wouldn't. Clara had observed that devotion when she'd helped care for him. "In exchange for your services, he'll not allow your theatre to be touched."

Clara sat there, silently contemplating all that . . . the woman's presence here, her proposal. And despite everything that had come to pass . . . there was the faintest stirring of something so unfamiliar she almost didn't recognize it—hope. Hope that the dream she had for herself might not be crushed by the heel of greed and power. Hope for her future and security, and for the security of all those who'd left reliable work to take on a new role at the Muses.

As quick as it came, however, reality dashed those foolish sentiments. "Lady Lila, given everything you heard during my conversation with your brother, I know you're aware of my past."

"That you were once a courtesan?" Lady Lila asked.

And as the young woman appeared wholly unaffected by that scandalous part of Clara's past, she clarified. "Not just a courtesan, but also a madam. A madam who worked in two of London's most scandalous gaming hells." To the young woman's credit, she didn't so much as blink or blush at Clara's admissions. "Your reputation would be ruined if you were to spend any time with me." Including this meeting now.

"Miss Winters," Lady Lila said softly, "I do not give ten damns about my reputation. I haven't cared about anything in so long I forgot what it was to be remotely interested about something. My brother would allow our relationship if I asked it because the alternative is that I disappear, again."

Danger. Everything about this discourse whispered of peril. The further interactions the young woman spoke of would invariably mean further interactions between Clara and Henry . . . Nothing good could come from that. Nothing.

Except that isn't altogether true, a needling voice whispered at the back of her mind. What Henry's sister spoke of . . . The opening of the Muses. The work for all those dependent upon her.

And she knew she was lost. Because for the security of each person—herself included—she would strike a deal with the Devil.

Clara pressed her fingertips against her temples. "I'll speak to your brother."

The young woman's smile returned. "Splendid. I'll be expecting you."

And with those words—an order, more than anything—Lady Lila stood, rushed out of the room, and left Clara sitting there feeling like she'd made yet another perilous mistake.

Chapter 16

Most gentlemen despised social events—balls, soirees, formal dinner parties—all of it.

Henry, however, had long proven the exception.

He'd always seen each event as an opportunity to further advance his political maneuverings of the moment.

This night was no different. A ball hosted by his recent political ally, Lord Peerson, with the intention of making clear to Polite Society the potential match between Henry and Lord Peerson's only daughter, Miss Newton. The night would bring Henry further down the path toward that permanent alliance and the goal he sought for a British police force. And yet, even with all that, this night . . . was different.

He didn't know what or how to account for the ennui. Or this inexplicable desire to skip the damned ball.

Yes, you do, you damned fool.

It was her—Clara Winters—and her kiss. Their kiss.

Do not delude yourself into believing it is now possible to think of any other woman. Not after he'd held Clara in his arms.

Have I horrified you, Lord Proper? I trust it is not every day a woman storms your office, knocks you on your arse, and downs your whiskey . . .

For the truth was, even as she'd jeered him with every word hurled like an expert plunge of a rapier tip, she'd been magnificent in her fury and passion, and he could not rid her from his thoughts.

"Ahem, my lord."

Staring into the bevel mirror, he caught his valet hovering at his shoulder.

Alas, he had to rid her from his thoughts. If he were to accomplish what mattered most to him and his family, and to the whole of England, he'd stop thinking about the slight hint of ginger and mint on her lips. Forcibly pushing aside any more thoughts of her, Henry collected the white silk cravat from the servant and, as he was accustomed to doing, proceeded to knot his own. Next, he accepted the maroon coat with a velvet-lined collar. The young man came around to begin buttoning the front of the jacket . . .

When Clara intruded once more.

I know you've never done this, but surely you might manage buttons and laces . . .

Henry stumbled away from his valet. "That will be all, Wilbur."

The young man, hands still stretched out as they'd been when he'd been tending Henry's buttons, stared back. "My . . . lord?"

By the shock reflected in Wilbur's eyes, Henry may as well have stated his intentions to overthrow the king.

"I have it from here," he repeated, dismissing the young man.

"You are . . . certain you have it, my lord."

And it was a testament to the valet's doubts that he, who was only ever obedient, challenged Henry.

Could he . . . Heat stained Henry's cheeks. "I'm quite certain," he said testily.

"As you wish, my lord." Wilbur lingered a moment more, and then clicking his heels like his elder brother, Henry's butler, the young man rushed off.

After he'd gone, Henry resumed dressing.

"Never done this, she says," he muttered under his breath as he wrestled with the bottom bronze button. "I've handled my own buttons. Plenty of times." Henry paused. Hadn't he? Surely he had? Except he couldn't recollect a single damned moment when he'd not had the benefit and aid of a servant—for any endeavor.

And what did that say about him?

It bespoke privilege that he'd never before given a proper thought to. He'd been born . . . with everything: wealth, landholdings, servants. Many, many servants. And had therefore only ever known that lifestyle.

Had he ever truly given a thought to how those outside the peerage lived their lives?

Oh, he'd drafted plenty of legislation pertaining to economic programs and banking which would benefit those of all stations, and yet . . . those men and women had existed in the periphery.

Something that felt very much like . . . shame . . . took root in his stomach. It was a sentiment he was not unfamiliar with, one he'd experienced too many times since his sister had been nearly killed and forever scarred at Peterloo.

Peterloo.

That fateful night, which, of course, anytime it slipped into his thoughts, brought him back to the task at hand: the police force. Lord Peerson.

Lord Peerson's daughter.

Drawing in a breath, Henry went and fetched his gloves. And resolved to begin securing that connection and political alliance. He'd quit his rooms and was starting for the foyer when a commotion sounded.

"By God, I said you'll not enter, and enter you won't." His butler's voice carried from belowstairs.

Bloody hell. What was it now?

Henry took off charging forward, knowing even as he did what would meet him when he reached the foyer. Or rather, who.

Sure enough, as he came to the top of the curved marble staircase, his gaze found her—

Clara stood at the center of the foyer with her arms folded at her chest. Ignoring the butler, she lifted her gaze up to where Henry stood.

All the air lodged in his chest, stuck there, making it impossible to breathe. God, she was—

"There you are, Henry," she drawled with all the disgust she might reserve for the grime she'd picked up on her boots.

His neck ran hot, an all-too-familiar embarrassment he was never without when in the woman's company. "Miss Winters," he returned, drawing on his gloves as he walked to meet her.

"My lord, I attempted to have this *woman* thrown—"

Henry lifted a hand, staying the remainder of his servant's profession, despising how the butler had wielded that latter word as if it were an insult. "That will be all. My office again, Miss Winters." Henry pointed toward the corridor, motioning her ahead.

Clara brought her shoulders back and swept past the trio of servants standing in wait.

The respectable part of him that had been fed propriety as if it were a dietary sustenance knew he should be horrified at her being here— again. That even as his servants were loyal and wouldn't talk, anyone could have seen her, and there would be only a scandal in an unmarried woman visiting his family residence. And yet he was unable to keep in the droll retort that left him. "We really must stop meeting this way, Miss Winters," he said as they walked side by side.

"And how should we continue meeting, Henry? With you beaten and bloodied in the streets of Seven Dials, with me there to rescue you?"

"Fair point," he muttered as they reached his office. Henry reached for the handle, but Clara was already pressing it, letting herself inside, and marching over to his desk. And by God, if she didn't continue her march right behind it and claim his seat as her own.

He cocked his head. Well . . . this was unexpected and unsettling. It wasn't every day a gentleman's home was invaded and his desk chair commandeered. Henry quietly shut the door behind them and then, returning to his desk, claimed the seat across from her.

"I trust you're here to discuss our previous business." It had been inevitable.

Clara released the Austrian crystal grommet at her throat and let her elegant cloak fall. The article slipped from her shoulders in an iridescent waterfall, leaving on display the plunging décolletage of her finely made silk gown. He swallowed hard. Or tried to.

"Actually, Henry," she purred, resting one elbow at the edge of his desk and leaning forward lazily. His mouth went dry. And words failed. Along with every other faculty. "I'm here to discuss altogether different business." There was a smile in her voice, a playful one. Coy. And slightly hardened. And together, that combination sent a suitable wariness through him. Even with the warning bells going off, the cloud of lust lingered.

"And what business is that, Miss Winters?"

By her deepening smile she both had detected the hoarseness in his voice and knew precisely the effect she was having on him.

"I received a visitor earlier."

A visitor . . . ? It took a moment for that pronouncement to sink in. He frowned.

"Aren't you going to ask me who visited, Henry?" She wrapped that query in her husky contralto, which would thereby steal any hope of sleep for any night in the foreseeable future.

He forced his brain to work and his lips to move. "And I trust the identity of that visitor is of particular interest to me?"

Clapping slowly, Clara leaned back in her seat. *His* seat. "Bravo, Henry. Yes, someone who is of particular interest to you." And just like that all her earlier teasing and mockery faded, so that all that remained was a palpable sadness that hung on her frame. "Your sister."

"My . . . ?" His ears went hot. What game did she play? "My sister is in the country for her confinement. Therefore, whomever said they were a sibling of mine was, in fact, lying to you."

"Not that sister, Henry." Clara cast a glance past his shoulder to the doorway. He followed her stare, more than half expecting to find someone there. "Lady Lila."

Lady . . . "Impossible. My sister does not leave . . . She hasn't left . . ." The words wouldn't come.

"Lady Lila. Dark, lovely, loose curls. Not unlike your own." Clara thought his hair lovely? "A slight jagged scar right here." Clara trailed a fingertip between her brows.

Henry surged to his feet. "What game are you playing, madam?" he said with a growl, stalking around the desk.

Clara was already out of her seat and quick to put his desk chair between them. "No game, Waterson. I don't jest." Her eyes narrowed. "And certainly not with gentlemen who threaten my livelihood."

His pulse pounded loud in his ears as all his senses tunneled on that revelation.

Lila . . . not only had left the townhouse but also had gone to the Dials and sought out a person who was a stranger to her. No matter how many ways in which he tried to make sense of that statement . . . he couldn't, and only one question remained: *Why?*

"Because she heard us." Clara's quiet murmur brought his musings to a screeching halt as he realized he'd spoken aloud.

"She . . . heard . . ." *Oh, good God in heaven. Our embrace.* Henry recoiled.

"All of it, Henry," the woman opposite him clarified. "*Allll* of it," she repeated, stretching that single word into several syllables. "She knows I'm a whore."

So wrapped was he in the horror of his sister having listened in while he'd held Clara in his arms, it took a moment for that last utterance to register. When it did, tension whipped through him. Something in hearing that vile word applied to her . . . to this woman, had him wanting to toss his head back and snarl like the beast she no doubt took him for. "Do not say that," he ordered, harshly. He'd not have Clara's name disparaged . . . not even by the woman herself.

A little frown tugged at the corners of her lightly rouged lips as she glanced to the doorway. When she spoke, her voice came quieter. "Very well. A courtesan. A madam. Whatever word you'd care to use, she knows, Henry."

"That is what you believe I'm offended over, Clara?" He searched her face. "Your usage of that word?" What manner of prude did she take him for?

Clara motioned to him. "You *are* ever proper, *Henry*."

"I'll not have you, a woman brave enough to take on a pair of assailants and then save my life, and proudly confront me now two times, speak of yourself in those terms."

"It's what I am. Dressing it up in fancy words will not change it. Either way. She knows and put a request to me anyway."

Good God, he could only begin to imagine what his youngest sister had asked of Clara. With the girl of old, it could have been anything—none of which would have been good or proper. With the shadow of a figure she'd become, he didn't have a blasted clue. "Go on." Henry crossed his arms at his chest.

"She wants me to provide her music lessons."

Music lessons . . .

His arms dropped, falling limply to his side. In the far recesses of his mind, the long-forgotten, just-remembered jaunty and oft-scandalous tavern ditty that had once filled the halls echoed there. *She should not be singing those songs, Henry. You need to speak to her, immediately . . .* How irate their mother had been at her daughter's playing. How displeased. And despite her maternal upset, Henry had been secretly amused . . .

And I urged her to stop, anyway . . .

What had it all been for? Demanding certain, strictest, ladylike standards for Lila, to what end?

Blankly, he wandered away from Clara and over to the windows overlooking the London streets. The moon's glow bathed the pavement in a soft light, illuminating the periodic carriage as it passed.

"It has been seven years," he murmured, clasping his hands at his back.

There was a faint pause and then the rustle of silk skirts as Clara drifted closer. "My lord?" she ventured.

"It has been seven years since my sister has played the pianoforte." Since anyone had played in this household. After Peterloo, the instrument had fallen as silent as his sister. And he'd deny Lila nothing now. Henry turned back. "She wishes lessons from you."

Her lips formed a pouty moue of her surprise. She'd undoubtedly expected him to reject even the idea of her working with Lila. And mayhap at another point in his life . . . seven years ago, to be precise . . . he would have. But no longer. He'd give anything for Lila to be restored to the woman she'd once been.

"I want you to rescind the cease and desist on my music hall, Henry."

Except that.

He could not give that.

"You're asking for the one thing I cannot give you," he rasped. "I can pa—"

"Don't you dare offer to pay me, Henry. This is about more than a damned payment."

Bloody hell. Why must she be so damned stubborn?

"If you take the funds, Clara, you can use them to purchase another establishment," he pleaded. "I'll buy you another blasted building."

She stalked over. "Don't you see?" Clara gripped him by his lapels and gave a light shove. "This isn't just about my establishment. This is about something I built from the ground up, with my hard work and vision, and with the support of those who are as reliant upon me as I am upon them. To cede any of this to you? To cede it to anyone—"

"For the love of God, Clara, it is in the Dials," he hissed. "Do you truly believe you can have a respectable theatre in the damned Dials? Those streets, they aren't safe."

Clara shook her head slowly and backed away from him. And there was such disdain dripping from her eyes, it carved a hollow space inside him. "You don't understand anything, Henry," she said quietly. "You never will. To you, people, their livelihoods, their businesses—they can all simply be purchased. Bought. And you can never believe those streets you revile, with the addition of honest people and respectable businesses, might be transformed into a place that is good. Or that the singers and actresses on that stage will be anything other than the whores they once were." Her chest heaved with the force of her emotion. "What I've created is a place where people who aren't born with a bloody silver spoon in their mouth are proud to live and call home." Clara was already starting for the door.

Panic set in.

From the truth that she represented, she was the one person who might help his sister.

From the reality that after she left this room, he'd likely never see Clara Winters again.

"Wait!" he called out as she reached for the door handle. *What am I doing . . . ?*

Bartering my soul to save my sister . . . "I'll speak to the other MPs." *My God, where did that come from?* For Lila. It came from a place where he'd do anything, say anything, and be anything to restore his youngest sibling to the woman she'd once been.

Clara whipped around. "What?" she breathed. Her eyes worked frantically over his face as if that clever gaze, heavy with suspicion, sought the veracity of his pledge.

Guilt needled at his insides, at the hope he saw there, and at the outcome he knew to be inevitable. "Give me one more day." He grimaced. "I'll speak to the gentlemen I would need to—"

"Reconstruct your house of cards?"

"Precisely," he said with a nod, ignoring her droll tones. "But I will . . . attempt a new round of negotiations. And in the meantime, I'll speak to the appropriate people to arrange a temporary halt on the closure of your establishment."

Clara was across the room in an instant and had his hands in her own. "You can do that?"

"Only temporarily." It was unlikely that any of his fellow peers, particularly Lord Peerson, would relinquish the terms they'd reached. "Until I have the matter resolved with the other MPs involved," he repeated in different words, needing her to hear and heed that warning, "I cannot promise you more." And certainly not from the man who sought a match for his daughter with Henry.

Clara eyed him for a long moment. "Very well."

"Very well?" What did that mean? His heart hammered erratically.

Clara stepped away, and her mask was perfectly in place once again. "Have your meeting. If you manage to secure me my hall, then you have your instructor."

A sound of frustration rumbled from his chest. "I cannot promise they'll agree to that request, Clara." His request hinged on pragmatic gentlemen who didn't give a jot about her business or his sister.

She lifted her shoulder in a careless shrug. "Then you don't have an instructor for your sister."

"You'd be so indifferent to my sister's well-being?" he asked, resentment stirring inside. And along with it . . . something else. Disappointment. The woman he'd taken her for was one who'd self-lessly help all—just as she'd done for Henry in the streets.

"Don't look at me like that, Henry," she chided, firm when any other person would have infused some chagrin into that response.

"Like what?" He was unable to keep the bitterness from creeping into that query.

"As if you're somehow let down by my making my services con-tingent upon your intervention in my affairs. Why should I selflessly help?" she pressed. "Because I'm a woman and that is what women do? Act selflessly, only caring for others? And yet"—she shook her head—"you don't see?"

He stared at her in abject confusion.

"That it is *because* I care for others that I'm setting the terms that I am. I care about the former prostitutes who'll not have to earn a future on their backs. I care about the guards who are former soldiers who've not found their way since they returned from war." She took a step closer, a challenge glinting in her eyes. "And yes, I care about me, Henry. I care about my future and my security, and that does not make me the selfish woman that you've painted in your mind."

Heat splotched his cheeks. "I didn't say you were selfish." *I am the selfish one. Because I want her to selflessly give for Lila's sake.*

"You didn't have to, Henry." Clara's lips twisted in a small, wry smile. "You wear your truth in your eyes."

Which was a good deal more than he could say for her. This woman, who was a mystery, whom he still knew next to nothing about, and yet whose favors he desperately sought.

Clara turned to leave once more, and this time when she walked out, it would be final: her decision and their time together. "Fine," he called out before he could silence that offer.

Do not. Do not. Do—

Clara whipped around. "What?" she asked, faintly breathless.

"I'll speak to those I need to, and if I save your club—"

"My music hall."

"Then I have your word that you'll help my sister," he continued over her interruption.

She flew back over to his side. "When will you meet with them?"

With Lord Peerson. All hopes for her business started and rested there, with the mastermind behind the Piety and Virtue laws. "Immediately. As soon as I'm able to secure an appointment." In the meantime . . . "Tomorrow morn, at eleven o'clock, I'd ask you to come and meet with my sister and me." And mayhap if . . . when . . . Peerson rejected her request, Clara would be compelled to help when she saw Lila once again. "I'll have an answer for you then."

"If you secure my business, you have my word." The siren held her hand out, and he stared at those outstretched fingers, encased in delicate leather. And he ached to tug that article off, slowly stripping each finger free, until he had her palm in his, and . . . "Generally, this is where one shakes on an arrangement, Henry," she drawled.

Resisting the all-too-familiar need around this woman to yank at his cravat, Henry swiftly placed his hand in hers. That electric heat, which burnt even through the scrap of fabric, made a mockery of his bid for control over his hunger for this woman.

She sighed. "Like this, my lord." Clasping her spare hand over his, she guided their fingers in an up-and-down shake before releasing him. "If you manage it, the deal is set. Daily lessons. An hour each day. Good evening, my lord."

With that, Clara stalked off like a whirlwind, leaving Henry swirling in her wake.

And as he remained rooted to his office floor, only one thought remained:

How could he bring Lord Peerson around to agreeing?

Chapter 17

"Well, *that* is . . . unexpectedly promising news," Reggie blurted.

The following morning, as Clara affixed one of her butterfly hair combs, she found herself agreeing with her partner. "Yeff," she mouthed around the other jewel-studded article. "Very good newfs." When usually everything went wrong for Clara Winters and, by default, for everyone connected to her, something had gone unexpectedly right. Or almost right.

Only temporarily . . . I cannot promise you more . . .

Nay, Henry had not made her any concrete guarantee, other than that he'd try and coordinate another means to achieve his goal while preserving her future.

Seated on the edge of Clara's bed, Reggie twisted her fingers over and over in a telltale gesture of unease.

Removing the other hair comb from her mouth, Clara placed it parallel to the first at the top of her loosely arranged curls. "You are a good deal less enthused than I'd expected."

Reggie sighed. "It's simply that we both know the dangers in bracing for the best. He didn't promise he could or would help. He merely promised he'd try."

Clara adjusted the jewel-studded comb at the left side of her head. "Well, this is certainly a reversal of roles. I'm generally the cynic and you the optimist." Annoyance soured the brief hope she'd allowed herself since leaving Henry. He wouldn't fail. He couldn't . . .

"Not all the time," Reggie pushed back. "I may have come to you with a vision for the Muses, but that dream would have stalled had it not been for you."

Yes, that was true. Reggie had been more worried about taking staff from the Devil's Den and setting herself up as any kind of competition for Broderick Killoran. In the end, however, the pair had found love, and the Muses had found a home in the Dials.

The bevel mirror reflected back Clara's darkening expression.

"I didn't mean to cast doubts on what you've accomplished," Reggie murmured from where she still sat. "It's simply that we both know firsthand how ruthless noblemen are."

It was another well-aimed point. "Nay," she said tightly. "Not all noblemen. All *men*." The devoted lover who'd sought her favors and then seen her cast out of her role at Drury Lane and reliant solely on her body to survive. She stared wistfully at her reflection. And yet—Henry was different. Wasn't he?

Were any men really different, though?

Enough!

Casting off those doubts rolling around, she faced Reggie with a smile. "All I know is that by that order we received, the Muses should be closed to us and our staff, and now it is not."

"What happens if he's unable to convince his fellow MPs to change their minds?" Reggie let her legs fall over the side of Clara's bed.

Clara gritted her teeth. "He'll manage it." He had to.

"Very well," Reggie went on with an annoying tenacity. "What happens if he is successful? You become his sister's music instructor? What happens when she tires of your lessons and he no longer has a need of you? Do you think he'll be as dedicated to helping our business remain open?"

That matter-of-factly delivered arrow found a place square in Clara's chest.

For no truer words had ever been spoken: eventually Henry would no longer have a need of her or for her, and from there, he'd cast her out. Such had been the fate with her first protector, and the ones to follow. Even Ryker Black, the man whom she'd called friend and business partner, had all but turned her out after he'd married and his wife had moved into the club.

This had to be different.

It can only end well.

"I hope it does, Clara," her friend murmured, and Clara started at having been caught talking aloud. As Reggie rested her hands on Clara's shoulders and leaned closer, unease lined her features. "But we should also be prepared."

For the worst.

That ominous warning hung there, not needing to be spoken aloud, coming clearer than had she uttered it.

Clara glanced back at the other woman. "Too much has gone wrong for both of us in our lives. This time, I'll settle for nothing other than absolute triumph." Spinning away from her friend, Clara collected her bonnet.

"Please be careful," Reggie called after her.

"I always am." Clara winked and started from her rooms inside the Devil's Den.

Avoiding those main floors of the clubs, Clara kept to the servants' stairs and made her way out the kitchen entrance. She'd not let Reggie's words weigh on her. Henry could have sent her to the Devil with her demands, but he hadn't, and she had to take hope in his power of persuasion.

As she stepped outside, the dank London air filled her nostrils, the pungent scents of dirt and waste all wrapped together, so familiar that she'd stopped noting them.

Until she'd paid her visits to Henry's residence and recalled how vastly different every aspect of life was for those outside the peerage—the air, the roadways, the pavement all marked a divide between the fortunate few and those born to lesser ranks. Reaching the end of the alley, Clara wound her way around a slumbering drunk sprawled between the buildings. That abject poverty also too familiar.

For the love of God, Clara, it is in the Dials . . . Do you truly believe you can have a respectable theatre in the damned Dials . . .

She bit the inside of her cheek. Hating that he was right. Hating that he'd spoken from a place that illustrated just how very different they, in fact, were.

Only, he didn't treat her like a common whore the way the rest of the nobility did.

Clara stopped midstride and stared over at the pair of noblemen ambling through the front doors of the Devil's Den.

Nay, any other one of those powerful peers would have had his footmen and butler toss Clara out, just as the servants had intended.

But Henry hadn't. He'd not only allowed Clara into his household and into his office but also allowed her to rail at him, accepting each insult she'd hurled as his due.

And not only that—he'd entrusted Clara to deliver music lessons to his sister. Her, a former madam and courtesan living in a gaming hell.

Clara dug her fingertips into her temples. *Damn you, Henry March. Damn you for being a conundrum I can't make any sense of.*

"Miss Winters?"

Clara dropped her arms to her side.

MacLeod, one of the lead guards at the Devil's Den, stared back. "Everything all right, ma'am?" he asked in his husked brogue.

Clara blinked slowly.

"Out of the way, ya fancy bird," a passerby spat, shouldering past her.

Bloody hell. "I'm fine," she said quickly, giving her head a shake.

The street-hardened Scot gave her a dubious look.

And why shouldn't he? Woolgathering like a starstruck country girl on her first visit to London.

"I'm fine," she repeated, hurrying the remainder of the way to the carriage. Accepting MacLeod's hand, she scrambled inside the Killorans' gleaming black conveyance. She ducked her head out. "Furthermore, I'm not in need of a guard, Mr. MacLeod."

"Take that up with the Killorans."

Clara jumped out of the way as he pushed the door closed in her face.

"Now *that* I'm more accustomed to," she muttered, settling back on the bench. Since she'd begun working in the Devil's Den three years earlier, every last guard, dealer, and servant had treated her with the wariness befitting one who'd abdicated her place at the rival establishment.

This new treatment, a product of her relationship with Broderick Killoran's wife, was still too foreign and went against how the whole world had generally treated her.

Except Henry . . .

Angrily swiping the velvet curtain back, Clara stared out at the passing landscape. "You're making more of it than there is. He only feels a sense of gratitude because you saved his life."

Only, he wasn't simply treating her as somehow lesser. He wasn't throwing her past in her face as so many before him had done. Instead, he was allowing her inside his residence and asking her to work with his sister. Asking.

"What manner of nobleman are you, Henry March?" she whispered, her breath lightly fogging the leaded-glass windowpane and hazing her view of the changing landscape outside. Clara, however, already knew the answer: he was a nobleman who genuinely cared for and loved his family. That was why he'd allow a former courtesan and madam inside his household. That devotion to his sister took precedence above all else.

And it was incredibly heady stuff, discovering that such a man, in fact, existed.

Groaning, Clara let her head fall against the wall. She knocked it against the lacquer. "Stop it. Stop it. Stop it." She'd but one purpose and goal: get in, do her work, and move on with her future secure.

There was no place in any of that for an enthralling earl, driven by honor.

Except, as their lives became intertwined in these passing days, she'd be wise to remember their time together was limited. That the basis of their relationship hinged solely on their own professional and personal goals.

Mayhap if she reminded herself enough of that, she'd begin to believe it.

The key to all negotiations was to always have the superior hand. To never find oneself a step below, asking for something, particularly something the other side had no intention of giving.

Knowing all that as he did, seated on the other side of Lord Peerson's desk, Henry also knew he'd set himself off to that very ignoble start.

The portly nobleman was a study in repose. His pudgy fingers, straining his gloves, remained clasped over his round belly. It was the perfect display of a casualness—for anyone other than Lord Peerson, that was.

There was nothing relaxed or casual about the gentleman. After all these years working opposite him in Parliament, Henry knew the stories—that other man hadn't so much as cracked a smile when his wife had finally conceived, giving him a child.

That same daughter whom Henry had failed to come 'round to pay attendance on last evening.

"Waterson, how very unexpected to see you here." Lord Peerson looked down his bulbous nose at him. An impressive accomplishment for a man one foot shorter than Henry's six feet, three inches. "You're looking unusually"—the viscount lingered his focus on Henry's right eye—"well."

Henry looped one foot across his opposite knee. "I assure you, I'm *quite* well." He could only begin to imagine which rumors had begun circulating regarding his latest blackened eye. "I'm made of far sterner stuff."

The man who'd likely be his father-in-law pounced. "Not such stern stuff that you avoided missing Lady Peerson's ball, eh?"

Bloody hell. A more obvious trap he couldn't have stepped into.

The viscount abandoned that pretense at nonchalance. "But I trust it was something *very* important that took you away, Waterson, hmm?"

"They were . . . *are* . . . matters pertaining to my sister," he said quietly, offering nothing more than that. Henry would sell his soul for the establishment of a police force, but he'd not trade his sister's dignity and the cloak of secrecy she deserved for her life and circumstances.

"*Ahh,*" the gentleman stretched out. "I see." The hard cast to his gaze revealed not a hint of humanity. Not that Henry either wanted or needed it from this man. What he did, however, require was his understanding.

"You are familiar with my family's circumstances at Peterloo and its subsequent role behind my latest drafted legislation."

"I know your leaning, Waterson," the other man said with an impatient wave of his hand.

"There was . . . is a woman who has had some success in . . . helping my sister."

"A w—"

The door opened, and a servant entered, carrying a tray. "Get the hell out, Pimbrooke. We don't need refreshments," the viscount snapped without even a glance for the liveried footman.

Without missing a beat, the servant turned on his heel and left.

"A woman, you say?" the viscount demanded before the door had even clicked shut.

Of course that was the bloody piece this man would hear and focus on.

"The woman is skilled in the arts, and she's agreed to serve in the role of music instructor for my sister." *She is also a woman whose mouth I had under mine, and whose lush hips and nipped waist I explored and ache to explore again.*

Lord Peerson narrowed those eyes that bulged slightly too much. "What does this woman have to do with me and my business, Waterson?"

"She is the owner of the Muses."

The viscount came out of his chair and made his way over to the oak Tantalus. Grabbing a decanter and two glasses, he hastily made two drinks.

Despite the other man's typically surly temper and bluntly spoken questions, he'd poured two brandies. It was a telltale gesture that spoke to the relationship they did have. One that was precarious, built on mutually beneficial goals they each held in Parliament, but a relationship nonetheless.

"The Muses," Lord Peerson repeated, his lip pulled back in a derisive sneer as if he'd been sullied simply by stating that name aloud. "Why do you say that as though it should mean something to me? Sounds like the name of a damned bordello," he muttered, carrying his drinks back. "As such, I'm not familiar with it, Waterson." He held out a glass.

The same man who'd attack Clara's establishment for being immoral had no qualms drinking spirits in the morning. Anger sluiced through Henry, and he forced himself to accept that drink. Made himself take a requisite sip while the other man reclaimed his chair. How casually and coldly the other man spoke of that place of pride Clara had built. A place that was anything but a bordello, and instead an establishment Clara had constructed to give hope to people . . . like her. "The Muses is the music hall in the Dials," he said when he trusted himself to deliver that reminder in even tones. By God, this was the man who'd ordered Clara's place closed, and he had no recollection of so much as the name. "The one you seek to close."

Peerson froze with his glass close to his lips. Then his eyes widened. "Of course. That's how I know it. Just one of many and w—" He set his drink down. "You've gone and hired the woman running that for your sister. How very philanthropic of you, Waterson. Have a care, though. If it were any other gent than you, some would misconstrue your motives as wicked."

If it were any other gent than . . . ?

Have I horrified you, Lord Proper?

Yes, that was how the world saw him, because . . . well, it was how Henry was and had always been.

Henry sat forward. "Mine was not an act of charity. I met Miss Winters by chance on the night I was assaulted. She intervened, without any worry for her own well-being, and inserted herself between me and the men who beat me."

"*Ahh*, so you feel a sense of . . . obligation, then." Lord Peerson chuckled. "I'd never have taken you for one who developed a heart."

Refusing to rise to that bait, Henry went on with the careful construct of his argument. "Miss Winters rejected my offer of repayment."

Lord Peerson waggled his thick, curled mustache. "And that there is why women have no place in business. Rejected your repayment," he scoffed. "You've offered her funds; you've offered her employment for your sister's instruction. You owe her nothing else."

Henry stared at the viscount as he took a measured sip of his brandy. How many times had Henry in his life dealt with such ruthlessness? And more . . . how many times had he behaved precisely as this coldhearted man across from him did now?

Shame, an all-too-familiar sentiment since he'd met Clara Winters, found a place in his belly.

Bastard that he was and had been, it was a marvel he'd had friendship with even Waverly. "The Muses is not a bordello," he said as Lord Peerson savored his fine French spirits.

"It is in the Dials?"

"It is," he said succinctly.

"Do they hire whores?"

"They . . ." *And you can never believe those streets you revile, with the addition of honest people and respectable businesses, might be transformed into a place that is good. Or that the singers and actresses on that stage will be anything other than the whores they once were . . .* "They are not," Henry said quietly. "They are performers, no different from the actresses and opera singers at Drury Lane theatres or the London Opera."

"*Pfft.* You're a prude, Waterson, which is one of the reasons I like you," the other man tacked on in a compliment that didn't feel so much like one, coming from this pompous prig. "But an actress and a whore is really just one and the same."

Clara, by the nature of her past, would be considered only a whore in this man's eyes. Hatred sang in Henry's veins at how the Lord Peersons of the world would see her in only that light forevermore. When she was so much more. When that was the least of which would ever, could ever, define a woman of her indefatigable spirit.

Henry's hands formed reflexive fists that left marks upon his palms. "Ah, but your box at Covent Garden is not but five from mine. And I've seen you numerous times with the honorable Lady Peerson and your equally honorable daughter."

The viscount took another sip and waved the half-empty glass as he set it down. "Entirely different. We lords attend them because our ladies are oblivious to the uglier vice that occurs at those theatres."

Henry stared incredulously at the portly fellow. Had Henry himself truly ever been so foolish to believe that about any of the women in his life? Something inside said yes. God, how he despised himself. The older version of this new, still unfamiliar skin he called his own. "I'd ask that we leave this particular establishment out of our agreement."

"Can't do, dear boy. Shutting it down. Shutting it all down."

"Shutting what down?"

"The vice," Peerson clarified. "The sin. And your police force will go a ways in helping to combat that corruption."

It was a none-too-subtle reminder of their reliance upon one another.

"This one needn't be shuttered," Henry persisted, setting his barely touched glass down on the other MP's desk. "I've an obligation to—"

"Me," the viscount interrupted. Resting his elbows on his desk, the other man leaned toward him. "Your obligation is to me, along with all the other MPs you've promised a vote to."

That black-and-white way in which Lord Peerson spoke was the principle by which Henry had lived his own life. There were no shades in between. Or there hadn't been. Until Clara. Clara Winters, who'd upended that dull palette and splashed an array of vibrant hues that both confounded and captivated. "Surely, allowing this one establishment to remain open isn't grounds for undoing everything we'd agreed upon?"

"Actually, that is precisely what it would be grounds for, Waterson," Peerson said flatly.

Henry balled his hands in annoyance. "I'd ask that we at least drop the cease-and-desist letter." There were two barriers to be brought down for Clara. Perhaps beginning with that letter was the place to start.

Peerson shook his head. "Can't do, Waterson. Do you think you're the only person I've made promises to?"

No, of course he wouldn't be. An MP was always politicking, and it was a cause that never ended.

That was the ruthless nature of politics. It didn't matter if the absolute good would come out of a piece of legislation. Ultimately, for each and every last bewigged MP, one's individual goals took precedence over any regard for the greater good. Because to each man, the issues one focused on were the only ones that mattered.

The viscount tugged at each end of his curled mustache. "You don't need me to tell you as much. You're not a green boy to Parliament. You've spent years learning how things work and adhering to that system." He scowled. "So do not now go about attempting to renege on our agreement."

Henry fought for control, keeping his mask in place so the viscount couldn't see his restlessness. Collecting his glass, he forced himself to take several casual sips. "I can look to others for my votes," he said nonchalantly.

Lord Peerson's brows stitched together in the only hint that he had heard—and was offended by that threat. "Go ahead and look, Waterson. You've been seeking to build your damned police force since '19." *Since Peterloo.* That was what had marked the great shift and the learned-too-late appreciation for having such a structure in place. "The only reason you've gained the ground you have these past months is because of me."

God, how Henry hated that the bastard was entitled to his arrogance. He'd never falter in his decision, and yet Henry could not simply concede. Not for Clara. He owed her too much. Henry sat forward in his chair. "I've two debts to this woman." Why did it feel, however, that this was, in fact, about more than obligation?

"And one to me. You decide which matters more."

Which matters more? Clara or . . . the goal he'd devoted his life to since Lila nearly lost her life at Peterloo? How could he simply abandon his vision for a universal police force? How, when it was inextricably linked . . . to Lila? And all for a stranger.

You know she's more than that, a silent voice jeered. *You're only making it out as though she's not to ease your conscience and make this decision easier.* Henry swiped a hand over his mouth.

She'd saved his life. "It would be dishonorable to deny her appeal for help." There had to be another way.

Peerson snorted. "You speak of honor?" He lifted an eyebrow. "You, who appear so very ready to go back on your word to *me.*"

Henry opened and closed his mouth. The other man was . . . correct. But Henry's pledge to him had come before. Before Henry had known the business owner whose establishment he'd shut down was, in fact, Clara. "It is . . . complicated now," he settled for.

The viscount sighed. "You're too honorable for your own good." He rested his elbows on his desk. "Why don't you simply make it right by the woman some other way? A way that preserves all."

"A way that preserves all," he murmured. "What could I—" Henry sat slowly upright. Why, there was a way to ensure both Clara's well-being and Henry's goals. Initially, he'd given her a payment for services rendered. But what if he gave her a *sizable* sum? Enough money to allow her to establish her business elsewhere—Covent Garden. In doing so, her music hall would be considered a music venture and not subject to allegations of immorality.

Lord Peerson waved his hand in annoyance. "I see those wheels in your head churning with a solution about that woman," the viscount said, distaste dripping from his tones. "I couldn't care less about that actress. What I do care about is the agreement between us."

The agreement . . . ?

It took a moment before that emotionless statement made sense.

Lord Peerson's daughter. The dynastic match Henry's mother had dangled before the viscount, before presenting that same possibility to her son. It was a courtship he'd also not brought himself to see to since he and the viscount had first discussed the possibility of a union between Henry and Miss Newton. Though, in truth, no sane nobleman in the whole of England would have ever believed "the possibility" had been anything less than a factual understanding.

"Unless I was mistaken about your intentions?" the viscount asked, as if he'd followed Henry's very thoughts. "Given your failure to attend Lady Peerson's ball last evening and your defense of this *actress woman*, perhaps I'd be wise to question your commitment to . . . me and the greater good."

The greater good of all England.

So why did Henry's every nerve blaze to life with fury at that slightly emphasized description of Clara? "You're not mistaken," Henry brought himself to say. "We're clear on our arrangement." And Henry was clear in what he had to do with regard to Clara—give her the fortune she was deserving of and hope that, in the time she worked with his sister, she might come to see reason. "I will, however, ask something of you."

Peerson nudged his chin in Henry's direction. "Well, what is it?"

"Time." Even as the request slid out, his muscles still went taut at his intentions. *Enough. She'll be better for this, in the end. Safer. More secure. And her business untouchable.*

"Time?"

How many hours of how many days would be necessary to bring a woman who'd been on the fringe of existence back to living once more?

"A fortnight. Call in your contacts, and see that all matters with the Muses are on hold for two weeks' time."

The viscount contemplated him a long moment. And then—

A slow chuckle rumbled from Lord Peerson's chest, the sound of his mirth slightly rough, as if he were unfamiliar with laughter. "That is why I like you, Waterson, and also why I've worked with you. You're as ruthless as I am. A fortnight," he committed.

Chapter 18

He'd kept her waiting.

It was not an unfamiliar position Clara had found herself in through the years.

Having dealt with lovers who'd been of the peerage and patrons of the clubs she'd worked who'd also been members of that exalted station, she'd learned early on that, to them, their time was more valuable than anything.

And hers was irrelevant.

Therefore, it should not surprise Clara.

It did, however, disappoint her. Because the gentleman who'd cared more about his sister's well-being than the scandal of Clara providing lessons to the young woman had spoken of a man different from those others.

Seated on the austere sultan sofa, Clara consulted the gilded clock atop the mantel.

"Twenty minutes," she muttered. He'd kept her waiting now for twenty minutes.

As a once actress, she'd been at the whim of divas who'd ultimately determined when a performance would go on. As a young woman who'd served as mistress to gentlemen, she'd accepted their practice of always being tardy.

As a woman who'd eventually given up whoring and vowed to never again sell her body, Clara had also made a vow to herself: her time was no less important than any man's of any station, and if any person believed different, she'd no use for them in her life. When she'd been kept waiting in the past, she'd left.

And yet here she found herself . . . waiting still.

Because you need him. That voice needled at the back of her mind. It was an unwelcome reminder of how precarious her situation was, and of how her hope for the future hinged on one man. It also hinged on Henry's willingness and ability to present a defense on behalf of her venture to his noble peers.

Given that, her circumstances seemed precarious, and yet Henry, the master builder of a house of cards, had managed to secure her agreement to serve as vocal instructor to his sister. Therefore, it would be foolhardy to doubt his capabilities.

That was the only reason she remained here still, despite being kept waiting.

You are here because some foolish, irrational part of you wants to be here . . .

What? Clara went absolutely motionless, unblinking. She couldn't draw a single breath through her frozen lungs. Where had that irrational thought come from?

She *couldn't* want to be here.

That was preposterous. Her interest in Henry stemmed only from his ability to intervene on behalf of her and the people she employed. Soon she'd be done here, and the business relationship they'd entered into would be finished, and she'd never again see him. Which was fine. Which was better than fine. She'd no desire to have any form of relationship—business or otherwise—with a proper lord.

Liar.

You do want to be here. You enjoy sparring with Henry. You admire that he's not treated you as a common whore, but rather as an equal in all your dealings.

Fear dried out her mouth, and she made herself swallow. Forced herself to exhale and inhale so that she was again breathing. It didn't help. Jumping up, Clara began to pace, her reticule swinging wildly at her side as she stalked past Henry's walnut-and-burl parlor table. This was bad. This was bad, indeed. *Worse.* She'd violated the most cardinal rule of kept women: never care for a nobleman. Over the years, Clara had corrected that to never care for *any* man. Because at the end of the day, men didn't have a use for a courtesan—reformed or otherwise. To have any feelings for anyone jeopardized one's heart and crippled reason.

"Ballocks," she whispered.

"What was that?" an amused voice drawled from the doorway.

Screeching, Clara stopped abruptly. Midswing of her reticule, she lost her grip on the beaded handle. She stared on with something akin to horror as the pale pink article sailed across the room.

Lounging with one shoulder lazily against the doorjamb, Henry shot his left hand out and easily caught the silk-and-ivory piece.

The bounder. "Of course you'd catch it," she muttered aloud, the words escaping her. He'd be so perfectly, coolly collected and triumphant that he'd catch the damned thing.

"Should I have let it fall, Miss Winters?"

Miss Winters, was she now. That only added to her ire that morn. "Hit you."

Henry cocked his head, and that slight movement didn't so much as send one of those expertly combed strands out of place. "Beg pardon?"

"You should have let it hit you."

He grinned, that lazy half smile better belonging to a rogue than a proper MP in Parliament. Her heart thudded. Had his smile always been that wickedly tempting—Satan's smile in that garden of eternal damnation? As if he'd noted her interest, his smile widened.

Clara's cheeks burnt hot. By God, she was not some silly ninny to stand anywhere agog over a blasted gentleman's smile. Especially this man, who'd shut down her business. "I am so happy you're able to finally join me, my lord," she clipped out, stalking angrily across the room. "I'll take that." She plucked her reticule from his fingers, ink-stained digits that bespoke a man who worked frequently with his books. Unlike the lazy sorts who let all those responsibilities fall to another. As soon as she had the beaded ivory handle in her grip, she took four quick steps away from him. Needing distance. "You are late."

"My apologies," he said automatically.

"And why was that? Hmm?" she pressed, not allowing him a chance to speak. "Because my time is somehow less important than yours, Henry?" she demanded, advancing on him.

His cheeks went ruddy. "Of course—"

"Do you think how you spend your time and your moments of the day are somehow more important?"

"I do not think that at all," he said calmly, like he was dealing with a fractious mare.

"Do not take that tone with me, Henry March."

Henry reached behind him and drew the door closed, which for some inexplicable reason added to her fury. Nay, it was because it reminded her once more that he was one hell-bent on living a decorous life . . . and how she would forever be his opposite in that regard.

Spreading her feet apart in a battle-ready position, Clara planted her hands on her hips. "You ordered me here for eleven o'clock."

"It wasn't truly an order as much as a request," he pointed out, adjusting his immaculately tied cravat. "Had you wished to meet at another time, then I would have readily adjusted that schedule."

Damn him. "That is not what you're supposed to say," she cried, her heart hammering.

"What am I supposed to say? You know I'm rubbish with"—he slashed a hand back and forth between them—"all this."

But he wasn't, and that was what was making each exchange with him so damned difficult. He was to have reminded her of her inferior station, told her that he was an earl and she was indebted to him. Only, he hadn't.

"It was a mistake to enter into a deal with you." Just not for the reasons she'd initially believed. She knew that now, and so she did what all wise commanders on the end of a losing battle did—she retreated.

He jerked like she'd slapped him. And damn her for being so pathetically weak that her conscience smarted at the evidence she'd somehow wounded him. "I respect you and your time, Clara," he said quietly, and that was the first time in the whole of her thirty-three years that anyone had uttered those words to her.

And it caused a greater shifting in her chest, and in her convictions.

He drifted toward her, slowly, as to allow her time to retreat if she desired it. But she didn't. Whatever spell he'd cast on those streets of St. Giles months earlier had only intensified this deepening hold he had over her. Henry lowered his head toward hers, and the crisp sandalwood scent of that masculine cologne filled her senses. *Weak. I am weak.* Tipping her head back, she raised herself to meet his kiss. "I was meeting with Lord Peerson," he said quietly, his breath fanning her lips.

Lord Peerson?

Lord Peerson.

The arrangement that had brought them together brought reality crashing back.

Feeling her entire body burn with a blush, Clara sank back on her heels. "Lord Peerson," she repeated dumbly.

Henry caught that lone curl she'd artfully left loose from the arrangement. He stared at the flaxen strand as if transfixed, and her breath stuttered as he rubbed the curl between his fingers. *"Mmm,"* he murmured in response to her inane utterance. His appreciation of that strand of hair more heady than the overt caresses she'd been the recipient of through the years.

And that was Henry March's power—and the danger of him.

Henry made to tuck the lone strand under one of her hair combs. "It was intentional," she whispered, her pulse thudding at their bodies' nearness and her awareness of him and even his lightest touch.

"What is that?" he asked hoarsely.

"That strand. I intended for it to lie there." She reached for the curl, and their fingers kissed; heat burnt, and logical thought fled. Clara caught the tress and draped it between the deep crevice of her satin bodice. Artfully, masterfully, she dragged the strands along the gold piping there.

Henry's throat moved wildly as his gaze drifted to the swells of flesh challenging the neckline of her elaborate emerald-and-gold-striped satin gown.

It was a siren's trick, one she'd employed before, but never because she'd truly wanted to and only because it had been expected of her. Until now.

Now, she twisted that curl between her fingers, deliberately tempting him. Wanting his arms around her once more.

And ultimately winning him.

With a groan, Henry covered her mouth with his; he devoured her, stealing the breath from every corner of her being as she returned each hungry slant of his lips.

Pressing herself against him, Clara kissed him back. Opening her mouth, she let him inside. And his tongue touched hers, burning her, branding her. And for the first time, she wanted to belong to a man. She ached to belong to *this* man.

Henry cupped her buttocks and dragged her to the V of his thighs, and moaning, she let her head fall back.

He was immediately tasting the sensitive flesh of her neck. Nipping at the skin. Suckling lightly. Clara mewled wildly. "I want your mouth, everywhere," she rasped, owning her wantonness and reveling in her body's hunger for this man and this moment.

Henry slid her scandalous satin neckline down a fraction, and that was all he needed to expose her to his gaze and worship. "You are so beautiful," he rasped, trailing a path of kisses along her right breast. Until he reached the swollen tip.

Clara bit her lip to keep from calling out as he drew that flesh in and suckled. A yearning pulled between her legs, an ache that was both agonizing and blissful glory all at once. Her hips undulated as she arched against him in a desperate need to get closer. He switched his attentions to the previously neglected tip, and a keening cry lodged in her throat.

Prior to Henry, Clara had moved methodically through lovemaking. Each act had been routine, without any of this thrill. Tangling her fingers in his hair, she mussed those previously perfect strands and held Henry close. "Henry," she keened his name, over and over. Urged him with words and her body's undulations to continue on. Pleading with him to never stop.

His breath rasped hot and hard against her chest, the slight hitch in his breathing a telltale mark of his like desire. Henry lifted her skirts, and the air slapped at the bared skin, a soothing balm to the heat raging within her. And also, with it, came the cold intrusion of reality.

Gasping, she stumbled out of Henry's arms, tripping in her haste to be away from him. Her pulse roared in her ears as she set to work righting her gown. Good God, what had she done?

What was this hold? What was this enigmatic pull that made her forget reason and made her see only . . . *him*? With fingers that shook, Clara finished straightening her garments.

"We should not have done that," she said, still breathless, her voice low and husked with unfulfilled desire. "That should not have happened." It was a reminder for herself, more than the man before her.

From the corner of her eyes, she caught a glimpse of Henry righting his own, still frustratingly tidy, garments. "I wouldn't . . . I'm sorry. Forgive me." She took pleasure in the slight quake to his own palms and his inability to string words together. "It was not my intention to take advantage of you or your role in this household."

She clenched and unclenched her fingers in her skirts. Never had any man before him made apologies . . . for anything. To them, Clara had simply been an object, no different from a fancy bauble, there for their pleasure, and her own desires and wishes . . . secondary.

And that was why this would never do. This was why she had to leave. Because of every way in which he was different. He was . . . honorable . . . when she'd ceased to believe a man capable of being so.

As she tended her garments, neither of them spoke.

Clara, however, felt his stare, taking in her every, even slightest, movement.

When she'd regained a semblance of control over her thoughts, she drew in a slow breath before speaking. "This is not what I agreed to," she said quietly.

He blanched. "I am sorry. It was never my intention to force you into a—"

Her sigh drowned out the rest of that apology. "No man has or ever will force me into a decision on sexual congress," she said flatly. "Not you, Henry. Nor any man." Men had tried—including Terrence Lowery, the bastard who'd seen her career ruined in a bid to secure her services as his mistress—and failed. Clara took a step toward Henry. "I kissed you because I wanted it."

Passion blazed to life in his eyes, and her heart quickened once more. *Stop it.* "But this"—she waved at him—"arrangement we've entered into isn't"—*safe*—"wise."

His gaze sharpened on her face. "What are you saying?"

"I'm saying that you yourself don't trust your sister alone with me."

His expression softened, and Clara glanced away from the gentle knowing in his eyes. "Is that what you believe?" he asked softly, erasing the short distance between them. Henry dusted his knuckles along her jawline. "That I somehow doubt the very woman who saved my life and cared for me despite her own reservations."

"This isn't about my having cared for you, Henry." His fingers caressed her jaw, and he was so tender in his touch that he wrought havoc on the determination she'd come to a short while ago. "This is about my past and your sister's reputation."

The ghost of a smile turned his lips. "Says who, Clara?"

All the oldest insecurities reared their ugly heads. With a sound of annoyance escaping her, Clara spun away from him, missing his touch even as she was responsible for its loss. "You didn't need to say it with words, Henry," she said crisply. "You said more than enough with your insistence that I not be given access to Lady Lila until you'd arrived." Unable to meet his piercing gaze, Clara went and retrieved her reticule, resting forlornly just a handful of feet away. When she again faced Henry, she braced for his onslaught.

After all, no lord was content at being thwarted—and certainly not by a former whore.

Henry remained where he was, directly in the path to the doorway. His hands, however, remained clasped behind him. "Is that what this is about?" he asked solemnly. "You're resurrecting that same argument, Clara?"

Yes. No. It was all jumbled in her mind. As such, she stood there in silence. "Any relationship between us cannot work." There, that much was true. As her past precluded her from a proper future, she was left with only one possibility with this man: becoming his lover. And the feelings this man roused in her told her that such a fate would never be enough. That was ultimately what this was about. And nothing she could ever admit to him.

"You were correct," Henry finally said after a pregnant pause.

"I was?" she blurted. Such an admission was a first in her lifetime.

"I had no right to put the favor I did to you. I owed you a debt for the time you cared for me in St. Giles."

She frowned. "I didn't care for you out of any debt."

"Which is why it was wrong of me to ask anything of you. You aided me without any thought of payment or favors given. I, in turn?" He swiped a hand down a smooth-shaven cheek.

Her fingers ached to follow the path his fingers had lightly traveled, to test the sharp contours.

Henry let his arm fall back to his side. "I, in turn, made my pledge to help contingent upon what you could do for me." He paused. "For my sister," he clarified. Something darkened in his eyes. "I . . . need you to understand . . . every decision I've made these past years has been with my sister and her experience at Peterloo in mind. All of it."

She caressed a palm down his cheek. "Why are you telling me this?" she asked softly.

"Because I wouldn't ask any person for help they didn't wish to give—except for my family." He briefly looked away. The muscles of his face contorted in a paroxysm of such emotion her heart folded unto itself.

No person, not even the mother who'd given her birth, had ever felt such devotion and love for her. Had there been someone to care about her with even a smidgeon of the depth that Henry cared for his sister, Clara would have never wandered from the path of respectability and built a life of comfort on her back.

When he met her gaze once more, the mask was firmly affixed, the one that gave no hint of vulnerability . . . but it was enough—she'd seen it. "I was delayed returning because of my meeting with Lord Peerson."

Lord Peerson.

The faceless MP so determined to bring down her future.

"You had your meeting?" And then energy whipped through her. She caught his jacket in her fingers. "What did he say? What did they say?" The questions came tumbling off her lips, frantic.

"He—"

"Yes?" she demanded, gripping him more tightly.

"He relented." His expression grew shuttered. "He . . . agreed to intervene and halt the closing."

Clara staggered back. Pressing a palm against her mouth, she stepped away. "He . . ."

Henry tugged off his gloves and beat them together. He tucked those leather articles in his jacket and then fished out a small scrap of paper. "The gentleman agreed." Wordlessly, he handed that sheet over.

Accepting it, Clara scanned the note . . . and choked. "What is this?"

"Ten thousand pounds," he said quietly.

Still euphoric at his revelation, Clara raised her confused eyes to his.

"It is an alternative, Clara. It is the option to start over."

"You'd offer me ten thousand pounds," she murmured. She stared down at that exorbitant sum . . . How very ironic that rich amount he'd settled upon should have also been the same amount that had been wrested from her by a swindler who'd stolen her first hopes of her club. In a peculiar way, she and her business had come . . . full circle. The dream had begun and been quickly dashed at the hand of one man, then fully restored with the help of another. And in that instant, Clara's heart was healed and beat anew . . . with love for this man. The only man of honor and convictions and integrity she'd ever known.

There would be time enough to panic about that discovery later. A time when he wasn't standing before her. Clara lifted the page. "Why are you offering me this?" she asked hesitantly.

"Because I had no right to put the request to you that I did. And now . . . I am offering you freedom from me and your circumstances. Allow me to hire your services outright. In turn, you can take that money and do with it what you wish in a different end of London."

Freedom.

Her heart paused, and when it resumed beating, the organ slipped to her toes. That she should discover her love for a man so willing to send her on her way was the story of her proverbial life. He was offering her an out of their arrangement that would see that they both continued their own ways. He'd not threatened her. He'd not held the Muses over her head the way Reggie's own husband once had, and that mark of Henry's difference warmed a heart she'd believed long cold and jaded by life. Rather, he'd put the choice to her.

He'd given her an out.

It was a wholly foreign and generous offer. One that marked Henry so *different* from the man who'd been determined to have her at all costs—*Lowery*. Lowery, who'd stripped her of employment and funds, all in a bid to break her.

Even resenting Henry's role in that damned cease and desist, this offer of a fortune on his part was one she couldn't make sense of.

Clara wandered over to the window, the long floor-to-ceiling panes that overlooked the fashionable streets of Grosvenor Square. At no point did Henry call her away; at no moment did he remind her that being spied at his window in itself represented scandal.

And it was because of that she remained at the edge of the whispery-soft pale-ivory fabric, staring out.

Since that note had been delivered with the orders against her music hall, she, for the first time, had everything she'd hoped for—the best of what she could hope for: freedom to carry on with her business, and a promise from a nobleman in a position of power to advocate on her behalf.

So why did she not just walk out that door?

Because of him. Because of who he is. Because he is a man who would offer you a fortune with no expectation of services rendered—not even the help he desperately seeks for his sister. Because of the sister he loves so deeply. And because of the sister who needs your help.

Clara pressed her eyes closed. "I already told you I don't want your money."

"This isn't just money, Clara. This is ten thousand pounds."

A fortune.

"Very well. I don't want your ten thousand pounds, either, Henry." And she didn't. The ten thousand pounds would indicate their time was complete, along with her dream. "Nor do I want to be in a different end of London." St. Giles needed to be transformed.

A guttural sound of frustration spilled past his lips in an unusual break in his armor. "Even if Peerson does not bring down your establishment, there will be others. Men who will take a music hall run by women in St. Giles as immoral."

Annoyance swelled. "That is nonsense. Why should it matter where it is?"

"Because it just does, Clara." He swiped the air with his palm as he spoke. "It matters to those who've decided that St. Giles and the Seven Dials, with its whores and pickpockets, is home to no respectable place."

Her mouth tightened. Wasn't that the way of the nobility? "Then I'll change their minds with my establishment."

His expression was pained. "My God, you are stubborn, Clara Winters."

Drifting over, she eyed him suspiciously. "Are you trying to renege on our agreement?"

Did she imagine the slight pause? "No."

Clara smoothed her skirts. "Very well, then. I promised you my services."

He winced. "Clara, you don't have to—"

She touched her fingertips to his lips, staying the rest of his response. "I don't have to do anything. I'm *choosing* to." Suddenly, it was very important that he understood. That he understood *why*. "I didn't want to be a courtesan," she revealed. "I was an actress."

Henry stilled. If he pressed her. If he put a single question to her, she couldn't get the words out. "I was not the greatest upon the stage. I was . . . good *enough*. But 'good enough' does not mean a woman can build a future that is respectable." Her gaze drifted to the urn, overflowing with pink blooms.

I want you, Clara. And I will have you . . .

Sadness filled her as she wandered over to the chintz vase and collected a full peony. Drawing it close to her nose, she inhaled the sweet, fragrant scent, and her belly churned as all those memories she'd kept locked away slipped out from that buried chamber in her mind. "A patron was determined to have me, and when I wouldn't be had, he used his money and his influence against me." She glanced over and tried to read something from him, but Henry may as well have been carved of stone.

"What did he do?" he asked with a lethal steel underscoring those tones.

And just like that, the tension weighting her frame eased, and in its place was a stunningly beautiful warmth. A soothing warmth. No one had ever been offended on her behalf. None of her lovers had cared enough to ask about her past. Only this man had.

"I rebuffed his repeated offers at a protectorship."

"Who was he?"

"Does it matter?"

His eyes darkened. "It does because if I know him and he's responsible for your suffering, then I'll see him destroyed."

And when thoughts of Lowery had always ushered in an icy chill, now there was only warmth. "He was a slaver, dealing in the sale and purchase of human flesh, and saw women no differently." A familiar hatred burnt through her. No matter how desperate she'd been, she would have never had any relationship with such a man. "And so when I rejected him, he did what any man with influence might do: he saw me barred from all of Covent Garden and Drury Lane."

Henry cursed, a splendidly inventive one.

"He ruined my name at every theatre." There hadn't been a stage job open to her throughout the whole of London. "I survived because a gaming hell owner offered me employment." And that had been the end of Lowery's harassment. At last she'd found safety in the Hell and Sin Club, and because of it, she'd felt indebted to the owner for the gift he'd given her. Clara had repaid him with the only currency she'd ever had—her body. She drew a breath in through her teeth and shook her head, dislodging those memories. "That is why this is so important to me, Henry. Because in the Muses, I'm in control." Or she had been until the law had been brought down upon her.

"Clara," he said hoarsely. He swiped his hands over his face. "You don't have to do this." His was a plea.

And understanding dawned. Her heart dipped. "You don't want me here." He'd changed his mind. He was always proper and had at last registered what she'd reminded him of all along. "Because of your sister." And that realization was like a lash upon her soul. "I . . . see." And here she'd erroneously believed herself immune to society's disdain? So why was it that this man's rejection hurt? She turned to leave, but Henry caught her briefly by the wrist and drew her close.

"It isn't that, Clara." And when spoken so gently, she could almost believe him.

"Then it is decided," she said with a forced smile. Avoiding his gaze, she smoothed her hands along the front of her striped skirts. "Now, I'll have certain rules laid out before I begin."

"Of course."

Yet again, he ceded such control to her.

Who was this man?

"I'll not be kept waiting, Henry. My time is of no less importance than yours."

"I agree." He agreed? Another dangerous shift occurred in her breast. "You have my word, Clara."

"I'll not have you present when I provide music instruction to your sister," she said before the desire to have him near won out over common sense.

He was already shaking his head. "I need to be there."

Need. Need versus want. She wanted him to want to be there. And yet, to have him there would be even more perilous. "You cannot."

He scowled, his features twisting in such a boyish annoyance that a smile pulled her lips. "There is an intimacy to music, Henry." As soon as that explanation left her, she felt the seeming wryness in her, a former courtesan using that word about song.

"Explain it to me," he murmured, drifting closer.

Move away. Keep your space. Keep your distance. Physical and emotional and every type of distance in between.

Except, as he stopped before her, his body close, so close heat poured from his powerful frame, she remained as she was.

"Music represents a woman's greatest connection to the joy she is feeling, to the hopes in her heart," Clara murmured. "To the . . ." She caught her lower lip between her teeth.

"What else, Clara?" he urged, stroking the pad of his thumb along the corner of her lip, and the tension left her mouth.

"To the regrets she carries," she whispered.

He slowly stopped that gentle back-and-forth caress, and she wanted to cry out at the loss of that touch which both tempted and soothed. "And are you a woman with regrets?"

"Too many to count." And she was perilously close to adding Henry March, the Earl of Waterson, to that great heap of errors.

"I know something of regrets myself," he said cryptically, and with that he brought them back to her role here.

"Your sister."

"Amongst others," he acknowledged, that veiled admission bringing questions to her lips. Those questions, however, contained answers she wasn't entitled to. *But I want them anyway.*

In the end, Henry made the decision for the both of them. "It is agreed. You will have complete access to my household and Lila. During your time here, I'll not . . . interfere. And at the end of it, regardless, the money is yours."

And a short while later, as Henry had a servant usher Lila in and join Clara, she could not fight another tugging of regret at her breast that Henry had capitulated to her request so very easily.

Chapter 19

Henry had prided himself on living a respectable life and doing so honorably. Along the way, he'd made missteps; he'd failed as a brother. But never had those failings been deliberate.

Until now.

Six days after he'd agreed to the terms Clara had laid out . . . again, he felt like the worst sort of bastard.

Not only had Henry not been forthright with Clara regarding his meeting with Lord Peerson, he'd flat out lied. He'd convinced himself that offering her a sizable sum that would see her set up in Covent Garden would be enough. For the first time in the whole of his life, he'd given his word on a pledge he had no right, or even an ability, to make. He'd sacrificed his honor . . . for Lila.

God, he hated himself.

Seated at the breakfast table, Henry stole a glance at the window.

She'd arrive soon, just as she did every day—she was ever punctual. She'd be attired in her shimmering gold satin cloak, just as she donned every morn. In it, she would be a glimmering Athena, and he would remain the mere mortal, wholly weakened by this ever-deepening need of her. For her.

"Oh . . ."

That quiet exclamation brought Henry's gaze whipping to the doorway. And he froze. All thoughts of Clara fled. His mouth moved, and he tried to get words out.

"Lila," he greeted dumbly, and then tardily, he jumped up.

His youngest sister hugged the frame, and for a moment he thought she'd leave. Instead, she took a tentative step forward, and then she was joining him at the table—two seats away and at the opposite end of the table, but joining him nonetheless. A vise cinched at his chest. For seven years, he'd sought . . . some acknowledgment from his sister. Be it anger, or disgust, or hatred for him and his having failed to call her back earlier or fetch her himself from Manchester, he'd craved any response.

A footman hurried over with a plate. The liveried servant set the porcelain dish down before Lila and then backed away, taking up his previous spot along the back wall.

Henry recalled that he remained standing and hurried to reclaim his seat. His fingers lightly shook, and he wrapped them around his cup of coffee. Raising the now tepid black brew to his lips, he took a drink.

All the while, his sister devoted her attention to the same morning fare she'd consumed since she was a little girl: two pieces of plain toast, one grilled tomato, and a poached egg. She still meticulously ripped her toast into four perfect quarters and arranged them along the top corner of her dish. His throat tightened under a swell of emotion. How very strange that the most mundane of tasks should have remained forever unaltered, while the woman across from him had been changed in every way that mattered.

"I did not expect you would be here," Lila said. Her voice came so soft that he struggled to hear.

He resisted the urge to drag his chair closer to the table. If he did, she'd flee. If he made a single mistake, she'd go silent once more. "I—"

"Are always at Parliament," she finished in those same hushed tones. "At this hour, you are off and holding your meetings and drafting your legislation."

"I didn't expect that you'd noticed," he said haltingly. What was she really saying? He sought to pick out any hint of resentment, but she was an impenetrable wall of emotionless repose. And there was something so very agonizing in that.

"Of course I noticed." Lila dipped a corner of her toast into the grilled tomato, and there was silence in the breakfast room once more. "I trust you are leaving."

He should be leaving. Mayhap that accounted for why she was here now, with him.

She'd been accurate in pointing out he had obligations that called him elsewhere. Work pertaining to votes he still required and needed to court amongst his fellow MPs.

And mayhap he, who'd believed himself only capable of holding the reputation of emotionless, purpose-driven lord—by even his own family—had changed in this regard, after all. Henry shifted his leather folio slightly away from his dish.

With her gaze, his sister took in that deliberate movement. And this time, she met his eyes.

Did he imagine the hint of a smile on her lips?

"How are your lessons with"—Clara—"Miss Winters?" he asked, the safest of topics for them, and also the only one he knew to speak with her on.

Her expression brightened. "She is marvelous."

"She is," he said quietly. *And I'm a damned bastard who'd betrayed her.*

Lila's eyebrows shot to her hairline.

Henry coughed. "That is . . . what I'd meant to say is"—*Clara Winters is brave and bold and forthright*—"Miss Winters is a marvelous instructor," he settled for lamely.

His sister dipped another corner of her toast into her grilled tomato. "Odd you should know as much when you've never attended a single one of her lessons."

He needed blacker, stronger, hotter coffee. Coffee. Lifting his cup, Henry motioned over a servant for a refill of his drink. "Miss Winters insisted that your lessons be conducted in private." And he'd been too much a coward to face her, knowing all the while that he'd less than a fortnight before she learned the depth of his treachery.

Tell her. She deserves the truth. Mayhap she'll forgive you.

But why would she? The answer was simple. She wouldn't. And then what would happen to Lila? Lila, who'd gone from a shadow in the household to a sister again taking breakfast with him. All that progress would be lost.

"And *you* agreed to Miss Winters's terms?" Lila asked, cutting into those guilty musings. His sister paused mid-dunk of her toast. "You. You, who've never ceded control of any decision, and certainly not to a woman, did so for Miss Winters?"

What a low opinion his youngest sibling had of him. And what was worse was that she delivered it not as a condemnation but rather as a matter-of-fact observation. Grateful for the brief break in discourse as a servant filled his glass, Henry murmured his thanks.

"And you're thanking servants?" Lila murmured wistfully. "You've . . . changed."

He had changed.

He, who'd never even changed how he took his morning drink. Except they both had been altered.

Sadness clouded Lila's eyes. "You've changed for the better," she added.

Is deceiving a woman into helping your sister truly for the better? a silent voice jeered.

"Unlike me," his sister said softly.

"You're wrong, Lila," he said gruffly. She had always been the good one. She and Sylvia. "I've only ever been a pompous, driven bastard." *And I still am.* "You, despite what happened, remain good and pure inside."

His sister gave her head a tight shake. "Mm-mm. I don't want to hear another word about who you think I am anymore, Henry. There's nothing else to say." She didn't wish to talk about that day at Peterloo, still. Lila nibbled at the corner of her toast. "Either way, I prefer this new version of you. You are . . . interesting."

And who would have imagined that even with this pressure weighting his chest, he could manage a smile. "Thank you."

"Even your nose is interesting now."

His fingers reflexively went to the slight bend in that once perfect cartilage. "Mother would disagree with you on that score," he forced himself to rejoin.

"At least she stopped crying about it."

"Oh, I'm sure now that Sylvia has had her baby, Mother's quite happily resumed the lamentations over my nose."

They shared a grin, even as a swell of emotion threatened to choke him. Sylvia had been safely delivered of her babe. Fear over his family's well-being was one he'd carried with him since Lila had nearly been killed. He'd come to appreciate how precarious life was, and how easily it could be lost. From that moment on, he'd committed to placing those he loved first.

Suddenly, Lila's smile froze on her face.

"What is it?" he asked.

"We are . . . smiling," she whispered.

Henry started. "We are." For the first time in so long.

Would either of them manage another smile when Clara learned the truth and quit this household and family? Henry picked up his cup and stared forlornly into the remainder of his coffee.

This time, when a silence fell between him and Lila, it was an easy one. One that had been brought about by Clara's influence, and as a result, Henry was undeserving of it.

When she'd stormed Henry's house and inspired Lila, she had brought his sister back to the living.

It was a debt which he could never repay.

And instead, one he'd match with a betrayal.

Is it truly a betrayal when she'll have the funds to set herself up elsewhere? When he would see her in a secure location where the Peersons of the world wouldn't again shatter her dreams?

Those same assurances he'd been repeating to himself these past days fell flat in his own mind.

Footsteps sounded in the hall, and he and Lila looked up.

Wright entered. "Miss Winters has arrived."

His heart hammered at the mere mention of her name. It was an all-too-familiar state for that organ whenever he saw Clara or heard her voice or thought of her. Which, sleeping or awake, was particularly pitiful in frequency, given the lady's complete lack of interest in him.

"She is early!" Lila exclaimed with an uncharacteristic brightness, and that pit settled in his stomach. That was the reason for his betrayal . . . The return of his sister's smile was why he'd bartered his soul. Seeing the fruits of that sacrifice did nothing to ease the tightness in his chest that came in betraying Clara. "Come, walk me to my lesson."

It took a moment for his sister's request to register. Another swell of emotion filled him, Lila had not brought herself to look at him these past years. She'd never asked him to join her . . . anywhere. And now, she did. Because of Clara. It was all because of Clara. A hungering to see Clara swept him. "I shouldn't. I have . . ." *To escape. To continue avoiding Clara like the coward I am.*

Lila glanced down at her unfinished toast. "I . . . understand," she said softly. "You've business to attend."

Yes, he did. He always did. As such, she'd offered him a true, and much-needed, excuse to make his leave. *Oh, blast and damn.* Henry climbed to his feet. "I'll walk you to your lessons." Even as he gathered his folders and started from the room with Lila at his side, guilt sawed away at him.

As they walked the corridors to the music room, he felt Lila's eyes on him.

He glanced down. "What is it?"

"I am . . . just surprised."

Nothing in her tone or blank gaze gave any indication of that shock she spoke of. Instead, it was the peculiar emptiness he'd come to expect from her. "I never expected you'd really join me. Not when Parliament awaits you, Henry."

"Ah, it was an empty invitation," he said dryly.

"You're thanking servants. You're worried after Miss Winters's time. I don't even recognize you anymore, Henry," Lila marveled aloud.

Nor he her. Swallowing past the emotions stuck in his throat, Henry forced a half grin. "It is no doubt the nose."

Lila's eyes rounded. "And you're making jests." Of all the changes she'd spoken of in Henry, with the astonishment underscoring her whisper, his sister had found that newly discovered ability to tease the most shocking of all.

Once more, it was another product of Clara's impact on his life. "Uh . . . yes, well, not very good ones. But . . . jests, nonetheless." *I trust you're not altogether familiar with being teased . . .*

Had he truly believed there wasn't a place for it in his world? Clara and his sisters had all been correct—he had been a stuffy, stodgy bore.

They reached the music room, and Henry motioned for his sister to enter ahead of him and then followed after her.

Seated at the pianoforte, facing him, was Clara.

Their gazes locked, the ten paces between them as inconsequential as air for the energy that hummed to life when they were near.

His pulse hammered away as it always did. Since he'd entered into a contract with her on a lie, he'd stayed away. It had been safer. Nay, the decision had been born of cowardice. God, how he'd missed her, and how he'd miss her when she was gone. "Cl—" That hoarse greeting came to a screeching halt as Lila spun back. "Miss Winters," he settled for lamely.

With the aplomb of a queen, Clara glided to her feet, and as she came out from behind that instrument, he let himself drink his fill. *A week*. It had been nearly a week since he'd seen her. Her black chintz dress, printed with crimson flowers, clung to her every curve and robbed him of all logical thought.

She stopped several steps away and sank into a deep curtsy. "My lord," she murmured, bowing her head slightly.

Curtsying. Bowing her head.

"My lording" him.

There it was. The reminder of the divide between them. A proper greeting delivered in the presence of his sister. *I want my name on her lips . . . always*. He didn't want the illusion of formality when there was . . . whatever this connection they shared.

A connection that he'd threaded together with a lie about her future. And here he'd believed it impossible to hate himself any more than he had after Peterloo.

His sister shifted a confused gaze over to Henry. "Henry?" she asked, breaking into those useless musings.

That reminder brought him back to the reason for his visiting this room she'd expressly forbidden him from entering while she was here. "Forgive me. I should let you begin your lesson."

Clara's lips, lightly rouged red, parted ever so slightly. Was it disappointment? Or was it simply his own longing that made him see that which wasn't there? "May I have a moment, my lord?"

"Of course."

"Lila"—Clara looked to his sister—"I've already set out our sheet music for the day. Why don't you begin?"

She hadn't even finished before Lila was hurrying over to the Broadwood grand piano. A moment later, the haunting strains of the unfamiliar song resonated through the room, soaring to the ceiling. Clara started for the doorway, but Henry remained frozen, rooted there by the song as it built in speed and cheer. The tune so at odds with the darkness that had lived within this household—within this family—and played so perfectly by his sister, who'd been so achingly broken by life.

He dimly registered the flutter of skirts. Clara returned, taking up a place at his shoulder. Just a handful of inches shorter, she arched her head and placed her lips close to his ear. "Magnificent, is it not?"

She was. She'd brought about every change he himself had been incapable of.

He managed a nod. Talk of music was safer . . . easier than the lie that hovered between them. "What is it?"

"It is 'Sonata in A minor for Arpeggione and Piano.' Franz Schubert," she murmured, the whisper of chocolate upon her breath tantalizingly sweet. "Do you know what I admire most about him? Schubert?" she clarified.

"What is that, Clara?" he asked, folding his arms at his chest and watching on as Lila played.

"He has no ego. He's never been one to show off. In fact, he'd compose pieces and simply place them in a drawer and close it." She mimicked that reaction with her fingers. "He marvels over Beethoven, and in his modesty truly has no idea of his own genius." Clara rested her fingers upon his sleeve in a touch that felt more an afterthought and would have shocked him for the impropriety of it . . . in front of his sister, no less. And yet, there was something innocent in it as well. A naturalness that spoke of an ease with one another.

He glanced down and found her gaze trained on her student expertly plying those keys. "You speak as one who knows him." It was an observation on his part more than a question.

"Knows his music," she amended. "My mother was a great soprano." Her gaze grew distant, and a sad little smile played about her lips.

Her words reminded him of how little he truly knew Clara. Largely because she'd kept herself a secret. She'd cloaked herself and her life in mysteries and denied him a right to them since she'd first rescued him in St. Giles. Waiting here, in silence, he feared she'd once again hold back those parts of herself. And when he confessed the truth, and she had no need for him, she'd leave, and he'd never know those secrets he craved.

Henry wanted to know everything there was to know about her. All of her: her past, what brought her joy. What dreams she'd abandoned that she deserved to again know and give new life to.

Panic dulled his senses.

His were thoughts of madness. They were worlds apart in every way . . . and even if they weren't, she'd been clear: she had no desire for anything respectable . . . or formal . . . with any man. And he'd never be one to put an indecent offer to her, because it would never be enough.

"Legendary musicians composed pieces in her honor," she went on, through the tumult clouding his head. A little laugh spilled past her lips. "Of course, every man who knew my mother was more than half in love with her, simply for her talent alone." Her smile faded. "Her talent never required her to sell herself to some undeserving gentleman to compensate for too-meager wages."

"As you yourself were," he murmured, more than half-afraid that in simply speaking, he'd kill this sudden, unexpected openness about her past.

Clara's lips pulled down ever so faintly in the corners in the hint of a frown that ripped at his heart. "As I myself was," she confirmed. "The truly great, like my mother, find fame and accolades and a comfortable existence." She gave a slight lift of her chin, urging him to follow her as they stepped outside the room. "But my mother's experience is not the reality for the majority of the working class, Henry. We don't have the luxuries of entailed and unentailed properties or inheritances. Or family jewels or pianos of a quality deserving of Beethoven."

Heat slapped his cheeks. "It was the . . ." He muttered the remainder of that nauseatingly out-of-touch admission under his breath.

"Beg pardon?" Clara cupped a palm around her ear. "What was that? It sounded as though . . ."

"Beethoven." The truth exploded from him. And he swiped his palms over his face. "The piano belonged to Beethoven."

She leaned close, her body arching toward his. "Is that what you believe? That I'd resent you for having the fine things you do have?" Disappointment colored her tone.

He'd failed somehow here. He'd failed at some test he didn't understand and couldn't make sense of. "I don't . . ." He lifted his palms up. "Why shouldn't you, though, Clara?"

While he and his family had lived a charmed life, she'd been forced onto an altogether different path. "Why is that? Hmm?" she murmured, the softest smile on her lips. "Because I became a courtesan?" He flinched. "Because I built a more secure future for myself by playing at mistress for other gentlemen?"

Other gentlemen, who'd not been him. Henry's hands formed reflexive fists. He'd not allowed himself to think about her past . . . because he'd hated every nameless, faceless man who'd had Clara in his arms. And whichever faceless stranger who'd one day earn her heart. Hopefully, it would be a man worthy of her . . . and Henry hated the mythical bastard anyway.

Clara dusted the tip of a painted fingernail down the uneven bridge of his nose. "I don't resent you for having things, Henry," she repeated. "I resent you and those in the ruling class who have those things but don't ensure that others are able to have those same privileges. Wages that allow us to not only survive but also *live* beyond just now." She moved her finger, trailing the tip of it lower to the silk cravat and the gold stickpin there. "Conditions that are safe, and laws in place so that employers don't abuse their workers." Clara circled one of his gold buttons with the pad of her thumb. "That is the reason I resent"—him—"those of your station, Henry." She glanced back toward the music room, and when she again faced him, her gaze and words marked the end of that thinly veiled scolding. "If your sister wishes for you to stay, would you care to remain and observe?" she asked, her question tentative.

His heart lifted in his chest. She wanted him here.

I want to be here. I want to be here with her, watching whatever magic she managed in this room. He wanted to sit and listen to a song fall from her lips, confirming a voice type he'd wager his soul was a husky contralto.

And yet . . .

Reality intruded.

"I cannot."

Her face fell. "Of course," she said quickly.

Henry caught her loosely by the wrist and drew her close. "Not because I don't want to be here." *With you.*

They spoke simultaneously.

"You wished—"

"Henry . . ."

He urged her to continue. "Please, you."

"I'd ask if you'd meet me later this evening at my music hall. Eight o'clock."

Her music hall. That business she so cherished that he'd been hopeless to see saved for her.

"Eight o'clock," he agreed.

She smiled softly at him . . . a smile he was undeserving of, and selfishly basked in anyway.

"I have to return," she whispered, and with a little wink, she darted back inside the music room.

And as he quit his residence, it wasn't thoughts of his legislative agenda or aspirations that consumed his thoughts—but rather her.

Henry March, the Earl of Waterson, had proven to be dangerous to Clara, after all.

Just not in the ways she had initially believed and feared.

Standing at the front of Beethoven's grand piano, Clara stole another glance at the doorway. Wanting another glimpse of him. Hoping he'd changed his mind and decided to join his sister's music lesson, after all.

Which was preposterous; Henry was entirely focused on his business. He'd been clear as day since the moment he'd been in her apartments that his responsibilities took precedence over all.

She sighed. It was her lot to love where she oughtn't.

"He likes you," Lila noted over her playing.

Startled, Clara looked over to her charge. "Beg pardon?" she blurted.

"My brother," the younger woman clarified from her place at the grand piano. Lila didn't miss a single stroke of the key. Each chord was struck at the perfect moment. "Henry doesn't like anybody. They're too flighty. Too silly. Too wicked. But you"—her fingers stilled on the keys, and the strains reverberated around them—"you, he likes." Lila commenced playing.

Somewhere between her first affair and her third, Clara had become a master of dissembling. Alas, every one of those skills now failed her. "I don't know what you're talking about."

Lila glanced across the top of the mahogany instrument. "The correct lie would be, you don't know *who* I'm talking about. But you do know because there's been just one person whom we've seen together."

And miracle of miracles, Clara felt herself blushing. *Do not betray your emotions.* She was being pressed by a young, innocent woman. She'd faced far greater interrogations in the course of her thirty-three years. "I like your brother, as well," she said calmly, straightening the sheets on the lyre-shaped music stand.

"And that is another thing," Lila went on. "No one likes my brother in return."

Clara frowned. "And whyever not? He is devoted to his family. He is honest, and—" She immediately clamped her lips shut. And she'd neatly stepped into it. She'd violated one of the most basic rules of St. Giles . . . never underestimate one's opponent.

Lila's gaze twinkled. "As I was saying . . . my brother likes you a great deal."

Clara's heart sped up and then resumed a normal cadence. Any number of men had liked her. None had ever loved her or felt any deeper regard than that. "Your brother feels indebted to me," she said softly.

"Because you saved him."

It wasn't a question, and yet she answered it as if it were anyway. "Because I saved him."

Lila ceased playing in an indication that she'd no intent on abandoning the wholly inappropriate topic of her brother's feelings—or lack thereof—for Clara. "Henry no doubt admires you for rescuing him . . . and is indebted, as well." The young woman swung her legs around the edge of the bench. "But that doesn't account for how he's changed."

"How he's changed?" Clara asked tentatively, wanting to learn about this man who'd stolen her heart.

"Many have called him pompous."

She scowled. "Pompous men do not keep company with . . ." She stumbled.

Lila stared at her expectantly.

"Former courtesans," Clara stated baldly, not eliciting so much as a blush from the woman across from her. "And they certainly don't allow their sisters in the company of them, either." And yet that was precisely what Henry had done. "Furthermore—"

Lila stared pointedly at her, and Clara made herself stop prattling her defense of Henry.

"You were saying?" she asked weakly.

"The world has seen Henry as pompous, but he's not. Rather, he's always been . . ." Clara waited as the other woman searched for the word. "Austere," she settled for. "Single-minded and driven in his purpose. And he's changed . . ." Lila stood, and Clara fought the urge to flee even as her feet twitched with the need for flight. "Henry's let his goals in Parliament rule . . . everything. And that drive came after . . ." A shadow fell over the young woman's face. She balled her hands at her sides and gave her attention to those curled digits a long while before she again met Clara's gaze. "Peterloo."

"His police force."

"Precisely," Lila confirmed with a nod. "It has been Henry's everything . . . until you. Now, he's set that goal second behind your music hall."

Because he was desperate . . . because he even acknowledged in his own words that he would have sold his soul for his sister's recovery. And then the other woman's pronouncement hit her. "How do you . . . ?"

"I may have . . . heard some of the terms you agreed to."

Another woman, a virtuous woman, would have been horrified at what else the lady might have heard. "Then you should know from that, you make more of our arrangement than there is." Henry didn't care about her. *But how I wish he did.* What would it be to have the love of a good, honorable man like Henry March?

Horror brought her mind to a standstill. For that naive dream she'd just allowed herself was better suited to a younger girl who'd not been scarred by life. A girl who had a right to dream—unlike Clara.

"Do you know, Clara? You may say that I'm making more of your arrangement with my brother," the other woman said as she reclaimed her seat at the bench. "But I don't think I am." With that, Lila resumed playing.

And Clara was grateful as the other woman let the matter rest and they settled on the far safer lesson. Even so, an hour later when the session concluded, Clara hurried out Henry's front doors with Lila's musings echoing around her head. *My brother likes you* . . . Clara hadn't allowed herself to entertain the other woman's speculations. But . . . what if Henry's sister was in fact correct and he somehow did care about her? What if the feelings that flared between them moved beyond desire?

And mayhap there could be . . . more . . .

Clara missed the bottom step. With a gasp, she caught the wrought iron rail and kept herself upright.

Of course there couldn't be more. Gentlemen like Henry married ladies. They didn't have any respectable relationships with courtesans.

Some did . . .

Why, the Countess of Jersey herself was one of the king's many mistresses. Granted, Frances Villiers had been mistress to a king, which put her in an altogether different class, but she'd been a courtesan, nonetheless.

Several gasps went up, cutting into those unhelpful thoughts, and Clara looked to the horrified pair of ladies staring at her.

Each carried two leashes in their gloved fingers, with four yapping pugs between them. With like-rounded cheeks and matched black ringlets, the plump pair, separated strictly by age, could only be mother and daughter.

The elder of the two muttered something, and then the ladies spun on their heels and marched off. It was an all-too-familiar response she'd received when she'd gone to the finest modistes on North Bond Street, but coming this moment, on the heels of her earlier musings, it only highlighted what a damned fool she'd been, daydreaming about a future with Henry.

There could never be a future with him . . .

She would settle for one night in his arms, and that would be enough.

It would have to be.

Chapter 20

Later that night, with a ravaged conscience after a final, failed round of negotiations with Lord Peerson and the other MPs, Henry sought out the only person he could trust.

"I require assistance," Henry said as soon as Waverly's butler, Chafter, drew open the marquess's office door.

Henry's frantic announcement was met with an awkward silence that blanketed the room and stretched into the hall.

Oh, bloody hell on Sunday.

With a little squeak, Waverly's wife, Lady Jane, scrambled off her husband's lap. Or attempted to scramble. Her burgeoning belly made it an impossible task.

Waverly easily caught his wife, saving her from a fall.

Henry directed his horrified gaze toward the ceiling. Arriving unannounced and nearly upending the expecting marchioness. Expecting again. Waverly and his wife were now on their sixth child. "My apologies," he murmured.

"The Earl of Waterson," Chafter drawled.

From the corner of his eye, Henry caught the servant's lips twist in a slight smile.

He was so glad someone was enjoying this moment. "I can return tomorrow." After he'd sent 'round a proper request to his friend. After all, that would be the proper thing to do, and he was nothing if not proper. Or he had been anyway. Before the minx with a teasing glint in her eyes and a saucy retort falling from her siren's lips had entered his life.

"Do not be silly," Lady Jane chided as she swept forward. "It is always a pleasure."

Given the state he'd interrupted the pair in, Henry rather doubted as much. Nonetheless, he was grateful for that generous response.

"Chafter, have refreshments readied."

As he entered the room, Henry held a palm aloft. "That won't be necessary," he called to the butler, who'd already turned on his heel. The servant froze and looked questioningly to the marquess and marchioness. "I assure you, I don't require any refreshments," he repeated for his unwitting but not unwilling host and hostess. "I've come . . . on a matter of business." Henry himself heard the lie in that admission.

Husband and wife exchanged looks, and then Waverly joined the marchioness. Catching her palms, the marquess raised her knuckles to his mouth and placed a kiss atop them.

It was a shockingly intimate exchange between them.

Henry's own parents had barely set foot in the same rooms. When his father had been living, the late earl and his wife had carried out entirely separate existences. She'd entertained, while his father had spent his days in Parliament and tending business. As such, this . . . closeness his friend had found was anathema to anything Henry had ever expected or wanted in his own someday marriage.

Or that had been the case.

Now, he stared on as an interloper, knowing he had no right to observe their exchange but unable to glance away.

The pair spoke in hushed tones, their bodies angled toward one another as they hung on to whatever words they now exchanged as if they were gifts to be cherished.

Theirs was a closeness Henry had never before known.

And for one dizzying moment where time stood still, that pair morphed and shifted in his mind so that Henry saw another woman there—taller, with hair a paler shade of blonde. Clara—he imagined Clara, her belly swollen with child. And in his mind's eye, it was his and her child.

A sheen of sweat broke out on his brow. "Uh, yes, well, I'll just be a moment," he croaked, desperately needing Waverly's wife gone so he could have someone to help him make sense of all this.

Lady Jane flashed him another smile; then, cradling her belly in her palms, she left.

As soon as she'd closed the door behind them, Waverly faced him.

"I need help," Henry said without preamble.

"I trust there's some legislative matter that requires my immediate consult," his friend predicted, because, well, any other previous unannounced visit had pertained to Parliamentary matters. "What is the bill?"

"It is not a bill."

"The act, then," his friend corrected, heading back toward his desk.

"I need help with a woman. Or it is about a woman. What I meant to say is, the reason for my visit is because of a woman," he rambled. *Good Lord in heaven, I'm running on like a chatty gossip.*

Without missing a beat, Waverly shifted course and made a beeline for the well-stocked sideboard. The marquess himself had never touched a drink as long as Henry had known him but kept spirits for when he entertained guests. Pouring a glass of brandy, Waverly carried it to where Henry stood in the middle of the room. "Drink."

"I don't need spirits."

"Drink," Waverly repeated in no-nonsense tones, and well, hell, Henry did need some kind of liquid fortitude.

He tipped the glass back and downed a long swallow. The spirits burnt a path down his throat, and he grimaced. "It didn't help," he muttered, and took another sip.

"I trust this is your lady savior."

"One and the same." Swiping his spare palm down his face, Henry stalked over to the hearth and deposited his glass there. "I lied to her."

"Yes, you said as much. In the name of good. Your police force."

"It isn't my police force. It is intended for the whole of England, and . . ." And his own self-assurances fell on deaf, guilty ears.

"And you've realized too late that you care about the lady?"

His mind stalled. Care about her? Clara had saved him, and he now knew he'd been lying to himself. These feelings he had for her . . . about her, moved beyond those nights they'd spent together in her apartments.

"What did you do?" his friend asked quietly.

"I . . . may have promised her that her establishment would be safe to secure her cooperation in working with Lila."

"Oh, good God," Waverly muttered, collapsing a hip onto the curved back of his leather button sofa.

Henry winced. There was no hint of assurance there. But why should there be? He was in the wrong, with no possible way to make it right. Sighing, Henry proceeded to give an accounting of the deal he'd struck with Clara, one he'd made on a lie with the help of Lord Peerson. When he'd finished, Waverly remained in the same repose. Silent.

That silence was far greater than any words the other man might utter in condemnation.

"This is . . . not good," Waverly finally murmured.

"I know that," Henry exploded. "Of course I know that. What choice did I have? Abandon everything I'd set out to build, everything that might help make England safer, all because . . . because . . ." Of her.

He couldn't even bring himself to utter the rest of that. Because to do so would lessen Clara and what she'd come to mean to him. Unable to meet his friend's disappointed gaze, Henry turned to the fireplace and gripped the mantel.

"After this, you'll have your votes, then, and you'll have your police force. By your own admission, there's nothing more to speak about." Waverly was correct. Wasn't he? The floorboards groaned, indicating the other man had moved. "And yet, if that was true? And if you were content in the decisions you'd made to secure those votes, then you wouldn't have stormed my house at this hour, pleading for help."

Pleading.

That was precisely what he was doing.

Only, no one could absolve him of his guilt . . . or shame. His shoulders sagged. "I don't know what to do," Henry whispered into the dancing crimson and orange flames.

"You tell her," Waverly said quietly. "You tell her everything, Henry."

Abandoning his death grip on the mantel, he spun around. "And then what?" he asked pleadingly.

His friend gave him a sad smile. "That I cannot give you the answer to. That depends on you and what you want more: your legislation . . . or a future with this woman."

A future with this woman. Nay, a future with *Clara*. Clara, who made him smile and laugh and who'd opened his eyes to how he'd previously viewed the world and everything he'd failed to see through those flawed lenses.

Only what Waverly spoke of . . . was preposterous. It was impossible. Wasn't it?

"Ahh," his friend said with a slight, knowing incline of his head.

"What?" Henry demanded.

"You haven't yet decided if you want a future with the young woman. I trust it is because of her past?"

"No," he said sharply, too sharply. And he hated himself all the more for the thinly buried lie in that adamant denial.

The other man gave him a long, knowing look. "Either way, Henry?" Waverly clasped his right shoulder and lightly squeezed. "Your doing what is right and admitting your lie and abandoning your plans in Parliament—none of that should be dependent upon whether or not you have a future with the young woman. Your decision to do the right thing should only have to do with your doing what is right, for the simple sake of right."

Henry's throat convulsed. "For seven years, since Peterloo, a universal police force has represented the start and end of every goal I set forth. How do I just abandon that? How do I give it all up without . . ." Failing Lila. He'd concentrated all his efforts and all his energies into crafting legislation to bring about that body because it had been something within his power. Something he could do after Lila had returned broken and scarred.

"Do you truly believe your sisters, either of them, would want you to sacrifice your honor to create something out of your own sense of guilt?"

"Is that what you think this has been all these years?" That query ripped from his throat. "My acting out of guilt."

"I do, Henry," Waverly answered with an automaticity born of truth that could only exist between friends who were closer than brothers. "Just as I know, if you go through with this and don't confide all in Miss Winters, you'll never be able to live with yourself."

Henry returned his focus to the hearth, and the truth slammed into him.

I cannot do this.

Creating a police force at the expense of his honor . . . at the expense of what he'd shared with Clara . . . proved the line that he could not cross. Not even in the name of that honorable goal.

He needed to tell her . . . *everything* . . .

Now. Tonight. His gaze went to the hands of the mantel clock. *Soon.* "I have to go," he said, straightening. Henry held a hand out. "Thank you."

Waverly caught his in a firm grip and gave it a shake. "Any time you require help, our doors are open. And Henry?" his friend called after him when he'd started for the door.

He glanced back.

"Something tells me following your appointment with the lady, you'll require another talk."

His stomach lurched.

For damned if his friend wasn't right about this, after all. And with a sick combination of dread and anticipation swirling in his belly, he set out to see Clara.

Seated at the last row of the music hall closest to the center aisle of the Muses, Clara should be attending to her performers onstage.

Not long until opening night of the music hall, she should be thinking of nothing else but that important evening.

And yet . . .

She stole yet another glance at the double doors that emptied out to the foyer, and consulted the timepiece affixed to the front of her gown.

He was . . . late.

Late when he'd vowed never to again be late. Henry, who was a man of his word.

And she could not escape the periodic dread that traipsed along her spine. An impending sense of peril . . .

For the love of God, Clara, it is in the Dials . . . Do you truly believe you can have a respectable theatre in the damned Dials? Those streets, they aren't safe . . .

She'd judged him for that blanket disavowal, but the truth remained—he wasn't an indolent lord who spoke of that which he didn't know. Months ago, Henry had learned firsthand the perils that lurked in these streets. That lesson had seen him with a blade in his side and a broken nose, and had very nearly cost him his life. But neither had he believed his attack random. He'd admitted to having enemies. Ruthless men who'd thrown bricks through his window. Some unknown, nefarious people who sought to harm him.

Do not think of it . . . Do not think of him in danger . . .

It signified nothing. Or she tried to tell herself as much. Clara forced her attention to the frantic strumming of the string section of the orchestra and the pair of ballet dancers twirling across the stage in expert time to each note. They spun in dizzying pirouettes.

She felt him before she saw him or heard him.

Clara brought her shoulders back and turned in her seat.

Relief swept through her. *Henry. He was here. Safe.*

And the sight of him did funny things to her pulse.

Breathe, breathe. Just breathe.

The reminder was useless.

His silk hat in hand, Henry lingered in the doorway. She stared on, not allowing herself to blink so she could just drink in the sight of him. Henry, with his midnight coat with multiple cape collars and high neckline, was a study in elegance.

Smile at him.

Only, where was that coquette's grin she'd mastered and practiced upon countless men?

Everything was different with this man. She was different with him.

Clara curled her lips up in a smile that felt hesitant and shy to her facial muscles.

He returned that silent greeting, his smile the crooked rogue's one that fit not at all with the man she'd first met all those months ago. He'd changed. Softened. It was as his sister had said. He'd shed that austere shell and presented himself honestly before her.

She angled her head, urging him over.

Henry was already striding down the aisle and claiming the empty velvet upholstered seat beside her.

"You are late, Henry."

"Forgive me." His cheeks flushed with color. "I am sorry." Two apologies from this proudest of men? "There was important business I had to attend."

Clara softened her earlier rebuke with another smile. "I was teasing, Henry."

That troubled glint remained in his always-somber gaze, however. "Clara," he began.

She lifted a fingertip to her lips, silencing him.

"I would speak with you—"

"This is why I asked you here," she murmured over him. Poor Henry. He was still a study in such self-control that he'd miss the beauty around him. He followed her gaze to the front stage.

"Clara," he repeated with a greater urgency.

She touched that same fingertip she'd previously touched her own lips with against his. "What brings you joy, Henry?"

That gave him pause. "Joy?" His gaze seared her; it reached within her soul, and for a sliver of a moment, she thought he might tell her that she was responsible for some happiness. Hers was a foolish wish. "I don't . . . What are you asking?"

"What is something that you do or see or feel that moves you so deeply?" she murmured, leaning close so that their arms brushed. "So much of your life is work. It is your role in Parliament and of earl and devoted brother and son, but what is it that fills you with joy?"

She saw him thinking, saw the questions he had of himself running through his eyes that revealed so much. He was always thinking, in full control of everything, including his own thoughts.

"Close your eyes, Henry," she urged softly.

He hesitated a moment before complying.

Against his ear, Clara sang from La Cenerentola sotto voce. Reaching up, she loosened the clasp at his throat, freeing him of the cloak. The garment fell around his shoulders. His eyes still closed, Henry swallowed; his throat moved wildly. "Awaken sweet passion," she sang. "Nobody knows more than me."

"Clara." Her name emerged half groan, half plea. And he opened his eyes. When they met hers, the passion blaring from those depths sent heat rolling through her.

"Mm. Mm," she urged, lightly dusting her palm over his face until his thick black lashes swept down, those long silken strands tickling her fingers. "The magic of music, Henry . . . is that it moves one . . . if one allows those songs or strains to enter them. You have to allow it. You have to listen." She caressed her fingers through the curls tucked behind the shell of his ear. "Ah, non reggo alla passione, Che crudel fatalita!"

"Ah, I can't bear this anguish, what cruel fate," he translated the fluent, flawless Italian.

Of course he should know multiple languages. It was the way for those born to his station. Only, he commanded those tones with an ease and accuracy to rival any one of the opera singers who'd hailed from Italy.

This time, when he opened his eyes and turned to face her, she didn't compel them shut. Shifting onto her knees, she angled her body toward his. *"Al suo palagio vi condurra, si canta, si danzera,"* he echoed those lyrics in his deep, melodious baritone. *He will take you to his palace; there will be singing, there will be dancing* . . .

And with the world melting away but for the music at the front of the hall, and their eyes locked, she could almost believe he spoke to her—of them.

Lost in the lesson she'd asked him here for, she swung her feet back to the floor. Capturing Henry's fingers, she slipped her hand into his. He automatically wrapped his palm around hers.

They sat there, this time in silence but for the voices of the singers that swelled to the rafters.

"On the stage, through song," she eventually whispered as the performance continued, "a person of any station might imagine an altogether different world for themselves. A song, a dance, a piece played upon a string instrument or pianoforte isn't about work, Henry. It is about the emotion in here." Clara reached a hand over and laid it against his chest. "Deep inside, one feels because of music." Under her palm, his heart beat hard, an erratic rate . . . because of her touch.

"I had forgotten that," she said, regret infused in that admission. As she spoke, Tremaine Anderson's deeper baritone swept over the room, to her and Henry's last-row seats in the music hall.

"Eppur mi, die Speranza is sapiente Alidoro—Yet wise Alidoro gave me hopes—"

"I had initially seen the Muses only as my future and the security it represented and offered me and the men and women here," she explained, looking at him squarely.

Henry stared, his gaze trained ahead on the performance unfolding at the front of the hall.

"*Che qui, saggio e vezzosa*—that a bride judicious and charming— *degna di me trovar sapro la sposa*—worthy of me, I could find here."

"But you helped me see the truth, Henry," she said, bringing his gaze back to her.

"The truth?" he asked hoarsely.

"When I nearly lost this." Removing her hand from him, she waved it toward the front of the theatre where the performers still glided about the stage. "You reminded me of what I once felt because of music. After I'd taken my first patron, I looked upon this and this world with jaded eyes, forgetting the wonder and beauty to be found here. And that, Henry, is something that all people, in any and every part of London, are deserving of."

The small orchestra built steadily to a crescendo.

"Clara, I would speak to you about our arrangement—" he began in those formal tones he reserved for talks of business.

How much she'd come to know this man and the nuances around him.

She shook her head. "I did not ask you here for business, Henry. I asked you to come and just watch . . . with me."

For the remainder of the rehearsal, they sat side by side as the performers moved through each song and dance.

And she knew the moment Henry was lost. The moment the world had melted away and he'd forgotten even her.

Belle wrapped the lyrics in her flawless coloratura, the warmth and tenderness to those beguiling lyrics coming forward with a swell of emotion that was impossible not to feel.

Henry had shifted to the edge of his seat, and for all the splendor of Belle's aria, the joyous bursts of intricate vocal work, Clara could see only Henry.

> "In this moment, so many feelings . . .
> So many feelings stir in my heart."

"Rossini wrote it for his wife," she said in hushed tones so as to not shatter his connection to the performance before them. "What must it be to know love that great?"

That pulled Henry's gaze over; he caressed her face with that heated stare before he settled his eyes at last upon her mouth.

Heat unfurled in her belly; a wild fluttering danced there in rapid time to the song soaring around the theatre. Of its own volition, Clara's head tipped slightly as she angled her neck, and body, closer toward him.

With a groan, he covered her lips with his.

They made love with their mouths in a primitive meeting, stripped of all gentleness and infused with an unadulterated hungering, and Clara luxuriated in that rawness.

"And I have no words to describe the immense joy I feel . . ."

Catching his hand, she lowered it to her belly, needing his touch on her. All over her.

She swallowed a cry when he broke their kiss.

Only the Henry of old, the one who'd been unable to meet her gaze in her apartments over two months ago, now caressed a palm over her thigh.

Her breath caught as he kneaded the flesh, his an erotic massage. Every nerve ending came alive as he stroked her leg back and forth in long, sweeping caresses.

The seductive pull of the music, in time to his touch, sent a sharper ache between her thighs.

"I dared not hope for such happiness!"

Clara lifted her hips, undulating as a deep, sweeping need took over her.

253

His gaze forward on the performance unfolding at the front of the theatre, Henry guided her dress up. Each move so slight, so subtle, as he gradually exposed her legs; the smooth rustle of her skirts, as he drew the garment higher, played as a wildly erotic melody that sent blood rushing to her ears. Clara's breath came hard and fast as the cool air bathed her hot skin.

There was something so heady, so erotic, in being caressed with the music soaring around them and a whole other world playing out upon the stage.

Henry's breath came at a harsh, heavy cadence, indicating that he was as aroused as she was by the wickedness of their actions.

She luxuriated in the sounds of his desire. Emboldened by her own hungering, she inched her skirts higher and let her legs splay.

"Oh, what a blissful moment!"

"Oh, God." Henry's voice was a whisper of a prayer and plea that melded with the husky contralto soaring to the rafters.

Collecting his hand, Clara guided it between her legs. Henry's breath hitched. Or was that her own? Mayhap it was theirs together. All logic and reason and clear thought had fled, to be replaced only with the heightened sense of just feeling. The thin, sheer layer of her undergarments served as the only divide between his fiery touch as he cupped her there.

"Henry." She panted his name. Clara lifted her hips into his touch, both hating and luxuriating in the rub of her satin drawers. Henry slipped his hand inside the opening in that fabric, finding the tangle of curls there, already damp from the erotic game they played.

"Ah! Who would have expected
To find so much happiness!"

Henry slipped a finger between the nether fold of her swollen lips and mercilessly teased her sensitive nub.

Clara bit her lips to keep from crying out. Trying to remain upright in her chair, trying to attend the performance at the front of the theatre.

To no avail.

Her head fell back, and she closed her eyes and surrendered to those rhythmic strokes as he caressed her. Tormented her. He slid his fingers in and out of her sodden cunny.

She needed to touch him, to feel him.

Clara crept her fingers to the front fall of his trousers, where his shaft, hard and long, tented the placard. Air hissed between Henry's teeth as she stroked him through the fine wool fabric, and she reveled in his lack of restraint.

"I adore you like this, Henry," she breathed, loosening his buttons and freeing his member. His erection sprang free, enormous and rock hard. An adoring purr climbed her throat, as she wrapped her fingers around him. He was satin and steel and a burning sun combined.

"Hard?"

A breathy laugh escaped her. Still literal, even making love. "Yes, that, too." As she stroked his length, Henry groaned and slumped in his seat. All the while he arched into her touch.

"How then?" his strangled reply teased a smile from her lips.

Even in the throes of passion, he was very much Henry, polite conversationalist, too gentlemanly to let a statement go unaddressed.

She pumped his length in her fist, wringing another faint moan from him. "With your restraints down. Reduced to simply feeling."

But this was not enough.

Clara ceased her strokes, and his hips lurched at that denial. She tucked his length back in his trousers, buttoned them, and then took him by the hand.

"What?"

"Come with me," she enticed, leading him by the hand down the long row of seats until they reached the far-left corner of the theatre.

"Where are we going?" he rasped, and not breaking her stride, she angled a look back. Pressing a fingertip against her lips, she urged him to silence and continued leading him through the hidden lair that was her theatre.

Chapter 21

Henry had prided himself on being a master of self-control.

The sins and vices that had so weakened other men had never been ones he'd succumbed to. Instead, he'd scorned those weaker, pitiable figures, a sea of weak Adams falling in their own individual gardens of temptation.

Now, with his fingers tangled with Clara's, all but sprinting through the dark, empty corridors of the Muses, Henry understood the depths of temptation that had driven the first man to sin.

Because Clara was Eve with that crimson fruit dangling from her fingers, and he would dance quite happily a jig on the fiery path to his own damnation for another bite of it.

She paused beside a doorway and hurriedly let them inside.

They tripped over one another in their haste to enter.

Twining her arms about his nape, Clara pressed herself against him, and he filled his hands with her waist, pulling her close.

Their mouths met again in a violent dance. Their tongues tangled, each hot stroke a fiery brand that would leave Henry forever marked for the glory of it.

Clara ripped at the front of his jacket, and a handful of gold buttons popped free and clattered at their feet. Together they struggled to rid him of the garment. With a breathless laugh, she wound her fingers through his snowy-white cravat and tossed it behind him.

"You find amusement in this, love," he rasped against her throat.

"Lord Proper comes undone," she said on a throaty whisper that sent another surge of blood rushing to his shaft.

"I trust you prefer me this way?" he asked as she yanked his shirt from his trousers and drew the garment over his head.

"I prefer you every way, Henry March," she whispered. "Which is why I'm so damned terrified of you." With that avowal, she sank to her knees.

Oh, God.

The air hissed between his teeth as she helped him out of his boots. His trousers were next to follow, and then she took him in her mouth.

Bliss. Pure, unfettered, unapologetic bliss. This was the joy she'd whispered of in his ear. The feeling he only knew with her, in her arms.

"Clara," he pleaded as her head bobbed in time to the lusty sucks she took.

I'm not going to last . . .

Squeezing his eyes closed, he concentrated on anything other than the web of desire she wove.

To preserve and advance the honour and service of Almighty God . . .

Clara ran the tip of her tongue up and down his length, trailing that tantalizing pink flesh around the mushroom-shaped head of his manhood.

. . . virtuously disposed, and which (if not timely remedied) may justly draw down the divine vengeance on us and our . . .

The minx paused in her ministrations and lifted her passion-laden gaze to his. "Henry March, are you reciting legislation?"

"Trying to. Distraction," he managed, unable to utter a coherent sentence.

Her gleaming lips curled in a pleased smile. And this time, when she lowered her head to him, Henry shoved his foot behind him and pushed the oak panel closed.

Clara's sultry laugh shook her frame and filled her throat, and drawing her up, he kissed her, consuming that sound.

"What is it?" he asked, kissing the corner of her luscious mouth and then moving his quest lower.

"Closing the door and reciting English law?" Her words emerged husked with passion and gentle amusement. "You are ever so proper, Henry March."

"Oh, is this 'proper'?" he breathed against her throat.

The muscles moved under his attention as Clara swallowed hard. "A tad, b-b-but not unwelcome or unappreciated."

Catching the edges of her puffed sleeve, Henry guided the neckline down. "What of this?" he asked, freeing the generous swells of her bosom from the constraints of her gown. He paused. And another surge of lust rushed to his shaft. *No chemise.*

He caught the knowing siren's smile on her lush mouth. "Insufferable minx," he teased, and lowered his head to her breast. "What of this?" he asked before drawing the puckered tip of a mound deep in his mouth.

Clara's legs buckled, and she gripped him by the shoulders, keeping herself upright. "B-better," she praised, her voice threadbare.

"Well, that is not good enough," he murmured, shifting his attentions to the other tip. And then gathering both orbs, he pressed them together and laved each nipple, teasing, flicking his tongue back and forth until Clara's head fell back and that loose, artful curl bounced over her shoulder.

"M-much b-better," she panted.

"Bah, I've not done anything differently." Henry's teasing scold emerged raggedly. Catching one of the clever laces down the back of her gown, Henry gave a tug.

"O-oh, it is v-vastly different," she panted.

The back of her dress fell open, and he shoved the loosened garment down her shoulders, lower, past her waist, and it fell in a shimmery satin waterfall around them. "Is it?" He slid the garment lower over her hips.

"Y-yes . . . it is . . ." He filled his hands with her buttocks and massaged those generous swells. "It is . . . titillating," she managed to squeeze out as she arched against him. Those reflexive movements caused her dress to slip lower. "The illusion of two tongues working together."

That gave him pause at that erotic imagery she painted with her siren's brush. "Duly noted," he managed to croak, ridding her—ridding them—of her drawers, until at last she stood naked before him.

Henry drew back and drank his fill of her resplendent in her nudity. Her shoulders thrown back and her arms at her side, she wore her nakedness with a deserved pride. Henry stretched a hand out, trailing his fingertips along the swollen crest of her right breast. "So beautiful," he murmured.

Clara's chest rose and fell hard and fast, that slight change in the modulation of her breathing the only evidence he had any effect on her. She was a lush fertility goddess come to life to tame the weak, lesser men around her, and he would gladly humble himself for a taste of her.

Henry swept her into his arms and eyed the small quarters, searching for . . . and finding a small cot against the back wall.

He didn't want to think about why she had a bed here but gave thanks that she did.

Carrying her over, Henry deposited her onto the narrow mattress.

Clara pushed herself up onto her elbows and watched him through thick, golden lashes. And even through those passion-heavy lids, he saw the challenge there.

Seated at the edge, Henry held her gaze. He ran his palm down the expanse of her leg, then slid her slippers off, first one, then the other, and raised her right foot to his lips. "Do you know I've longed to kiss your ankle since you stood before me in St. Giles?"

"I did not know that," she said, faintly out of breath. "Do you admire all women's ankles, Lord Waterson?"

"Only yours, Clara. There is only you."

Her eyes went soft, radiating a tenderness that scared the hell out of him for the depth of that emotion.

And coward that he was, Henry redirected his focus to worshipping every inch of her exposed skin. Crawling onto the bed, he trailed a path of kisses up the length of her long leg; that satiny-soft limb went on forever.

Until he reached the apex of those golden curls that shielded the depths of paradise from view. He lowered his head and breathed deep of her musk, filling his senses with the gloriously wanton smell of her. Sliding his hands under her buttocks, he guided her closer to his mouth.

Clara lifted her hips a fraction as she angled herself upward, closer to him, but he held back.

"Tell me, Clara," he breathed against her silken curls, damp from her desire. "I must know."

A whimper, guttural and desperate, tore from her throat, and he thrilled at the sound of her desire—for him. Her gyrations took on a frantic rhythm.

"Uh-uh, love," he teased, even as the restraint from denying himself that which he craved sent a bead of sweat trickling from his damp brow. "This is where you ask what I must know."

"What must you know, Henry?" Those words tumbled from her, faintly pleading. Sexual repression coated her query in frustration.

"Is this proper?" he tempted, pressing a kiss to her mound.

"I . . ." She clenched her eyes shut.

"Still proper, then." He forced a sigh and then settled his face between her legs, slipping his tongue into her wet folds.

Clara cried out. Her elbows went out from under her, and she collapsed against the mattress.

A primitive masculine thrill of triumph went through him at the evidence of her desire. And he continued his erotic worship of her, suckling at the nub buried there until her incoherent half sobs, half moans soared around the room.

"Am I getting better, love?"

"Yes," she hissed. "Yes."

"Splendid." Henry darted his tongue in and out; her juices coated his tongue, and he feasted on the womanly taste of her.

"Henry, Henry," she cried, nothing more than his name falling from her lips. She tangled her fingers in his hair and anchored him close, with words and the glide of her hips telling him exactly what she craved.

And he obliged.

"I'm close," she wept. "So close. Please. Please."

He shifted so that he lay between her legs, and with a hoarse shout, he plunged himself into Clara's passage. She was soaked with her desire, and he slid deep inside.

She cried out and wrapped her legs about his waist. Not breaking rhythm, he began to move with hard and feverish strokes, and Clara met every frantic thrust.

She clung to him, biting at his shoulder like a wild mare, scraping her nails over his back, leaving her marks upon him.

Henry drove harder inside. Faster. He fought for restraint.

Reform their ill habits and practices, and that the visible displeasure of good men toward them may, as far as it is possible, supply what the laws (probably) cannot altogether prevent. And . . .

"You are perfection." Reaching between them, he found her with his fingers and caressed the top of her mound. "You are all that is beautiful," he said between pants.

"I want your mouth on me," she pleaded, already gripping his damp hair and guiding his head to her breast, claiming for herself that relief she so craved.

He suckled at the sensitive tip, worshipping that bud and wringing cry after desperate, keening cry from Clara's swollen lips.

"I can't . . . please . . . Clara," he begged, his thrusts becoming more frantic, unbridled.

And then she stiffened in his arms. She came with a piercing cry that rang in his ears and soared around the room. That sound of her release shredded the last of his control, freeing him.

Throwing his head back, Henry came in a blissful wave of ecstasy that went on forever. White light flashed behind his eyes as he was blinded to anything but her slick channel clenching and unclenching around his shaft.

Gasping, he collapsed, catching himself at his elbows to keep from crushing her.

They lay there, limbs entangled and their bodies sweating.

"Mmm," Clara moaned like a contented kitten as she brushed her lips over his temple. "That was magnificent and not at all proper, Lord Waterson."

A lazy, sated half grin played at the corners of his lips. "I am so happy to please you, Miss Winters." Flipping over, he drew Clara atop him so she lay draped over his chest. A tangle of golden curls fanned his chest, silken soft and bearing the hint of lavender.

And as he allowed his heart to resume a normal cadence, Henry just held her. No words were necessary as he ran a hand in a tight, slow circle along the small of her back. How right this felt: this moment. He and Clara together.

"You would be even perfect in lovemaking, Henry March," she murmured in sleepy tones that were so at odds with his suddenly alert mind. Her breath teased the light matting of hair upon his chest. "No doubt practicing until you mastered every inch of the female form."

He briefly stilled his hand's caress before resuming to stroke her smooth skin. "You were the first." As soon as that admission slipped from him, his hands tightened.

Clara stilled in his arms and then swiftly picked her head up. "What?" she blurted.

Heat climbed his neck. The lone lit sconce, however, kept the room bathed in darkness, and for that, Henry was thankful. "You were the first woman I've ever been with, Clara."

There was an audible intake of her breath, which he didn't know what to make of . . . or want to, and so he, Henry March, master of self-control, proceeded to ramble. "My father died when I was still at Oxford, and the moment I graduated, all responsibilities, they immediately fell to me: my seat in the Lords, my sisters, my mother. I'd vowed to not . . . to not . . ." He winced. Bloody hell, he sounded pitiable to his own ears. Henry tried again. "I vowed to wait until I'd married." Nearly every other fellow student had built reputations as carousers, gentlemen who'd bedded widows and actresses, and while they'd been carrying on those wicked existences, Henry had been singularly focused in his responsibilities. "But there was no bride. No marriage," he said lamely.

Clara scooted closer so their eyes met, and there was no escaping the directness of her gaze. Cupping his face in her palms, she took his lips in a gentle meeting. "Thank you," she whispered against his mouth.

He angled his head. "For what?"

"For choosing me when that gift you gave belonged to another woman."

A strangled groan choked off his response. He pressed a finger against her lips. "Do not," he said gruffly. "*Do not* lessen your own worth." She was everything that was honorable and good.

She gave him a gentle smile. "I'm a whore, Henry," she said without inflection, and it was that—the matter-of-fact acceptance of who she was . . . what she was—that cleaved at his chest.

He sat upright, and she tossed her legs around his hips so that she straddled his lap. "You believe your past is all that defines you, Clara." She made a sound of protest, and he continued over her. "That decision was made for you." It was why her control of her own fate mattered so much . . . and Henry had come to understand and appreciate that, too late. "The truth is, some bounder stole your options and maneuvered you down that path." And by her own admission, it was a decision she'd never wished to make. "You did what you needed to do, and there is no shame in that." Unlike Henry, who, for his betrayal, deserved every burn of self-hatred now tearing him up inside.

"Oh, Henry." She sighed, resting her forehead against his. "Having dedicated your life to being proper, you'd make me into something other than what I am."

"*Mm. Mm.* This is *not* about me." Mayhap once upon a lifetime ago, before this woman, her charge would have been accurate. No longer. Her past mattered not at all. Who she was, inside, was all that mattered. How could he make her see? "You are Schubert."

Clara sank back over her heels. "I am what?" she asked, perplexity coloring her voice.

"Not 'what,' but rather, 'who.' Schubert, the Austrian composer who—"

With a laugh, she swatted at him. "What are you on about?"

"You don't see, Clara." He caught her by the shoulders and drew her upright. They sat facing one another. "You have tucked yourself into a drawer, like Schubert's music; you speak of yourself as if you're somehow second to anyone, when not even the damned sun could compare with you in brightness. The same way Schubert underestimated himself is what you've done, and you are, you are," he repeated, caressing his palms down her arms, "superior to all, Clara Winters." One night with her would never be enough. He wanted forever.

His heart did a somersault within his chest. *My God, I—*

"I love you, Henry." A sheen of tears filled her eyes, and she blinked them back.

She . . . ? "What?" he whispered.

"I love you, Henry." Then ever so gently, she took his face in her hands and kissed him once more.

I love her.

He loved her strength and her cleverness and her ability to tease him. She'd opened his eyes to the narrow view he'd held of the classes and the world, and she made him want to be a better man.

Clara touched her lips to his chest. "Your heart is racing."

Of course it was . . . because she'd flipped his world upside down in every best way possible.

On the swift heels of that, reality came traipsing in, ugly and stark.

Their arrangement.

Nay, worse than that—his lie to her, which made moot everything they'd shared before.

As they settled onto the bed, Henry held Clara until she fell asleep. And there with her in his arms, he stared overhead at the plaster. She'd never forgive him for his treachery, but he had to tell her. She deserved the truth.

His throat moved.

Tomorrow. Tomorrow would be the beginning of the end of his happiness.

Chapter 22

In the nearly fourteen years since Clara had traded her career as an actress for one as a courtesan, she had never *slept* with a single lover.

Most had left after their lust had been slaked.

Many others had slumbered after they'd had all they needed from her.

But in those early hours, with those gentlemen sleeping in her bed, Clara would quit her rooms and take herself any other place but there.

Her decision had been a deliberate one. It had been a reminder that each relationship she'd had, each gentleman she'd allowed into her life, and whatever residence she called home at a given moment, was a temporary fixture.

There was no permanency to them or their role in her life.

Her connection to each one of them, including Ryker Black, the man who'd saved her, had been purely transactional, based on physical need and security.

"Until you, Henry March," she whispered. Clara stretched her fingers out and glided them through the dark, endearingly sleep-tousled strands that hung over his brow and cheeks.

Of course the one man she should have fallen so helplessly in love with and broken countless self-imposed rules upon should be a conservative MP. He'd proven himself different, not only from those starchy politicians she'd played mistress for but also from any man.

He drew in a light, shuddery snore. A faint shadow marred those perfectly chiseled cheeks, heightening his masculine appeal. She liked this side of him, even in sleep—relaxed. His guard down. "You are trouble for me, Henry. Pure trouble," she murmured, caressing his cheek.

Henry turned into that touch as if, even in sleep, he sought to be closer.

Clara let her hand fall and then lay down, once more.

Only, there was no closer than . . . this—what they'd shared.

And yet this was all they'd share. There was nothing more than this. Not for women like her. Not for anything between the two of them, together. Henry might have adamantly defended her honor and spoken of her worth, but the truth remained—he was first and foremost a respectable nobleman with a mother and two sisters' reputations to look after. As such, there was no place for Clara or a woman like her.

Nor did he give you words of love, as you gave him.

She bit the inside of her cheek, concentrating on—and welcoming—that sting.

Of course she hadn't made that profession expecting anything from him; those words she'd uttered only once in her life, and they had been for him. That did not stop her from wanting those words in return.

Nay, she didn't just want the words. She wanted them and everything that went with them.

I deserve them.

She stilled.

Henry had been right. All these years, she'd convinced herself that she'd accepted the decisions she'd made. But she hadn't. Not really. She'd kept her past as a barrier to keep others at bay. Accepting that honorable men didn't marry former whores meant that she'd also accepted that there was no other relationship she could expect from anyone.

You don't see, Clara . . . You have tucked yourself into a drawer, like Schubert's music . . . The same way Schubert underestimated himself is what you've done, and you are, you are . . .

Tears filled her eyes. No one in her life had felt that way about her, and because of it, she'd not allowed herself to see anything more in herself, either. Henry had helped her to see her own worth, not linked to his opinion or anyone else's.

And when their time together was done, that would be just one of the gifts she took with her. It would be enough.

"It has to be," she whispered into the silence.

Refusing to let reality intrude on these moments with him, Clara burrowed against his side. So natural, in sleep, Henry looped an arm around her and drew her close.

She closed her eyes—

When a shout went up from somewhere in the theatre.

Her eyes flew open.

Of course, yelling was not at all uncommon in St. Giles. It was not, however, a fabric of the business she'd built with the company of men and women performers.

"Ya canna simply come in here . . . ?" Anderson thundered, that bellow echoing faintly from down a distant corridor.

"Do you know . . . am?" Distance ate away part of that sentence.

"Ya 'ave to wait."

What in blazes? Clara darted over to the small armoire and dragged out a pair of drawers. She hurriedly stepped into the silk garment. Next, she grabbed the first dress her fingers touched. "Henry," she said on a loud whisper, "wake up."

A moment later, a light scratching sounded on the panel. "Miss Winters?" Collette called hesitantly.

With one foot in her gown, Clara froze. She darted her gaze from Henry to that oak panel. *Oh, bloody, bloody hell.* She hurried across the room. Clara took one slow, steady breath and then opened the door a fraction. "Collette," she greeted in surprisingly even tones.

"I'm sorry to bother you, ma'am—"

"No bother."

"But—" The young actress peeked over Clara's shoulder, and Clara drew the panel closer, cutting off any hint of a view. "Er . . . there's someone to see you."

"I don't have any appointments."

"Tried to send him away, ma'am?" Collette whispered. "But he seems like the important sort. Said he wasn't going until he spoke with you." Collette paused. "Something about the desistness?"

Desistness? Desistness?

"Or cesist . . ."

Clara's mind raced, and then she gasped. "Cease and desist."

Collette nodded. "Yea, ma'am. That one."

"Don't send him away," she said frantically. What business could she possibly have with him? Her business had been saved. "Tell him to wait."

"Anderson is with him now?"

Anderson, who'd been yelling at the gentleman. Clara swallowed a groan. "*You* wait with him."

With a snore, Henry flipped over, and the mattress creaked.

Collette directed her gaze to the ceiling. "I-I'll try and distract him, ma'am. But he said he won't be kept waiting, Miss Winters," she added as the door was closed in her face.

No, a powerful man wouldn't be kept waiting. Not for her.

There was, however, one certainty: as a proprietress, she could not be discovered in her offices in a state of dishabille . . . with a man who'd intended to shut her music hall down for impropriety. Indiscretions would be forgiven any man, but if a woman were caught in such a flagrant state, her business acumen and moral standing and honor were all called into question.

"Wake up, Henry," she snapped as Collette's footfalls petered off.

"What in God's name?" Henry mumbled, his voice heavy with sleep.

With her spare hand, Clara swiped Henry's trousers and shirt off the floor. "I admire your ability to sleep soundly, Lord Waterson, but if you can put these on," she muttered, hurling the rumpled garments at him. "Someone is here."

The lawn shirt hit him in the face. "I am certainly *not* a sound sleeper." His voice came muffled around the fabric. Henry swung his legs over the side of the bed, and Clara froze with her fingers clutching her dress as she drank her fill of him. Then he yanked the article from his face. "What was that?" God, he was magnificent in all his naked splendor. In the light of day, she appreciated the contoured planes of his chest, his flat belly.

"Someone is here, and you can't look like that." She grabbed her dress and, as she spoke, scrambled into it. "We cannot look like this. Here." She presented her back to him.

His fingers fumbled with the ivory pearls.

"Oh, bloody hell. I thought you had mastered buttons and laces," she muttered, stepping away as he'd secured several of them.

"I—*oomph*."

"Here," she repeated, shoving his garments at him. "Get up." She was already dragging him to his feet, and Henry struggled to retain hold of his sheet.

"I'm not waiting," someone said sharply from out in the corridor, those crisp, flawless English tones belonging to only a noble.

Henry froze.

"I'll see her myself."

The door burst open, and a rotund, silver-haired stranger stormed into her office with all the conceit of one who owned it.

"Good God." Henry and the unfamiliar gentleman spoke in unison, like horror wreathing their faces and voices.

All the color leached from Henry's cheeks, leaving him an ashen shade of grey.

Clara clutched her partially buttoned garment close. Bloody noblemen and their easily offended sensibilities.

"I beg your p-pardon," she sputtered, with a surge of indignant fury that had come from a lifetime of being seen as less to those of his exalted station.

She, however, may as well have been invisible.

The silver-haired lord reserved all his attention for Henry. "Ah, now it makes sense, Waterson," he said coolly, his gaze dripping with rage on Henry. Henry, whose naked form was hidden by nothing more than a sheet.

She puzzled her brow. Henry? "What makes sense?"

"Let us conclude this discussion somewhere else," Henry clipped out, his stare sliding briefly beyond the gentleman and over to Clara. The emotion there—regret, horror, fear—sent unease racing along her spine and, with it, an impending sense of dread.

"Who are you?" she asked flatly.

Finally, the stranger looked at her. "Who am I?" He peered down the length of his bulbous nose in a snub that had grown all too familiar. Henry had been the only nobleman who'd never looked upon her with disdain as if she were an inferior to him because of her birthright and past. "Viscount Peerson."

Lord Peerson.

Her tongue felt heavy in her mouth. Lord Peerson. This was the man who'd been behind the closure of her business, and the one Henry had relied upon for securing votes for his police force.

The viscount turned to face Henry, giving Clara a deliberate cut direct. "You must take me for a damned fool, Waterson," he hissed.

Henry took a step and promptly stumbled over the bottom of the sheet. "Not at all."

Lord Peerson blanched.

Presenting his back to the doorway, Henry released the white satin covering and struggled into his trousers.

"Telling me your relationship with the woman was because of your need to help your *sister*." A jaded, empty chuckle shook the other man's frame. "And here I was fool enough to believe that rot. And why shouldn't I?" He slashed his cane through the air. "None would ever dare suspect that the priggish, proper Earl of Waterson was all the while worried about pleasing a *mistress*."

Clara's shoulders went back. A mistress was what she'd been, and yet Henry had opened her eyes to her own self-worth, and she'd not be disparaged by this Lord Peerson—or anyone.

"That is not what this is. That is not how she is," Henry rambled, so at odds from a man in full command of . . . everything. "Miss Winters is not my mistress."

She curled her toes as that statement inadvertently brought the viscount's hate-filled focus back her way.

"*Of course* she's not." By the exaggerated emphasis on those two words, the viscount no more believed the veracity of that claim than he did Henry was fully attired.

Clara whipped her gaze back over to Henry. "What is the meaning of this?" she demanded of either man, even as terror unfurled in her belly.

It was falling apart.

Henry's life.

His happiness.

And, worse, Clara's trust.

And he was helpless to stop it. Even as Clara stood there with befuddlement in her eyes, it would soon give way to an understanding—and hatred.

He'd failed Lila, first at Peterloo, and then during the years she'd spent recovering from her trauma.

This failing, however, was different. This was one of his own making. One that had been preventable, and one from which there could be no absolution.

Panic swelled in his chest.

"I would have expected this from any number of rogues or scoundrels, but *you, Waterson*?" Lord Peerson spat.

"Expected *what*?" Clara's voice came slightly pitched with a timbre of panic in that question that cut through him.

"Clara, will you allow me a moment?" Henry asked, faintly pleading.

"Expected *what*?" she repeated, her tone increasingly strident.

Lord Peerson ignored her and took several long strides over to Henry. "I need a fortnight, you said. It's for my sister, you said. And when my wife and daughter discovered this woman leaving your familial residence, I assured them there was nothing at all untoward in her being there."

And yet, the other man had somehow discovered the truth.

"Only to arrive here and find your damned carriage in wait."

Henry made another attempt at having this exchange in private. Clara would learn the truth, but not like this. It couldn't be like this. *I waited too long.* "Peerson, I believe it best we continue this—"

"Alone?" Lord Peerson gave his cane another thump. "So you can feed your plaything some other lie."

Clara paled.

Rage pumped through Henry's veins, and he was across the room. Peerson took a hasty step back. "Miss Winters is no plaything," Henry seethed. And yet, from his state of undress—bare chested and attired in nothing but his trousers—what else would the other man believe?

Lord Peerson snorted. "The woman is a former madam, and by the current state of you and that bed, she is nothing respectable."

Henry caught him by his cloak and dragged him close. "Shut. Your. Mouth," he bit out. She was the first, last, and only woman he would ever love. He'd never deserve her, and he'd be damned before he allowed anyone to besmirch her.

The viscount's cheeks turned florid. "Unhand me this instant, Waterson."

Henry abruptly released the other man. Lord Peerson stumbled and then hurriedly righted himself. "What a touching display," he said coolly, smoothing his palms along the immaculate folds of his cloak. "Perhaps for another man, who was not supposed to be your father-in-law."

Clara drew in a shaky breath, and the pounding of his own heart in his ears muffled but did not blot out that sound. "What?" Coward that he was, Henry could not bring himself to look at her.

"Why don't you tell her, Waterson? Hmm? Tell her of the arrangement we agreed to."

"What arrangement?" Clara asked, her question threadbare.

His heart cracked in his chest. "Clara," he entreated, holding an outstretched palm toward her, "I can explain." Except it was another lie. He couldn't.

"He'd get your services, and I'd hold off on transferring your establishment to the rightful owner and ending your indecent plans for it. In exchange, he'd have his—"

"Police force," Clara whispered. She swayed, catching the back of the cane-and-carved chair at her desk, and kept herself upright.

His heart hammering, Henry took a step toward her, wanting to help her stand, but she leveled him with a black stare that went through him.

Lord Peerson nodded. "Precisely. He'd have everything he really wanted: the votes he needed in both houses and a music instructor for his sister. Or was that another lie?" he demanded. "Were there really any music lessons for your sister, or was that just another ploy to have this one in your bed?"

Clara's entire body jerked like she'd had a blade thrust between her breasts, and in a way . . . she had. *And I am responsible for that betrayal.* She looked to him, and in her eyes, there was a pleading there. One that asked him to counter every vile word that dripped from Lord Peerson's lips. Only, that was one gift he could not give her.

Clara glanced away, but not before hatred sparked in those depths, and it ripped a hole inside Henry's chest.

"Well?" Lord Peerson barked. "What do you have to say, Waterson?"

"What he has to say matters not."

Henry's and Lord Peerson's gazes swung to Clara.

"I want you gone," she ordered, ice coating that command. She was a proud Athena ordering about mere mortals, and so very glorious in her indignation.

The viscount pursed his mouth. "This is not done, Waterson," he vowed. He glanced once more to Clara. "But you are finished. Your den of iniquity here is through." With that, Lord Peerson marched off and slammed the door in his wake.

A heavy silence blanketed the room, tense and volatile like a life force, and neither Henry nor Clara moved. Time stood still, ceasing to mean anything. Minutes or millennia may as well have passed for the irrelevance of time. And even as the moment stretched on forever, Henry could not muster a single meaningful word for her.

"Is it true?"

Of course a woman who'd taken down his assailants and managed to bring his sister back to the living should also have the courage and strength to speak first.

"I never meant to hurt you," he whispered.

She chuckled, and this was a dark, cynical laugh he'd never once heard fall from her lips, and it shredded his already broken heart all over again. "How very unoriginal of you, my lord." *My lord.* It was that form of address that marked an end of intimacy and the fragile bond he'd not treated with the reverence it had been due. And it was another loss he'd forever mourn. "I never meant to hurt you," she spat. "Tell me, then: What did you intend, Henry?" Her throat moved spasmodically, that telltale evidence of how desperately she fought for control.

"There is nothing I can say—"

"Goddamn it, Henry, at least try?" she cried, flying over and taking him by the shoulders. She gave him a hard shake. "Try?" she begged.

"You were adamant that you would not take on teaching my sister. I believed the funds I'd give you would see you set up and safe somewhere . . . afterward."

Even as he said it, he heard the selfishness in them. They were words enough to inspire self-loathing. "I made a decision for you that I had no place making, but for seven years I was unable to help my sister, and you represented my one hope for her."

"Lies," she whispered to herself, her gaze going through him. "Everything was a lie."

His chest ached from the pain of losing her. *Nay, you lost her long before this moment.* "There was only one lie." He winced as soon as he uttered that dastardly admission.

Clara's eyes formed wide circles. "Oh, my, and here I'd begun to question your honor, Lord Waterson. Just one lie. One lie. One lie about my whole future and every dream I had." Grabbing his boots, Clara hurled one at him. It landed hard at his chest, and he grunted. She tossed the next, and the remainder of his garments followed. "Get out."

"Please, Clara. I—" *I love you.* Except those words had come too late. She'd deserved that truth long, long ago.

Her lip peeled back in a sneer. "You spoke of my worth and railed over the man who'd stripped me of my career as an actress and ruined my life. But you're no different, Henry."

His entire body jerked.

"You are no different from him," she repeated. "You took what you wanted and broke me down in the process." Then the fight seemed to go out of her; her shoulders sagged with a weight that Henry had put there.

"Get out," she cried, and then her tears fell. Those crystalline drops of her misery ran down her cheeks, unchecked, each one a token of his betrayal.

I will not survive this . . .

"I am so sorry," he whispered, stalking over to her. Wanting to fold her in his arms and make all this right. He reached for her.

Clara brought her arm back and cracked him across the cheek with her open palm.

He welcomed the sting of that deserved blow; agony radiated up his jawline.

Fire burnt from her eyes and scorched him with the hatred glimmering in those cerulean depths that had once radiated happiness. "I said get out, my lord." Her chest heaved with the force of her emotion. "We are done."

Not, *We are done here.*

But, *We are done.*

Numb, Henry backed out of the room; with every step, he kept his gaze on her. Committing each plane of her cherished face to memory. Wanting her. Needing her.

And ultimately leaving.

They were done.

Chapter 23

There wasn't a single drop left to cry.

Since Henry March, Lord Proper, had ripped her heart out and stomped it under the heel of his immaculate boot, Clara had been left empty.

Which, had she the energy for it, would have stirred a deserved fury . . . with herself. For everything she'd lost, for the dreams she'd had for the future, and for the hope she had for the Muses, for her, and for everyone else who was to have been employed by the theatre, it was Henry's betrayal that left this great, gaping hole in her heart.

"Fool. Fool. Fool," she whispered into the floral coverlet.

She'd always made missteps where men were concerned. Underestimating Lowery. Trusting Ryker Black. And now she could add Henry March, the Earl of Waterson, to that list of names she'd be content to never hear again.

She forced her eyes open, and her gaze collided with the same leaded-glass windowpane that she'd stared out of for the four years she'd resided in the Devil's Den. The thick, obscuring mist of the London fog shielded any hint of the night sky. From those dangerous streets of

St. Giles, the ribald laughter of patrons making their way into the club for the evening drifted up.

Her life was to have been different.

She wasn't to have lived in a place of vice and sin, but one where music was what drew men and women of all stations in.

And Henry had orchestrated both the theft and the lies surrounding the fate of her music hall.

Tears sprang behind her lashes and trickled down her cheeks. She'd been wrong. There apparently were more of those damned drops to shed. For a man who was so undeserving of them. "Damn you," she whispered into the pillow. Except having uttered the words more times than she could recall since that morning, they'd lost some of the sting and emotion. Now that curse was as empty as Clara herself.

A light rapping on her bedroom door filled the quiet.

Go away, she silently pleaded. *I don't want to talk about . . . any of it.* She wanted to forget all the ways in which she'd deluded herself into believing Henry could . . . and did . . . care about her. What was worse . . . even as she hated Henry March for his betrayal, she remained in awe of the love he carried for his sisters. He'd sacrificed the honor he held dear to see Lila happy. That depth of emotion she'd hungered for from him—but for herself.

"You're a damned fool," she mouthed into the quiet.

Reggie knocked again. "Clara?"

Clara rolled onto her back. She'd hidden away long enough. Reggie deserved to know all, not just because she was Clara's friend but also because she was Clara's business partner.

And I assured Reggie that everything would be fine. Clara had been the optimist and Reggie the realist, just as she'd said when she'd sought to warn Clara against trusting Henry.

There was another knock. "Clara?" Reggie called, her voice muffled by the panel.

Mayhap if she feigned sleep, the other woman would go away, and Clara would be spared from reliving everything that had happened this day and what all that misery meant for her future.

Reggie, however, had been patient, allowing Clara far more time than she deserved. Wiping her eyes and nose on the edge of her pillowcase, Clara forced herself to sit up. "J-just a moment." She stole a glance at herself in the cheval mirror. The pitiable creature with swollen, red-rimmed eyes and pale cheeks was a stranger to the woman she'd prided herself on being these past years. She'd made herself strong by keeping people at arm's length. Henry had been the one person she'd truly let in, a man she'd shared not just her body with but also every part of herself. Because of that misplaced trust, she'd become a shadow of her former self. Ignoring Reggie's call, however, would not undo any of those mistakes or regrets. "C-come in," she finally made herself reply.

Almost as if she feared Clara might change her mind, Reggie immediately let herself in. The young woman made to close the door, but she froze the moment her gaze landed on Clara.

Clara curled her fingers so tight her nails left marks upon her palms, and she braced for some pitying remark.

Reggie, however, simply closed the door with a calm Clara would never again be able to feign.

Folding her hands behind her, her only friend in the world leaned against the door. "Do you want to talk about it?"

"Not particularly." Clara attempted a smile, but her muscles failed at that basic task and her lower lip trembled.

"Doing so might help," her friend persisted.

And this time, a laugh exploded from Clara's lips. "Only an act of Parliament and the services of London's finest barrister would help."

"I wasn't referring to the Muses, Clara," the other woman said gently. Reggie moved away from the door and ventured over to Clara's side. "I was speaking about . . . him. The gentleman."

"Gentleman," Clara scoffed. "What does that mean, anyway? The name itself suggests that they are men who are gentle. But they're incapable of kindliness or even basic decency or humanity or—"

She caught Reggie's gaze, and Clara's diatribe faded on a sigh.

"May I?" Reggie murmured.

Clara nodded once and waited as the other woman joined her. And then Reggie looped an arm around Clara's shoulder and drew her close.

The dam broke once more.

Clara's shoulders shook with the force of her tears, her sobs silent as she simply took the support that her friend offered. There was no recrimination. There were no placating words. Reggie solely offered that quiet, unconditional support, and that loyalty wrenched the remaining tears from her.

Until they abated once more and only silence remained.

Reggie reached inside the pocket along the front of her gown and withdrew a white kerchief. Wordlessly, she held the scrap out.

Sniffling, Clara accepted that offering. She raised it to her nose but paused, her gaze caught on the embroidered initials there: *BK.*

Broderick Killoran.

Reggie's husband.

And I wanted that with Henry.

She hadn't allowed herself to truly acknowledge that, even to herself, but a place inside her that had still believed she was worthy of love and a future had wanted a loving, loyal husband in it, with children.

"He lied to me," she said softly, fiddling with the dry edges of the scrap of fabric. Clara went on to share everything with her friend, leaving nothing out and including every joyous moment to the last agonizing one that had cleaved her heart in two. "He made me a promise, on a lie to help me . . ." Nay, it hadn't just been Clara. "To help us."

When she'd finished, Reggie remained silent for a moment. "Oh, Clara."

Clara stiffened, braced for those hated words of apology. Reggie sighed. "Men . . . They are oftentimes ruthless and single-minded in their purpose. They'll do anything to achieve a goal they believe more important than any other in a given moment."

The other woman spoke as one who knew.

Reggie added, "Broderick was not dissimilar in his quest against me and subsequently you and the Muses."

"It isn't the same," she said, her tones deadened to her own ears. In fact . . . "It is *entirely* different."

"How so?" Reggie asked, leaning back on her elbows.

"You were friends long before you were anything else with Broderick." Once more, Clara wiped at the residual moisture on her cheeks.

"And you didn't, at any point in your relationship with the earl, consider him a friend?"

"No. Yes. No." Everything was confused in her mind. There'd never been any idea that she could or would have a friendship with any man. Every man she'd known had sought and claimed only the use of her body. Only . . . there hadn't been any intimacy with Henry . . . until just last evening. Their every kiss had been initiated by her.

Her breath caught on a quiet intake. He'd not simply wanted her for his own sexual pleasures.

On the heels of that dizzying realization, reality came crashing in.

Clara stared blankly at the window. "My relationship with Henry was only ever constructed on our mutual need of one another at given points in time," she said.

"Ah, that is right. He sought your assistance with his sister." There was a slight pause. "And he offered you ten thousand pounds to begin again."

Clara frowned. Did she imagine the undertones there? "Surely you're not defending his actions or my decision to help or not help?"

"I'm not doing any such thing," Reggie said, sitting upright. "There is no excuse for betrayal or treachery." She paused. "There are, however, sometimes reasons that help us to understand why a man like Broderick, or perhaps your Henry, might have done what he did."

Your Henry. "He isn't my Henry." Her voice faded. "He was never my anything." Furthermore, her heartbreak over Henry March was secondary to all those who'd depended upon her . . . including this woman.

"Do not," Reggie said sharply, almost simultaneously anticipating Clara's next words.

"I'm so sorry, R-Reggie." Clara's voice cracked. There were so many she'd let down, but this woman, who'd been like a sister to her, was the most acute part of her failing.

"Oh, stop it," Reggie said, giving her arm an impatient swat. "You'd think of me at this time? If you believe for one minute I'm worried about myself or the Muses, then you don't have that high of an opinion of me as a friend."

"The people dependent upon us? Upon the Muses? What of them?"

Reggie worried her lower lip. "Well, those individuals I am concerned about as well. But Broderick has promised to find placement for each employee until . . . until we sort all of this out."

And God rot her soul for being so very selfish, but Clara ached for the devotion and love of a good man who'd so fully support her and the dreams she had.

"Listen, Clara, you were the one who told me broken furniture could be fixed."

"This isn't just furniture," Clara said tiredly. *It is my heart.*

"And when I blamed myself," her friend went on, relentless, "when Broderick threatened to take it all and I told you that you were better off without me, what did *you* say, Clara?"

She'd vowed to stand by her.

"This is different," Clara said, flying to her feet. She began to pace. "I wanted this, Reggie. We deserved this. A new beginning from something we created without any help from Broderick or any man." And they'd been so very close to having that.

Reggie sighed and pushed herself to stand. "Oh, Clara. You still haven't figured it out."

Figured what out? She no longer could make sense of up from down.

"You showed me there was no shame in taking help where I need it, and yet you've lived your own life by different standards; you see it as a weakness in your own self to ask for or accept help. But needing support and being too proud to take it? That is what is truly weak."

Those words hovered in the air, ringing with a palpable clarity for the accuracy in them.

"Do you know what I believe, Clara?" Reggie murmured, drifting closer.

She scrubbed a hand over her cheek, still damp from tears. "What?"

"You've hung everything upon this location. It has come to symbolize your desire for control when you, and I, and so many in these parts of London are without." Reggie offered a gentle smile. "But this? This isn't *really* about the Muses as much as it is about the Earl of Waterson and your broken heart."

A denial sprang to Clara's lips.

You've hung everything upon this location . . .

Only there was truth to so many of her friend's words. Clara had sought control above all else. After Lowery had destroyed her career and future, she'd craved a semblance of mastery over her life. And she'd been so very close to it . . . until Henry had ripped it from her grasp.

To help his sister . . .

It had never truly been about Clara, and selfishly, she'd wanted that level of devotion.

Nay, you wanted it from Henry.

Reggie gave her a sad smile before starting for the door. "Oh, and Clara?" she asked, her fingers on the handle. "I will forever hate what the earl did, but if you love him, I have to believe you saw something good and honorable in him, and mayhap he can be . . . redeemed."

Redeemed. Clara balled her hands into tight fists. "When the late Queen Caroline is resurrected and reconciles with her sod of a husband."

Reggie's lips curved in a slight smile. "Well, that is certainly inventive and emphatic."

And why shouldn't it be? She'd given Henry her heart, and he'd taken that special gift and stomped it under the heel of his exalted boots. All the while, he'd had intentions for another woman. A respectable lady with noble blood running in her cold veins. Which had always been Henry's fate.

Oh, God.

"I am so sorry, Clara," Reggie said gently.

"Thank you . . . for everything."

Her friend lingered as though she wished to say something more, then let herself out.

After she shut the door behind her, Clara remained motionless in the middle of the room, unbreathing.

And then in the still of only her own company, the depth of all she'd suffered . . . and lost . . . hit her all over again. Clara sank down slowly and drew her knees close to her chest. Looping her arms around them, she rested her chin on the smooth satin skirts.

She didn't want to think about the fact that Henry had made the decision he had for a police force that would make London safer . . . or for the sister he loved so much he would have lied for her.

"Don't you do that," she whispered. "Do not make excuses for him."

And yet, as she sat there in silence well into the night, she hated that a part of her loved him for being a brother who'd sacrifice even that deeply held honor he so prided himself on.

Chapter 24

His head was pounding.

As Henry forced bloodshot eyes open, his gaze collided with a blurry stack of ledgers.

He blinked back the lingering effects of too much drink.

To no avail.

He slowly closed his eyes once more and attempted to straighten—without success.

The pounding persisted.

His cheek still pressed against his desk, Henry winced, then forced his head up.

Even that slight effort proved excruciating. He touched a hand to his temple.

So that was the source of the pounding.

His stomach promptly pitched, and he drew in slow, steady breaths to keep from vomiting.

Good God, he was dying. This agony hammering away at his head was going to kill him when even London street toughs hadn't managed the feat.

Except . . . with that, the memory of Clara came rushing back in and, with it, the pain of losing her and the only joy he'd ever truly known in his life. With a keening moan, Henry rested his forehead against the surface of his desk—and then promptly regretted both of those actions.

KnockKnockKnock.

Nay, that pounding was different from the skull-crushing agony left by his drunken stupor.

Someone was at the damned door.

"Get the hell out," he called weakly, and his gut roiled all over again. He didn't want to face anyone.

"Excuse me, my lord?"

Sacked. The other man was asking to be sacked.

Mustering a reply to that query from the until-now-loyal servant proved wholly beyond Henry's abilities.

"I hesitate to interrupt you."

The servant already had.

"And I wouldn't dare persist in knocking unless I'd absolute reason to do so. Particularly as you said last evening that under no circumstances were you to be bothered . . ."

Through those ramblings, Henry closed his eyes again. Mayhap they'd been looking for the wrong culprit all along. Mayhap the person who'd tried to off Henry resided under his damned roof and answered to the name "Wright."

"My lord?"

Henry squinted. At some point his butler had stopped talking. "What?"

"It is just that . . ." Wright lowered his voice to a whisper that was largely lost to the oak panel. ". . . arrived."

What in hell was the fellow talking about? He wasn't expecting anyone. He . . .

Heart racing, Henry sat up so quickly the room spun and the throbbing in his head temporarily blinded him. Clara.

And ignoring the holy torture that was his head, he jumped up and raced across the room. He yanked the door open, and Wright tumbled inside.

"Where is she?" Henry rasped. "Why didn't you show her in immediately?"

"Uh . . . they're only just disembarking from the carriages."

The carriages?

They?

Henry's heart plummeted. "*Who* has arrived?"

Wright stared back with abject confusion in his eyes. "Why, Her Ladyship, the Countess of Waterson."

"My mother," he repeated dumbly.

Wright nodded enthusiastically, smiling like Henry had solved an impossible puzzle. "Precisely, my lord. Her Ladyship, along with Lady Norfolk."

His sister had arrived, too? "Lady Norfolk?" he said too loudly and winced.

"Your sister, my lord. That is also correct." The carriages had arrived sooner than Henry had expected. "I thought you should know." He sniffed the air and then nudged his chin none too subtly at Henry. "Immediately."

"Tell them I'm seeing to business," he said tiredly.

"Very well. Very well." Wright repeated that telltale echo that marked his nervousness.

The last thing Henry cared to do was indulge his mother's questions and demands over the damned title and need for heirs and a spare and a proper wife. And then he said, "I need a drink."

Wright blinked several times. "I'll see a tray of coffee is . . ." The other man's voice faded as Henry walked over to the sideboard. "Is . . . is . . . it is brandy *you require*. Uh . . . yes. Yes . . . of course." His suddenly loquacious butler paused. "At ten o'clock." Another distinguishable beat. *"In the morning."*

In response Henry reached for a bottle. Wright's rambling faded to a distant hum in his ears as Henry picked up the bottle of whiskey.

"Maybe you are daft, after all," Clara breathed, and took a long drink of whiskey.

Henry drew the decanter close to his chest and cradled it as he let the memory of the night she'd stormed his offices slip back in. "Wh-whiskey," he whispered, his voice breaking. *Oh, God.* She was everywhere, and until the moment he drew his last breath, he would carry the memory of her and them together.

"Ahem," Wright said, clearing his throat. "Is there anything else you require?"

Clara Winters. A chance to begin again. "Nothing." With a ragged sigh, he yanked the stopper out and tossed it atop the sideboard, where it clattered against another bottle, the crystal ringing and compounding his devilish headache. "Just be sure Her Ladyship does not . . . pay me a visit."

His butler hesitated, and for a moment Henry almost expected the servant to debate him on the propriety of failing to greet his just-arrived family. And more than a small part of him wanted that. Henry wanted to be seen and treated not as an earl or MP or stodgy gentleman, but as just any other man. His stomach muscles spasmed. *The way Clara was with me.*

"As you wish, my lord." With that, Wright bowed and hurried off.

The moment he'd gone, Henry finished pouring his drink. His butler had been correct in his opinion. Henry *should* meet his mother and sister and new nephew at the front steps. He *should* be properly shaved, bathed, and in finely pressed garments.

There was, however, a whole host of things he *should* have done these past weeks . . . and he'd failed there.

Soon, he'd transform himself back into the son and brother and earl they and the world expected. But not now. Now there would be whiskey. More of it.

And then, God willing, a blissful slumber from the pain ravaging his damned head.

With his glass in one hand and the whiskey in the other, Henry found his way to the corner of his office.

He set the decanter down and then claimed a spot on the sofa; the Italian leather groaned as he kicked his legs up onto the fabric. Then, resting his glass atop his chest, Henry turned his face toward the fireplace and stared into the crimson-and-orange flames dancing before him. At some point when he'd been asleep at his desk, a servant—likely Wright—had found his way in to stoke the fires. Heat radiated from the fireplace, bathing Henry's office in a comfortable warmth.

It was the simplest of luxuries, and yet . . . it wasn't. Not truly.

A warm household and a regularly tended fire had just been a comfort he'd taken for granted. He, as Clara had rightly charged, had never paid proper thought to the men and women who were born outside the peerage. Oh, many had benefited from legislation he'd written and pushed through to a vote. But he'd not seen them as people. He'd not considered what life was truly like for those who lived in St. Giles and the Dials, scraping to survive and walking streets that were riddled with danger.

Until Clara.

Clara, who'd not only saved him but also cared for him in her modest apartments. She'd faced adversity and fought for her security and future, struggling in ways he never had nor ever would. And all because he'd been fortunate enough to have been born into the nobility.

And had it not been for her, he'd have continued to be the same self-righteous prig she'd accused him of being.

Angling his head up, Henry took a long drink of whiskey, welcoming the burn of the liquid as it streamed down his throat. He'd not gotten soused enough last evening. The pain of his mistakes and regrets was as sharp now as it had been then. He rested the glass against his breastbone once more and closed his eyes, cowardly seeking the brief escape that had come from his drunken stupor.

Boom.

The sharp crack of the door striking the wall brought Henry jerking awake. His glass toppled sideways, soaking his shirt and staining his sofa.

Bloody hell.

"Have a care, please," he muttered, rubbing at his temples—to no avail. Wright was useless. Utterly useless. Though in fairness, when the countess was in one of her tempers, not even the king himself would have been able to silence her. Henry, however, had never found himself the recipient of her maternal ire—until now.

"What is the meaning of this, Henry Winston James March?" his mother demanded, and in an act he would wager his soul was a deliberate statement on his previous request, she slammed the door. Those reverberations sent a fresh round of misery to his head.

"Mother," he drawled.

Yanking her gloves off, she stalked over. "The last thing I should expect was to find—" She blanched. "My God, you smell like . . . you smell . . . like a bottle of spirits."

"In fairness, you did startle me into dropping a glass of whiskey upon myself."

"Whiskey?" his mother squawked in shrewish tones that were surely a mother's revenge against a drunken son who'd consumed too many spirits. "Whiskey? Gentlemen do not drink whiskey. You do not drink whiskey. You do not drink any spirits."

There was no avoiding this meeting. "No," he agreed, and reluctantly swung his legs over the side of his seat. The situation, however, had merited a good sousing.

"What have you done, Henry?" his mother asked, pleadingly. "What have you done?" She yanked a note from the front of her gown and thrust the paper at him.

He cringed. "Egads—"

"Oh, hush your mouth, Henry. If you're drunk on whiskey and smelling like a distillery, then you aren't permitted offended sensibilities." She lowered her voice to a much more forgiving whisper. "Furthermore, desperate times call for desperate measures."

As such there could be no doubting the subject of the note in his hand. Henry unfolded the page, but before he could read, his mother launched into him.

"You were bringing a courtesan into this household, Henry. Allowing her near your sister. And . . . and . . . you were caught . . . caught . . ." If his mother's cheeks flamed any redder, she was going to set her hair afire.

So Peerson's first act had been to involve the countess.

His mother sank onto the chair beside him. "But Lord Peerson has been gracious enough to allow you to make it all right."

Make it all right?

Furrowing his brow, Henry at last read the note.

> We came to an agreement about our children, Hettie.
> Your boy, however, has been fraternizing with a courtesan. Lord Peerson had the horror of seeing with his
> own eyes the pair of them engaged in flagrante delicto.
> We've managed to convince Dorinda nothing untoward has happened. Your boy better not blunder this
> again. Get. Home.
>
> With Sincerest Respects,
> Lady Peerson

There it was, his circumstances as they'd appeared to the world, laid out for his mother. And even knowing what they did, Lord and Lady Peerson would still seek a match between their cherished daughter and Henry.

If I were a father, I'd cut the bounder with the ancestral March broadsword for daring to hurt my daughter . . .

A girl who'd have pale-blonde tresses like her mother.

Oh, God. He wanted that future. He wanted Clara as his wife. And children. He wanted children with her. Only her.

"You should look as though you're going to cry," his mother said flatly. "Shameful. Just shameful what you've . . . done in my absence." His mother took the note from his hand, and carrying it over to the hearth, she tossed it into the flames. "Now," she said as she turned back, calm enough to rouse a deserved suspicion, "I will not lie and say I am not disappointed in you, Henry. Very disappointed."

Odd—it was the first time in his nearly forty-two years of life that she or his late father had ever uttered those words to or about Henry. And yet . . . her opinion on this didn't matter. His own disappointment in what he'd done, and the treachery he'd enacted, was sharp enough to wound.

"But I . . . understand it," she murmured, returning to his side.

She . . . ? "What?"

"You are proper, but you are still a man. As such, this courtesan you've taken up with has quite captivated you. As long as you use discretion, your wife, and the world, will understand. But carrying on as you have been, Henry?" She shook her head. "That must stop."

Fury pulsed within him; it brought his hands curling and uncurling. "Clara."

His mother angled her head. "Beg pardon?"

"Her name is Clara Winters, and she is no courtesan."

Holding her hands up, his mother stumbled away from him. "Oh, my goodness. Oh, my goodness." Horror filled her eyes. "Do not say it. Do not—"

"I love her," he said quietly, coming to his feet. "And if she would have me, I would—"

"*La-la-la.* I cannot hear you. I do not hear you," she repeated in a singsong voice, her hands clamped over her ears.

"Look at me." When she gave her head a firm shake, he repeated those words on a sharp command. "I said, look at me."

Shaking, the countess let her arms fall to her side.

"I'm not marrying Peerson's daughter. I love Clara, Mother," he repeated. "She came into this household, even as she didn't wish to, and helped Lila. Lila sings and plays again. And takes breakfast with me and teases."

"What?" she whispered, pressing a fist to her mouth and catching a sob.

He nodded. "Clara . . . Miss Winters . . . provided music lessons, and she is the person we have to thank for Lila's return." After the hell she'd seen and been part of at Peterloo, his sister would never be completely healed, but she was journeying back to the living. And it was all because of Clara.

"Why didn't you tell me?"

Because she would have asked questions about whose services he'd employed with her cherished daughter, and she'd have never been content without herself meeting the person working with Lila. "I thought it best you see for yourself when you returned," he settled for.

Tears filled his mother's eyes, and ever the too-proud countess, she presented her back to Henry and discreetly dabbed at the corners. Several moments passed before she faced Henry once more. And gone were all hints of vulnerability, as her mask of aloofness was firmly back in place. "I am . . . grateful to this woman, but that does not change her past, or her unsuitability, or the fact that you have an obligation to Lady

Peerson's daughter and the goals you set out for yourself in Parliament. See to it, Henry."

And uttering those words as a command, she swept out.

See to it.

Which was a thinly veiled alternative of, "Marry Miss Newton." Marry where his heart was not engaged. Marry for political reasons and legislative aspirations. And in fairness, those goals would have once taken precedence over all—particularly marrying for love. Simply, he'd not allowed himself to think of a marriage as anything more than a business transaction.

Only to find out too late that the only way he wanted marriage was with a woman he loved, respected, and admired.

There was a light rap at the door.

Before he could call out, the person on the other side opened it a fraction. Lila dipped her head in. "May I join you?"

"Of course," he said quickly, coming to his feet. "Mother was—"

"Looking for me? Yes, I know. I took the opposite corridor," she said as she closed the door behind her.

And then it occurred to him: Clara. Lila's lessons. He'd not told her that those had come to an end. "Lila," he began.

"Miss Winters is no longer coming," she interrupted, joining him at the sofa.

He hesitated.

"I gathered as much when she didn't arrive this morn, and then there was your . . . conversation with Mother."

His heart spasmed. "Oh, Lila. I am so sorry."

"For what?" she asked matter-of-factly.

Puzzled, he stared back.

"Are you upset about not having told me? About my lessons with Miss Winters ending?"

Henry dropped his head into his hands. "All of it," he whispered. What had become of him? He'd been a master of self-control, his life ordered. Now, he was responsible for disappointing all those who mattered most to him, those he loved: his sister. Clara.

Lila inched closer. "And what of Miss Winters?"

"What of her?" he asked tiredly.

"Are you sorry for having deceived her? By the stench of you and your untidy state, I'd venture yes."

He sucked in a breath. Yet again she'd heard more than he wished to discuss with her—or anyone.

"Henry, I've learned to move with the shadows. There are no secrets in this household." She gave him a long look. "None."

His neck heated.

"You hurt her." It was a statement, and coming from his sister, it hurt all the more for the disappointment in her tone. He was a constant disappointment to her.

Henry briefly closed his eyes. *You are no different from him . . . You took what you wanted and broke me down in the process . . .* "I did."

"Because of me," Lila said flatly.

"No." Henry's denial tore from him, and he ignored the sharp stabbing in his skull at having raised his voice. He'd not allow her to try and own his sins. "This is not because of you." He was the sole person responsible. "This is because—"

"You were wanting to help me at all costs." Lila caught his fingers and gave them a squeeze. "But you still haven't realized, Henry . . . you like an ordered existence and want life to be and go a certain way, but you have no control over that. None of us do."

Her words ran through him, freeing, feeling very much like . . . an absolution.

"You can only control what type of person you are and how you live your own life."

A pained chuckle rumbled from his chest. "In changing, one cannot undo"—what he'd done to Clara—"what's come before."

"No," Lila said simply. "But you can also try to earn forgiveness and start again."

She was speaking of him and Clara, raising the possibility of the life he wanted but didn't deserve with her. "Not in this. Not in what I've done."

"You're not one who simply quits, Henry. The same way you were resolved to have your police force, you shouldn't give up on the hope of Miss Winters or of helping her keep her establishment."

He froze as those words cut through that place of regret and self-pitying. He'd been so agonized over losing Clara and fixed on the wrongs he'd committed against her that he'd not considered any other option to help her take on Peerson.

"There," Lila said with a smile. "That is much better. Now, I have an idea for you to win back your Miss Winters."

He whipped his head so he could face her squarely.

His youngest sister let out a bemused smile. "There was a time when you'd never speak with me or Sylvia or Mother on matters of import. I prefer this new version of you, Henry."

It was all because of Clara. He'd spent so many years trying to protect the females in his life that he'd never allowed them a place to use their voices as they deserved. "I'm listening now. What is your plan?"

"I—"

Whatever sage advice his sister intended to give was cut off by a hard knocking at the door.

Crying out, Lila jumped up and raised her arms protectively over her head.

"Quiet," he bellowed in a bid to halt that frantic rapping, and at last the infernal thudding stopped.

"M-my apologies," Wright's voice came, muffled.

Despite that immediate cessation and the silence ushered in, Lila continued to quake.

Oh, God. A weight crushed his chest at that unnecessary and always visible reminder of how his youngest sister had been forever altered. "Lila," he said quietly.

Shaking and huddled into herself, his youngest sister finally picked her head up. She stared at him through half-mad eyes. "Henry," she whispered, "I'm so—"

Rap-Rap-Rap.

She jumped. "Answer it," she said with a surprising calm in her voice.

"It doesn't matter. Whatever business Wright has can wait." Would he have ever before placed his family above whatever business he had? Had he even sat and spoken with his sister until these past weeks?

Rap-Rap-Rap. "My lord?" Wright called again.

Damn it all to hell. Stalking across the room, he reached for the door handle. "Bloody hell, someone had better be dead or dy—oh . . . Steele."

The hard-eyed detective stared back.

Wright swallowed loudly. "I am ever so sorry to bother you, my lord. However, Mr. Steele"—the butler motioned to the man beside him as if the point needed clarifying—"insisted he speak with you. I—"

"I would speak with you about . . ." Steele paused, his gaze going to Lila.

Henry followed his stare. Aside from Clara, his sister had ceased all engagements with . . . anyone. And for all the progress she had made with Clara, his sister was still only just finding her way back to the living. "Will you excuse me a moment?"

Wordlessly, his sister sprinted from the room, dashing past Steele.

"Come in," Henry urged, starting for the sideboard. "May I—"

"I've determined the identity of those behind your assault." The detective had never been one for wasting time with niceties.

Henry spun around. From the time he'd spent with Clara to the moment yesterday when he'd lost her, Henry's thoughts hadn't been on himself or the nameless enemy responsible for his attack. Except now his foe wasn't nameless. "Who?" he demanded, stalking over.

"A wealthy slaver." A memory stirred. . . . *He was a slaver, dealing in the sale and purchase of human flesh, and saw women no different . . . And so when I rejected him, he did what any man with influence might do: he saw me barred from all of Covent Garden and Drury Lane . . .* "He's made his fortune in the sale of human flesh and has a deep-seated distrust and resentment of the peerage."

It was because of Henry's legislative attempts to abolish the slave trade.

His gut churned.

And yet . . . there was something he could not shake.

"Who is he?" he asked, his voice slightly hoarse.

"Terrence Lowery. In my search into the gentleman and his past," Steele went on, "I discovered he has links to a woman of your . . . acquaintance."

The floor fell out from under him. "Oh, God," he exhaled his horror.

Clara.

His skin broke out into a cold sweat.

"A Miss Clara Winters." Henry's heart lurched. "It would appear the gentleman has harbored resentment toward the woman for some years . . ."

A patron was determined to have me, and when I wouldn't be had, he used his money and his influence against me . . .

"And I believe there's reason to be concerned for Miss Winters' safety."

Oh, God.

She was in danger.

Thundering for his horse, Henry raced from his offices.

He needed to find her.

Chapter 25

Goodbyes had never much bothered Clara.

As one born to the stage, she'd been accustomed since birth to people being transient, moving in and out of her life. Time with anyone and in any place was fleeting. That had held true in her years as a courtesan.

This goodbye, however, proved the hardest of all.

The slight taps of her heels echoed off the walls as she walked the rows of the Muses.

There were no singers and dancers rehearsing for their performance—a performance that would never be.

There was no bickering between Old Maeve and Anderson.

There was just an eerie, empty silence.

Sheets of music lay upon the stage as if they'd been hastily abandoned when the Muses had fallen apart once more.

Clara continued walking until she reached the front row and then sat. Closing her eyes, she breathed deep of the crisp finish on the parquet floors she'd been so insistent upon. Fresh paint. The faintly stinging bite of apple cider vinegar, which had been used to clean the residual dust left by the builders.

It was over.

"Before it even began." She spoke into the quiet, her voice bouncing around the empty theatre.

Those archaic rules would subvert her property rights over to the gentleman who'd sold her the place, and then he would undo all this. And somehow that ownership had bypassed Broderick, reverting over to the proprietor before him.

"It's because of whomever is in control," Clara said tiredly into the quiet, needing to hear her own voice so she knew she wasn't alone. Whoever their nameless, faceless foe in fact was, this had been the desired outcome all along. And if they fought, that battle would drag on, with only Clara and Reggie losing funds, and then in the end, they'd lose their fight, anyway. The laws and rules could always bend but they could only be bent by the ones truly in power. And no matter how much money they had, people of her and Broderick and Reggie's station invariably failed.

She'd blamed Henry for this loss, but the truth was, all the world was to blame. The world that established their one-sided laws in favor of men and those of the highest stations. They were the ones who profited and thrived, and the rest of the people, the majority, got by as well as they were able. He'd lied to her, but he'd also spoken on her behalf. He'd tried—and failed—to secure the votes necessary to keep the Muses open.

Nay, it wasn't the closure that she blamed him for—but the lie.

"It would have been wonderful."

Clara glanced back.

Reggie stood at the doorway with Broderick at her side. The couple exchanged words for a moment; then Reggie hurried down the aisle.

"I thought you weren't coming back," Clara said as Reggie took the seat next to her.

"I wasn't going to." Reggie loosened her fichu and let it fall. "I'm rubbish at goodbyes."

Clara laid her head along the back of her chair and stared at the enormous crystal chandelier directly overhead. "Yes, I know something of that."

Her friend rested her head in like repose. "I wasn't going to come, but it felt important to look at this, at what we did, so that we both know."

Clara glanced at her friend.

"That we did it once and we can start something from the floor and build up all over again."

We?

A frown puckered her friend's mouth. "Surely you didn't believe I wasn't going to warrior on to our next venture?"

"I . . . I . . ." Clara's gaze fell to Reggie's swollen belly, and the other woman's hands went to cradle that place where her child rested.

"You believed because I'm married to Broderick and expecting a babe that I shouldn't involve myself in business?"

"Well . . . well . . . that is generally the way." For women of Reggie's wealth—they didn't generally take on any work, either before and certainly not after a child was born.

Reggie scoffed. "Why can't I do both?"

"You can do anything, Reggie."

"We can." She paused. "And we shall." Reaching inside the reticule on her lap, she fished out a note.

"What is this?" Clara asked, already reaching for and unfolding the letter.

"They are properties that are both vacant and available for purchase in both the Dials and St. Giles." Reggie sat forward in her seat. "More importantly"—excitement threaded through her friend's words—"it

304

includes very specific workarounds that would see us fully compliant with the—"

"Proclamation for the Encouragement of Piety and Virtue," they both said as one.

"Yes, yes. Precisely. This is how we begin," Reggie said, stabbing a finger at the page.

Clara read the detailed provisions contained within the note, and she felt that rare-for-her sentiment—*hope*. And for all these years she'd spent resenting Broderick Killoran, she'd been proven wrong once again where the proprietor was concerned. "Who did Broderick—"

"Broderick did not do that."

Clara paused halfway down the page and looked up. "What?"

Reggie shook her head. "That"—she pointed at the handful of pages in Clara's hands—"arrived, addressed to the both of us." Her friend paused. "From the Earl of Waterson."

The pages slipped from Clara's fingers and rained down in a noiseless flutter about her lap and feet.

Reggie reached down to rescue the sheets.

"What?"

"The Earl of Waterson." The other woman's words were directed at the floor as she picked up the notes.

Clara's heart thumped slowly. "What?"

"Lord Waterson," Reggie repeated.

Henry had done this? What? Why? When? All the questions rolled around her mind, confused. "I don't understand."

"I think it should be simple," Reggie said, handing over the small stack. "I suspect because he was not as comfortable with how he behaved as you might believe."

And then Clara let her gaze fall to those pages written in Henry's meticulous scrawl. Of course even his handwriting should prove perfect. "It was guilt," she whispered, toying with the corners of the top note. "Henry prides himself on being a man of principle and honor."

"If he were heartless, he wouldn't give a jot what happened to the Muses. And he certainly wouldn't spend his time drafting guidelines to ensure we're compliant with the law."

Clara bit the inside of her cheek, hating that she so desperately wanted to cling to Reggie's optimism. And yet . . . She laid the papers down once more. Henry hadn't come for her. The notes had been addressed to and delivered to both her and Reggie. It was a silly, nonsensical detail to fix on, and yet . . .

I wanted him to come . . . I wanted even this to be more than business . . .

"It was always just business," she said into the quiet.

"Bah. You are being stubborn. The man you describe, Clara, isn't one who is coldly indifferent. But rather a man who made a mistake and is trying to make reparations." With that sharp rebuke, Reggie stood. "I'm not telling you how you should or should not feel about the gentleman. What I am trying to do is help you see that which, in the face of betrayal, might not be so clear to you."

Standing, Clara looked down at her notes once more. "Thank—"

"If you thank me, I'm going to thump you." Her friend gentled that by leaning over and kissing her on the cheek. "Regardless of your Lord Waterson, our future is a bit clearer than it was yesterday."

Yes, it was.

Because of Henry.

"Will you return with me?" her friend offered, drawing on her cloak and fastening the clasp at her throat.

Clara shook her head. "I'm going to stay a bit longer."

Her friend hesitated and then edged out from the aisle and continued the long walk to where Broderick Killoran waited at the back of the theatre. The moment she approached, Broderick claimed Reggie's hands and raised each knuckle to his mouth for a kiss, as if the handful of moments they'd been apart had been an eternity.

Clara told herself to look away from that intimate exchange, and yet, she could not. She stared on, longingly, selfishly aching to have that bond . . . wanting to have someone at her side through the triumphs and also the struggles.

I want that with Henry.

She'd only ever wanted it to be Henry.

Clara forced her focus to the notes he'd sent until the pair of footfalls faded and then disappeared.

As soon as they'd gone, Clara slid back into the chair. From the corner of her eye, she caught the fluttering of a delicate scrap of white. She caught Reggie's fichu and held it in front of her eyes; the translucent fabric dimmed the clarity of that beloved stage the performers had rehearsed upon. She lowered it just below her eyes until the color shifted into perfect clarity and then moved the cloth over her eyes once more.

Clara repeated that distracted movement over and over.

Mayhap Reggie was correct and Henry's betrayal didn't truly alter who he was inside as a man, but muted the qualities she'd come to love and admire in him.

At the faint tread at the back of the hall, Clara stopped. "I would have returned with it," she said, climbing to her feet. She turned to greet Reggie—and froze.

The fabric slipped from her fingers, along with those notes. Ice skittered along her spine and chilled her from within. Time had left him remarkably . . . untouched. With the same rounded, pale-white cheeks with their perpetual blush better suited for a baby and his paunchy frame, he may as well have been the same gentleman who'd seen her out of work years earlier.

"You," she breathed.

"Clara Winters, you've not changed a day." One might hear the high-pitched timbre of his voice and mistake him as boyish in innocence.

She'd learned the peril of underestimating the evil that lay within him.

"Neither have you," she said coolly, running a condescending stare up and down his padded frame.

He smiled as if she'd handed him the highest of praise.

"What do you want?"

"You wound me, Clara." He meandered over. "You always did, though." He spoke softly to himself. Before he could trap her, Clara slid out into the aisle so she could face him squarely.

"I rejected your advances and rebuffed your offer of protectorship, and for being truthful you wounded me." He'd fed lies about her to the theatre owner and then set himself up as a patron of the arts all over London with the sick, single-minded intention of blocking her from having any future on the stage. "You took away my choices."

"Choices," he scoffed. "You weren't an actress ever, Clara. You were a whore. A whore to the nobility and yet turned your nose up at me because I'd been born without a fancy title."

The shame that she'd fought but carried for all these years simmered within her, and she gripped the sides of her skirts.

You believe your past is all that defines you, Clara . . . That decision was made for you . . . The truth is, some bounder stole your options and maneuvered you down that path . . . You did what you needed to do, and there is no shame in that . . .

Clara forced her palms open. "I was a performer," she said quietly, bringing her shoulders back proudly. "I was an actress." And now she was the proprietor of her own business. For even if it could not be this one, as Henry and Reggie had accurately pointed out, there would be another—as long as she wished it. "What were you, though, Terrence? Hmm?" she murmured, wandering a path around his pudgy frame.

He stiffened as she circled him.

"You were a man who resented the peerage for having what you would never, ever have." He'd been too blind, too much a fool to see the greatest gift of security and wealth he'd had and therefore never really needed anything more. "I could never have as my lover any man so loathsome, who didn't even like himself."

His large nostrils flared ever so slightly in the only indication he'd heard her. "Hurl your insults, Clara, because they are just words." Confidence infusing his spine, he tugged at his lapels, and this time, he went on the advance, ambling closer. "Whereas I, Clara?" Several inches shorter than her, he tipped his head back to glare at her. "I've seen that you pay for those slights."

Clara had faced down more life-hardened men than the one before her. She'd be damned if she cowered or gave in to any fear over this one.

"You lost your acting career. You lost your ten thousand pounds."

She drew a sharp breath in through her teeth. She'd known it had been him. Even as common sense would have said with the passage of time he would have moved on in his petty quest of vengeance, he'd never been sane or logical. He'd always been there . . . lurking. Waiting to land another blow.

"Nothing to say? Hmm?"

Clara smiled coldly at the madman before her. "You took everything, and I still triumphed."

"Is this triumphing?" he boomed, tossing his arms wide and gesturing to this cherished place she and Reggie had built. "You were *swindled* out of your savings, and then used what you were able to scrape together for this place?" His arms fell back to his sides. "And you've lost this, too, Clara."

Except . . . she hadn't. Not really. She'd seen this physical structure as the start and end of every dream she had. But it wasn't. She was capable of rebuilding her life. She'd done it before, and she would do it again.

Reggie had been correct.

And Henry. He'd helped her to see that, too.

"Go to hell, Lowery." And with that Clara started past him.

He shot a hand out and caught her by the wrist.

Clara gasped. "Unhand me, Terrence," she hissed, struggling against his surprisingly strong grip.

"We are not done here," he whispered, sticking his face close to hers. "You do not get to decide when we are done."

"I assure you, you are done here."

Clara's heart stopped beating as she found the cherished owner of that voice.

Henry.

She squinted.

That was . . . a rumpled, unkempt version of the always-in-control earl.

He moved down the aisle with purposeful strides, his gaze focused squarely on Terrence, and as he drew closer, rage burnt from that gaze. "Release her now, or I will happily sever your hand from your person and choke you with it."

This Henry was as she'd never before seen him—volatile, with a gaze that promised death.

For me.

Why is he here?

Terrence Lowery's skin went ashen, and he abruptly released Clara. She immediately rushed to Henry's side, and he did a quick once-over before returning his attention to the man opposite them. "You," Lowery spat.

At that familiarity, Clara glanced back and forth between the two gentlemen. "You . . . know one another."

They ignored her.

"Of course the bastard I intend to bring down should also find himself lover to the only woman I ever wanted." Lowery removed a pistol from his jacket with more alacrity than she would have believed the rotund gentleman capable of.

Cursing, Henry stepped in front of Clara.

"Stop it this instant," she gritted, sliding out from behind him. By God, she'd not let him be killed for her.

"Clara."

"Touching," Lowery snapped. "Just . . . touching." He waved the gun back and forth between them. "Odd, how these two moments in my life converged, eh? It was as though the fates and the universe brought everything I loved and hated all together."

She gasped. "You are the one who attempted to kill Henry."

"Mm. Mm," Lowery corrected. "A number of men I hired attempted to." He grinned like the cat who'd just swallowed the canary. "I am the one who will kill Lord Waterson. Lord Waterson, leading the charge for a military force to suppress those not born with his illustrious rank. Drafting seditious laws limiting speech. Authoring laws abolishing slavery and the purchase of slaves." It was the sinful mark by which Lowery had built his fortunes. "All of it was about oppressing the masses. Oppressing me."

Clara lifted her gaze to Henry. "You drafted laws to abolish slavery?" It was the mark of a man who drafted laws not for control as Lowery thought but for his sense of moral right. Her heart swelled anew with love for him.

Henry shrugged. "It was wrong." He leveled a steely gaze on Lowery. "No man has the right to own another." How casual he was on that accomplishment, when nearly every other man would have considered only profit earned off the backs of others.

"Either way, I'll have my revenge now against the both of you. With your little row over this . . . place." Lowery swept his pistol over the theatre. "You've provided quite the perfect setup. Miss Winters, the determined courtesan, lashing out at the lover who stole her theatre, killing him in a fit of rage. But there is enough of this talk—"

"And what then?" Henry asked, inching closer to Lowery. "Do you think you'll have Miss Winters then? Do you believe she could ever be anything to you after this?"

That gave the other man pause. "She will need security. In time she will grow to love me as I love her."

"You are mad," she breathed. Henry shot her a warning look, and she ignored his unspoken bid to silence her. "You didn't love me," she said, disgust sliding into that retort. He'd wanted her and her body and entry to what he believed she represented. "You wanted control and entrée into a world you'd never belong to, Terrence."

"I wanted you," Lowery cried, his voice pitched. "Do you know how much I've gone through these past years to have you? And this time, this time my efforts were without error. I saw you divested of your funds and then saw that cease-and-desist letter that should have been enough."

Henry cursed. "You're working with Peerson."

"I am," Lowery said, not bothering to glance at the other man.

My God, there'd been no end to Lowery's ruthlessness. She peered down her nose at the man who'd been behind so much of her misery. "You are a vile, empty-hearted man whose soul is blackened for trading in human flesh as though people were a commodity." And in a way, it was no different from how he'd seen her . . . there for his pleasure, to take without a regard for her no. "And I would rather starve in the streets than take you as a lover."

His eyes took on a maniacal gleam as he leveled the muzzle of his pistol at Clara's chest and drew the hammer back.

Henry surged forward, launching himself at Lowery.

The thunderous report of gunfire echoed.

"No," Clara cried.

Henry dropped the other man with a solid right hook to the jaw. He landed a swift blow behind it, and the sharp crack of his nose breaking, followed by Lowery's wails, filled the hall. Henry continued beating the other man as blood sprayed from the shattered appendage.

Clara raced over. "Henry," she pleaded. "Henry!"

He was a man possessed. His hair fell over his eyes as he battered Lowery over and over.

She dimly registered the heavy fall of footsteps. A broad bear of a man made to drag Henry from the unconscious Lowery. Ophelia Killoran's husband—Steele.

Her shoulders sagged as he pulled Henry off the other man. "It is done, Waterson," Steele said quietly.

Henry staggered to his feet.

"Henry," she cried, rushing forward, and launched herself into his arms.

He grunted and staggered back under her weight. "You came for me," she whispered against his temple.

Henry's arms came up around her as he cradled her close. "Of course I did," he said simply, panting from his exertions. "I love you. I am so, so—"

She kissed that apology from his lips. "Don't you dare apologize."

His thick lashes swept low. "I wronged you."

"That one mistake does not undo all the world of good you've done and all the joy you've brought me. I love you."

Henry fell to a knee, and Clara pressed her palms to her mouth. "What are you—"

"Clara Winters, will you marry me? Will you allow me to spend the rest of my life trying to fill your life with laughter and not teasing—"

"Yes," she cried. Once she would have believed herself unworthy of a traditional life as his countess. With his help, she'd come to see and appreciate her own worth. "I will."

"Not teasing," he went on, his voice growing threadbare, "because I'm really not that fu-funny."

"You are, though. You . . ."

And then Henry held a hand to his side.

Her happiness died a swift death. "Oh, my God. You were shot."

"I'm *fahhh* . . ." His assurance faded as his eyes rolled to the top of his head and he fainted.

Chapter 26

The first thing Henry became aware of was that damned throbbing in his head. A vicious pulsing that wrapped around his entire skull and radiated pain up to his temples.

I'm dying.

Yet again.

Then it came back to him: the bottle of brandy and then whiskey he'd consumed.

Alas, it would appear he was dying by his own hand this time. Except . . . he didn't know much about spirits and the aftereffects of drinking them, but the burning at his side was an unexpected misery for that indulgence. An indulgence he would never again make. Not even the oldest, finest bottle of French brandy was worth this.

Only, something was not right. There was something he was missing.

What was it?

Henry forced his eyes open and stared into an inky darkness. Silence cloaked the room so that the only night sound was that of the dissonant ring from the hum of the quiet. He winced and closed his eyes once more as that faint whining exacted another round of torture on his head.

And then the memories rushed forward: Lowery. Clara.

His eyes flew open.

"You're awake." That beloved voice, cherished and beautiful, washed over him.

Henry turned his head and found Clara seated at a chair next to his bed.

"You fainted."

"I'll have you know I do not faint."

Her lips formed a watery smile. "Your sense of delivery and timing with jest-making remains horrid, my lord." She caressed his cheek, gentling that rebuke.

"Surely I've gotten better at it?" he returned, his voice hoarse.

"Slightly," she conceded. "Which says more for how poorly your previous attempts at teasing, in fact, were, than any real improvement."

He glanced around his chambers. "Where—"

"Is your family? I assured them I would remain with you and call them when you woke."

He stared at her. There was something he was missing. Something she was not saying. "And my mother abandoned the room."

Clara nibbled at her lower lip. "I might have suggested she leave until you awakened."

And despite the searing agony from his injuries, he felt his lips twisting up with amusement. "There's a story there."

"She may have continued saying, 'He is going to die,' over and over, and I, believing that you did not need to hear that while you recovered, thought it might be best if she remained . . . elsewhere."

"And she went?" he asked incredulously. His mother's worry over the Waterson title superseded all, mayhap even her worries over his sorry arse.

"I may have coordinated a distraction with your sisters that required your mother look after a distraught Lila."

"Clever," he murmured approvingly. "I'm fairly certain you're the only one who's managed to maneuver my mother, the master chess player, into . . . anything." Henry shifted, and that slight movement caused another wave of misery to his damned side. He hissed, concentrating on breathing.

All earlier lightheartedness gone, Clara jumped up. "I'll fetch the doctor."

"No," he called, staying her. "I don't need or want the doctor." Not yet. He wanted only this woman and these stolen moments of silence. "Sit, Clara," he urged.

As soon as she sat, her face crumpled, and she buried her head in her hands.

"No," he murmured, struggling to sit up. "What is this?" Tears from her? "None of that."

"Lie down, Henry." Her fingers muffled that command, but he'd be a fool to fail and heed the warning there.

"I am fine, Clara."

"You are not *fine*. You were shot. You placed yourself between a bullet and me." Her tears continued falling. "You've thrown your political aspirations into turmoil and risked your own life . . . *for me*."

"And I'd do it again," he said without missing a beat.

She sobbed. "No o-one has ever believed my life was one of value, and then y-you'd give up all." *For me* . . .

The words hung there as real as if she'd spoken them aloud.

His heart ached. She deserved to know how special she was. She should have lived only an existence where she'd been valued and loved. "I love you," he said softly. How could she not realize just how much she meant to him?

Clara's tears continued falling. "You were bleeding, Henry. *Bleeding*. And even so you were fighting him anyway."

Even with his wounds, he managed to preen. "Impressive stuff, no?" he asked in a bid to end her sadness. "For a stuffy, pompous lord that—"

Letting her arms fall to her lap, she glared at him.

"Still not amusing?"

"Still n-not." Her voice broke through her tears. "I thought y-you were going to d-die, Henry."

"Oh, Clara," he said softly, linking his hand with hers. Raising her fingers to his mouth, he brushed a kiss along that sensitive seam where her wrist met her hand. "Don't you see?"

She stared at him, a question in her tear-filled eyes.

"Without you, there is no reason to live. There is no happiness. You have made me a better man, and I only wish that I'd been a better man before you, so that I was deserving of you. I—"

Resting a knee on his mattress, Clara leaned forward and kissed him. "I love you," she whispered against his mouth, their breath tangling.

"Did I dream you agreed to marry me?"

She narrowed her eyes. "Are you attempting to get out of that offer, my lord?" The playful smile on her lips tempered that teasing response.

There was, however, a slight pause, a hesitation that he heard even through his pain. "What is it?" he asked quietly, searching her face.

"What of . . . Lord Peerson's daughter?" she asked hesitantly.

She still did not know how much she meant to him. *I want to spend the rest of my life showing her.* "I paid a visit to Lady Peerson's home, drunk and disheveled."

Her lips twitched. "You?"

"Oh, yes. And the young lady and her mother were none too pleased with me or my state."

"Lord Peerson's daughter jilted *you*?"

"Yes, but in fairness, I hadn't asked and only after she fainted," he said dryly. "I'm fairly certain I can't count on Peerson's vote anymore." In fact, he knew as much.

Her levity fled. "Your police force." Clara's gaze fell to his chest.

Yes, that dream had been lost . . . for now. "All I've known"—he grimaced—"All I *understood* is Parliament and lawmaking. I failed my sister . . ." He spoke over Clara's protestations, needing her to understand. "In my eyes, I did fail, and I needed to accomplish something to atone for those mistakes. I allowed the ends to justify the means." Henry caressed her cheek. "Until you showed me the truth."

"The truth?" she whispered.

"Loving someone isn't about controlling them. It is about loving them and supporting them." Somewhere along the way, he'd ceased truly interacting with his family and focused only on providing for them. "And I am unwilling to sacrifice my honor to advance my political aspirations, no matter how beneficial those acts or laws might be." Unlike Peerson, who'd sold his soul to cement deals by working with a blackguard like Lowery. How close he'd been to becoming just like the viscount.

Clara's lips trembled. "And this from one of the greatest MPs."

"No vote or act ever mattered to me more than you," he said solemnly. Not long ago, that was all he'd cared about. How empty his life had been—before her.

Clara drew in a breath. "There is still the matter of my music hall."

At that unexpected shift, Henry creased his brow. "What of it?"

"I still want to run my business and provide employment for those in East London, and I don't want to give that up. I want it all." She grimaced. "And marriage with you, even as it is unconventional. Uh . . . not marriage to you, though that is, too, I suppose, given my former status and—"

Henry touched his fingertips to her lips, silencing those ramblings. "Clara," he said quietly, "do you truly believe I would ask you to give up on your dreams and your business?"

She gave him a look.

"Fair point," he muttered. "Old Henry very well may have had difficulty with a wife who was—unconventional."

She sidled into the bed beside him. "And the new Henry?" she murmured, lingering her lips near his, nearly touching but not kissing.

"And the new Henry would want my wife . . . would want you . . . no other way," he whispered.

And, lowering his mouth, Henry kissed her.

About the Author

Photo © 2016 Kimberly Rocha

USA Today bestselling, RITA-nominated author Christi Caldwell blames authors Julie Garwood and Judith McNaught for luring her into the world of historical romance. When Christi was at the University of Connecticut, she began writing her own tales of love. She believes that most perfect heroes and heroines have imperfections, and she rather enjoys torturing her couples before crafting them a well-deserved happily ever after.

The author of the Wicked Wallflowers series, which includes *The Bluestocking*, *The Governess*, *The Hellion*, and *The Vixen*, Christi lives in southern Connecticut, where she spends her time writing, chasing after her son, and taking care of her twin princesses-in-training. Fans who want to keep up with the latest news and information can sign up for Christi's newsletter at www.ChristiCaldwell.com.